Readers are LOVING

MY KIND OF HAPPY...

'Inspiring and uplifting'

★★★★★

'If a book can offer you something that
continues after you've read it, it's done
a wonderful job...'

★★★★★

'Cathy just gets better and better...'

★★★★★

'Like a dose of sunshine on a dismal day...
you can't help but smile!'

★★★★★

'As always, Cathy's ability to create a
vivid story puts you right into the action'

★★★★★

'A feel-good story!'

★★★★★

'Draws you in from the beginning...
a fabulous, well thought out plot'

★★★★★

'Finished it in one go...
I laughed and cried my eyes out!'

★★★★★

Cathy Bramley is the *Sunday Times* Top Ten bestselling author of *A Patchwork Family* and *The Lemon Tree Café*. Her other romantic comedies include *Ivy Lane*, *Appleby Farm*, *Wickham Hall*, *Conditional Love*, *The Plumberry School of Comfort Food* and *White Lies and Wishes*. She lives in a Nottinghamshire village with her family and a dog.

Cathy turned to writing after spending eighteen years running her own marketing agency. She has always been an avid reader, never without a book on the go and now thinks she may have found her dream job!

Cathy loves to hear from her readers. You can get in touch via her website www.CathyBramley.co.uk, on Facebook @CathyBramleyAuthor or on Twitter @CathyBramley

Cathy Bramley

MY KIND OF HAPPY

ORION

An Orion paperback

First published in Great Britain in 2020 by Orion Fiction
This paperback edition published in 2021 by Orion Fiction,
an imprint of The Orion Publishing Group Ltd,
Carmelite House, 50 Victoria Embankment,
London EC4Y 0DZ

An Hachette UK company

1 3 5 7 9 10 8 6 4 2

A CIP catalogue record for this book is
available from the British Library.

ISBN (Mass Market Paperback) 978 1 4091 8679 3
ISBN (eBook) 978 1 4091 8680 9

Typeset by Born Group
Printed and bound in Great Britain by Clays Ltd, Elcograf S.p.A.

www.orionbooks.co.uk

Hello dear reader!

Before you dive into the story, I thought I'd give you the background to 'My Kind of Happy'...

In July 2018, I was sitting on the terrace of a hotel in Scotland shortly before my sister's wedding and a TED talk by someone called Sebastian Terry popped up on my Facebook feed. I watched it, completely entranced. Following a life-changing incident, Sebastian had asked himself a hypothetical question: If today was my last day on Earth, would I look back and think that I'd lived in a way that made me proud and happy? There was much more to it than that, but even this basic question made me think about my own life. What are the things that make me happy, and am I doing them?

My sister Nikki married Tim and we all had a lovely day, and in the background my brain was whirring away, thinking about that talk. Sebastian's slogan is what's on your list? and when I got back home I started to write my own happiness list. There are lots of things on it, but the one which spoke to me most of all was volunteering overseas. I didn't know where or when I'd achieve this, but I was determined to do it.

And miraculously an opportunity came my way! In November 2019, I set off to Nepal alone to meet up with a group of volunteers. We'd raised money to build a computer classroom for a small rural school and for two weeks, we joined the building contractors to finish the project. It was probably one of the happiest, most fulfilling things I've ever done, and I can't wait to do it again!

In 'My Kind of Happy', Fearne is at a crossroads in her life and needs to discover her own path to happiness just like I did. I hope you enjoy her story and maybe it'll inspire you to write your own happiness list too!

Much love,

Cathy

xxx

Part One

Chapter One

'I think I've died and gone to heaven,' I said with a contented sigh.

Laura looked at me uncertainly and whistled under her breath. 'Talk about glam. Hope they let us in.'

We were gazing around the foyer of the Enchanted Spa, Derbyshire's newest luxury health resort.

There was something special in the air, as if the staff knew just what a fabulous day you had in store and could hardly contain their joy at sharing their workplace with their clientele. Young, old, fat, thin; gym bunnies or couch potatoes, everyone received the same warm and celebratory welcome at the front desk. I could feel my body slowly unfurling at the prospect: a spa day with my best friend. What a perfect way to spend a grey Saturday in March.

'Oi, speak for yourself.' I tossed back my blonde hair. 'I can do glam.'

Although having said that, I had noticed a rather unattractive dark parting this morning. Time to book into the hairdressers for some overdue highlights. I hadn't been for ages. In fact, I'd hardly been anywhere for ages.

Perhaps today would mark a fresh start? A chance to get my life back on track and moving forward again . . .

Laura snorted. 'Tell that to your joggers, I hope that's only mud up the back of your leg.'

'Whoops.' I peered down at the mark; almost definitely mud. It had still been dark and damp when I'd taken Scamp for a walk this morning, I could have splashed through anything. I wiped the front of my trainer against the back of my leg and prayed I wasn't making things worse.

Although I was only half an hour from home, it felt like I was a million miles away from reality. Crystal chandeliers glittered above us, the polished marble floor sparkled and harp music played softly in the background.

I caught the perfume from two enormous flower arrangements and exhaled with pleasure; my shoulders dropped from their usual place around my ears. 'I feel relaxed already.'

'Ditto.' Laura squeezed my arm as we both gazed around us, taking it all in. 'I've got loads to tell you later.'

'Can't wait!' I answered contentedly. 'And we've got all day, nothing to rush for.'

Just then the sliding glass doors behind us swished open and a huge group of women entered, all kitted out in sashes and tiaras, and we were pushed towards the reception desk on a tidal wave of over-excited hen party chatter.

Ten minutes later, we'd been handed fresh fruit smoothies, fluffy gowns and slippers and a lady called Bernice, one of the smiley young receptionists, was showing us to the changing rooms.

'Is today a special occasion, ladies?' Bernice glided ahead of us along a thickly carpeted corridor as if she was floating on her own cloud of happiness. Her lipstick matched her nail polish exactly, I noticed. I tucked my own ragged nails into my palms and tried to remember the last time I'd even worn make-up.

'Not really,' I answered, straightening my spine to copy her immaculate posture. 'Just spending a day together. We haven't seen each other for ages.'

'Celebrating life then.' Bernice turned and gave me a twinkly smile. 'Can't fault you.'

'Er . . . I guess so,' I said vaguely.

Today was about *escaping* my normal life. And here, where no one knew me except Laura, I was hoping to forget my sorrows for a few hours. Or did that make me sound uncaring? Because I cared very much. Always would. Oh God, now I could feel tears pooling in my eyes. *Fresh start, Fearne, remember?*

Bernice gave me a quizzical look and I felt Laura's reassuring hand on my arm.

'I'm an accountant,' she said, forcing Bernice to divert her stare from my less than celebratory face. 'So the start of the year is always hectic for me, doing people's last-minute tax returns. I'm exhausted.'

Poor thing, I thought, snapping myself out of my reverie to note the dark shadows under her eyes. We'd been friends since we were sixteen, so I was used to her ridiculously long hours in January. Mind you, this year must have been exceptionally busy because I'd scarcely seen her in February either. And seeing as I'd become a bit of a recluse over the last seven months, so far this year had been pretty quiet. If it wasn't for her and my brother's best friend Hamish checking up on me regularly then the majority of my conversations outside of work would be with the dog, Scamp. And he wasn't even mine, I was looking after him for my elderly neighbour, Ethel, while she recovered from a broken hip. Scamp did his best to keep up his end of the conversation, but I must say I was looking forward to chatting with an actual human for a change.

'Tax returns. Urgh.' Bernice pulled a face as she opened the door to the changing rooms and led us inside. 'Sounds tough.'

'It's over for another year though, thank goodness!' said Laura, doing a fist pump. 'Besides, it's Fearne who's most in need of some pampering, she really *has* had a tough time.'

A knot of frustration tightened in my stomach. She was half right. But I hadn't *had* a tough time; I was still having one. If my best friend didn't understand how I felt, what chance did anyone else have, I thought glumly. I'd been there when her mum died ten years ago just before we graduated from university and it had been a full year until she stopped bursting into tears at the most inopportune moments. Grief was inconsiderate like that, it didn't work to a deadline and my grief appeared to be going on long after other people thought I should be over it.

'Oh? Sorry to hear that.' Bernice tilted her head, waiting for me to elaborate.

'Thanks.' I looked down at my muddy trainers. No way was I going to open up to a stranger.

'So how do these lockers work?' Laura asked, coming to my rescue again. She sent me a look of apology.

Bernice demonstrated how to activate the wristbands we'd been given to open the lockers. Then she gave us a smile. 'Righto, ladies, now all you have to decide is what to do next.'

'I fancied doing a class first,' I said, scanning the activity schedule. 'Before getting into my dressing gown.'

Laura's brow lifted with shock and I felt a flush of warmth to my face. I'd resisted her attempts to get me to go to Salsa (and every other sort of exercise class, and I'd bailed out of book club). I didn't know why she bothered with me these days: I'd always been the sociable one, always up for a drink or a shopping trip, an impromptu party. Now I avoided group situations like the plague.

'Great idea.' Laura looked at the fluffy robe over her arm longingly. 'As long as it's nothing too strenuous.'

We both looked at Bernice for ideas.

'Hula-hooping at eleven?' she suggested, circling her hips.

Laura shuddered. 'Tried it once at the gym and my hips wouldn't gyrate like everyone else's. I looked like Mr Bean dry-humping his imaginary friend.'

I giggled. Laura was petite and pixie-like, with short coppery hair and large brown eyes and looked absolutely nothing like Mr Bean.

'Hmm, OK, let's have a look.' Bernice peered over my shoulder at the sheet. 'How about Nordic Walking then? Fresh air and a tramp in the woods?'

'Who's she calling a tramp?' Laura muttered wickedly.

I coughed to cover my mirth.

'Nice thought, but I've already done some of that this morning,' I said, showing Bernice the dirt up the back of my leg. My trainers must have been muddy as well because now there was a mess on the spotlessly clean floor around my feet.

'That's mud, allegedly,' Laura piped up.

Bernice laughed nervously and took the schedule from my hands.

'I've got it!' she said triumphantly, a moment later. 'Crystal Healing. It starts in a few minutes in the dance studio; you could do that if you hurry?'

Laura and I exchanged dubious looks.

'That's a real class?' I asked.

'Oh yeah.' Bernice nodded earnestly. 'Crystals are powerful things. They can do wonders for your physical and emotional needs. You get your chakras balanced and everything. All you have to do is sit down for an hour with a blanket over your knees. It's fabulous; you'll feel like new women after that.'

'Sounds interesting.' I nudged Laura. 'I was saying only last week that my chakras were all over the place.'

'Ditto.' Laura was chewing her lip, trying to keep a straight face. 'And I'm sure one of mine is heavier than the others.'

'There you go then.' Bernice pursed her lips. If she was aware she was being teased, she was too professional to comment on it. 'It'll be perfect for you.'

She glided back to reception and Laura stared at me in amazement.

'You nut job. We're not really doing it, are we?'

'We are,' I said shoving my stuff in the locker. 'It might be a laugh. It's ages since I've had any fun.'

Neither of us was into any of this new-age, deep and meaningful stuff normally. But I reckoned it had to be worth a try, I'd been stuck in a rut for months now and couldn't see a way out of it. Perhaps getting my chakras shaken up would do the trick.

Laura opened her mouth, a protest forming on her lips. I grinned at her and her face softened.

'You're right, let's do it. And then we do need to talk about something.' She cleared her throat. 'Something important.'

I smiled indulgently at my dearest friend, watching while she folded her own belongings neatly into the locker below mine. It would probably be another self-help book, or website or support group. Laura was on a one-woman mission to mentor me through my loss and while I knew it wouldn't help me, I loved the fact that she kept on trying, because it meant that she still cared.

'Sure.' I locked my locker and linked her arm through mine. 'Straight after this. Promise.'

★

The dance studio we'd been directed to appeared to be empty at first except for four chairs which had been arranged in a circle, a folded blanket placed squarely on each seat. But as Laura and I entered, we saw a woman with a head of tight white curls crouched over a CD player on the floor. She pressed a button and the sounds of wind chimes and waves softly lapping the shore filled the room.

Laura cleared her throat and the woman turned, her face lit up with a welcoming smile.

'Hello, come in, come in, take a seat!' She stood and waved us to the chairs. She was wearing what looked like a long tapestry rug and her fur-lined boots squeaked on the rubbery floor as she crossed it to close the door behind us and dim the lights.

'I think it might just be us,' I whispered, tucking the blanket over my knees. 'This is going to be so awkward.'

Laura eyed the door shiftily. 'We could do a runner?'

'We can't do that to her,' I said with a horrified giggle.

'I can,' she muttered.

Just then the woman joined us in our circle of two. She smelled of cloves and eucalyptus; it was exotic and mysterious and exactly how I imagined a crystal healer should smell. She sat down, placed a velvet bag on the floor by her feet and regarded us both intently.

'I'm Maureen Sinclair,' she said in a voice as smooth as warm honey, 'welcome to this crystal healing session. You are good friends, I think?'

We nodded.

'Then this will be a wonderfully intimate session for you both.' Her fingers were adorned with silver rings and her thumb was stroking them rhythmically.

9

'Great!' Laura announced with a note of hysteria in her voice. She'd pulled her blanket up to her chin and looked about eight years old.

'Yes, lucky us!' I pinched my lips together, trying not to laugh.

Maureen lifted her velvet bag onto her knee and looked at me as if she could read my soul, as if my innermost thoughts were etched on my heart in bold for her perusal. I felt a flush of heat to my cheeks. It already felt intimate and she hadn't even produced a crystal yet.

'Introduce yourselves and tell me what you are hoping to get from this session,' she asked softly.

Laura gave me a look as if to say *good question*.

'Well, I'm Fearne,' I said confidently, trying to remember what was on the write-up about this class, 'I definitely think my chakras needed balancing.'

Laura let out a snort and quickly turned it into a cough.

Maureen leaned towards her and gave her an intense look. 'We can certainly do that. Any particular issues you'd like to address?'

'I'm Laura and I need my brain to calm down after a busy month and I haven't been sleeping well,' Laura said meekly.

Maureen listened so carefully, it was almost as if she was straining to hear another voice, inaudible to the two of us. She nodded slowly before turning her attention back to me.

'And you, Fearne?' she said softly, 'I'm sensing a sadness behind that smile.'

I shrank back in my chair, feeling an instant prickle of perspiration under my arms; I wasn't comfortable being under this kind of scrutiny. I didn't want her to be able to read me like this.

'I've had a lot to deal with recently,' I said in a small voice.

Maureen held my gaze for a second longer than I'd have liked and delved into the bag. Getting to her feet, she placed a large pink stone on the floor in the centre of our circle and around it she dotted others in white, green and more pink ones.

She tipped some smaller crystals out into her hand and held them out to us. 'If you'd like to hold one during the healing, help yourselves.'

Laura and I exchanged sceptical glances. Maureen's eyebrows flickered with interest as we made our choices. Mine was a smooth white stone shaped like an egg which seemed to have a light coming from its centre. Laura's was blue flecked with gold.

'Close your eyes and relax . . .'

I did as I was told. This is what I had come for: complete relaxation, for body and mind. A rest from the angry thoughts which had been tormenting me for the last eight months.

Let them go, Fearne, just let them go . . .

Chapter Two

Maureen asked us to imagine a sandy beach, a hammock, the gentle sound of the waves and warm sun on our skin, her words soft like a lullaby. My breathing slowed and I felt the steady beat of my heart in my ears.

'And now, I will come to both of you in turn and begin the healing,' Maureen murmured. 'Concentrate on the area in your life or in your body where you need my help.'

As I let go of all the remaining tension in my muscles, I could sense that she had crossed the circle and was behind Laura. Normally this sort of thing would send me into a fit of giggles, but this felt really important. Laura had put up with my mood swings, my tears, my listlessness without comment and I'd done very little to repay her. Now I sent her my love telepathically and thanked the universe for her friendship.

I don't know how much time passed but suddenly, I felt Maureen's light touch on my shoulders. It was my turn; my stomach fluttered with nerves.

All at once, colours danced inside my eyelids: red, green, blue like fireworks exploding in my brain and all the doubts I'd had at the start of the session melted away. Even if these crystals didn't have any effect, just sitting here, meditating and thinking good thoughts felt like a very good way to pass the time.

I sensed Maureen moving behind me, that heady aroma growing stronger and I heard the faint chinking sound as she selected crystals from the bag. After that initial contact, she didn't touch me again, but I knew she was there and I knew she was trying to help me, to ease the sadness which she'd sensed so intuitively.

When will I feel normal again, Freddie? When will I wake up in the morning without my stomach dropping, remembering that your room is empty and you're not coming back? When will I stop fearing for everyone I see riding a motorbike, wanting to shake them and tell them how stupid, how dangerous they are? Life just isn't fun any more, grief feels like such a heavy load to carry day after day. First Dad left us and now you. I can't bear it; I can't bear losing people I love. Perhaps that's the answer, perhaps I shouldn't love anyone at all and save myself the heartache.

An image floated through my mind, a memory of my big brother and me playing on the altar in the little Welsh chapel where Granny was in charge of the flowers. We were obsessed with a board game called Operation at the time and we would take it in turns to operate on each other while Granny created huge arrangements of lilies and gladioli and chrysanthemums with the other ladies. I missed Granny so much, but her death had felt like the natural order of things. Not like Freddie's stupid, stupid accident. I didn't think I'd ever reconcile myself with that, no matter how long I lived.

Other memories began to flash up, happy ones: summers spent making daisy chains in the meadow behind Granny's cottage, making the journey at dawn to the market in a van bursting with the perfume of cool fresh flowers, pinching pieces of fern – my favourite foliage of course – and other small flowers and making fairy bouquets with offcuts of ribbon from the haberdashery stall . . .

The sound of rustling fabric interrupted my thoughts. Maureen had moved away and was back in her own chair.

She spoke soothingly, bringing our attention back to the room and after a few moments, invited us to open our eyes. Laura stretched her arms above her head and I blinked to refocus my vision.

My face was wet with tears and when I looked across at Laura, so was hers.

'How do you feel after that?' Maureen held out a box of tissues and we both took one.

Laura wiped her cheeks. 'Good. Relaxed. I didn't realise it had made me cry.'

'And what brought on those tears?' she probed.

Laura twisted the tissue round and round and stared down at her hands. 'Guilt, I think.'

My heart melted for her; what could she possibly have to feel guilty about? She was good to her dad, a hard worker and a saint when it came to dealing with me.

'You have a good heart and a great capacity for love,' said Maureen kindly, 'but don't forget that you are also worthy of love. It's fine to let others lean on you, but value yourself and remember that your happiness is just as important as theirs.'

Laura flushed and a fresh crop of tears appeared in her eyes. 'Do you think?'

Maureen inclined her head. 'I *know*.'

'I'm probably to blame.' I gave my friend a watery smile. 'Laura has been my rock just recently.'

'I can tell,' said Maureen. She tilted her head. 'Fearne, what was going through your mind during the healing?'

'Oh . . .' I shrugged casually, not meeting her eye. 'Memories. Games I played with my brother. Things I used to love doing. Happy times.'

'Would you say your life is happy now?' she asked in a soft voice.

Her direct question put me on the back foot. I felt the familiar constricting of my throat.

'I can't . . . I don't . . .' I flicked a glance at Laura, hoping she might step in but she simply nodded encouragingly. I took a deep breath. 'No, it isn't.'

'Perhaps you've lost sight of what makes you happy,' she persisted.

I nodded, tears blurring my vision. My brother had lost his life and I hadn't worked out how to fill the gap he'd left behind.

'My advice to you is to be kind to yourself, allow yourself to find your way back to happiness. Maybe you've put up barriers to protect yourself but don't be scared to connect with people and let them into your heart.'

I stared at her, unable to voice my feelings. A wave of annoyance flared in my chest: if only it was that simple. I was ready to leave now, I needed some air. I hadn't expected to be affected as deeply by this session, but I felt totally exposed as if my skin had been peeled back and Maureen could see everything about me.

'Thank you, that was really . . . useful,' I said hurriedly, getting to my feet. I handed her back the stone I'd been holding. 'Is that quartz?'

She didn't take the crystal from me, she held my gaze instead. 'You chose selenite. It's a calm stone. It brings a deep inner peace, perfect for someone who might be grieving.' She folded her hand over mine. 'You keep it. A gift from me. I wish you well for the future, Fearne.'

My voice had evaporated but I managed to smile and nod my thanks.

'And this?' Laura held out her blue stone. The metallic flecks twinkled where they caught the light. 'What did I choose?'

Maureen smiled knowingly. 'Sodalite. It eliminates mental confusion and improves communication to help you verbalise your feelings. I hope it has helped?'

Laura's eyes flicked briefly to mine. 'I think so. I'll certainly try.'

Maureen insisted on Laura keeping her crystal too and after clasping both of our hands and wishing us well, she sent us on our way.

Once we were out in the corridor, we headed for a squishy sofa and both collapsed onto it with relief.

'Never again.' I groaned, pressing the heels of my hands into my eyeballs. 'How weird was that? So apparently I'm a misery guts and you need to work on your communication skills.'

I shoved Laura's arm playfully, expecting her to join me in poking fun at what had just happened. But when she met my eye, her face had gone deathly pale.

'There's something I've got to tell you.' Her voice shook. 'Something I've been trying to tell you but I haven't had the courage.'

A trickle of fear ran down my spine, a hundred awful possibilities whirring through my head.

Please don't be ill. Please.

My mouth had gone dry. 'What is it? Tell me?'

'It's not a bad thing, it's a good thing, at least . . .' She swallowed as if she might be sick. 'I hope it is. Because if you didn't think it was, then . . .'

'Jesus, Laura, my heart is going like the clappers here.' I gripped her hands. 'Put me out of my misery.'

'It's Hamish and me,' she blurted out. 'We're seeing each other.'

I was lost; what was so earth-shattering about that? 'Well that's nice for you, when?'

'No,' she said slowly, 'I mean we're together; as in I love him.'

Laura and Hamish? *My* Laura, and my brother's best friend.

My jaw dropped open. Of all the things she could have said, that one hadn't even crossed my radar. They'd known each other for years, but not well and there'd never been a spark between them. Or at least so I'd thought. And I saw them both separately all the time and neither of them had mentioned it.

Laura was staring at me, waiting for my reaction, but I was so stunned I *couldn't* react.

'Well, that's unexpected,' I managed shakily. 'Since when?'

There was a beat of silence.

'We swapped numbers at the funeral and—'

My gasp stopped her in her tracks.

Freddie's funeral. July last year. The worst day of my life. Correction: second worst. The day I found out he was dead was off the scale.

I sat back against the sofa, taking this in. Laura squeezed my hand but I slid my fingers from her grasp and turned my face away. While I was burying my big brother, our two closest friends were setting up their first date. I felt physically sick.

'How could you?' My voice was barely audible, and tears spilled down my cheeks. I shook my head, trying to remember the events of the day. 'Of all the places. And as for Hamish, I thought he was genuinely cut up at the funeral. But now it turns out he was working on his chat-up lines.'

'It wasn't like that, I promise.' She held her hands up, pleading with me. 'Initially we thought we should stay in contact because we were worried about you. I didn't even see him again after that until December. We just texted each other or talked on the phone.'

'What happened then?' I said stonily.

'Hamish found tickets to some Christmas party he'd been supposed to go to with Freddie and he got really down. He rang me to tell me how much he missed his best friend and I suggested we met up.'

I folded my arms. 'He could have rung me.'

'How could he?' Laura sighed. 'You were suffering yourself, he didn't want to burden you with his grief.'

My heartbeat was thumping so loud that I could hear it whooshing in my ears. 'And all that time you never thought to tell me?'

'A million times,' she groaned. 'But we wanted to be sure that it was serious before we told you. It hasn't been easy to find the right moment.'

We, we . . . already they were a couple. A pair. And three was a crowd, everyone knew that.

I should have been happy for her, for them both. But all I could feel was betrayed. The two people who'd been my closest allies, by my side, helping me through the last few months, had secretly been dating, laughing behind my back, having fun, having *sex* even . . . Bile rose in my throat. I'd never felt so alone in my life.

I glanced around the spa pointedly.

'And you think this was the right moment?' I tried to keep the emotion from my voice, which resulted in an icy staccato tone that sounded nothing like me at all. 'When we're supposed to be having a nice day together.'

She reached towards my arm. 'Maureen gave me the courage . . .'

'Stop.' I shrugged her off me and jumped up. 'I can't listen to this. I'm going to be sick.'

I stormed off along the corridor and Laura ran to catch me up.

'Fearne, wait! Please be happy for me. Remember what Maureen said, that I deserve happiness.'

It was true. Even through the mist of my anger I knew it was true. Laura did deserve to be happy. I hated that I was behaving like this: angry and selfish. But right now it felt like another loss. Only this time I was losing both Hamish and Laura, to each other.

'Please leave me alone,' I said in a shaky voice, reaching the door of the changing rooms. 'I'm going home.'

'Maureen was right,' Laura said sadly. 'You *have* forgotten what makes you happy. And until you find it you'll never be able to move on with your life.'

I whirled round to face her.

'Why are you so obsessed with me *moving on*?' I drew air apostrophes over the words. 'And what exactly am I supposed to be moving on to, anyway?'

'Oh, Fearne.' Laura's shoulders slumped.

I pushed the door open and went inside; the wounded look on her face nearly undid me. If she spoke, I didn't hear her, which was just as well. Because I simply wasn't ready to hear it.

Chapter Three

The row hovered over me all the way home like my own personal rain cloud. I felt wretched; I'd never quarrelled with Laura before. If it hadn't been for Scamp, I'd have probably made a den under my duvet and stayed there for the rest of the weekend, curled up with my own misery.

I was ashamed of my reaction to her news; of course Laura deserved to be happy and she deserved my support. But I was hurt too. We'd always been there for each other; I didn't have any secrets from her and I couldn't believe she had fallen in love with someone and not confided in me. And not only was Hamish in on the deception, he was the cause of it, which made me feel more isolated and despondent than ever.

My spirits lifted a little as I pulled up outside our – *my*, I corrected myself automatically – house, a pretty little Victorian terrace on the outskirts of Chesterfield; there, perched in the front window was Scamp. Ears pricked and front paws, one white, one black, resting on the back of the armchair I'd put there especially for him to keep a lookout. I was pretty sure that he was waiting for Ethel to come home, which melted my heart and made me perhaps a bit over generous with the dog treats to compensate.

Freddie and I had bought the house between us seven years ago; we'd had the best fun doing it up and for a time it had been known as party central among our friends. For the months following his death, I'd hated the special kind of silence Freddie had left behind him. Having Scamp to come home to had helped No. 78 Pineapple Road feel like home again.

'Hello, you gorgeous boy.' I crouched down to let Scamp give me his usual enthusiastic welcome and felt my phone buzz in my pocket. I took it out and read the screen: text messages, from both Laura and Hamish. I wasn't ready to listen to them. Not yet. Instead, I cancelled the dog walker who'd been due in at lunchtime and took Scamp out for a long walk.

'You're the best thing to happen to me this year, you know,' I told him as we stopped at a pedestrian crossing. He looked up at me adoringly, two chocolate brown eyes under expressive bushy eyebrows. The crossing started to beep and Scamp tugged me across the road, eager to get to the park on the other side. Once through the gate, I let him off the lead, laughing as he lolloped off to the spot where two months ago he'd found a discarded sausage; he never gave up hope of finding another. I envied him his optimism.

Ethel had left me a letter asking me to look after him if anything happened to her. *A dog fills a space in your heart you didn't know was there*, she'd written. And she'd been right; Scamp had quickly worked his way into my affections as well as my home, and I was simultaneously looking forward to and dreading the day that Ethel returned to her house next door. Scamp ran back to me, his tail wagging wildly, and dropped a filthy tennis ball at my feet. I picked it up gingerly and Scamp yelped with glee as I threw it for him. Part Border collie, part Jack Russell, he had longish legs, wiry fur and perky ears. Despite his arthritic hips and advancing years he raced after the ball with all the enthusiasm of a puppy. At least I was making someone happy today, I thought wistfully, thinking of Laura alone at the spa.

So much for our lovely day of pampering. I wondered whether she'd left after I did, or maybe she'd phoned Hamish and asked him to join her. I shook the image of them both from my head for now. At some point I'd have to get in touch with them, but until I worked out what I was going to say I needed to keep myself occupied.

There was one obvious job I could do: sort out Freddie's room. Until Christmas, I hadn't been able to clear any of his belongings; his coats had still hung on the hook in the hall, a heap of discarded trainers below them. The shelves in our little living room had bulged with his books and DVDs and his dumbbells still served as a doorstop. Since the start of January, I'd been tackling a room at a time, gradually removing traces of my big brother. All that remained was his bedroom. I'd been putting that off until last; it was such an intimate space and it was going to feel like such an invasion of Freddie's privacy. Hamish had offered to help me and I'd accepted. Now it looked as if I was going to have to do it alone.

Or . . .

I could get some work done instead. Perfect, I thought briskly. Work it was; Freddie's room could wait for another day.

I called to Scamp, clipped his lead back on and we set off for a lap around the lake before heading home. Data crunching might not be the most thrilling way to spend the day, but at least I'd get ahead on the big project my team was delivering to clients next week. And, maybe working on a Saturday would give me some extra leverage with my boss, Bernie, because I had a favour to ask. Again.

★

By six o'clock that evening my eyelids were beginning to droop from staring at the screen for so long. But as a distraction tactic it had worked – every time I'd found my thoughts returning to Laura and Hamish, I'd given myself a shake and focused hard on my report. I'd squirrelled away in comfort: in front of the fire, with Scamp pressed to my thigh and my laptop on my knee. I'd work this way every day if I could, I thought, stretching my arms above my head before composing an email to Bernie, my boss, to give him an update.

Tuesday was D-Day for our big annual presentation. Clients from Japan, Portugal, Germany and South Korea would be tuning in to a video call to watch what we at Zed Market Trends were predicting would happen in the world of office paper over the next five years.

Being a senior market analyst in the paper industry might not sound thrilling; in fact, everyone I told about my market niche had a habit of glazing over. Until, that was, I got them thinking about the supply chain (or paper chain as I jokingly described it). From forests in Indonesia, to paper mills in Scandinavia right through to the UK's stationery retailers, billions of pounds were invested to keep our home printers supplied. And it was the trend-predictions made by my company that helped steer that research and development across the world. Heady stuff . . .

OK, well, I found it interesting anyway.

I emailed Bernie my PowerPoint slides ready for Monday and a second later a reply pinged into my inbox:

Working on a Saturday? Very dedicated! All we're waiting for now is the data from Seattle and I can work on the summary.

I typed one back:

> That should be in by Sunday night. There'll be plenty of
> time on Monday for the team to have a run-through
> before the presentation on Tuesday.

The presentation which I had no intention of delivering.
The prospect of all those international boffins hanging on
my every word filled me with dread. Giving presentations
used to be a piece of cake for me, but now I abstained
from cake completely whenever I could. My heart sank as
another email popped up from Bernie:

> Fearne, you are going to deliver this presentation, aren't
> you? Because it's time you got back in the saddle. It's
> been a long time since Frankfurt.

Frankfurt.

I shuddered so violently at the memory that Scamp
scooted closer and pushed his nose onto my lap.

It had been on a work trip to Frankfurt that I'd felt the
full force of losing my brother. After Freddie's funeral I'd
crunched up my grief into a tight ball, pasted on a smile
and headed off to a trade show in Germany with Bernie
to give a talk to Norwegian engineers about 3-D printing.
As I stepped from the taxi outside the conference centre, a
motorbike courier pulled up in front of me. He swung his
leg over the bike and pulled his helmet off to reveal a close-
cropped blond head. He could have been Freddie's twin.

'Freddie?' I'd gasped, grabbing the sleeve of his leather
jacket.

As the complete stranger stepped back from me in alarm,
the world had spun and gone black.

I came to, clammy and confused, surrounded by a group of Germans and a very worried Bernie with his arms around my shoulders. I recovered quickly, or at least I thought I had, until an hour later, when Bernie and I had commenced our presentation to the Norwegians. Grief exploded like an airbag in my chest and I couldn't breathe, let alone talk. Bernie had been brilliant. He'd organised a taxi to take me back to the hotel and given the presentation without me. Since then, the thought of speaking in public brought me out in a cold sweat.

My stomach was still churning as I typed a response to Bernie.

> I could, but I've been thinking. Gary wants more responsibility and he knows this project inside out. Why don't we give him a chance to shine? This presentation is standard stuff; I don't think there'll be any surprises for the client. Perfect opportunity for Gary to cut his teeth in the boardroom.

I bit my lip, waiting for his return message, but instead my mobile flashed up silently with Bernie's number.

Damn it. There was no way I could avoid answering his call.

'Hi, Bernie,' I said wearily.

'We need *you* there, Fearne.' Bernie cut straight to the chase. 'You can't cherry-pick the parts of the job you like the most forever. I can't keep making allowances for you.'

This sounded like a reprimand. An official one. The subtext here was: *OK, your brother died, it was awful and you were grieving, we cut you some slack, but enough is enough.*

'Of course you can't, not forever,' I said forcing a smile into my voice. 'But just this once?'

Bernie sighed down the phone.

'The clients are expecting you. You're the senior analyst.'

'I can't, I just . . . can't.'

There was silence down the line and I held my breath, hoping he'd take pity on me.

'Maybe if getting back in this saddle is beyond you just now, then maybe you need . . .' He paused and gulped so loudly I could almost see his Adam's apple bobbing. 'To look for another saddle.'

'You mean another job? Are you sacking me?' I was stunned; I hadn't seen that coming.

'No. And I don't want you to leave. You're a brilliant analyst. In ten years' time you could be eyeing up my job. Imagine that!' Bernie enthused.

'Yes, imagine,' I said faintly.

The prospect horrified me. I'd worked at Zed Market Trends for a decade since leaving university; I liked routine and I felt comfortable there, but the thought of another decade and then another: suddenly it felt like a life sentence.

'Exactly. But at the moment . . .' He hesitated again and when he spoke, his tone was more gentle, 'Let's just say, your current behaviour hasn't gone unnoticed by the directors. Your unwillingness to give client presentations, I mean. Yours is a client-facing role and when you abstain from delivering the end result of the project, well, you're not fulfilling the terms of your contract. The rest of the team can't carry you indefinitely. You're either on board. Or you're not.'

'I understand.' I felt the blood drain from my face. So much for Saturday working giving me extra Brownie points; instead I felt like I'd been given an ultimatum.

We ended the call shortly after that with him telling me to think about it carefully and me promising I would. I powered down my laptop and sat for a moment in shock.

This was dreadful; I wasn't up to thinking about a new career at the moment, I was just about coping with the one I'd got. Or maybe I wasn't even doing that.

Your current behaviour hasn't gone unnoticed . . .

I reached automatically for my phone to call Laura and tell her what had happened before remembering. Not only had I alienated two of my closest friends today, on top of that it seemed I was in danger of losing my job.

'What a mess, Scamp,' I groaned, smoothing the fur back from his face.

His anxious expression reminded me of the look Laura had given me just before I'd turned my back on her and stormed off.

Poor Laura, I'd treated her terribly; I was consumed with shame. I was envious, plain and simple. Her life was sailing full steam ahead on a sea of love while mine was marooned on misery island and rather than be pleased for her like a true friend would have been, I'd shouted and stomped off in a huff.

'Right,' I said, purposefully, picking up the phone yet again. 'I'm ringing her. This situation has gone on long enough.'

Before I'd even had a chance to scroll to her number, Scamp began to bark. He leapt up from the sofa and onto his look-out chair. The curtains were drawn against the dark evening, so he couldn't see out and he did an impatient dance until I opened them for him. But other than the headlights of a passing car, I couldn't see anything.

'Who's there, Scamp? What did you hear?'

The dog jumped down and went to the door, his tail circling enthusiastically just as the doorbell rang.

I went out into the hall and grabbed hold of Scamp's collar before opening the door. A sharp gust of cold air greeted me, as did one of my favourite people in the world: Hamish.

My heart pattered nervously while I tried to gauge his mood.

Scamp strained to get to him, almost dragging my arm out of its socket. I let him go and he launched himself at Hamish's legs.

'I come in peace.' Hamish thrust out a bunch of black-eyed pink and purple anemones and eyed me cautiously.

'Thank you. They're gorgeous,' I said staring at the flowers awkwardly. Scamp sniffed the air hopefully.

Hamish scratched behind Scamp's ears and then pulled a leathery-looking chew from his pocket. 'And I believe you like these?'

Scamp sat down in a flash, managing to be as still as a statue and yet quiver with anticipation at the same time. We both laughed and some of the tension dissipated.

What would I do without that dog, I thought, with a stab of love: he could diffuse a sticky situation, simply by being there. He kept his eyes trained on Hamish until the treat was his and then padded off to enjoy it in private.

'I'm probably the last person you want to see right now, but may I come in?' Hamish, hunched up in a ski jacket, blew on his hands, reminding me that he was still standing out in the cold.

'Of course.' I stood back to let him pass.

He kissed my cheek as he drew level with me. 'I knew bribing you with flowers was a good idea.'

'Oh, Hamish. You'd have been welcome anyway.' I dropped my head on his shoulder and he wrapped his arms tightly around me. 'I'm so ashamed of myself, I've behaved appallingly today. I'm happy for you and Laura really. It was just a shock.'

28

Hamish peered at my face. 'Do you mean that?'

I nodded. 'I think you'll make a great couple. I'm so sorry.'

I really meant it. They were well suited: both kind, loyal, hard-working and good fun. I wondered why it had never occurred to me before.

'No apology necessary,' he said. 'Laura can't forgive herself for letting our news ruin your spa day.'

A rush of shame flooded through me.

'I was just about to ring her when you called,' I said. 'Because I *do* need to apologise. She didn't ruin the day. I did.'

Hamish ran a hand through his thick mop of red hair. 'Laura and I don't come out of this well either. We're not proud of keeping our relationship secret from you. In hindsight, perhaps we should have involved you right from the very beginning. Truth is, we felt guilty that Freddie's funeral led to something so wonderful.'

I nodded slowly, appreciating how difficult it had been to tell me anything recently. There was so much about my brother's death that didn't make sense. I had questions that I'd probably never get answers to. What he'd done that night was so out of character that I didn't think I'd ever understand what had been going through his mind. Sometimes it made me angry, at others I was simply heartbroken. But now Hamish and Laura had found love through him and while it wouldn't mend my heart, it certainly helped.

'You know something?' I said with a watery smile. 'This is the first positive thing that has come out of losing him, so I'm going to celebrate it. Come here.'

I hugged him again, this man who'd become like a surrogate big brother to me. Not just since last summer but ever since Freddie had first introduced us after meeting Hamish at uni.

'I've never loved anyone like I love her,' he said now with a goofy grin.

'You'd better look after her,' I warned, tapping a finger to his chest. 'Or you'll have me to answer to.'

Just then Scamp pushed his bony head between us and breathed his hot chew-flavoured breath up at Hamish.

'And him,' I added.

'I promise,' he said, pressing a fierce kiss to my forehead. 'So are we good?'

I nodded and sent up a silent thank you to the powers-that-be for the gift of Hamish McNamee in my life.

'Thank heavens for that,' he said with evident relief. 'Because Laura's in the car. I was sent ahead as the peace envoy. If I'd got short shrift we were . . .'

I didn't hang around to hear the rest. I handed him the anemones and fled from the house.

My best friend was here and I couldn't wait to make it up to her.

Chapter Four

I ran out onto the pavement in the dark and looked left and right, searching the line of parked cars along Pineapple Road until I found Hamish's. Laura was already out of the car by the time I'd reached it, her worried face lit by the orangey glow of the street lamps.

'Friends?' she asked softly.

'Always.' I threw my arms around her neck and drew her close. 'Forgiven?'

'Always,' she replied.

And we both sighed with relief.

My spirits lifted. Sometimes things could be that simple. We headed back, pausing to collect Scamp who'd gone to sniff his old front door. In the kitchen, Hamish had put the flowers in the sink in water and was making tea. Laura went straight to him, touching the nape of his neck tenderly and then pulled me into their orbit for a group hug.

I pushed down the thought that from now on I'd be the third wheel in this relationship and concentrated on the happiness that was radiating from them both.

'I'm glad we've cleared the air,' I said. 'But sad it needed doing.'

'Ditto,' said Laura. 'And I promise if we go to that spa again, I'll even go hula-hooping with you.'

'Deal.' I grinned and we both laughed at Hamish's startled face.

'And now we're going to clear Freddie's room,' he said, clapping his hands together. 'Because that's another thing which needs doing.'

I blinked at him. 'Right now?'

'Yep.' He handed us mugs and strode purposefully out into the hallway and up the staircase.

'No time like the present,' said Laura, grabbing my hand. 'Before you have a chance to talk yourself out of it again.'

Scamp, excited by such unusual activity, danced ahead of us.

My pulse speeded up as Hamish paused outside Freddie's closed door. He was right; I'd been avoiding this job for months. And doing it spontaneously meant that I wouldn't have time to think about it.

He looked at me steadily. 'Ready?'

'Ready,' I said gruffly.

Laura's comforting hand squeezed my waist.

Hamish twisted the doorknob, the heart of my brother's domain opened up and a tremor of emotion rippled through me. Laura and I followed him inside. She snapped on the light and Hamish crossed to the window to close the curtains.

It was cold in here; the radiator had been turned off and both Laura and I shivered.

The leather and aftershave and engine oil that had made up my brother's unique scent still lingered.

'It smells like he's still here,' I murmured, turning around to see everything.

His double bed had been stripped and the duvet and pillows had been piled at one end of the mattress. Mum had done it the week of the funeral, before I'd begged her to leave the rest of his room intact. The magnetic board above his desk had overlapping layers of notes and ticket stubs and photographs pinned to it; a row of battered trainers formed a border underneath the window. A wardrobe, some drawers and a bookshelf, all crammed with Freddie's possessions, possessions which I'd never in a million years have rifled through without his permission.

I felt dizzy thinking about it. Laura appeared back at my side.

'You OK?'

'Not really,' I said, with a ghost of a smile. 'Maybe we'll just do one drawer tonight if you don't mind?'

'I'll go and find bin bags from the kitchen,' said Hamish and bounded back out of the room.

The thought of piling Freddie's things into a bin bag stole the breath from my lungs. I sat down heavily on the chair at his desk. Suddenly I just wanted this over with as quickly as possible. Scamp slunk in and after investigating the only room in the house he'd never been in, he flopped down at my feet. By the time Hamish had returned with a roll of bin bags, Laura and I had pulled out the bottom drawer of Freddie's desk and were staring into it.

'On the basis that the bottom one has the least interesting stuff in it, this seemed like a good place to start,' I said.

'Sounds like a plan,' said Laura cheerfully. 'Shall we make piles to keep?'

I made a face. 'Keeping things is easy, it's choosing what to get rid of which will hurt.'

'We shouldn't find anything of great importance,' Hamish said, tearing a black sack from the roll. 'I've already dealt with his financial stuff and passport, etcetera.'

'But it's all important,' I replied, gazing at the melee of loose photographs, countless pens and keyrings and at least three torches. 'Because it's all I have left of Freddie.'

Hamish winced. 'Yeah, 'course. I didn't mean . . . I just meant—'

33

'I know what you meant,' I said, sighing. 'This is just hard, you know? Letting go. And being in here seems such an invasion.'

Laura's hand found mine. 'I felt the same when Mum died. Listen to your heart and if you don't feel ready, we'll walk away and do it another day.'

I nodded, grateful for her experience. Her mum had passed away only weeks before our university graduation ceremony and her dad had gone to pieces for a while, leaving Laura to deal with the arrangements.

My fingers found a small box, I pulled it out and removed the lid to reveal a pair of silver cufflinks. Freddie was a T-shirt, jeans and leathers man; I couldn't remember the last time I'd seen him in a suit.

'They're gorgeous,' whispered Laura.

'I remember those, I had a matching pair,' said Hamish. 'For a mate's wedding. All the ushers had the same ones. I lost one of mine.'

'Then take these.' I handed him the box quickly as if it was scorching my fingers. 'He'd be pleased about that. And you're more of a cufflinks man than he ever was.'

A sharp pang twisted at my insides, threatening to drag me back to the darkness of grief.

Freddie would never get married in a suit wearing silver cufflinks, he would never turn to watch the girl of his dreams walking down the aisle to meet him, would never do all of the things that Hamish no doubt would achieve so easily in the years to come. And the sheer waste of his beautiful life stung.

'I'll treasure them.' He tipped them out and turned them over in his hand, twisting his mouth into a smile. 'Laura says I look hot in a suit. I've bought two new ones since our first date.'

'Have you!' Laura gasped with embarrassment and covered her cheeks. 'That is so sweet!'

It was on the tip of my tongue to ask about their first date but I held back. It would be something she and I could giggle about over a glass of wine one night.

'A word of warning; Laura also thinks Spiderman's hot,' I said. 'If she starts talking about all-in-one Lycra bodysuits, run for the hills.'

Hamish and I teased Laura for blushing and I felt the first hopeful shoots; maybe them being a couple wouldn't be as bad as I thought after all.

'So far we've removed only one item and the bin bag is still empty,' said Laura. 'I think we're going to have to be a little more ruthless.'

For the next few minutes, we delved through the bottom desk drawer and managed to clear it out, salvaging only a university keyring which Hamish wanted to keep and a pen with four coloured inks in it which Laura said would be handy for work. Scamp had shown an interest when we'd uncovered half a biscuit but I'd quickly disposed of it before he could snaffle it; goodness knows how long it had been there.

Laura and I both eyed the middle drawer of the three while Hamish stuffed the rejected items into the black bag.

'Only if you're up to it,' she said.

I puffed my cheeks out and opened the drawer. 'If not now, then when, as the saying goes.'

At first glance the contents seemed similar to the last drawer: a mishmash of things which, although not obviously important, clearly were important enough to Freddie to warrant drawer space.

Underneath a pile of leaflets that Freddie had had printed when he'd first started as a motorbike instructor was a small hardback notebook. It had lots of pieces of paper slipped between the pages. I lifted it out and Hamish's eyes widened.

'No way!' he whistled. 'I remember that book, he wrote all the details of our India trip down in there: flights, hotels, things we definitely wanted to see.'

At the end of their degree course, Hamish and Freddie had gone on a crazy road trip across India on motorbikes and had had the time of their lives. When they returned, tanned, thin and brimming with stories, Freddie announced that he was never going to work in an office or be weighed down by corporate life. The thrill of discovering the world on a bike far outweighed the prospect of job security and a pension. For the next fifteen years, he had worked as a motorcycle instructor, earning just enough to pay for the next trip. Hamish, on the other hand, said he never wanted to ride a bike again. He worked in London for a talent agency before returning to the north to set up on his own. He was now a successful sports agent with a roster of footballers, cricketers and boxers on his client list. Despite their different life choices, they'd remained close.

I flicked through the pages, my heart twisting at the sight of Freddie's terrible handwriting: all in capitals and written so firmly that I could make out the indentations of the letters on the back of each page.

'Can I see?' Hamish was itching to take the book from me.

As I handed it across, something papery fell out from inside the back cover and landed on the carpet. Scamp's nose was on it immediately. Laura rescued it before he had a chance to chew it.

'It's a letter to you.' She handed it over, puzzled.

The envelope had my name on it but no stamp. I turned it over in my hands, intrigued.

'I think I remember him writing that,' said Hamish, nodding thoughtfully. 'We definitely bought paper and envelopes with the idea of writing proper letters home.' He laughed. 'I never did in the end. A few postcards were all I managed. It looks like Freddie might have written that and never posted it.'

It sounded plausible; and knowing Freddie, he'd have been so caught up with telling everyone about his adventures when he returned to England that the notebook and the letter within it had probably slipped his mind.

'Shall I open it?' I whispered. My heart had begun to race. A letter from Freddie. Written over a decade ago. It was like uncovering hidden treasure.

Hamish put an arm around my shoulders. 'If not you, then who? As the saying goes.'

I set it on my lap, my hands already clammy, and took a calming breath. 'OK. Right. I will then.'

Hamish got to his feet. 'I'm ready for another cup of tea.'

'I'll help,' said Laura, scampering after him.

They were giving me some privacy and I was grateful for their thoughtfulness, although part of me didn't want to be alone.

Come on Fearne. I laughed at myself under my breath. Stop over-dramatising it; it's probably just a bog-standard 'wish you were here' holiday letter.

But as I removed the flimsy sheets of paper with fluttering hands and began to read, I realised that this letter from beyond the grave might just change my life.

5 July 2004

Hey little sister!
We've reached Agra and it is OUT OF THIS WORLD! You have to travel. You HAVE TO! And when you do, come HERE I think you'd love it.

Being so far from home, with no one else to rely on but ourselves has opened my eyes to what a safe and cosseted life I've had until now. Everything here is different, even the air, the sun and definitely the food – I love it all (although what I wouldn't give for one of Mum's Yorkshire puddings right now). The skies are vast, the roads either gridlocked or deserted and as far as modes of transport are concerned – anything goes. The other day I saw an entire family including the dog clinging on to a scooter. Cattle pull wagons, bicycles pull carts, lorries with bald tyres are held together with string and sticky tape; every day is like some crazy episode of the Wacky Races cartoon show.

I wish you could have seen the maternity hospital we came across yesterday on the outskirts of a town. It wasn't much more than a hut made from a patchwork of materials and a wriggly tin roof. About twenty or thirty pregnant women were squatting down calmly at the side of the road outside in the blistering heat. We stopped our bikes to have a drink and asked what they were doing. Someone told us that they were all in labour but weren't allowed inside until the baby was actually coming, because there wasn't room for them all. Some even had younger children with them. Imagine that!

I think about how we in Britain complain about waiting times when we go to the hospital, about the quality of the food, or the lack of nursing staff. Next time I will remember the quiet acceptance of these mothers and I will shut the hell up. We have no idea how lucky we are.

This morning, we stopped to buy fruit from a street-seller who was probably only about fifteen years old. He must have grown out of his shoes because he'd cut open the toes to give his feet room. The shoes looked so uncomfortable that I gave him my spare pair of trainers and Hamish gave him a T-shirt. The boy shouted out so loud that I thought we'd done something wrong and when two older men appeared we almost jumped back on our bikes and rode off. But they turned out to be the boy's uncles. They shook our hands and insisted on piling as much fruit as we could carry into our rucksacks – they were so grateful for our simple gesture. Fearne, I have about eight pairs of trainers that all fit me, it was nothing to me but to them it was a massive deal. I can't tell you how good that made me feel. This trip has thrown my own greed and vanity into sharp focus.

But that's normal for us. Having stuff is what everyone does. You earn money and you buy stuff. You and me and millions of other British kids have been conditioned to work hard and get good grades, so we can get good jobs, so that – you've guessed it – we can buy more, bigger, better stuff. Leaving home to go to uni seemed like such a huge deal. I thought I owned the world when I moved out. I had the best time. Three years away from home, living with my mates and studying English. Now I realise that until I came to Asia, I knew nothing. I am twenty-two and I have spent those years wearing blinkers, staring straight ahead and sticking to the path that I am expected to be on.

Now the blinkers are off and the future I thought I wanted for myself seems far too small. The idea of coming home to start working a forty-hour week in a job which doesn't excite me fills me with dread. I don't want to waste my life.

And here's the thing: I don't have to. Because I get to choose. We get to choose. What we do, where we go, who we love, it's all up to us and no one else.

(Are you still reading this epic letter? Are you thinking I must be drunk, or high? I bet you're wondering why I'm telling you all this stuff!)

I've made a decision about the rest of my life and I'm so ecstatic and that's why I'm writing it down. I'm ignoring what family and society and the university careers office expect of me. From now on, it's MY moral code which matters. I'm going to live my adult life doing what makes me happy. Some of the things on my list –

Riding my motorbike through new places
Sunrise from mountain tops
Barbecues on the beach
Buying fresh food in local markets
Meeting people from other cultures
Putting a smile on someone else's face
And a million other things I haven't even thought of yet

So there you have it. Your big brother has a plan and it's not the one I thought I'd have. I might be an ordinary human, but I'm determined NOT to have an ordinary life.

And I want you to promise me, little Sis, that you'll think about this. Don't just settle. As the saying goes, go big or go home. I think you only chose to study Business Studies at Manchester because Laura was going there.

But what does Fearne Lovage REALLY want??

If I could give you one gift it would be to choose happiness over habit every time – do things because they make you happy, not just because it's a habit you've fallen into. I know it's a cliché but we really do only get one life and you and I are only just beginning ours, so let's live it to the max.

Be happy, Sis, don't let me down on this.
Lots of love Your slightly crazy brother
Freddie xx

When Hamish and Laura returned with our tea I'd pulled Scamp onto my lap, my tears soaking his fur, Freddie's letter on the floor beside me.

'Oh, Fearney.' Laura dropped to my side and hugged me close.

'You need to read this.' I handed her the letter and she and Hamish read it together while I mulled over Freddie's words. What a powerful letter. At the age of twenty-two, Freddie had set out the code for his life. And for the rest of his time on earth, the short fourteen years which had followed, he'd lived his life exactly as he'd planned.

But as well as that, Freddie had asked me a very important question: what does Fearne Lovage want? Perhaps the time had come for me to find out.

Chapter Five

I could easily have walked to the graveyard where Freddie was buried; it would only have taken me half an hour from Pineapple Road. But Scamp was still getting used to travelling by car and the ten-minute journey was a good length for him: long enough for him to have a nap and short enough for him not to get anxious.

'See,' I said, releasing him from his seatbelt harness and clipping on his lead. 'That wasn't so bad, was it?'

I was bleary-eyed and shivery after getting very little sleep last night. Hamish and Laura had stayed with me for a couple of hours after the discovery of Freddie's letter. We'd talked and shared our happiest memories and funny stories about Freddie and I'd woken with a sudden urge to put some flowers on his grave.

The morning had a bite to it, there was a layer of frost on the grass and I was glad I'd brought my gloves and put Scamp in his new fleecy coat. Ethel would be outraged, I thought, smiling to myself, she didn't believe in 'dogs being dressed up as dolls'.

I lifted the bunch of flowers I'd brought with me from the back seat, locked the car and together Scamp and I made our way to the far side of the cemetery, the new bit, the saddest bit. Scamp was delighted to be out in the fresh air; he snapped at tufts of long grass at the edge of the path and stopped every few paces to sniff something interesting.

There were a few other people about but I managed to avoid eye contact and reach Freddie's grave without entering into conversation. There was a man on a bench deep in thought, another with a camera zooming in on a Gothic monument, an older lady kneeling in front of a newly dug grave and a woman rocking a pushchair backwards and forwards to soothe a crying infant inside it.

The floral tributes dotted here and there, on the other hand, always caught my eye: fresh funeral wreaths, little bunches with notes tucked inside, gaudy and bright artificial bouquets, bowls of narcissi. I loved the messages conveyed within the blooms – *I'll never forget you*, *you are still loved*, *we will always care*. The cemetery may be a place for the deceased, but there was also a lot of life and love to be found here.

And now here I was with a message of my own. For the brother I'd never forget.

At thirty-six, with so much of life still ahead of him, or so he'd assumed, Freddie hadn't left any special wishes about his funeral. I was sure he'd have wanted to be cremated, quick, fuss-free, efficient, or maybe that was just because it was what I wanted for myself when the time came. But Mum had insisted on having him buried. The pain of losing her child was already so much for her to deal with, I didn't have the heart to contradict her.

But now, as I looked down on the tidy pea-gravel covered plot with its simple white granite headstone, I was glad to have a physical place to be near him. Mum had moved away from Derbyshire soon after he died. She lived by the sea in Norfolk now; 'a new start with new faces' had been her way of moving on with her life. That and the support group she'd set up for other women her age who had lost children.

It had been the same after their divorce. Witnessing her gradual metamorphosis from a besuited loss adjustor for an insurance firm to a purple-haired vegetarian café owner had been baffling for me as an eight-year old. The café hadn't lasted long and since then, Freddie and I had grown used to Mum changing jobs as often as her hair colour. Perhaps that was why I'd stayed in my job so long, I mused; a subconscious rebellion against the instability I'd felt growing up.

Her current job was in a second-hand bookshop and she was so busy these days I hardly saw or spoke to her. Her efforts certainly seemed to be helping her to get over Freddie's death. I was proud of her achievements and although Freddie and I had moaned about her at the time, I missed the way she used to interfere in our lives at every opportunity.

I didn't especially miss Dad. He'd never featured very strongly in my life, even before he'd decided that married life wasn't for him. Within eighteen months of leaving us, he'd moved in with a dental nurse and they were expecting their first child. I didn't resent Dad starting again, but I'd probably never forgive him for missing Freddie's funeral because he couldn't get a flight back in time from his holiday.

There was a tap near the end of the row. I filled the vase I kept there and took the flowers out of their plastic bag.

'Hello, Freddie,' I murmured, brushing some fallen leaves from the gravel. 'I've come for a chat. Hope you don't mind.'

My breath misted the air as I arranged the bouquet in water: early tulips from the corner shop, plus daffodils, pussy willows and evergreen foliage plundered from Ethel's garden.

Scamp lay down on the path patiently. I felt in my pocket for a treat and told him he was a good boy.

Later in the year, perhaps I'd plant some bulbs: snowdrops and tête à tête and cyclamen, or maybe grape hyacinths and perhaps sow some nigella seeds for summer flowers. Anything to detract from the stark truth: beneath this cold frozen ground lay Freddie. I took his letter out of my pocket and scanned the words, although I almost knew them by heart already.

'So, I found your letter. Bit of a shocker.' I spoke quietly even though there was no one within earshot. 'I was going to say I wish I'd found it sooner, or that you'd actually posted it at the time you wrote it. But maybe it wouldn't have had the same impact. It was a fantastic letter, it made me so happy to see your handwriting again. And I know this is a bit cheesy but it felt like the perfect gift at the perfect time. It's made me hold a mirror up to my life and I don't like what I see.'

I lifted up the vase to check the arrangement for symmetry and then settled it into the gravel where it would be steady. The sight of flowers brought a smile to my face as ever. Fresh flowers in the house had been a regular indulgence of mine, although I hadn't bothered for months. Freddie had always marvelled at my creations; he loved flowers but reckoned his fingers were built for motorbike handles, not easily bruised flower stems. But now, with Hamish's bunch of anemones brightening up the living room, it reminded me how much I missed them.

Scamp nudged my leg with his wet nose and brought me back to the moment. I squatted down beside him and felt for his wiry ears.

'You, on the other hand, Freddie . . .' My voice came out as a croak. 'You cracked it. All my memories of you are happy. All of them. You had a bloody short life, but you lived it to the max just as you wanted. But you got one thing wrong in your letter: you weren't an ordinary man, Freddie, you were extraordinary. And I loved you.'

I felt in my pocket for a tissue. Scamp licked his lips hopefully. I gave him another treat.

'What do I do, Freddie? Is my grief just a habit that I can kick? I hate feeling like this. I hate that every time I think I'm taking a step forward, I manage to take an even bigger one back. My emotions are up and down like a see-saw and I've cut myself off from most of my friends because I'm afraid of bringing the mood down. Even Maureen the crystal lady worked out that I've forgotten how to be happy. I feel like I'm stuck in a rut. I wish you were here to help me. Can't you send me a sign? Like a robin landing on your headstone or the sun breaking through the crowds or something, so I know that you're listening?'

Scamp retched and coughed up a ball of chewed grass and I grinned.

'Not quite the symbolic gesture I was hoping for,' I said, bending to stroke his head. 'But it'll have to do.'

The dog wagged his tail, proud of himself.

'So that's it, Freddie, I just wanted you to know that your letter has given me plenty to think about. I don't know what comes next, but I do know that I don't want to let you down. I'll come and see you soon, tell you how I got on.'

I blew a kiss into the air and turned to leave but Scamp had lifted his back paw and tried to scratch his side.

'Is that fleece irritating you?' I said as he pivoted on the spot to reach his itch. I unpeeled the Velcro strap under his tummy and pulled it over his head. 'Don't tell Ethel I made you wear this.'

Scamp's wiry eyebrows lifted at the sound of her name and he let out a gentle woof.

'Ooh!' I bent and kissed his nose. 'That, my furry boy, is a very good idea indeed.'

A visit to Ethel's care home was just what I needed.

'Worst thing about being stuck in here is not having a proper cup and saucer,' said Ethel, gazing with dismay at the two earthenware mugs I set down for us on the table. 'Tea tastes better from bone china, and hotter.'

We were sitting in the reception area of The Beeches Care Home, she and Scamp in a large armchair and me on the end of an uncomfortable sofa. Thomas, the nice man behind the reception desk, caught my eye and smiled. He'd told me the first time I met him that most of the clients here weren't happy unless they were moaning about something. It was visiting hour and people were coming and going all the time but nobody bothered us in our quiet corner.

'But looking on the bright side,' I said, pulling out a packet of chocolate digestives from my bag with a flourish, 'there's more room for dunking in a mug.'

I smiled to myself as Ethel's eyes lit up. Before she'd had the fall which had put her in here, she'd been more or less housebound and I'd popped in regularly throughout the winter to have a cup of tea with her. There would always be biscuits set out on a plate and she had always polished off most of them while repeatedly saying she didn't have much of an appetite these days.

'Now you're talking. What a treat. We only get plain ones here,' she grumbled. 'Chocolate makes a mess apparently and we get mugs because a cup and saucer makes double the amount of washing up. Efficiency rules in this place.'

'There are worse things than efficiency,' I pointed out, taking in all the spotless surfaces.

'*Humph*,' was Ethel's only response to that.

Reception was the only part of the building where Scamp was allowed. I don't know what either of the old companions would have done if he hadn't been permitted entry at all. Ethel had been very low when she'd arrived two weeks ago after a stint in hospital. At that point she hadn't seen her dog since the accident. I'd come over after work that same day with Scamp and pleaded with them to let her see him despite the 'no dogs' policy.

Their joyful reunion had had all of us in tears including the no-nonsense manager, Deidre. After that, it was clear to everyone that time spent with Scamp in her arms was the best medicine Ethel could possibly have. It was obvious that the staff at The Beeches put the residents' happiness at the forefront of their care; and it put Ethel's son and daughter's minds at rest to know that Ethel was in good hands.

It was too chilly for Ethel to be outside at the moment, but when the weather picked up we'd be able to take him into the gardens. Assuming she was still in here of course; she could be back home by then.

Scamp was in seventh heaven. Despite his size, he was determined to cram as much of his body onto Ethel's knees as he could. She insisted she wasn't uncomfortable but I had a suspicion she'd gladly endure pain just to feel Scamp's familiar warmth and inhale his doggy smell as though she was at home again.

'But you're all right, aren't you,' I said, sipping my tea. 'You like it here?'

'Move over, you bony beast,' said Ethel, nudging Scamp out of the way as she reached for her mug. 'I am perfectly fine, dear, thank you for asking. Despite being pushed and pulled and made to exercise every five minutes at my age.'

I suppressed a smile. 'Do you mean your daily physio-therapy to help you stay mobile?'

'I shouldn't grumble, I suppose.' Ethel sipped her tea and confided that although she wasn't used to such a regimented life, she felt safer than she'd done in Pineapple Road, just knowing there was someone on hand if she fell.

She patted Scamp's head fondly. 'Feels a bit odd not having this old boy on my bed but . . .'

'You told me he wasn't allowed on the bed!'

'Yes, well.' She looked shifty. 'He isn't officially. But I can't help it if he creeps up in the night. What about at your house then?' She pursed her lips. 'Sleep in his basket, does he?'

'Sometimes,' I replied.

We both laughed at my blatant lie.

'Anyway,' she continued, running her hand over his head. 'I think I've adjusted well to captivity. The only downside to living here is that Scamp can't join me. I do miss him.'

Her voice had gone a bit quavery, but I knew better than to draw attention to it. She was like me in that respect, didn't always like to discuss her feelings. And of course she missed her constant companion. He'd only lived with me for a few weeks and already I knew that the house would feel empty without him.

'Perhaps you should have thought of that before you decided to go climbing on chairs in your bedroom.' I raised my eyebrows sternly at her and offered her a biscuit.

She took two.

'I was thinking of you. I wanted you to look at my photograph albums. The ones of George and me mountain climbing on the Continent. I thought I might inspire you to get out and see the world.'

'Hmm, well, breaking your hip wasn't very inspirational and I think that chair escapade might have put paid to your mountain climbing for good.'

'Don't care.' She dipped the edge of the biscuit into the hot tea and closed her eyes with pleasure as she bit into it. 'It's you I'm concerned about. Still watching films of other people having adventures, are you?'

The night before her accident, I'd called around with provisions and showed her the DVD I'd bought about a woman who sets off on a dangerous journey to find herself.

'I wish I'd never told you about that. Besides, I can't swan off having adventures now, can I?' I said playfully. 'I'm busy looking after your dog.'

Ethel's face fell. 'If you don't want to have him any more then just say the word, I'll make other arrangements.'

'No way!' The thought horrified me. 'I love having him.'

A shadow passed briefly across her face before she turned it into a smile of relief.

'That's a nice thing to hear, you are a kind girl.' She squeezed my fingers, slid her hand from mine and picked up another biscuit. 'Now that's enough about me, I want to hear what you've been up to. You look thinner.'

'And you look plumper,' I replied, watching the biscuit descend into Ethel's tea. 'I can't think why.'

'I'm ninety-four,' she said briskly. 'If I want to stuff my face I shall. You should see some of the old dears in there.' She jerked her head towards the day room. I bit back a laugh, wondering how many of the residents were older than Ethel. 'Like skeletons, they are. I eat like a horse these days. The dinners might be a bit on the mushy side but it beats having to cook for yourself.' Her smile faded. 'Cooking for one gets a bit boring.'

'It does.' I nodded as my chest tightened with recognition.

Freddie and I had shared the cooking; either chatting over our day together in the kitchen or taking it in turns when one of us was going to be late in. And there had always been a dish of something leftover in the fridge or extra portions stuck in the freezer. Recently, I'd become over-reliant on ready meals or something to simply fill me up like cheese on toast. It wasn't good enough, I thought. It was time to take myself in hand.

'Fearne.' Ethel's voice was hesitant. 'I wouldn't be surprised if The Beeches was the last stop on my life's journey.'

'Rubbish,' I protested. 'A few more weeks to gather your strength and you'll be back in Pineapple Road.'

'And if it is, I won't be sorry,' she continued. 'And I don't want you to be sad either. I've no regrets, there's nothing left on my to-do list. Really there isn't.'

I felt my eyes grow hot with the effort of holding back tears. 'I'm glad. And you are an inspiration. There's plenty left on my to-do list.'

'Good!' Ethel cried, waking Scamp up from his nap. 'That's as it should be! I've been waiting for this. So go on, tell me, what adventures does the future hold?'

'Not sure yet.' I pulled a face. 'I spent most of last night asking myself the same question.'

'Oh, my dear.' She nodded wisely. 'I knew there was something on your mind. Come on, spit it out.'

I don't know who was more surprised, her or me when I did just that. She sat as quiet as a mouse while I told her about the fiasco at the spa, and then about my boss's ultimatum. She gasped in surprise when I told her Hamish and Laura were now an item and how hard that was to deal with. And finally I shared the unexpected pearls of wisdom I'd found in Freddie's letter to me and how much his words had affected me.

'The things Freddie wrote,' I began, 'it made me realise something. He set out at twenty-two to focus on doing the things he loved and he succeeded. Freddie's life might have been short, but he loved every second of it. I don't think if he had his time again, that he'd do anything different.'

Ethel smiled softly. 'And there's comfort to be had from that, dear.'

'I am comforted. But . . .' I groaned. 'I still can't accept his death. I can't move on. The crystal healing lady was right. I've forgotten how to be happy. Now I'm moody and antisocial, I pushed my boyfriend away and I'm even in danger of losing my best friend. I used to be such a happy, sunny person. Good at my job. And I was actually nice to people. But that Fearne has gone.'

'You are still all of those things,' Ethel said, brushing biscuit crumbs from the front of her dress. 'And that's the most you've ever said to me about your grief, take heart from that small step. I saw the spark in your eyes dim when you lost your brother. In my long life, it has happened to me many a time when I've lost people I've loved. But the good news is that the spark doesn't go forever. And grief isn't a bad thing.'

I looked at her surprised. 'Isn't it?'

'Oh no, not at all,' she exclaimed, her voice as warm as sunshine. 'Grief is . . . well, it's just love with nowhere to go.'

Love with nowhere to go.

I nodded slowly, taking in her words. 'That's a wonderful way of putting it.'

'Grief never truly leaves you, it changes you. And at the moment I think you are stuck in a rut. Find that love somewhere to go: put it into new places, new adventures and let new people into your life and into your heart.'

Freddie had asked me in his letter to promise that I'd choose happiness over habit. He'd be all in favour of Ethel's advice.

'But what do I do?' I murmured. 'Where do I start?'

Ethel thought for a moment and then her face lit up. 'You said he made a list of things which made him happy, why don't you do the same?'

I smiled at her. 'Why not? I'm partial to a list. Let's start now.'

There was a tiny notebook and matching pen in my bag and I pulled it out and turned to a clean page. I jotted down a title, underlined it and wrote a number one in the margin.

Ethel chuckled at my enthusiasm. 'So what'll be top of the list?'

I was still contemplating that when one of the care assistants approached the reception desk, handed Thomas a big bunch of flowers and walked back down the corridor, waving as she passed us.

'Great.' Thomas said, rolling his eyes good-naturedly at us. 'I'll just add flower arranger to my job description, shall I?'

'Gift from an admirer?' Ethel asked.

'Don't joke,' Thomas replied archly, 'I've had plenty of those since working here. No, these were given to one of the residents, Cynthia, but they're making her sneeze. I've been told to display them on reception instead.'

'A right Lady Muck, that one,' Ethel whispered to me as he rummaged under the desk and reappeared with a vase. 'Thinks she's staying at The Ritz.'

We watched as Thomas peeled off the cellophane and dumped the stems unceremoniously into the vase where they all flopped to one side; he hadn't even added water.

'Voila.' He cocked his head, studying his efforts. 'That'll have to do for now.'

The bouquet must have cost a fortune; I couldn't leave it like that.

'Allow me to help,' I said, setting aside my list and getting to my feet.

'Be my guest,' said Thomas, gesturing to the vase with a flourish of his hands.

He directed me to a sink where I washed the vase thoroughly. Granny's instructions came back to me down through the decades as always: *these flowers have come a long way, give them a fresh, clean start and they'll repay you for your kindness.*

Back on the reception desk, I surveyed the contents of the bouquet. Large-headed white roses, pale pink ranunculus, silvery foliage, the big blue thistles . . . it would create a wonderful display to greet visitors.

I separated the stems into groups. 'Ruskus, eucalyptus, eryngium—'

'Sounds like you're chanting a spell,' said Thomas, glancing up from his computer.

I laughed. 'And the magic has only just begun.'

Ethel looked on proudly from her armchair. 'She's a marvel with flowers. I just bash the ends with a rolling pin and hope for the best, but Fearne's an artist.'

I batted their compliments away. 'I can't do anything fancy but my granny was a florist, she taught me a few basics when I was a little girl and I've used them ever since.'

I quickly stripped away the excess leaves, snipped stems to the right length and began with the foliage. The largest blooms went in next, followed by the smaller flowers to fill the gaps. Then, I turned the vase around, checking for anything which needed tweaking. Finally, I stood back to look at the arrangement from a distance.

'That'll have to do,' I said.

It was nothing elaborate; I'd have loved to be able to do those big hand-tied bouquets I'd seen at posh florists with spiralled stems which you could simply take home and pop straight into water. Or big modern arrangements with single exotic blooms framed by an arch of steel grass. Or even something like the huge displays Granny used to make for her church which at the time were bigger than I was.

'Beautiful.' Ethel gave me a round of applause and Scamp wagged his tail to join in.

'I'll say,' said Thomas, whistling through his teeth. He pulled the vase towards him. 'I might pretend it's all my own work.'

'It's easy, you could do it yourself,' I said happily. 'Start with the foliage. That forms a structure to support the stars of the show. Then just pop in the flowers, making sure each one gets room to shine. Simple.'

'*Simple*, she says.' Thomas winked at Ethel.

'Easy,' Ethel echoed and they both laughed.

I found myself blushing. 'You can say so much with flowers.'

'You already have,' said Ethel, beckoning me back over to her.

'What do you mean?' I moved my notepad from the sofa cushion and sat back down.

'You've got your first thing for your list,' she motioned towards the pad.

Of course. A spark of joy lit me from within. My list didn't have to be made up of big adventurous things like Freddie's was. My list was for me, what made me happy.

'Number one on my happiness list,' I said aloud as I picked my pen, 'is flowers.'

With a jolt I realised that quite inadvertently, thanks to Cynthia's sneeze, I might just be at the start of something wonderful, something for me, and something which quite possibly could help me look forward to life again.

A life without my big brother.

I brushed away a stray tear and smiled at Ethel.

For the first time since Freddie died I felt a stirring of excitement: there was a light at the end of the tunnel and I was heading towards it.

The next morning, I woke up feeling brighter than I'd done for months. I bounced out of bed and shoved my feet into my slippers. Without moving from his half of the bed, Scamp opened one eye and gave me a solitary thump of his tail as if to say that he was very pleased for me but he wasn't quite ready to be quite so enthusiastic for a Monday.

But I was. Today felt different. I hadn't done anything with my list yet, and I only had one thing on it, but it was already working its magic. It was forcing my mind to consider the future instead of constantly dragging me back to the past. And today, as soon as I found the right moment, I was going to ask my boss for a couple of weeks off. I hadn't had a chance to find anything yet, but my plan was to go and do something 'flowery', some sort of flower-arranging workshop. Because flowers, I acknowledged with a little smile, made me happy.

After breakfast and a walk with Scamp, I made it into work early to tidy up some loose ends. I spent a productive thirty minutes on my own until my boss arrived.

'Morning, Fearne.' Bernie perched his plump bottom on my desk and helped himself to one of my mint toffees.

'Hi, Bernie.'

The toffees served two purposes: they reminded me of my granny who always kept a few in the pocket of her body warmer which she always wore on market days; plus, they had a tremendous capacity of shutting people up when they outstayed their welcome in my tiny corner of the open-plan office.

'Have you had a chance to think about what we spoke about on Saturday?' He picked up a printed graph from my desk, scanned an eye over it and put it back down.

This was it; a thousand butterflies began to flap their wings in my stomach.

'I did,' I said taking a deep breath. 'And you were right. I can't carry on as I am. So—'

'Excellent! I knew you'd come round! I've booked the boardroom and ordered in sandwiches.' Bernie's eager face said it all; if ever there was anyone who loved his job more, I'd yet to meet them. He unwrapped the toffee and threw it up into his mouth as if he was catching popcorn. 'And you'll be great, you know, it's like riding a bike.'

I had to bite my lip; we'd be back to his 'back in the saddle' metaphor in a minute.

'Actually, with your permission, I was hoping not to come in at all tomorrow. I'd like to take some annual leave. Immediately. I think the time off will do me good, give me a chance to think.'

'I'm confused.' Bernie took his glasses off and polished them on his sleeve. His eyes looked tiny without being magnified by the lenses.

'I don't want to do the presentation.' I gave him a look of apology. 'I've already primed Gary.'

He gave a laugh of disbelief. 'I thought I'd made the company's position clear.'

I felt the thrum of a pulse in my ears as my mind raced feverishly ahead.

Choose happiness over habit.

Freddie had been wiser at twenty-two than I was at thirty-four. This job was a habit. It didn't fill my soul with joy, and I certainly wasn't happy at the thought of another ten, twenty years chasing promotion.

I'd been planning on simply asking for some time away from the job. But perhaps it was time to move on from here completely. There was a whole world out there if only I was brave enough to discover it.

But was I brave enough? My chest tightened. Was I over thinking this happy list, was I being too literal with Freddie's advice? I hadn't thought it through at all and yet here I was, on the verge of quitting my job. My livelihood.

A memory flashed up of Freddie and me charging into the estate agent's office and making an offer for our house on Pineapple Road. And it turned out to have been one of the best decisions we'd ever made. I could almost hear Freddie's voice cheering me on: *Go big or go home!*

'Bernie, you're right, you did.' I stood up, my heart pounding with the enormity of what I was about to do. I held out my hand to shake his. 'Please accept my resignation with immediate effect.'

'Whoah, now hold on a minute.' Bernie blinked. He looked like a disorientated little mole who had popped his head up from underground into bright light.

I shook my head firmly.

'There's something I need to do. For my brother, but most of all, for me.'

Chapter Six

I pulled up outside a pretty white cottage with a thatched roof and a plethora of tubs brimming with tulips lining the garden path. The wisteria winding its way up the walls wasn't in bloom yet, but even without it, the cottage had a fairy-tale feel to it and I felt my shoulders relax.

I read the wooden sign fixed to the wall aloud. '*Wisteria Cottage Flower School*; I've made it.'

It was late March and spring was in full swing. Two weeks had passed since I'd resigned from Zed Market Trends and several major things had happened in that time. Not least the fact that I'd followed my heart and decided to immerse myself in the world of flowers for a whole week, starting today.

Ethel had been all for it. In fact, she'd insisted on paying for the course for me as her way of thanking me for taking in Scamp permanently. 'There are no pockets in a shroud,' she'd said, foisting a cheque written in her wobbly writing into my hand. 'And I can't think of a better person to invest in.'

My dear old friend had made a big decision of her own: after a month at The Beeches, she'd come to the conclusion that being waited on hand and foot was far preferable to living alone in Pineapple Road and had taken up a permanent residency there. Independence lost its allure, she'd confided with dignified defeat, when all your friends were dead and you lived in fear of falling downstairs and lying in agony undiscovered for hours. And so although Scamp would always remain her dog in his canine heart, he'd be sharing a bed with me for the rest of his doggy days, a fact which made both her and me shed a tear.

'But you are definitely happy here?' I'd questioned as we'd ventured out into the gardens over the weekend with Scamp in front of us sniffing the path diligently.

'Of course! All to do with mindset,' she'd said stoically. She'd shunned the wheelchair one of the carers had brought out to reception for her and was clinging on to her walking frame for dear life.

'I've told myself that it's an adventure and I shall enjoy it just as much as the adventures which have gone before. Now let's head back inside, I promised to help Arthur with the crossword this afternoon and then there's an old Ronald Reagan film I want to watch and rumour has it that the kitchen has been making custard tarts for tea . . .'

Satisfied that my old friend hadn't had so much to occupy her for years, I approved of her decision and hoped that Scamp didn't mind being stuck with me. I cooked him some liver for his dinner just to cement my place in his affections.

Other big news was that Laura had moved in with Hamish. It was impossible not to be swept along by their happiness. Scamp and I were their first dinner guests and I came away feeling that both of them might just have found 'the one'.

And then there was my news. I'd stuck to my guns and wouldn't reconsider my decision to leave Zed Market Trends. And thanks to an empathetic Bernie and some remaining annual leave, I had officially left the company last Friday. My time was now my own.

I was giving myself a year's sabbatical from my career. I didn't quite know how I was going to fill it yet, but the sheer act of doing something radical and giving my life a shake-up had already given me a glimpse of the old Fearne. The Fearne who knew how to be happy. The Fearne who'd also inadvertently called a flower school looking for a beginner's workshop and had found herself handing over her credit card details for a five-day professional floristry course . . .

A course which was about to start any moment. There were several cars already filling the driveway and I wondered if I was the last one to arrive.

The cottage door opened and a woman wearing a long grey apron waved energetically to me.

'I'm Fiona and you must be Fearne,' she said, bustling over to shake my hand as I got out of the car. 'Come along, everyone's here and chomping at the bit to get cracking.'

'Pleased to meet you,' I said, following her to the front door. 'Before we join the others, can I just reiterate that I have no plans to be a professional florist, this is just a hobby. So I might not be as good as the others.'

Fiona's eyes sparkled. 'All my students enjoy themselves, they just happen to learn a great deal at the same time. And you never know, you might surprise yourself.'

I smiled. This was going to be fun, and since normally at this time on a Monday morning I'd be catching up with my research contacts in south east Asia, I had already surprised myself.

Following my tutor, I took my first step into Wisteria Cottage. The scent of fresh flowers drew me in. I was doing it, I thought, I'd stepped away from my ordinary life to do something which would make me happy. I was completely out of my comfort zone; Freddie would be proud.

Fiona led me along a hallway into a bright and airy studio dominated by a long wooden table. At one end, wide glass doors looked out into the pretty cottage garden and at the other was a workbench covered with tall buckets full of flowers. Bending over the flowers, mugs in hands, were the other three students.

'Karen, Claire, Harriet,' announced Fiona, gesturing to each of the women in turn. 'Meet Fearne. Now, there's a lot of theory to get through this morning, so Fearne, help yourself to coffee, take a seat, everyone and we'll begin.'

Two hours later my head was spinning with everything I'd learned and so far, we hadn't even touched a single petal. I'd learned about the giant flower markets in Holland and how to order from them, I'd heard about gerberas from Kenya, carnations from Columbia and roses from Ecuador, I'd discovered how to 'condition' flowers to keep them at their peak. And we'd discussed the difference between supermarket flowers and their superior counterparts at the high street florist.

Everyone else looked similarly overwhelmed. Karen and Claire, two sisters from Cheshire with grown up children of their own, were pooling their resources to open up a florist's shop in the village where they lived now.

Harriet, who looked about my age, had made copious notes in the pad we'd each been given. She'd done flowers for a few weddings as a hobby, she admitted but was planning on turning it into a full-time career.

Fiona disappeared into the kitchen to prepare something for lunch, leaving us a container each and instructions to select flowers for our first arrangement: a table decoration using flower foam. Harriet and I headed straight for the buckets of roses, while the sisters were still finishing their notes.

'Some flowers die if you don't keep them cool enough, some die if you don't keep them warm enough. Not in a draught, not in direct sunlight,' said Karen with a groan. 'At this rate the only place in our shop suitable for storing flowers will be the loo.'

'You and your weak bladder can keep them company then,' said Claire, scratching her head with her pen. 'But you make a good point. It seems the biggest challenge in floristry is preventing premature death of the flowers.'

I smiled to myself as a long-forgotten memory popped into my head.

'It's a race against time,' Granny used to say, hunched over the steering wheel as we'd bombed along country lanes in her flower van, the chiffon-pink sky heralding the dawn of another perfect day. 'From the moment we set up the flower stall, these blooms are starting to decline. It's my job to flog them before they keel over. Or else it's butter sandwiches for supper.'

'And did she say don't use bleach to clean the buckets or do?' said Karen, peering over her sister's shoulder. 'My poor menopausal brain has forgotten already.'

'Do,' I said. 'Unless the bucket is for roses. Then don't. Roses hate bleach.'

'Arrgh,' said Claire, flinging her pen down. 'We're doomed.'

'It's only our first morning,' I said. 'I'm sure it'll all make more sense by the end of the week.'

'It'll have to,' said Karen, getting to her feet. 'Come on Claire, leave the details. We can always google it if we need to know anything. Let's get onto the nice bit.'

'I don't know about nice,' said Claire, popping a huge sprig of eucalyptus followed by a fistful of sweet williams in her container. 'I'm all fingers and thumbs when it comes to anything creative.'

Becoming a florist seemed an odd choice in that case, I thought.

'When do you think you'll open the shop?' Harriet asked. She chose three beautiful lilac roses and placed them reverently into her container.

'Six weeks,' the women answered in unison. 'We've already signed the lease.'

There was a moment of stunned silence broken by Fiona's footsteps tapping along the tiled corridor.

'Now,' our tutor said brightly. 'How are you getting on? Does anyone need anything special?'

'A miracle?' said Karen hopefully and we all laughed.

The rest of the week flew by and soon it was Friday. Not only did I make three new friends, I made every sort of flower arrangement a modern florist would ever need, from handtied bouquets to bridesmaids' posies, corsages to head-bands and, as a team, we even decorated a moongate which was a huge metal hoop used at weddings. The moongate would be used at the wedding show that Fiona was exhib-iting at the following weekend, but we had been able to take the rest of our handiwork home with us. There were beautiful arrangements in every room of my little house now and I could scarcely keep the smile from my face as I walked from room to room. I loved every second of the week; the freedom, the instant beauty of our creations, the satisfaction of seeing my ideas coming to life and the sense of peace which came over me while I was concentrating on my work. And socialising felt good and as the week progressed, I could feel a bit of the old Fearne coming back.

I had no plans for the following week, but it would have to be pretty spectacular to beat the first week of my sabbatical. Maybe I should add something new to my happy list, or maybe I'd book a trip to Holland and visit the world's biggest flower market myself? Who knew; the world was my oyster.

As the last day was coming to an end, Fiona brought tea and cakes into the studio to have while we were finishing off our contemporary designs. Harriet's was the best. She was the undisputed star pupil of the week. She'd created an asymmetric structure of twisted willow, stargazer lilies and glossy dark green leaves. Any bride who picked Harriet to do her wedding flowers was in for a treat. Claire had decided that she was going to let Karen do the lion's share of the flower arranging after discovering her clumsy fingers would cost them a fortune in snapped stems and bruised blooms.

I'd gone for a white theme, calla lilies and hydrangea with a delicate arc of steel grass giving it an architectural feel. I was finishing it off with a sheaf of grass tied around the vase in a bow.

'That is stunning,' said Fiona, stepping around my arrangement and checking it out from every aspect. 'Your best yet. You had a natural gift for floristry when you began on Monday, but now your talents are shining through. Well done.'

The other women gave me a round of applause.

'I think it's a bit lumpy and I should have trimmed the lilies more, but thank you.' I felt my cheeks colour with everyone's attention on me. But for once I didn't feel the need to hide away or escape from view, or brace myself for a well-meaning comment which would lead on to how well I was doing following Freddie's death.

'Your shoulders were wedged up by your ears when you arrived on Monday,' Claire pointed out. 'And now you are glowing and relaxed.'

'You're lit up from within, Fearne.' Harriet looked up from her creation and tucked her hair behind her ears. 'I think flowers are sunshine for the soul.'

'I think you're right,' I replied softly.

Maybe, I realised with a surge of hope, maybe this really was the start of a new phase in my life. Could it really be that simple? The kindness reflected back at me warmed my heart and I was going to miss the three of them. Happy tears welled up in my eyes and I turned away to blink them back.

'Bloody hell,' said Claire, gesticulating at her sister. 'Write that down, Karen. We can have that on a blackboard outside the shop.'

We all laughed and I sent a silent thanks to Claire for changing the subject.

Over the course, we'd opened up to each other a little more each day and yesterday I'd told them about losing my brother and the letter I'd found over a decade after he'd written it. I'd been worried that it would open the floodgates for everyone else's personal bereavement stories, something which I'd struggled to cope with since losing Freddie. But to my delight the thing everyone wanted to talk about was my happy list and what they would put on theirs.

It was almost time to leave. We'd taken hundreds of photographs of our flower creations in Fiona's studio and even outside in her pretty cottage garden and now, reluctant to leave, we were swapping numbers and Facebook names.

'I'm so glad you managed to persuade me to attend the week-long course instead of one afternoon workshop,' I said, taking my apron off for the final time. 'It's been a wonderful experience.'

'Glad to hear it. It's called upselling,' said Fiona with a naughty giggle. 'The secret weapon in a florist's arsenal.

Never push a customer to spend more than they can afford. Just give them some options, make it easy for them to increase their budget if they want to.'

'Good idea,' said Karen with a sly smile. 'But there are a lot of elderly people who live in our village. And ours will be the only shop for miles. We've got to stock a bit of everything: milk, bread, stamps—'

'And wine,' Claire put in. 'All the essentials.'

'So our shop will be more than a florist,' Karen continued. 'It'll be the hub of the community, we hope.'

'What about you, Harriet?' Fiona asked, as we filed outside to our cars. 'What's next for you?'

'My sister is getting married here,' she replied, getting her phone out to show us a photo of the venue. 'So I've offered to do her flowers to give me some more experience. And then, I hope to do as many weddings as possible. My wedding day was the best day of my life and I want to help other brides have the day of their dreams just like I did. The cake, the dress, the flowers are the holy trinity of things people remember most about a wedding. I want to create flowers that no one will forget.'

I gave her an encouraging smile. 'I'm sure you will.'

'That's another good one,' Claire nudged her sister. 'You can put that on the business cards.'

'Tell you what,' said Karen, scribbling Harriet's wise words on the back of her hand with a biro. 'If your wedding business goes tits up, you can always go into writing motivational slogans.'

Harriet laughed. 'I think that's a compliment.'

'If that's your business ethos, Harriet, then I don't see how you can possibly fail,' I said, feeling proud of them all. 'All of you have such good intentions for your floral skills. I've only done this course to make myself happy. I feel a bit selfish.'

'Absolutely nothing wrong with that,' said Fiona firmly. 'As Oscar Wilde once said, "A flower blossoms for its own joy" and yes, Claire, you can have that one as well.'

We all hugged goodbye after that. Karen and Claire drove off first, followed by Harriet. As I started the engine in mine, Fiona knocked on the glass and gestured for me to open the window.

'I hope you will cultivate your new skills, experiment with different containers and practise, practise, practise until you're spiralling stems for a hand-tied bouquet in your sleep.'

I gave her a lopsided smile. 'I will. I've learned so much this week, but I've only scratched the surface and I want to keep improving.'

'We all carry on learning our whole lives,' she replied. 'But flowers have a way of making people smile, even when a project seems impossible. All you have to do is let the flowers do the talking and have a little faith.'

I drove back home feeling happier than I'd done in months. Fiona was right. Flowers had already made me smile and life seemed a lot brighter for it.

Chapter Seven

'Over here!' Laura waved to me across the crowds outside the busy café. I waved back and headed over to where she and Scamp were waiting at the only empty table.

It was Saturday, the day after the flower course had finished and much as I loved having flowers in every room, I decided to share the love. Scamp and I had already dropped in on Ethel and given her a jug arrangement for her room and then we'd called at Hamish and Laura's house to give them one of the large bouquets for the dining table. I'd found Laura on her own, researching recipes for simnel cake ready for Easter weekend next week.

Hamish was stranded in Paris after a fire in the Channel Tunnel had delayed all the trains back to the UK. And as she was on her own, I'd suggested a walk in the sunshine to the nearest café.

'One chai latte and a cinnamon bun for you,' I said, setting the tray down. 'Tea and a giant shortbread biscuit for me.'

Scamp's ears pricked up at the 'b' word.

'Of course I didn't forget you.' I took a Dentastix out of my bag, which the vet had suggested might help his antisocial breath, and held it out to him.

He eyed it glumly before ignoring it and slumping under the table next to it in disappointment.

'Sorry, mate, you can sulk all you like,' I said sticking it back in my bag. 'But the honeymoon period is over, I've got to be a responsible dog owner now I'm providing your forever home.'

'That's how I feel about living with Hamish,' said Laura.

'Like a sulky dog?' I said, accidentally-on-purpose knocking a chunk of my shortbread off my plate. Scamp hoovered it up before it hit the floor. Well, he was twelve years old, what harm could it do?

'Haha,' she said drily. 'No, the honeymoon period bit. It still feels like I'm playing house, and the food he cooks! Oh my word! I think I've put on half a stone since moving in with him.'

'In ten days?' I raised an eyebrow. 'That's some going. What's he doing, force-feeding you?'

Laura eyes softened dreamily. 'He's cherishing me. That's what it is, I feel cherished. And content. I love it.'

'It shows,' I said. 'You look radiant. I'm happy for you. I'd have been happy for you months ago if you'd told me sooner.'

'Really?' She gave me a quizzical look.

'OK, perhaps I'd have still behaved like a spoiled brat,' I admitted, cringing at my full-on strop at the spa. 'But let's put that behind us. I'm glad it's out in the open. Just don't forget your best friend. We can do this whenever you're at a loose end. I'm happy to fill the Hamish-shaped hole in your weekend.'

'How could I forget you? Anyway, I'm not going to squeeze seeing you into the times when Hamish is busy,' she said with an admonishing look. 'Sisters before misters, remember? Although my weekends might have more Hamish-shaped holes than I'd like. With the number of football players he represents and the matches he has to attend, I'm already a Saturday sport widow.'

'You've got to be married before you can be a widow, remember.'

She blushed and leaned forward. 'I'll let you into a secret. I've been practising my married signature. Mrs Laura McNamee.'

I snorted. 'You're not still doing that! Remember that boy—'

'Paul Leggett! Don't!' Laura covered her face in embarrassment.

We both collapsed in a fit of giggles at the memory. Laura had been so obsessed with Paul Leggett in sixth form that she'd scribbled Laura Leggett everywhere. Which was absolutely fine until our English teacher held up a piece of homework at the front of the class and asked whether it was Paul's or Laura's or was it in fact a team effort. Paul never did ask her out after all that.

'You haven't changed,' I said, shaking my head fondly.

Laura's face grew serious for a moment. 'But you have. I feel like I'm getting my best friend back. I've missed going places with you. Like book club and yoga and drinks with the girls.'

I smiled awkwardly. 'You are getting your friend back. And I'm sorry I've been away so long. It's just that it has been easier to avoid public situations.'

She covered my hand with hers; I knew she understood. It had been hideous for her when her mum died. 'People are on your side,' she said. 'They just don't always know how to show it, or what to say.'

'And then it becomes the elephant in the room,' I said with a shudder. 'Until someone cracks and feels the need to address it. I can tell when they're about to launch into some crappy platitude and I can feel my porcupine spikes ping into action.'

Laura pulled a piece off her cinnamon bun and laughed. 'You have been a bit porcupine-y. Good image.'

I grinned. 'I thought so. But seriously, how can someone think that telling a grieving sister that things happen for a reason was ever going to improve matters?'

She rolled her eyes. 'Ugh. Or my personal favourite, which made me want to stab them in the eye. "She did what she came here to do, it was her time to go." *If that was true*, I wanted to yell in their faces, *Mum would never have booked a holiday which she never got to go on, so put that in your patronising pipe and smoke it.*'

Until Freddie died, I'd only lost Granny. I'd cried at the time, but I'd got over it fairly quickly. I think I'd been just as upset when her cottage in Wales had been sold to pay for her care home. I was a teenager then and although I loved her, selfishly my world revolved around me and my friends; dying was what old people did. But brothers weren't supposed to die and neither were women Laura's mum's age.

'Was I a terrible friend when your mum died?' I asked.

She blinked at me, surprised. 'Not at all. You listened without butting in. That was all I really needed: someone to listen to my ranting and raving. You were a great friend. Still are.'

She squeezed my hand and we were quiet for a moment, lost in our own thoughts.

'Ditto,' I said. 'Although in my case, I didn't want to talk at all. Which isn't like me.'

She grinned. 'True. But no one knows how they'll react until it happens. That's why "I know how you feel" is so bloody annoying. No one can possibly know how you feel. And you'll talk about it when you're ready.'

She held my gaze for a moment, giving me the chance to speak if I wanted to and then stirred the remains of her latte slowly, staring into the milky foam.

'I've resisted talking about my feelings because I didn't want them to be real,' I admitted, feeling under the table for the reassuring solidity of Scamp's body.

Laura stayed perfectly still, but gave me an encouraging smile. I swallowed. Already my throat was tightening, making it hard to form my words. But if I could manage to talk to my new friends at the floristry school, the least I could do is open up to my oldest friend.

'Freddie has just always been there,' I began. 'My earliest memory is of him stealing the ice cream off the top of my cone. I must have only been about two. Greedy sod.'

Laura laughed. 'Sounds about right for big brother behaviour.'

'It didn't matter where I was, he was always with me. When my dad left us, Freddie was the one thing that remained constant. Mum's attitude to life changed over-night, not that that was a bad thing, but it took some getting used to. Dad we rarely saw even before he moved away. But whether I was at home or at Granny's, Freddie was always with me, shaping the memories of my life. Even my first house purchase was done with him.'

'I always envied the relationship you had with him.' She tore off a piece of her bun and ate it. 'You were lucky to have a sibling. Being an only child isn't half as much fun.'

'None of the new memories I make will have him in them,' I said. 'And I don't want that to be true. I haven't wanted to move on because I'm worried about leaving him behind.'

Laura frowned. 'You know, I think he'd be really sad about that.'

'I know. I can't stay in denial forever, I accept that. I need to find a way to live without him, to live alone and still be happy.'

'*Without* him, yes,' she said, briskly, 'but not alone, there's no need to banish other people completely.'

'I never want to miss anyone this much again,' I said. 'It seems the best way to do that is not to let anyone in.'

'Just keep your mind open,' she said. 'You won't always feel this way, I promise.'

'What if I fall in love and lose them? Look how badly I've coped with losing a sibling. I don't want to go through this again ever.'

'I'll always miss Mum but I try not to dwell on all the things she hasn't been part of; instead I remember the times that she was there. And I do believe I carry a piece of her in my heart always.'

'Same with me and Freddie. And now that I have that letter from him, I feel even closer to him than before.' I gave myself a shake and forced a laugh. 'How did we get so maudlin all of a sudden? Let's change the subject.'

'OK.' Laura cast about for a second and then slapped the table. 'Let's talk about your happy list. Number one on the list is flowers. What's your number two going to be?'

'Not sure,' I said with a frown. 'Freddie's big thing was travel, different cultures, different scenery. But I'm quite fond of England. I like cottages and cream teas and now I've got a dog, I quite like country walks. I know, I know, I'm boring!'

'You're *you*,' said Laura loyally. 'Nothing wrong with this green and pleasant land.'

She picked up a discarded newspaper from the table next to us and pointed at one of the headlines. 'You can travel *and* stay at home. Look at this article in the *Derbyshire Bugle*: ten villages which the locals don't want you to know about. There you go. You've got a whole year at your disposal, you could travel around, discover undiscovered England, stay in cottages and eat your way through cream teas.'

I took it from her and turned to the article mentioned on the page.

'This isn't a bad idea, actually,' I said. 'I could go away for a few days, find a cottage to rent. I haven't got any plans for next week and Scamp would love it.'

I was in the fortunate position of not needing very much money to live on. Freddie and I had taken out an insurance policy when we bought the house so that if either one of us became seriously ill or died, the mortgage would be paid off. So now I owned the house in full and that, coupled with a conservative attitude to savings since childhood, meant that I could get by for a while without the need to earn a wage.

'That's you sorted then. Do you want another drink?' Laura pointed at my empty mug.

'Better not. Scamp will need to go out for a wee soon and I promised him a long walk before I start boxing up more of Freddie's stuff.'

She got her purse out and tried to give me money for her share of the bill, but I waved her away.

'My treat. It's the least I can do after everything.'

She sighed in defeat. 'Thank you. But no more. You've already given me a beautiful bouquet and you've apologised a million times anyway,' said Laura, putting her purse down.

'Just one more thing,' I said, smiling. 'If you and Hamish do ever get married—'

She gave a bark of laughter. 'You want to be my maid of honour. Yes of course, goes without saying.'

'Well, thank you. But I was going to say I'd like to do your flowers. As my wedding present to you.'

Her eyes widened. 'Oh, Fearne. That is the loveliest offer I've ever had. I'd love that, thank you.'

'All you need now is the groom to pop the question.'

She beamed. 'Of course, and there's no rush. No rush at all. Although I might have a scroll through Pinterest, just to pick up a few ideas.'

'You might as well,' I said with a grin, 'seeing as you've already perfected your signature.'

A few minutes later, we were ready to leave. Laura headed to the loo while I stayed put with Scamp. I turned my attention back to the article on undiscovered villages in the newspaper to see if any of them were close by. There was one that stood out immediately:

The picturesque village of Barnaby nestled in the heart of the Derbyshire Dales will charm the pants off you. With its traditional village green, narrow streets and chocolate-box cottages, it's so beloved by its tiny population that property rarely comes onto the market. Locals, however, welcome visitors with open arms and the Lemon Tree Café in the centre of the village is dog-friendly and serves delicious Italian delicacies, making it the perfect destination for a weekend hike.

Was visiting two cafés in one day really greedy, I wondered. Because suddenly the thought of being cooped up at home clearing yet more of Freddie's things held no appeal at all.

Scamp thumped his tail vigorously against the table leg, alerting me to Laura's imminent return.

'This one's actually not far away.' I tapped the page while she read it over my shoulder.

'Barnaby? Sounds idyllic,' she agreed.

I folded the newspaper and stuffed it into my bag. 'I shall report back and let you know if it makes it onto my happy list.'

She stared at me, amused. 'Are you really going to go?'

'Yep. Right now. Next stop the Lemon Tree Café.'

Chapter Eight

According to the satnav, Barnaby was about half an hour away from home. Not far, but before I'd had Scamp, I hadn't really been into walking so I didn't know the Derbyshire Dales well. But by the time I'd negotiated tight bends and up and down hills I was already a teeny bit in love with it. Scamp behaved himself perfectly and after turning a few circles on the passenger seat, settled down for a nap while I enjoyed the scenery.

I passed the village sign informing me I'd reached Barnaby and my heart skipped with delight; whoever had written the article in the *Derbyshire Bugle* was right. It was love at first sight; the village was charming the pants off me.

Everywhere was in bloom: trees were covered in pink blossom, cottage gardens were brimming with tulips, daffodils and grape hyacinths, and the village green was dotted with clouds of bluebells and cowslips. I slowed down after passing a little school and edged carefully down the main street which was partially blocked by parked cars outside the church. In my peripheral vision I was aware of a row of shops opposite. The Lemon Tree Café and its famous Italian delicacies were probably over there, but I carried on until I found a space to park, intending to take Scamp for a walk before eating anything else.

Once Scamp had completed his full range of yoga stretches, I attached him to his lead and we set off. A signpost ahead promising a riverside walk drew me towards it and before long, we were passing through a wooden kissing gate and underneath a canopy of hawthorn blossom. A small patch of woodland stretched ahead of us; new growth swished in the slight breeze and filtered sunlight made a fluttering mosaic on the ground. I stuck to the fairly dry path, but Scamp, his tail waving like a furry flag, tore from left to right, hoovering up the delicious smells of damp earth and brittle sticks and clumps of wild garlic. Overhead an orchestra of birds serenaded us with the sound of springtime and I breathed in deeply, feeling incredibly smug with my spur-of-the-moment excursion.

We emerged from the trees and joined a towpath bordered each side with swathes of long grass sprinkled with dandelions, one side of which sloped down towards the river. We walked past a hotel where people were sitting out on the terrace enjoying drinks in the sunshine. Off to the side, as if awaiting a wedding party, was a large white marquee decked out with bunting. In front of the hotel was a small wooden jetty where a row of brightly painted narrowboats were lined up end to end.

'England's green and pleasant land, eh, Scamp,' I said, remembering Laura's words. I picked up a stick and flung it as far as I could. 'We approve, don't we?'

I smiled, watching him delve into the tufty grass after his stick. I honestly couldn't think of a single thing I'd rather be doing right now than this. This unexpected expedition might well earn a place on my happy list.

Because I *was* happy.

Doing this simple thing with the dog had made me happy. It seemed so straightforward, too easy almost, but it felt as if there was a shift in the burden of sadness I'd been under and light was beginning to find its way through, like the sunlight through the trees. Perhaps it was just timing; perhaps I'd have been feeling better by now without coming across those words of wisdom from Freddie. I'd never know. But that letter felt like a lucky charm, a talisman to live my life by.

The weather was warm for the time of year and I was beginning to feel the sting of sun on my pale face. Scamp had begun to pant and was eyeing up the river longingly. I had no idea if he could swim or not and had no desire to find out just at the moment.

I called him over and clipped on his lead. 'Let's head back and get you a drink. Perhaps that dog-friendly café will have a bowl full of water for you. And then we can explore the village.'

We retraced our steps and were soon back at the car. I collected my bag and shook out a lump of dried liver from a tub for Scamp. I'd parked a couple of hundred metres or so away from the village green and I could see it in the distance. Small groups of people were clustered together posing for photographs, others were milling about chatting while children played around their parents' legs. Even from my position, I could see that the number of cars near the entrance to the church had swelled to almost gridlock proportions. The church bells began to ring and people sprang into action, gathering little ones, adjusting buttonholes and straightening hats.

It had to be a wedding, and what a perfect day for it. I stowed the dog treats back in my bag and we set off towards the church. With any luck I'd get a glimpse of the bride and I was interested to see the wedding flowers. We'd made all sorts of wedding arrangements at the Wisteria Cottage flower school: bridesmaids' bouquets, garlands, table decorations and even the pièce de resistance – the moongate. If I managed to get close enough, I'd take some photos and send them to Harriet.

'Come on, Scamp,' I said, picking up my pace, 'let's try and find somewhere to lurk before the bride arrives.'

There was a beautiful ancient lychgate at the entrance to the churchyard and a floral swag made from various types of narcissi had been wound around one of the old oak beams. I took my phone out to take a few pictures quickly and had just managed to zoom in on a gorgeous detail of twisted willow and variegated ivy when Scamp's tail began flapping against my leg, alerting me to the presence of someone else.

I turned to find myself face to face with a man with unruly brown hair and amused eyes. He was dressed in a suit and holding a professional-looking camera.

'I'd get yourself seated inside, if I were you.' He nodded towards the road. 'Here comes the bride.'

Sure enough an old-fashioned cream Rolls Royce was creeping at a snail's pace towards us.

'I'm not a guest,' I said.

He grinned. 'I'm not a photographer either, so wish me luck.'

Odd, I thought, watching as the man leaned into the road as the wedding car came to a halt. He snapped away at the bride who waved and smiled from the back seat. Next to her, an older man, the father of the bride presumably, looked beside himself with pride.

The driver opened the bride's door and the man who claimed not to be a photographer squatted down and took some more pictures. The bride was on the opposite side of the car to me so I couldn't see much other than an awful lot of ivory lace veil, but I could hear her laughing and saying that she couldn't move in her dress and had anyone got a winch.

Aware that Scamp and I looked rather conspicuous standing there like lemons, I opened the lychgate and slipped inside the church grounds out of view. There was a sudden clatter and yell behind me and I turned to see a long-legged dog with a bow around its neck hurtling towards us and a small boy in hot pursuit trying to catch the end of the dog's trailing lead. Scamp raised his eyebrows and bounced on the spot at the prospect of a new playmate.

'Catch Hugo for me please!' shouted the boy.

Hugo, tongue wagging, made a beeline for us. He looked delighted with himself for breaking free from church. As he and Scamp began the ancient ritual of bottom-sniffing I grabbed the end of Hugo's lead and held on to it tightly.

'Good boy,' I crooned to the dog who looked like a cross between a spaniel and a Labrador and had the most gorgeous fluffy ears.

'That was close,' said the little boy, pretending to wipe his brow with relief. 'Thank you.'

'You're welcome.'

He took the lead from me then glanced up and saw the wedding car. 'Yikes, Mummy's arrived. I'd better get back in there. Come on Hugo, we've got a job to do. Bye!'

'Bye,' I replied with a grin.

What a sweet boy; I was no expert but he must have been about eight years old. He looked very cute in his outfit: trousers, white shirt and a full-length adult tie which poked out from the bottom of his waistcoat. He had a yellow and white buttonhole pinned to his chest. As he and the dog headed back towards the church, something fell from his pocket.

'Wait! You've dropped something,' I called, stepping forward to pick it up. It was a ring box.

'Yikes again!' His eyes widened, as he dragged the dog back to collect it from me. 'Dad would ban me from the Xbox for life if I lost the rings.'

'Let's make sure that doesn't happen,' I said, smiling at his earnest little face. 'Tuck it away safely. Are you an usher?'

He puffed his chest out, shaking his head. 'I'm the best man. I've got to do a speech at the party and everything.'

He put the ring box in his pocket and then froze. 'Oh no.'

'What is it?'

His chin started to wobble. 'My speech. It was in my pocket and now it's gone.'

I cast about on the ground looking for it, but couldn't see anything vaguely speech-like.

'What's your name?'

Before he could answer, the bride and her father appeared on the other side of the lychgate, thankfully still being occupied by the man pretending to be a photographer, but they'd be through that gate any minute.

'Noah,' he whispered, his face getting more crumpled by the second.

Scamp and Hugo were still trotting around in an endless circle and getting their leads tangled.

'I bet you'll give a great speech,' I said, unravelling the leads. 'Even if you have to make it up on the spot. Just say that the bridesmaids look beautiful, they'll like that, and then tell a funny story about the groom.'

'That's my dad,' Noah nodded thoughtfully. 'I suppose I do know quite a few funny things to say.'

'There you go then,' I said, keeping an eye on the bridal party.

'Like the time he farted in church and tried to blame Granddad.'

I managed to keep a straight face. Well what did I expect? He was a small boy; Freddie's favourite toys when he was a similar age were a whoopee cushion and a fake dog poo. 'Hmm, anything else, maybe not about wind?'

'Not wind.' Noah thought for a second. 'There is one about snow.'

'Much better,' I said with relief.

His eyes sparkled mischievously. 'Daddy's car got stuck in the snow driving up the hill and he was so scared he did a little poo.'

'Whoops,' I said, swallowing a giggle. 'Perhaps you'll find your speech in time.'

'What's your name?' he asked warily as if suddenly realising he was talking to a stranger.

'Er . . .' I hesitated, not wanting to get the blame for the amount of toilet-related humiliation about to be heaped on the poor groom by his son.

I was saved from having to answer by the gate being opened and the bride walked through on the arm of the man I assumed was her dad.

'Hello darling!' she said to Noah, a huge smile visible under her veil.

Also visible, although not as huge was a bump under her dress; she was definitely pregnant. Her flowers were amazing: a rustic bouquet of pale yellow ranunculus, white roses and sunshine-centred daisies, wrapped in ivy.

'Hi Mummy, hi Granddad, I just brought Hugo out for one minute,' he said, shooting a nervous glance in my direction, probably hoping I wouldn't grass on him about the escaped dog, dropped wedding rings and mislaid speech. I smiled evenly, hoping that the bride didn't want to know who I was. 'And now I'm going back in. Bye.'

'That's a good lad,' said his granddad.

He ran off, with Hugo scampering ahead, then stopped, pulled out something from his other pocket and turned around to me, with a wide grin.

'Found it!' he yelled, waving a scrunched-up piece of paper at me.

I gave him a thumbs-up; what an adorable boy.

'Gorgeous flowers,' I said to the bride, squeezing through the gate and pulling Scamp with me. 'Have a fabulous day!'

I left the wedding party to it and crossed the green, heading towards the café. It had a striped yellow and grey awning and a sign with 'The Lemon Tree Café' picked out in delicate pale grey lettering. My stomach rumbled; it had been a long time since that shortbread and I was in the mood for something substantial.

As I drew closer, my heart sank; all the lights were off inside and the café was deserted. A handwritten note on the glass door gave me the bad news: it was closed for a family wedding. In fact, now I looked carefully, I could see that everything was closed up except the pub but I didn't like sitting in pubs by myself, even with a dog for company.

'Back to the car then, Scamp,' I said with a sigh. Even he looked disappointed.

Next door to the café was a flower shop called Nina's Flowers. There was a small card stuck to the door. I bent closer to read it, expecting it to be a notice about the shop being closed for a wedding, but it was an advertisement for a job vacancy. I stepped forward to peer inside when a flash of movement caught my eye. I shielded my eyes from the light so that I could make out the interior. A small dark-haired woman was leaning over the counter, a mountain of ivy fronds piled up beside her; it looked like she was crying. I couldn't hear anything over the church bells but next to me, Scamp cocked his head to one side.

'Someone doesn't seem very happy, do they?' I said, scratching his neck.

I almost walked away and left her to it; after all, it was none of my business, but at the last second I changed my mind. I knocked briskly on the glass and the head on the counter flipped up to stare at me.

'We're closed!' shouted a sob-weary voice.

'Are you OK?' I shouted back, trying to inject as much compassion into my raised voice as I could. 'You look like maybe you could do with some help?'

For a long moment the woman didn't move but then she peeled herself from behind the counter and dragged herself across the shop.

The door opened just enough for me to note the puffy eyes beneath a heavy dark fringe, sore fingers holding the door frame and the edge of a pretty cream dress printed with soft pink peonies.

'Whoever you are, you're very kind, but unless you're a florist, there's nothing you can do.'

My head told me to smile sorrowfully and head back to the car. But my heart . . . my heart couldn't bear to see such sadness when there was something I could do to help.

I crossed my fingers behind my back. 'Then it's your lucky day.'

Well. I didn't exactly lie.

Chapter Nine

The woman clung to the edge of the door as if she might collapse if she let go. 'But we're strangers, why would you want to help me? I can't even pay you.'

There was a tiny chink of hope in her eyes and my heart went out to her.

'Karma,' I said simply. 'What goes around comes around. Maybe one day I'll be in need of assistance and someone will come to my rescue. I'm Fearne and this handsome devil is Scamp. And I'm guessing you must be Nina?'

She nodded, adding flatly, 'Pleased to meet you.'

She looked exhausted; she had hollows under her eyes the size of moon craters, not helped by smudged eyeliner and streaks of mascara.

I looked past her into the shop. 'So how can I help?'

I hardly needed to ask: the huge quantity of flowers, which incidentally had the most amazing perfume, and the stack of white packing boxes on the floor were a bit of a giveaway: it looked as if she had a large order to fulfil and was behind schedule.

She sighed. 'I'm doing the flowers for a friend's wedding and everything that would possibly go wrong has.'

I chewed my lip, trying not to show my dismay. A wedding. And for a friend. No wonder she was stressed.

'Oh dear, well I'm here now,' I said brightly. 'Let's get stuck in. When is the wedding?'

Just then the church bells fell silent. Nina's face crumpled in horror.

'Now. It's literally starting now the other side of the green.' She brushed a tear from her face. She opened the door wide enough for us both to enter. 'Oh balls. Not only have I messed up Rosie's wedding, I've actually missed it as well.'

She was a guest as well as the florist? I tried not to show my panic. What a nightmare.

Nina said something else then, but it was more of a wail and I couldn't make out the words. Scamp's eyebrows were moving from left to right and I could tell he was picking up on Nina's anxiety. It was time to take action.

'Why don't you sit down while you give me some instructions?' I handed her some tissue paper from a roll on the end of the counter.

She dabbed at her eyes, making the mascara even more smeared.

'There's no time for sitting,' she muttered, but didn't put up much of a fight when I nudged her into a chair.

As soon as she sat down, Scamp, ever game for some fuss, rested his chin on her knee and gazed up at her with worried eyes.

'And I hope you don't mind,' I said, 'but Scamp and I are parched. Do you have anything to drink?'

'Through there.' Nina pointed to an open doorway at the back of the shop through which I could see a tiny kitchen.

'He's impossible not to love,' said Nina, when I returned with water for all three of us.

I smiled. 'He was a rescue dog, although in reality, it was he who rescued me. OK, where do we start?'

Nina took a sip of water and then began to tell me what was what.

She was about twelve hours behind schedule. Partly because her assistant, Kelly had left without working her notice to take up another job and she hadn't yet found a replacement. And partly because the fire in the Channel Tunnel yesterday – the same one which had left Hamish stranded – meant that her flower order hadn't been delivered and she'd had to buy up what the wholesalers had spare and they had only arrived late yesterday evening.

'I've worked through the night,' Nina said with a wan smile. 'I managed to get the buttonholes and the bouquets for the bride and bridesmaids and the swag for the church lychgate done. But the marquee for the reception is totally flowerless.'

'Is it the marquee at a pub near the river?' I asked, thinking back to our walk earlier.

'The Riverside Hotel, yes,' said Nina.

She told me that after the service, the wedding party would have photographs in the church grounds, then travel on to the hotel where champagne was to be served on the terrace before everyone would retire to the marquee for the wedding breakfast at four.

'I met the bride a few minutes ago, and the best man.'

Nina gasped. 'And? How did she seem? Was her bouquet all right?'

'All the flowers were gorgeous; in fact, I loved them so much, I took pictures to show a friend.' I pulled out my phone and showed her the photos I'd taken. 'And she looked radiant, blooming actually.'

Nina made a whimpering noise. 'Her baby is due in July, the last thing she needs is stress.'

'Look,' I said hurriedly, conscious of the time. 'All is not lost. We've got a couple of hours before the wedding breakfast. If you're quick, you can still get to see them tie the knot.'

She blinked at me, wide-eyed. 'And leave you here alone?'

'You can trust me,' I promised. 'But if it makes you feel better . . . There you go.' I held out my car keys to her. 'Now I can't escape with your stock.'

'*Bloody hell!*' Nina said shakily, refusing to take them. 'I've never, I mean, how kind, that's just . . . Oh God.'

'Don't cry again,' I said flapping at her. 'Now go. Or you'll miss the kiss.'

'*The kiss,*' she squealed, yanking on her apron strings to remove it. The full short skirt of her dress sprang out. 'Literally can't wait to see that. Such a gorgeous couple.'

Scamp, buoyed by the new energy in the room, started to bounce around in circles, barking at his tail. I caught his collar before he knocked Nina over.

'Thanks so much for this.' She planted a fierce kiss to my cheek. 'You're an angel.'

'See you at the venue,' I said, feeling slightly hysterical with all this excitement.

She chucked me the shop keys, grabbed a pink corsage from the counter and dashed out of the door. 'Good luck,' she yelled over her shoulder. 'And thank you again.'

Scamp and I watched her sprint towards the green while simultaneously trying to pin the corsage to her dress. Once she'd disappeared from view, I turned back to the scene of floral devastation in the shop.

My stomach flipped at the size of the task ahead and the limited time I had to accomplish it. How would Fiona, the flower school teacher, tackle it? Only one way to find out. I found her number and called her.

'Heavens above!' Fiona cried when I brought her up to speed with the job in hand. 'When I told you to practise, this wasn't quite what I had in mind.'

'Me neither,' I said, surveying the vast quantities of spring flowers awaiting my attention. 'Where shall I start? And how do I prioritise?'

'OK,' said Fiona, clearing her throat. 'Grab a pen and make notes . . .'

I did as I was told and for the next couple of minutes I scribbled down as many instructions, including the main priorities and some brilliant cheats, as Fiona could think of.

'So in short: maximum impact with minimum effort,' I repeated, counting on my fingers. 'Concentrate on the areas which will appear in most of the photos and anything which will only be seen from a distance, fudge it. Got it. I hope.'

'Do you remember what I said yesterday?' Fiona said lastly.

Her comment brought me up short; I'd only graduated from flower school twenty-four hours ago and now I was in charge of someone's wedding.

'Let the flowers do the talking and have a little faith,' I said, pushing down a shiver of fear. 'I'll do my best. And thank you.'

'No, thank *you*. Seeing my students blossom is my greatest reward,' Fiona declared, then adding timidly, 'And if you wouldn't mind tagging the flower school in the photos . . .?'

I said I would, I ended the call and took a deep breath.

What had started with Laura handing me a random article about undiscovered villages had morphed into possibly the biggest, most nerve-wracking challenge of my life. The funny thing was, I realised, that I might be out of my comfort zone, but I was enjoying every second of it.

You can do this, Fearne, said a small voice in my head, sounding very much like Freddie.

'Go big or go home,' I said firmly and tied on Nina's apron.

It felt a bit like one of those cookery shows where the contestants are given a mystery bag of ingredients and have to invent dishes without being able to look up the recipes. But after a very quick exploration of what I had to work with, I managed to form a plan. Nina had been halfway through a long and complicated garland which I'd got no hope of finishing but I'd use it somewhere. There was also a box of white bowls and circles of flower foam cut to size which I presumed were for table decorations. But I wasn't going to use them, I had a new idea which would be far quicker and simpler.

Fiona advised me to do the flowers *in situ* so Scamp and I ran back to fetch my car and I crammed aluminium buckets full of flowers into every available space.

Then grabbing ribbon, string, scissors, wire and any other tool which looked remotely useful, I coaxed a bewildered Scamp into the front seat and off we drove, with me steering around every bump and pothole in the road to minimise spillages.

The bells were ringing again by the time I skirted the village green and I was vaguely aware of a crowd emerging from the church. But there was no time to stop and watch them, the clock was ticking. Finding the Riverside Hotel by road was straightforward and thanks to a friendly member of staff who was stationed at the front doors ready to direct the wedding guests (eek!) I was able to drive right up to the marquee.

I left Scamp in the car for a moment while I went inside. I had no idea what the protocol was for bringing a dog to work with me, although I couldn't leave him in the car in this sunshine for long, but for now, I needed to get my bearings without him tugging on his lead to investigate this new and exciting place.

And exciting it was.

As well as a long top table, there were ten round tables, each laid with eight place-settings: glassware sparkled and silver cutlery shone. There was a serving area at one end and a dance floor at the other and beside that was a pretty white structure resembling a huge bird cage and set inside that, on top of a table was a three-tier wedding cake.

It was already beautiful.

'But you ain't seen nothin' yet,' I murmured.

I turned to head back to the car, my pulse racing with a sudden burst of adrenaline when a group of staff arrived carrying ice buckets on stands.

'Can I help you?' asked one of them: a woman, in a smart black suit and crisp white shirt.

'I'm Fearne, the florist,' I said. 'I'm about to decorate the marquee.'

The other members of staff smiled and carried on with their preparations.

'Where's Nina?' she said, striding over on spiky heels which sank in the grass. Her red hair had been scraped back so tightly into a ponytail that she'd given herself a facelift. 'Is she OK? I heard what happened with her flower delivery. If that was me I'd have topped myself. I mean, you don't want to let someone down on their big day do you?'

'Not really, no,' I said drily.

I explained that I was helping Nina who, although having a stressful time, hadn't yet felt the need to commit suicide and was probably throwing confetti over the bride and groom as we spoke.

'I'm the events manager for the hotel,' she said, shaking my hand. 'You've got an hour, tops, to get the flowers *in situ*. After that, the catering team will be in and you'll have to leave.'

'Oh crap,' I muttered under my breath. A beginner like me would need an entire day to do a good job.

The woman grinned. 'Wedding flowers are always a crap job.'

Just then a lanky teenager with a shaggy haircut and a soft fluffy moustache sloped into the marquee pulling a trolley loaded with crates of drinks. I eyed the trolley longingly.

'Could I borrow that do you think?' I asked. 'It would be perfect to ferry the flowers from my car.'

'Sure.' The events manager relayed my request to the young man who set about emptying it for me. 'I'm Kelly, by the way. If you need any help, give me or one of my team a shout.'

'Thank you,' I said, wondering if 'help' extended to flower-arranging. Her name rang a bell . . . 'Are you the Kelly who used to work for Nina?'

Her face flushed. 'Yes.' She glanced over her shoulder to check none of her team were in earshot and lowered her voice. 'Why, what did she tell you about me?'

I considered the million and one flowers in the back of my car and ticking clock and decided to be creative with my answer. 'Only that she misses you and that you're really talented with flowers.'

Kelly frowned. 'Nina said that?'

That frown was slightly alarming; maybe I'd overdone it with 'talented'. However, beggars couldn't be choosers . . .

'She certainly misses you.' I nodded earnestly. 'So if you're serious about helping, I'd be honoured. I am rather against the clock.'

She sucked in a sharp breath. 'This is my first wedding in my new job. The last thing I need is for Nina to cock it up for me by not being ready. OK, I'll muck in for a bit, this lot know what they're doing anyway.'

She peeled off her jacket and chucked it over the back of a chair. 'Right, where's your workbench?'

My vast inexperience hit me in a tsunami of doubt. I hadn't thought about where I'd actually create my flower displays and I certainly hadn't realised I'd need a workbench. I had a flash of nostalgia for the long wooden table at the Wisteria Flower school where we were allowed to create as much chaos as we wanted. 'Um . . .'

Kelly was waiting for an answer, a bemused smile making her cherry red lips twitch.

I drew myself up tall. This time last year, I'd delivered the keynote speech at a conference for Scandinavian timber merchants about the future of global paper consumption. If I could hold my own in front of them, I could certainly handle leave-in-the-lurch Kelly. I gave her a tightly efficient smile. 'Nina said you'd have a trestle table set up for me?'

'Did she?' Her eyes darted left and right as if scrolling through her memory for that detail.

I nodded.

'Arses.' She stomped off to sort it out.

I let out a breath. Today was turning out to be a good deal more nerve-racking than planned, I thought, heading back to the car to release Scamp. I was well and truly out of my comfort zone, and, amazingly, I was enjoying every second of it.

Chapter Ten

Kelly wasn't the most delicate of florists, plus she was accident prone and potty-mouthed. In the first five minutes she managed to knock a full watering-can over her shoes, stab herself with secateurs and snap the heads of several precious peonies, while supplying everyone with an expletive-heavy running commentary on her woes.

In spite of that, I don't know what I'd have done without her. Within minutes, she'd purloined a trestle table for us to work on which we set up behind the marquee just out of sight of any early guests. She cajoled several of the waiting staff to bring water for us to fill all my hotch-potch collection of vessels (I hadn't even considered where I'd be getting water from) and she even had a glass of lemonade and a sandwich plus doggy snacks for Scamp sent out after declaring that my rumbling stomach sounded like someone had pulled the plug out of a full bath and she was sick of listening to it.

We tackled the easiest job first: displays for each of the round tables. With Scamp sprawled out on his back in a patch of sunshine, I filled an assortment of jugs, bottles and old jam jars with water. The marquee was very white and I had a vague notion of softening the space with relaxed, fun and casual flowers in quirky containers. I gathered bunch after bunch of blowsy peonies, feathery gypsophilia, fragrant stocks and plump hyacinths and popped them into water, while Kelly finished them off, tying lace ribbon and twine around the containers and setting them straight onto tables. We couldn't achieve perfection, working at this speed and I had to resist the urge to fiddle with the stems. Kelly felt no such urge.

'I might have stayed with Nina if I'd known you could take short cuts like this,' she said, impressed when we'd provided three vases of flowers for every table. 'What next?'

'On to the top table,' I said, gazing worriedly at the half-finished garland which Nina had been working on when I'd found her. Between us we carried it through the marquee and set it in the centre of the long rectangular table in front of where the bride and groom would preside over the room. But no matter how much we fiddled with it, it didn't quite work.

Kelly wrinkled her nose. 'Looks shite. Not long enough and you'll never have time to finish it.'

Annoyingly she was right.

'Arses,' I said flatly.

Kelly's lips twitched into a smile.

I carefully lifted it out of the way and set it to one side under the arch on the wedding cake table.

Kelly opened her mouth to impart more wisdom.

'It's just temporary,' I said curtly. 'While I, er . . .'

I was about to say 'while I decide what to do with it' but thought better of it.

But Kelly had clocked my hesitation. She gave me a sharp look. 'You do know what you're doing, don't you?'

'Of course,' I said, willing my face not to blush. 'I'm going to make a table runner of flowers which looks like a spring meadow: natural, pretty and unfussy. Masses of foliage peppered with flowers.'

'Right.' Kelly lifted one slender eyebrow. 'And the arch?'

'One thing at a time,' I said, my mind whirling with Fiona's advice. The arch was over to one side and wouldn't be in people's eyeline. The top table, on the other hand, would feature in everyone's wedding photos so that was the priority.

'You're the boss,' she muttered dubiously.

'You grab as much greenery as you can and arrange it in a wide stripe along the entire length of the table. And I'll poke loads of flowers into it.'

Kelly did as she was told and even managed to get two waiters to help cart the foliage inside for us. We started at one end and while she made a deep foresty bed of ivy, ruskus, eucalyptus and fern, I selected a hundred or so flowers and tucked them into the foliage. Roses in shades of white, pink and creamy peach, blue lisianthus and corn-flowers, trumpeting narcissi and frilly-edged tulips . . . the beauty of the flowers was making my heart soar. Although thinking about it, that might have been nerves.

'Nina normally makes me wire every stem,' said Kelly, marvelling at how fast the display was coming together. 'Most mind-numbing job on the planet.'

'The theme is more rustic for this wedding though,' I said, brushing aside my pang of doubt.

There was no time for wire and besides, Fiona had drummed into me that these flowers only had to look good for a few hours. 'And just think, at the end of the night, the bride can give bunches of flowers away to her guests.'

'At the end of the night, this bride will only have one thing on her mind,' Kelly smirked. 'And that's bed.'

'Let's stay professional about our clients, shall we?' I said primly, noticing that two of the younger lads had overheard and were now elbowing each other.

'You and your dirty mind.' She hooted with laughter. 'I meant she'll be knackered. She's five months pregnant. Mind you, the groom is well fit.'

We reached the end of the table and walked round to the centre to survey our work. My heart was definitely soaring with happiness this time.

'Wow,' I said, feeling a lump in my throat. 'It looks incredible.'

I knew my hours of scrolling through Pinterest would pay off one day.

'Not bad,' she said, with a sniff. She took her phone out of her pocket and took a few pictures. For the hotel website, she told me. I took some for Nina. I had no idea whether she had a website or not, but I felt I should.

'Wedding cars are here,' announced a breathless waitress from the marquee's entrance. Behind her a line of staff appeared carrying silver serving dishes.

'Shit the bed!' Kelly yelled.

'Stay calm,' I said, feeling very proud of myself. 'All we need to do is tidy up around the top table and –'

'I'm supposed to be out there, greeting them.' Kelly flapped about trying to find her jacket. 'Doing my actual job, not yours.'

Not my job either, I thought, but didn't say anything. Instead I held out Kelly's jacket for her and she slid her arms in.

'Thanks for your help,' I said. 'I couldn't have finished in time without you.'

'You haven't finished.' Kelly nodded to where I'd left Nina's abandoned garland. 'You haven't done the arch.'

I blinked. 'The arch is supposed to have flowers on it?'

She gave me a quizzical look. 'Duh. Yes. It's one of Nina's wedding props. Major focal point for photos.'

98

'You're kidding me.' I groaned.

That had been one of Fiona's top three rules: prioritise the focal areas. Now what was I going to do? I'd got plenty of flowers to spare but no time.

'Tut, tut. Call yourself a professional florist?' Kelly teased.

'No, I don't actually,' I said flatly. 'This time yesterday I was still in flower school. I've only done a five-day course.'

From behind us there was an enormous gasp. Kelly and I turned to see Nina frozen to the spot, mouth open in horror.

'Got to go,' said Kelly, sidling out of the marquee.

'You told me you were a florist.' Nina jammed her hands on her hips, her face flushed and jaw set grimly. 'I'd never have left you in charge of Rosie's wedding flowers otherwise.'

I shifted uncomfortably, aware that all the staff in the marquee had paused in their tasks to watch the drama.

'I am. I've done a course, I like flowers, therefore I'm a florist. Just not . . . a professional,' I said weakly. 'Does it matter?'

'*Of course it matters!*' Nina raked a hand through her hair. 'I'm such a plonker; my friend's wedding and I've left the flowers to . . . what even are you?'

'I have a degree in business studies and for the last ten years, I've been a data analyst, in the paper industry.'

At that, Nina's eyes glazed over; an expression I was used to.

Scamp, deciding I needed support, rolled over from where he'd been lying under the top table and sat down proprietorially on one of my feet. His faithful presence gave me a boost and I decided to style it out.

'Look, I can see you're annoyed but you needed help and I stepped into the breach,' I pointed out. 'Do you like what I've done? Kelly helped.'

Nina's eyes slid sideways to the spring meadow table runner and pursed her lips. I sensed her soften towards me. 'It looks charming,' she admitted.

'Thank you,' I said relieved.

If I hadn't turned up she'd probably still have been sitting in a puddle of tears, the marquee wouldn't have any flowers at all and she'd have missed the actual wedding.

Through the entrance of the marquee, I could make out the bridal party in the distance. The little boy, Noah, was running around with his dog and the photographer was organising people into groups.

'I'm quickly going to do something with the arch,' I said steering her towards the entrance, once I'd removed Scamp from my foot. 'Why don't you go and be in the photographs, while I finish off. If you trust me, that is?'

Just then a diminutive white-haired woman bustled into the marquee, pursued by an old man.

'*Santo cielo!*' she cried, clapping her hands to her cheeks. 'Look atta this!'

'Oh balls, now we've had it,' Nina muttered, shaking my arm off from around her shoulder and striding up to the old couple.

'I can explain, Maria,' said Nina, hanging her head. 'I accepted help from this woman who told me she was a florist and it turns out she's not a professional.'

Maria wafted Nina away, walked to the nearest table and bent over a jam jar of flowers to smell it. The old man checked over his shoulder anxiously. 'Maria, I think they want us for a photograph.'

'*Un momento*, Stanley,' she replied, walking over to the top table. She shook her head in awe. '*Perfetto, bellisimi fiori.*'

'It's true. I don't have much professional experience,' I said hotly, frustrated that Nina had changed her tune again. 'But I've been around flowers since I was a little girl helping at my grandmother's market stall. Flowers are my passion.'

'Passion.' The old lady pointed at me, nodding in agreement. 'Worth ten times any papers.'

'But there are skills, techniques,' argued Nina. 'And it takes longer than five days to learn them.'

'You like my biscotti, *si*?' Maria asked her.

Nina looked confused. 'Yes, but . . .'

'Not once you say to me, I not eat your biscotti till I see your papers. No. They look, they smell, they taste. Passion come from here.' She banged her chest. 'You don't learn it in cotton blue cookery school.'

'It's *cordon bleu*, my dear,' said Stanley, with a twinkle in his eye.

'No, I learn from my grandmother, like her,' Maria said, ignoring him. She reached for my hands. '*Brava, cara*. Whoever you are, this come from your heart.'

'I'm Fearne,' I supplied.

She smelled of lemons and vanilla and lavender and I felt a wave of nostalgia for summers spent with my granny.

'When me and my Stanley get married, I want flowers like this. From the heart. Now, come on Stanley, we gotta go.'

She held her hand out to Stanley who tucked it under his arm. The two of them walked away, leaving Nina and I staring awkwardly at each other.

Nina chewed her lip. 'I'm so sorry, Maria's right, your flowers are *bellisimo*. And I've been incredibly rude and ungrateful.'

With a jolt, I remembered the arch and without replying, I made to leave the marquee, Scamp trotting loyally behind me. Professional or not, I wasn't a quitter and I was determined to decorate it somehow, though perhaps not with the finesse it deserved.

'Wait!' Nina caught me up. 'Don't leave like this.'

'I'm not,' I said, distractedly. Instead I surveyed the remaining foliage. I couldn't decorate the whole arch, but maybe that semi-complete garland could go across the top and then I could have tumbling fronds of ivy wound around the sides.

'OK, look, the job is yours.' She beamed at me, clearly expecting me to be thrilled.

'The job?' I looked at her blankly.

'The vacancy for assistant manager?' She raised her eyebrows mischievously. 'That's why you came to the shop, isn't it? Because you'd seen the ad in the newspaper.'

'Um . . . well . . .' Technically, I'd gone to the café for sustenance before my day had taken such an unexpected turn. Walking past Nina's Flowers had been purely as a result of it being next door.

She held up a hand. 'No, I insist. This has been your interview, practical task and references all rolled into one. You've passed. With flying colours. Plus, you've impressed Maria Carloni, grandmother of the bride, which is in itself quite a feat.'

'Well. Thank you,' I replied, slightly dazed. 'I suppose.'

'Fab.' She threw her arms around me, taking my gratitude for job acceptance. 'Welcome to Nina's Flowers.'

This was the point at which I could have told her that I was having a year's sabbatical to work on my happy list. That I didn't want a job, I wanted to experience new things and get out of the rut I'd fallen into. In essence, to find a new way to live without Freddie. But a golden glow of happiness was spreading through my body and instead of turning Nina down I was smiling back at her.

'I can only commit to three months,' I blurted out.

'Hmm.' Nina narrowed her eyes thoughtfully. 'How about four?'

I shrugged. 'OK, four. But Scamp will have to come with me.'

'Done.' She stuck her hand out and we shook on the deal. 'Ring me on Monday and we can talk money etcetera. Now if you really don't mind finishing the arch by yourself, I must get back to the wedding.'

And with that she dashed off across the lawn to rejoin the bridal party. I stared after her, stunned into silence, and then looked down at the dog.

'Looks like we've got a new job,' I said.

I laughed in surprise and Scamp wagged his tail eagerly in response.

Freddie would definitely find this funny, I thought wistfully, as I carted the rest of the ivy inside. His list had been full of sunrises, beaches and new places, I couldn't imagine that spending four months in a small village shop would have found a place on it. But this was my kind of happy, my choice and my life. I didn't know what Monday was going to bring, or in fact the next four months, but for the first time in my entire life, I was taking a leap into the unknown just for the fun of it.

Would Nina's Flowers be my chance to let happiness back into my life . . .?

Part Two

Chapter Eleven

A little over three weeks had gone by since the wedding and I was back in Barnaby with Scamp, ready for my first day as assistant manager of Nina's Flowers. It was a quarter to nine on a beautiful Monday morning and the smell of spring was in the air, all fresh and frothy with new life. The sun was shining, swathes of bluebells nodded in time with the breeze on the village green and the morning rush – such as it was – was in full swing.

Although taking a job in a flower shop hadn't been on the agenda, I was excited to see what the opportunity would bring, and today felt like the perfect day for a fresh start. Even Scamp was full of the joys of spring, tugging me towards the stream which bordered the village green.

As soon as it was safe to do so, I unclipped Scamp from his lead to let him stretch his legs and burn off some energy before going indoors. He did a couple of enthusiastic circuits around me and then ran off to explore. My new boss hadn't turned a hair when I'd asked to bring him to work with me. It had been supremely generous of her, not to mention trusting. Scamp was a laid-back old boy, but I wasn't sure how he'd react to spending the day cooped up in a shop, nor indeed what he'd make of a constant stream of strangers through the door. I hoped he wouldn't let me down.

There was a group of silver-haired ramblers crowded around a bench on the green, pouring steaming drinks from Thermos flasks and they waved as we passed by. Scamp went over to wag his tail cheerily at them and was rewarded with a piece of biscuit. Several other dog walkers were out on the open space, and I stopped and spoke to a couple of them who wanted to know Scamp's name and what breed he was. Having a dog was a great ice-breaker.

'Dog or bitch?' called a friendly lady from a distance. She was clutching the collar of a rotund Labrador whose tail gave a stately wag.

'Dog,' I called back, supressing a giggle.

'Righty ho.' She let go of her dog's collar and the pair came closer. 'Always have to check. Churchill might be advancing in years, but he's constantly on the lookout for an eligible bitch, if you get my drift. I'm Biddy.'

I introduced myself and Scamp and the dogs gave each other a cursory sniff. Then side by side, they stared at us as if they were now a team awaiting instructions.

'New to the village, eh?' Biddy pushed wiry greying blonde hair behind her ear and smiled welcomingly.

I explained about my new job with Nina and she sighed wistfully.

'Such a fragrant shop. I'm quite envious; mine smells of rabbit droppings and dried fish.'

I raised my eyebrows, not knowing how to respond.

'I own the pet shop across the green.' She delved into the pocket of her crocheted tunic and produced a money-off voucher for a mini-doggy-pedi. 'Take this for when Scamp needs his claws clipping. Cheerio!'

She marched off with Churchill waddling leisurely behind her and we carried on doing a circuit of the green, passing a group of younger women who were standing chatting. Mums, possibly, who'd dropped their offspring off at the little primary school. They made a fuss of Scamp who flirted shamelessly with them until I rattled a couple of treats in my hand which sent him running back.

'Looks like you've made lots of new friends,' I said, breaking a treat in half for him.

The village had a friendly vibe and already I was detecting a strong sense of community. So far, the place which I'd only discovered because it had featured in a magazine article about undiscovered villages was working its magic on me.

As the church bells chimed the hour, I spotted Nina waving to me from the doorway of the florist's shop and I picked up my pace.

'Scamp!' I called. 'Time for work.'

I jingled the lead. Normally, this was enough to have him return to my side. But just then, with a raucous quack and a flap of its wings, a duck landed in the stream.

'Nooo,' I yelled in dismay, as, before I could grab his collar, Scamp launched himself into the water after it. The duck took flight again leaving the dog splashing backwards and forwards across the stream, sniffing the air.

'Come back!' I shouted, patting the pocket of my jacket, where he knew I kept his treats.

Scamp scrambled back up the bank, dripping wet and looking mightily pleased with himself.

'Great,' I said, half-laughing as he shook the water out of his fur, covering me with droplets. 'A wet dog, just what every shop needs.'

I snapped his lead back on and quickly doubled back to the car to towel him off. By the time we finally reached the florist's, I was fifteen minutes late for work.

'Thank goodness,' Nina said beaming. She flung the door open and flipped the sign from closed to open.

'So sorry,' I said, 'not an auspicious start, is it? I'm late and I'm bringing a smelly damp dog with me.'

Nina waved my apology away and pumped my hand up and down in hers enthusiastically. 'I saw you head back to the car and I thought, oh no, she's changed her mind!'

'I wouldn't do that!' I said, not quite meeting her eye.

I *had* wondered if I was crazy to be taking this job. But a small voice cheered me on and told me that this was the most spontaneous, unlike-me thing I'd ever done, and it might not be as adventurous as trekking in Nepal but it suited me and I should embrace the change. Once again, the voice sounded surprisingly like Freddie's. So here I was.

'Phew,' she said, her brown eyes shining with relief. 'Because you've no idea how glad I am to have just the right person on board. Uncanny, how you turned up at the time of Rosie and Gabe's wedding, just when I needed help. Like a guardian angel.'

'A series of happy coincidences.' I said cheerfully and explained how the article in the *Derbyshire Bugle* had brought me here that day. 'And believe me, I was happy to help.'

It had been a while since I'd felt useful and needed by another person. Looking after Ethel had filled a big gap in my life after Freddie died, but since she'd gone into a home, I'd missed the daily contact of having someone to check on.

'And you, handsome boy, can be our guard dog,' said Nina, bending down to Scamp and raking her fingers under his chin, which unbeknown to her was one of his absolute favourite things in the world. I could already tell he was in love. And full marks to her: she didn't flinch at the lingering pong from his early morning dip.

'I've brought his bed, and his water bowl and his favourite toy,' I said, looking for a corner out of the way. 'Do you mind where I put them?'

'By the window,' she said, moving a little wooden stool which was being used to display some delicate potted primulas. 'Prime position. He can keep an eye on unwanted visitors.'

I looked at her, amused. 'I can't imagine you get many of those?'

'Ooh look, customer,' she said, nodding towards the door. A woman in her sixties was striding purposefully our way. 'That's Mrs Derry, chairwoman of the Women's Institute and chief organiser of the church flowers. Loves a yellow chrysanthemum. All yours.'

Nina chucked me an apron as the door opened and just like that, I was officially a florist.

The morning flew by in a blur of new information and instructions. The first job had been 'conditioning' the new stock, which I knew from my week at the Wisteria Cottage Flower School meant unwrapping delicate stems from their cartons and reviving them in a mix of water and a special type of flower food. The flowers had arrived in Barnaby from all over the world. Granny would be amazed; I was pretty sure none of the flowers on her market stall would have travelled across several continents.

'It's called quick dip,' said Nina, adding a capful of liquid to a bucketful of water. 'Caffeine for flowers. Never ceases to amaze me that flowers can be dry-shipped from places like Africa without a drop of water. Then boom, plunge them into this and they blink their bleary eyes and come to life again.'

'Like me after the first coffee of the day,' I said, eyeing the kettle.

Nina grinned. 'Coffee? Thought you'd never ask. Milk and one sugar, please.'

Coffee in hand, Nina gave Scamp and me the grand tour of her adorable shop.

It had all been such a rush last time I was here, and there had been so many flowers crowding the space, that later when I'd tried to visualise the interior of the shop, I couldn't conjure up a clear picture. Now I was able to look around properly I knew I was going to enjoy spending my days here: there was a vintage garden shed theme to the decor; mini aluminium watering cans with calligraphy slogans, pots in the shape of wellies and piles of vintage wooden crates of varying sizes which gave a rustic, earthy feel to the displays.

'It's bigger than I remember, it's like a Tardis,' I'd said when we'd finished exploring.

Only the front half of the space was visible from the street. There was a brick archway separating the front and back sections of the shop. The back half contained the kitchenette, the cold store and a large empty space. A rear entrance led to a yard where Nina had parked her van. I didn't think she was using the space properly; there was so much unfulfilled potential here. But it wasn't my place to tell her, at least not on my first day.

As if reading my mind, Nina sighed.

'Dead space really. Almost too big.' she said, wrapping her hands around her mug and leaning against the archway. 'And the rent certainly is. But what can you do? No point increasing the amount of stock; we struggle to sell what we've got as it is.'

My eyebrows lifted. 'The shop isn't doing well?'

And if it wasn't, why recruit me, I wondered.

'No, not exactly.' Nina's eyes slid away from mine and she scuffed the toe of her Converse on the floor. 'Just, you know.'

I didn't know, but neither was I going to pry. Besides, I was doing this job because I wanted to, not because I needed to. So if the shop was in trouble, it wasn't the end of the world, at least not for me. And perhaps there was something I could do to help the business. Maybe Nina and I could learn from each other. I could use the four months to indulge my passion for flowers, while she could benefit from my experience in analysing market trends. I could easily delve into the shop's customer database and check for patterns in spending. That way we might identify potential areas for growth. The thought gave me a happy glow.

Nina mistook my silence for disquiet about what she'd just revealed. 'Are you worried you've made the wrong decision, taking this job?'

'Not at all!' I protested. 'And my mum thinks it's a good idea, so I'm doubly sure I'm doing the right thing.'

'Oh good, because we are very busy, let me tell you about how we work . . .'

She began to give me a potted history of the business and I felt my attention drifting.

That was true about my mum. She had barely batted an eyelid when I'd told her I was leaving Zed Market Trends. Hardly surprising given that she herself didn't believe in staying anywhere long. Scamp and I went to stay with her last weekend and when I told her about my job offer from Nina, she'd been delighted.

'I've often thought you'd make a good florist,' she'd said, chuckling. 'Nimble fingers and a sharp eye for colour. Just like me.'

We'd been walking along the quay at the time, watching children brave the chilly morning to catch crabs with bacon and string and her comment had brought me up short. Freddie and I had always stayed at Granny's cottage without Mum, so I didn't associate her with Granny's market stall. But whereas we only spent school holidays in Wales, Mum had grown up there. Flowers would have been an even bigger part of her childhood than mine.

'You didn't fancy a career in flowers?' I asked, tightening my grip on Scamp's lead before he jumped off the quay and into the water.

She shook her head. 'No. I wanted the complete opposite of my mother's life. Something else you and I have in common,' she'd added with a knowing smile.

'I've never thought that . . .' I began to protest but my words faltered.

Gosh, I'd realised, reddening, *maybe I had*. Was that why I'd stayed in the same job for ten years? As a response to Mum's peripatetic lifestyle?

'Anyway,' she cut in, taking my arm. 'Granny would be very proud of you for giving it a go. And so am I. And so would Freddie.'

'Thanks.' I swallowed the lump in my throat and hoped she was right.

I'd given her Freddie's letter to read that night and we'd talked about what we missed most about him and had a little cry.

Scamp and I only stayed a couple of nights. Mum's apartment overlooking the sea was cosy but only had one bedroom and the novelty of sharing the sofa with Scamp was quick to wear off. As we were leaving, Mum tried to give me the money she'd got from selling off Freddie's motorbike collection. Again.

'Mum, please!' I'd begged her.

'It's just sitting there,' she said, looking vexed as I stuffed my fingers in my ears and refused to listen. 'He wanted you to have it.'

Freddie's new Triumph had been written off but his Harley Davidson, Honda Gold Wing and his Kawasaki had fetched a decent amount. Maybe one day I'd need it enough to overlook the fact that it felt like blood money. But right now my brain was refusing to believe that a skilled and experienced rider and a fantastic motorbike instructor to boot could have made such a stupid error.

'Fearne?' Nina was grinning at me. 'Have I bored you to death?'

'No, no, not at all,' I stammered, wondering what I'd missed. Thankfully, I remembered something I'd noticed earlier. 'I meant to ask, you don't have a computer?'

Nina wrinkled her nose. 'Not in the shop. I used to but it was always playing up and then Kelly spilled water on it and that was that. All the online orders from Fone-A-Flower come through on my phone. Plus, emails. It's all I need and it's always with me.' She fought through several layers to pull her mobile phone from her back pocket. It flew out of her wet hand and bounced off the corner of the counter before hitting the floor, shattering the screen into a million pieces.

'Balls,' she said blithely. 'Not again.'

She picked it up and examined it. 'Still works.'

I bent down to check for any glass splinters; the last thing I needed was for Scamp to get any in his paws. He, of course, had to come and see what I was looking at; I stroked his ears and he padded back to his basket, content.

'Just a thought,' I said. 'But why don't we have a tablet in the shop? That way, either of us can log the new orders when they come in, plus I could set it up to accept and make phone calls.'

'Can't afford it at the mo, but good plan.'

'We, I mean, *I've* got a spare one,' I said, picturing Freddie's iPad in a drawer underneath the TV at home. 'I can bring it in tomorrow. Won't cost you a penny.'

She chewed her lip. 'Thanks, but what if it gets dropped or soaked?'

I shook my head, laughing. 'My brother used it to run his motorbike school from. The case is so thick, he even rolled the wheel of his bike over it once and it didn't crack. It'll be fine in a florist's.'

'Then I accept, thanks. I guess your brother is as accident prone as me?' she said, rolling her eyes.

My stomach swooped. That was the stupid thing: Freddie had been such a careful rider. Which made accepting what had happened even harder.

'Miss Lovage?' The police officer's face had been impeccably professional, but he hadn't been able to disguise the look of pity in his eyes. 'I'm afraid there's been an accident involving your brother. Can I come in . . .?'

I swallowed down the memory. 'Just the one.'

Nina gave me a curious look, inviting me to expand on my comment but the phone rang and she answered it, scribbling down an order in the big diary which sat on a shelf under the counter.

'You know,' said Nina, once she'd finished taking down all the details and I'd selected some flowers for an all-white bouquet for a birthday order. 'I've got a really good feeling about you and me. I think we're going to make a great duo.'

Scamp chose that moment to remember just how amazing his tail was and chased it round his bed for a mad thirty seconds, while growling at it menacingly.

Nina laughed. 'Sorry, Scamp, was I ignoring you? I meant to say great *trio*.'

'A great trio,' I echoed, and let out a breath of relief. Like Nina, I had a good feeling about us too.

Chapter Twelve

Apart from popping outside to take Scamp for a comfort break, Nina and I stayed busy until lunchtime. There weren't many customers, which Nina said was normal for a Monday, so after brie and cranberry paninis bought from the café next door (her treat as it was my first day), I concentrated on the two telephone orders we'd received, with Nina looking over my shoulder and making suggestions.

Fiona at the flower school had let us take as long as we needed to create each arrangement, allowing us to start from scratch with a howl of dismay every time something went wrong. Working in a commercial environment was a whole different kettle of fish; the labour cost had to be incorporated into the price of every bouquet. Nina worked on thirty per cent labour, thirty per cent flowers, the rest taken up with the fixed costs of running the shop and presumably with a bit left over for profit. But I was so slow that the bouquet ordered by the vicar had probably cost Nina more than he was paying us for it.

'That'll have to do,' said my boss, sitting on her hands to stop herself from interfering.

I held the flowers at arms' length and examined it. 'This one at the back is still facing the wrong way. I'll just move it.'

'Nope.' Nina shook her head sternly. 'Finish with a ribbon, add the card and stick it in the back, ready for delivery later on.'

'Fair enough.' I suppressed a sigh and tied some raffia around the bouquet of lilies, gerberas and spray roses and apologised for my lack of speed.

'You'll get faster,' she said, generously, adding when she thought I was out of earshot, 'I hope.'

By four o'clock, Nina had been out in the van and done the deliveries, I'd cleaned the kitchenette, swept the floors and was now topping up the water in the buckets in the window. Outside the shop, people were milling about again in the late afternoon sunshine and the tables under the awning of the café had filled up with groups of parents sipping mugs of tea and children tucking into smoothies and slabs of cake.

Nina joined me in the window and yawned. 'Sorry. Early start to the flower market.'

'I thought you had your flowers delivered from Holland?' I frowned. The late delivery of wedding flowers had been the reason I'd found Nina in floods of tears that day, and ultimately, the reason why I was now working for her.

Nina scratched her nose. 'I did. Do. But, well, we sort of fell out.'

'I'm not surprised,' I said indignantly. 'Suppliers should have contingency plans for logistical problems, not simply turn up late.'

'Hmm,' said Nina reticently. 'Anyway, I'll be making market trips for the next couple of weeks.'

'I'd love to come one day.' Fiona's talk about the giant flower auctions in Holland had made all of us students want to visit.

'It is fun,' she said, smiling broadly as the door opened and a man came in, before continuing, 'choosing exactly the right flowers for your customers from the millions on offer from the wholesalers is heavenly.'

'And talking of *heavenly* . . .' said the man, who looked as if he'd stepped directly out of a Noël Coward play. He held out his hand to me so daintily that I wondered whether to shake it or kiss it. '. . . I'm Lucas from the Heavenly Gift shop, next door but one. And you must be the fairy godmother Nina told me about, who stepped into the breach on our darling Rosie's wedding day?'

'Not sure Nina still thinks that way, given my snail's pace work speed, but I'm Fearne.' I shook his hand, instantly warming to him.

'Oh the delicate fern,' he said, clasping his hands to his chest. 'Frilly-edged, unfurling in spring like seahorses, hiding their feathery fronds in the patches of summer shade, flower-less foliage whose beauty dazzles even the hardest of hearts.'

'Gosh,' I said taken aback. 'How poetic!'

Nina snorted. 'Please excuse my friend,' she said, giving him a swift hug. 'He's prone to be over-romantic.'

I'd looked into the gift shop window earlier and thought how beautifully put together all the displays were. Meeting the owner explained it all; Lucas was the epitome of sartorial elegance, from the triangular tip of his handkerchief poking out of his jacket pocket to the shiny toes of his polished brogues below ankle grazer chinos.

'Someone needs to be,' he said pointedly. 'And who's this handsome fellow?'

'Scamp,' I said watching as my shameless dog flipped onto his back and presented his pink tummy for approval. 'Most important man in my life.'

'Oh dear,' Lucas pursed his lips. 'Not another single lady in need of Uncle Lucas's dating advice?'

I shook my head firmly. 'I'm focusing on myself for a while, doing what makes me happy. A boyfriend would only get in the way of that.'

'Ooh, a challenge,' he said, smiling with mischief. He eyed me from top to toe. 'Well at least we've got good material to work with. Excellent hair, sparkling green eyes, beguiling smile. And an irresistible pooch is always a bonus. Shows you don't shy away from commitment.'

'Lucas is my go-to dating guru,' Nina explained. 'When I've got a date, he helps me pick out outfits, advises on menu choices and gives me conversational starters in case of awkward silences. Not that I have many dates, and I am still single.'

'But maybe not for long,' said Lucas, with a cheeky wink. 'It was me who suggested Nina should go on—'

'*Tinder*,' said Nina loudly, making him jump. She folded her arms. 'I'm on Tinder, which is about as depressing as it gets for a thirty-six-year-old whose entire friendship group is coupled up. Just as well you don't want to meet someone, Fearne, because being a florist is the worst occupation for meeting a potential partner.'

I met my last boyfriend, Steve, on a dating app, a really nice guy. The first few dates had gone so well; I remembered telling all the girls at the book club that this one had real potential. That had been in June. Freddie had died in July. Our relationship hadn't been strong enough to withstand that sort of test. I'd clung to him for support initially, but as the months dragged on, I think the only thing preventing him from breaking it off was pity. So we limped on into the new year, by which time I'd become so withdrawn from him it was a relief when he finally called it a day.

I smiled to myself, acknowledging just how much better I was feeling now. Not ready to embark on anything romantic, but happier to be around others.

'Florists love flowers,' Nina continued, crossly, 'yet everyone assumes that because they're surrounded with them all day, they wouldn't want to receive them. Wrong! Who wouldn't love to be wooed with a posy of lily of the valley or some colourful tulips wrapped in brown paper? Not that it matters because all the men who come in here are generally already in love.'

'But surely romance should be blooming among such a backdrop of beauty?' I said, amused by this side of her.

'Oh, now who's poetic!' said Lucas dreamily. 'I like this one. Far more class than Kelly.'

He plucked a bunch of pale yellow and lilac freesias from a bucket and counted out the change to pay for them which Nina waved away.

'Although Kelly did come up trumps in the marquee for us,' I pointed out. 'I couldn't have managed without her. Why exactly did she leave?'

Nina flicked her eyes momentarily to Lucas. 'She wanted the job as assistant manager but I wouldn't promote her. She thought I was being unreasonable, so she walked.'

Lucas pursed his lips as if to say that he couldn't possibly comment.

'And yet you gave it to me, and I'm completely inexperienced.'

'For Kelly it was just a job, she didn't care if she was selling flowers or fish. But you love flowers, anyone can see that. Besides, you proved yourself trustworthy by helping me out with Rosie's wedding.' Nina untied and retied the bow at the front of her apron for apparently no reason. 'I need someone who can work unsupervised, if say . . . I had to go away for instance.'

I stared at her warily. 'And is that likely?'

'Um . . .' Nina went pink. 'Nothing on the horizon.'

'Must dash. *Ciao*, ladies,' said Lucas, holding the flowers to his nose. 'Glorious fragrance.'

'He's fun,' I said with a laugh, watching him collide with another man on the pavement and make him smell the flowers he'd just bought.

'Adorable,' Nina agreed, bending over the freesia bucket and rearranging them.

Lucas scurried back to his own shop and the other man looked straight at me through the window.

Oh my, I murmured, under my breath. This one wasn't the least bit like Noël Coward. He was tall and broad, with thick honey blond hair and a strong jawline enhanced by stubble a shade or two darker. And he was heading our way.

'Coffee?' Nina shouted from the back.

The bell above the door jangled as he opened it.

'Hello?' Smiling eyes met mine. I was a sucker for nice eyes. And his weren't just smiley, they were startlingly blue. Like the deepest bluest sea.

'No thanks!' I yelled, still staring at him. I was speaking to Nina, obviously. But he wasn't to know that.

'You don't even know what I was going to say.' The man grinned and a dimple appeared in his cheek. Smiley eyes and a dimple. My stomach hadn't flipped like this at the sight of a man for a long time. This was so unlike me; I didn't even recognise myself.

I grinned back inanely. 'Well, just in case you were going to offer me coffee, I don't want any.'

He laughed out loud at that. 'Got it. Look, I'm Sam Diamond. I don't think we've met. In fact, I know we haven't.'

Agreed. Because he wasn't the sort of man you'd forget in a hurry. Behind me I heard the back door close softly.

'No,' I replied with a squeak.

'No,' he repeated. 'Are we still talking about the coffee?'

'We haven't met,' I explained. 'I was agreeing with you.'

He stretched out his arm. I thought he was trying to shake hands but when my fingers met his, I realised he'd been offering me his business card which I promptly knocked out of his hand.

'Whoops. Fearne Lovage.' I blushed as I said my name. I wasn't normally a blusher, but this man had made every cell of my being sit up and pay attention.

Sam picked up his card again and handed it to me to read: *Sam Diamond, Senior Advisor, Hogg Property Services commercial estate agents.*

'This your dog?' He looked at Scamp, who was lying on the floor, one eye shut, the other one trained on the new visitor, his tail thumping rhythmically against the wooden floorboards.

I nodded. 'That's Scamp. We're both new.'

'I guessed.' He looked past me to the far end of the shop. 'Is Nina in?'

'Sure,' I said brightly. *Damn.* 'I'll fetch her for you. Excuse me.'

I don't know why I was disappointed. The chances of a gorgeous single man wandering into the flower shop and being interested in me on my first day were pretty slim. Especially given Nina's declaration that this was the worst place to meet someone. Besides, what had happened to the Fearne who ten minutes ago had insisted that a boyfriend would only get in the way of . . . er, something or other; whatever it was, it had slipped my mind.

I backed through the archway, still smiling at him. He scratched his chin as if hiding his amusement.

A thought struck me. Maybe Sam was the reason why Nina might not need Lucas's dating advice any more? Perhaps she only said she was still single, because it was still early days . . .

'Is the dog allowed treats?' he called as I disappeared into the back.

'He is,' I replied, 'as long as you don't mind him never leaving you alone for the rest of your life.'

I heard Sam laugh as Scamp's paws scrabbled across the floor towards him.

Smiley eyes, a dimple *and* dog treats. There must be a catch, because right now Sam Diamond was too good to be true. Oh yes, I remembered; he was here to see my boss.

'Nina?' I hissed, not spotting her; she was probably quickly putting some lippy on and removing stray leaves from her hair.

I checked the kitchenette, the loo and the cold store. No sign of the boss. I was wondering what on earth could have happened to her when her face popped up at the window from out in the yard. Her eyes were wide and she had a finger clamped to her lips, urging me to be quiet.

I opened the back door and poked my head out. She was tucked into the small gap between the wall of the shop and her van.

'Are you all right?' I asked.

She shook her head, still with her finger in place.

'Sam is here to see you,' I whispered.

'I know. Get rid of him,' she hissed, flapping her hand at me to go back inside. 'I'll explain later.'

'OK.' I was so taken aback I didn't even question her.

When I got back to Sam, he was crouching down stroking Scamp. Scamp had invaded his personal space and the two of them were almost nose to nose. Sam stood up.

'No Nina?' he remarked as if he'd been expecting that to be the case.

'Sorry,' I said. 'You just missed her.'

'Thought I might.' His lips twitched.

He had nice full lips. I wondered if his stubble would tickle my face if I kissed him, I mean if *someone* kissed him. Like Nina. I gave myself a shake. This wasn't like me at all, what was going on? Crushing on my boss's . . . whatever he was, was hardly going to get myself into her good books.

'How about you leave a message with me, and perhaps a bunch of flowers?' I was really proud of this suggestion, given Nina's complaint. 'Florists don't often get flowers, you know.'

He coughed and glanced down at the floor as if covering his amusement. 'Thank you. I'll take a rain check on the flowers this time, but tell Nina that the rent is overdue and my boss isn't the sort of man who takes kindly to being owed money.'

I stared at him confused. 'Rent? So you're not, you and Nina aren't . . .? You're the landlord?'

He nodded grimly. 'As my card says, I work in commercial property and Hogg Property Services lease the building to Nina. She's in arrears with the rent. Again.'

And I'd just advised him to buy her some flowers. I groaned mentally.

'Oh, I see.' I couldn't think of anything intelligent to say; I hadn't been expecting that.

'Please inform Nina – when she reappears – that she's got one week.'

'Until what?' I said, not sure I wanted to hear the answer. 'You won't be back with baseball bats and a big lorry will you?'

'No, look . . .' An expression I couldn't quite name passed across his face, but whatever it was, he didn't look happy. He raked a hand through his hair and frowned. 'Just tell her.'

Chapter Thirteen

Sam climbed into a car with Hogg Property Services down the side without a backward glance and Nina crept in through the back door.

'Has he gone?' she hissed, hiding behind the archway.

'Yes. Until next week.' My casual tone belied the fact that I had quite a few burning questions.

Nina paced backwards and forwards, swearing to herself, while I made myself useful sweeping the floor.

Finally, she flopped down onto a high wooden stool, propped her elbows up on the counter and dropped her head into her hands. 'I know this must look bad, but I can explain.'

She looked as if she had the world on her shoulders and her chin was doing that crunched up, wobbly thing which told me that tears weren't far away. I couldn't make her out: five minutes ago, she'd seemed bright and bubbly as if nothing could possibly get her down. She reminded me of myself after Freddie died: all smiles one minute and devastated the next. If anyone ought to be sympathetic to a bit of erratic behaviour, I was that person.

'It's your business.' I said, kindly. 'You're not obliged to tell me anything.'

Her shoulders heaved. 'I know. My business, my problem, right? The buck stops here.'

Scamp looked at me, raising one eyebrow at a time; even he was worried.

'Hey, that's not what I meant.' I put my arm around her. 'I thought we were a team, a *trio*, you said? A problem shared and all that.'

She lifted her head and swiped the tears from her face with the back of her hand. 'Why are you so kind?'

I grinned. 'I'm not, I'm just nosy. I want to know all the salacious details, everything. Like how much debt are you in, what you plan to do about it and most importantly, I want to know everything there is to know about Sam Diamond.'

Nina's mouth curved into a smile. 'Lucas will be delighted; I thought you were sworn off men.'

'I am,' I said innocently. '"Know thine enemy". Isn't that what the Bible says?'

'No, that was someone else,' she said with a giggle. 'The Bible says you should *love* your enemy.'

'Either way I need details,' I said, holding my arms wide. 'Now are you going to tell me what's going on, or not?'

She groaned and covered her face again. 'It's a long story.'

'My favourite kind.' I gave her a nudge. 'Come on.'

'I'm in the shit,' she gave me a rueful smile. 'I never even wanted a flower shop, I wanted a farmer. And it all began in London.'

For the final time that afternoon, I put the kettle on to make some comforting hot chocolate, while Nina told me the truth about her wilting flower shop.

Her first ever business was a flower stall outside a busy tube station in central London just after leaving college. It had been the perfect pitch. She collected the flowers from Covent Garden each morning, buying only what would sell in the space of two hours. The odd blooms which were left, she'd quickly twist into buttonholes as little freebies to give to her regulars. Costs were low and job satisfaction was high. This took place *before* work. Because at nine o' clock, she'd pack the stall away and head into the office where she was a trainee graphic designer for a marketing agency. One day, she and the senior designer were asked to visit new clients in Derbyshire: a beef farmer and his son who were launching a new farm-to-fork business called SteakOut.

The farmer's son was called Andrew and the two of them hit it off instantly. He invited her to stay for the weekend and by Sunday night she was smitten. A month later she handed in her notice, sold her flower stall and moved lock stock and barrel to the Midlands. She found a job in an office, and a room in a flat.

'It was all such a whirlwind and so exciting.' She took a sip of her hot chocolate and smiled her thanks. 'I grew up in a big city. But even as a little girl, I wanted to marry a farmer and live on a farm. Still do if I'm honest.'

'I'm guessing it didn't work out with Andrew?' I pulled up a stool and joined her at the counter. Scamp sat alert in his bed, watching as people passed by.

She wrinkled her nose. 'Nah. He cheated on me after a month, I felt like such an idiot. I couldn't face going back to London with my tail between my legs. So I stayed. Eventually I missed being creative, so I took a second job in a florist at weekends. Fast forward a couple of years, then the lease on this place came up and I thought, why not?'

'Why not,' I repeated slowly. How brave, how adventurous. 'You've made a great job of it, Nina. The shop is lovely.'

She looked at me pointedly. 'Tell that to Sam Diamond and his boss.'

'Oh, forget them,' I said airily, waving my hand. 'Be proud of yourself. I've stayed in the same job for ten years out of habit. Or, if my mother is right, to be as different to her as possible. At least you've been out there having a go.'

'I've been giving it a go for five years and not once in those five years have I turned a profit.' She gave me a wry smile. 'Won't win any business woman of the year awards, will I?'

'Do you regret opening the shop?' I said, giving her a direct look.

'Yes. No.' She squirmed on her stool. 'Sometimes. I have actually thought of just locking up one night, packing a suitcase and flying off to New Zealand.'

'New Zealand?' I laughed. 'That's very specific.'

'Yeah.' She smirked. 'Thought I might find myself another farmer there. But I can't just run away from my responsibilities. Being in business on your own is hard. There's no one who cares about it as much as I do. No one to share the burden with and no one to keep me going when my spirits flag.'

'Except you've got me now. So,' I said briskly, sitting up tall. 'First, we have a week to pay off the rent arrears and second, we need to find a way to make the business flourish.'

'It's hard to make a profit in floristry,' Nina warned. 'Cash flow is a nightmare. And so many things can affect sales.'

'Like what?' I frowned. 'Surely the gift market is pretty steady?'

'Birthdays, Christmas, Mothering Sunday, Valentine's Day still happen, if that's what you mean, but I've been hit from all sides by other suppliers: internet subscription services, supermarkets, flowers by post and some of the market has even gone to artificial flowers. Silk ones are so good you have to look twice to tell they aren't real.'

'When you put it like that . . .' I said, pulling a face. 'So why take on an assistant manager when you're struggling to pay your bills? If business is slow, shouldn't you try and work on your own?'

'Probably.' Nina stared hard into her mug. 'But I'm so tired. I haven't had a holiday in five years. The longest break has been three days. I love my job, I do. But everyone deserves to get away now and again, or at least take a day off.'

A tear rolled down Nina's face but she didn't move to brush it away. My heart went out to her: the poor girl was exhausted with nowhere to turn and no light at the end of the tunnel. Weird how flowers had been right at the top of my happy list, but were the thing causing Nina so much stress.

'OK, listen.' I crossed to the door, flipped the sign from open to closed. 'A few weeks ago I read a letter from my brother about choices and how it's up to us to choose what we do, how we live, who we love. A moment ago you said you don't have a choice when it comes to running this shop, but you do. Maybe you just need some help to get it back on track.' I paused to get her attention. 'Or maybe this business has served its purpose, maybe you're ready for a new adventure?'

'Your brother sounds amazing,' she quirked her lips into a smile. 'Not single, is he?'

My chest tightened. I hated this moment, when mortification crossed the face of the person who'd just put their foot in it. 'I'll tell you all about him soon, I promise. But for now, I think you need some time off; give yourself some headspace and see how you feel in a couple of days.'

'*Time off*? As in not come to work?' She stared at me as if I'd suggested cycling naked around the village green.

'Exactly.' I laughed. 'Scamp and I will mind the shop. As you would say, why not?'

Nothing like throwing yourself in at the deep end. But I could do this and she'd feel so much better after getting a rest.

'Really?' Her eyes shone with gratitude. 'That would be amazing.'

'That's settled, then,' I said boldly. 'And while you're gone, I'll ask my best friend for some advice. She's an accountant.'

She got to her feet, rummaged in her bag and handed me a set of keys. 'Keys to the shop and keys to the van. I'll drop it off tomorrow morning and I'll find everything, all the accounts, all the books, the lot. Lucas was right, you are a guardian angel.'

Which was why the following Sunday, Laura and I were sitting in my kitchen with several box files of loose papers, two shoe boxes stuffed with photos of flower arrangements and a long metal spike with at least one hundred receipts speared onto it.

'Is this all the paperwork she has?' Laura asked, surveying the chaos.

'Apart from a box of diaries, which she writes the orders down in, yes,' I said.

Laura looked bewildered. 'No spreadsheets, no cash flow projections, no bank reconciliations?'

'She's more creative than logical,' I said loyally. 'She doesn't have time for computers.'

'And people wonder why they get in a pickle,' Laura grumbled.

'Thanks for helping,' I said, giving her arm a squeeze. 'I'm sure you've got more exciting things to be doing on a Sunday.'

'Are you kidding?' She tipped out one of the boxes with relish. 'My best friend disappears off for a walk in the country and returns with a new job, a crusade to save a little shop and pollen stains on her fingers. I'm dying to know what has put such a spring in your step.'

I inspected my fingertips and made a mental note to google how to get rid of the yellow.

'Well . . .' I leaned forward, ready to tell all.

'Shush, I'm concentrating,' she replied, sifting through a stack of invoices, adding a few moments later, 'She uses a lot of Milton's sterilising fluid.'

'It's for cleaning vases.'

'And ribbons,' she marvelled, unfolding a huge till receipt. 'Look at all these.'

Nina had an entire set of map drawers dedicated to the stuff. I was going to have to ban her from buying any more until we'd used the current stock up. 'Yeah, each bunch of flowers is finished off individually.'

'Etsy, Etsy, Etsy . . .' Laura muttered under her breath, making a pile of invoices from each seller.

'Display props and little bits and bobs to resell,' I said. 'Look, are you going to let me tell you about the business's problems?'

'No!' She looked blankly at me. 'I can discover it myself; this way is much more fun.'

'You weirdo.'

'Right.' Laura saved the document she was working on and stretched her arms above her head. 'I have some observations to make.'

For the last couple of hours, I'd kept Laura topped up with tea, Marmite on toast and coconut macaroons. In between catering duties, I'd been flicking through Nina's diaries and looking at the orders she'd taken over the years. They made fascinating reading and some of the messages which must have been dictated to Nina to write on the accompanying gift cards had touched my heart.

'And me.' I sighed, closing the diary I was reading. 'People are so thoughtful. Flowers come with such love and kindness. And that's what matters at the end of the day, isn't it?'

'Hmm.' She gave me a sideways look. 'Didn't Steve dump you with flowers?'

Steve had come round with a bunch of daffodils one evening not long after Scamp had moved in. Scamp didn't like him much and the feeling was mutual. Daffodils were Granny's favourites: their cheery arrival in the garden, trumpets the end of winter, she used to say. And I still thought of her whenever they appeared in springtime. I was impressed that he had remembered how much I liked them, but this particular bunch of daffodils hadn't brought much cheer; as he handed them over, Steve informed me apologetically that he thought it best that we went our separate ways. Scamp had clung to me protectively for the rest of the evening.

'True,' I said. 'But even that was an act of kindness. One of us had to call time on the relationship. We only stayed together because I couldn't deal with any sort of emotions at all and Steve felt too guilty to dump me when I was grieving. I don't think it would have gone on past the summer if . . .'

'Hey, it's OK.' Laura squeezed my hand. 'You don't have to talk about it.'

'I think I do,' I said, 'I think it might help me to say things out loud instead of bottling them up.'

Her eyes flickered with a mix of shock and pride. 'That's the spirit.'

'Also. Not talking about Freddie is doing his memory a disservice. I blocked out his accident for a long time because I wasn't ready to accept it as my new reality.'

Laura smiled encouragingly. 'And now you are?'

I puffed my cheeks out and thought about that for a moment. 'My heart is still in my mouth every time I see a speeding motorbike, or I think a car driver hasn't seen the approaching motorcyclist in time, or I spot a biker on the motorway not wearing protective clothing.'

'You don't have to remind me,' Laura said with feeling. 'I've been there, remember?'

'So you have.' I smiled sheepishly.

She'd driven me to the vet when Scamp had torn one of his claws. On the way back, an impatient van had tried to overtake us and nearly wiped out an oncoming motorbike. Laura had swerved towards the kerb, the van dropped back and luckily the biker had lived to tell the tale. The incident was over. But I'd flown into a rage, wound down the window and sworn like a trooper at the van driver. I'd written down his registration plate and yelled that I'd get him arrested for dangerous driving, at which point Laura intervened and threatened to eject me from the car if I didn't calm down.

'Freddie's gone and I don't think I'll ever come to terms with that.' I tucked my hair behind my ears and frowned. 'But what I can do is to be happy that he loved life, he lived it his own way and he wouldn't have changed a thing. I want to be like him. I don't want to get to the end and think *if only*. So my new mission is to make my life as good as it can be.'

For a few seconds we just sat there, blinking away tears until I cleared my throat and nodded at her laptop.

'Now come on, Little Miss Bean Counter, tell me how to save Nina's Flowers.'

She turned it so I could read the screen. 'I'm afraid there's no magic wand and you could probably have worked this out for yourself. But the business needs to cut costs, find new markets and increase profit margins.'

'Thanks, Laura,' I said glumly. 'That's all very helpful.'

Cutting costs wasn't going to be easy with a novice like me making up bouquets at half the speed of Nina. And finding new markets was a tough one; we had lots of competition and a virtually non-existent internet profile. As for increasing profits, if Nina hadn't made a profit in five years, it was unlikely that I'd be able to come up with a quick solution.

'Are you absolutely sure there's no magic wand?'

'Well, Nina does have one ace up her sleeve.' Laura said slyly.

'Oh?' I leaned forward, all ears.

'You!' she said punching my arm playfully. 'Market trends, forecasting, advising on how people can future-proof their business. It's meat and drink to you.'

I blinked at her. 'For the global paper market, yes, but . . .'

'Oh, so you can advise international corporations but you can't possibly help a florist,' she scoffed.

I opened my mouth to argue and closed it again. If Nina's Flowers were a client, what would I do? I'd . . . well, I'd gather data, talk to people about their wants and needs, find exemplary business models in the floristry industry . . .

Laura was smiling. 'You're already formulating a plan, aren't you?'

'OK, clever clogs, you're right,' I admitted. 'I'll see what I can come up with. But a market research project takes time and that's something we haven't got a lot of. Nina's on the verge of throwing the towel in.'

'Poor woman.' Laura drummed a pen on the table, her eyes focused on the ceiling while she pondered. 'It's only a small thing, but, look at this.' She tapped on the keyboard and brought up a graph showing the last twelve months on one axis and money on the other. 'This red line is costs and the blue line is sales. See these cash flow dips here?'

She pointed to the places where costs outweighed the sales.

I nodded. 'What's happening there?'

'Weddings. It looks as if Nina gets carried away doing the wedding flowers and then doesn't pass the cost on to the bride.'

'It's like you know her.' It sounded exactly the sort of thing Nina would do.

'If I were you, I'd avoid weddings like the plague.'

I shrugged. 'I'll suggest it, but Nina won't like it.'

'Nina needs to get her head out of the sand and borrow enough money to pay the rent and cover next month's expenses. How long has she got?'

Sam Diamond had said he'd be back tomorrow and this time I didn't think he'd be so easily fobbed off.

'Twenty-four hours.' I felt queasy at the thought, although a tiny part of me was quite looking forward to seeing him again.

Laura whistled. 'I've seen the bank statements, she's already at the upper limit of her overdraft. What's she going to do?'

There was one solution which had been niggling at me all week. It had even woken me up last night and made me go back through my conversations with Mum about the amount of money she was keeping for me from the sale of Freddie's bikes. There was more than enough to bail Nina out, but was it the right thing to spend the money on?

Laura's eyes narrowed. 'You're hatching a plan.'

I hesitated to tell her the truth; she would almost certainly advise against it. But then again, I was thirty-four and completely entitled to do what I wanted. I'd read Freddie's letter so many times that I'd memorised it word for word and one line in particular came back to me now: *it's my own moral code which matters. I'm going to live my adult life doing what makes me happy.*

I pulled a pile of papers towards me and shuffled them into a neat stack. 'What would you say if I told you I was going to lend her the money?'

She made a noise somewhere between a gasp and a laugh. 'As your accountant, I'd suggest that wouldn't be advisable.'

'And as my friend?' I said with a twinkle in my eye.

She shook her head fondly. 'If it makes you happy, then go for it.'

'Correct answer.' I gave her a warm hug. 'Now I need to phone Nina and give her the news.'

Chapter Fourteen

The following morning flew by in a blur of planning, phone calls and excited squeals from Nina, who'd been overwhelmed with relief by my offer and after thinking about it for half an hour had phoned me back and asked me to be her business partner.

And so now, after serving only one week as her new assistant manager, I'd been promoted to 'the board'. Mum, completely unfazed at my change of heart, transferred the lump sum to me, I sent it straight on to the florist's bank account after which a big chunk of it winged its way to the landlord to pay three months overdue rent. It had happened very fast, there was still some legal stuff to do, and both of us had agreed that there should be a cooling off period just in case either of us had a change of heart.

But judging from the new bright-eyed and bushy-tailed version of Nina, I didn't think she'd be backtracking on the deal any time soon.

'You can't imagine how much better I feel,' said Nina, twirling in a circle. Scamp, sensing an opportunity to play, danced around with her, his tail brushing perilously close to a glass display bowl.

'I think I can,' I said, looking up from the bouquet I was making. 'Because you look like you're going to start singing about the hills being alive with the sound of music any second.'

The bouquet was part of my new initiative. I'd come up with the idea of making up some arrangements at several price points; that way, if someone came into the shop with a budget in mind, they could simply select the flowers to suit without having to ask how much everything was.

'I love the idea of your happy list,' she said, shoving her hands into her apron pockets and finding a treat for Scamp. 'And it sounds as if your brother was a very special person.'

I nodded. 'He was.'

I'd called her last night and told her everything – well almost everything, I still wasn't up to thinking about the details of his accident, let alone recounting them to someone else. But I had explained that finding Freddie's letter had made me reconsider every aspect of my life, take stock and make some changes in order to bring about a life lived without regrets, a life with the pursuit of happiness at its core.

'I suppose I could have a day off every week now, can't I?' she said. 'I think that would make me happy.'

'I insist on it,' I said firmly. 'Work – life balance is essential. And proper holidays. Although if you could possibly wait until I've got a better handle on the flower side of things before leaving the country, that would be marvellous.'

'You'd be fine without me,' she said, 'the bouquet idea is already going to simplify things.'

'You sound as if you've got a trip in the pipeline.'

Nina opened her mouth and then quickly snapped it shut. I stopped what I was doing to stare at her, suspecting she was keeping something from me. It was unlikely given that she'd told me that she hadn't had a holiday in five years, but perhaps her time off last week had given her pause for thought.

'You're entitled to do whatever you like,' I prompted.

'Nothing in the pipeline,' she said, fiddling with an alstroemeria in my bouquet which was protruding slightly. 'A pipe *dream*, that's all. And if I do go away, you'll get plenty of notice.'

'Glad to hear it.' I breathed a sigh of relief and popped the finished bouquet in water.

Even after so few days working together, Nina and I had already found our roles. She was the flighty one, generous with the stock and with only a vague handle on profit margins and I was the sensible one, reminding her of the cost of everything and keeping on top of orders. Although my jobs seemed to be the more boring ones, I could already see that we worked well together. My floristry skills had improved in leaps and bounds in the space of a week and just being in an environment I loved made me feel lighter and freer than I'd done in years.

I glanced out of the window; I might feel full of the joys of spring, but the weather was doing its best to clash with my mood. The sunshine of last week had vanished and in its place a thick swirl of gloomy cloud hung over the village green. There weren't many people about either, although still a smattering of cars parked outside. But no car with Hogg Property Services painted on it.

'Looking out for anyone in particular?' Nina hoiked up her eyebrows and waggled them.

'No.' I answered quickly. 'Just surveying the clientele, seeing who's about at noon on a Monday.'

'So, not looking for a certain property agent?'

'God no! Hopefully he won't need to pay us a visit for some time.'

'But he did tickle your pickle,' Nina reminded me with a snort.

I blushed. 'He intrigued me, that's all. I don't normally go for the sharp suit type but . . .' I broke off, wondering whether that was still true. Leather jackets, jeans and T-shirts had been more my thing – the standard uniform of a biker. I'd never owned my own bike, but most of my boyfriends had and I'd happily ridden on theirs. Freddie had been forever trying to persuade me to get one. I shuddered at the thought. Never. I'd never even *go* on one again.

'But?' Nina prompted.

'. . . I don't know,' I said, dragging myself back into the moment. 'There was something about him; he looked out of place in his clothes, as if he felt trussed up. Maybe it was his broad shoulders, or the chiselled jaw and I did like his stubble, I admit, just enough to be sexy, but not bushy.'

'Not that you've given him much thought, obviously,' said Nina folding her arms, amused. 'I suppose we could always break something accidentally on purpose and then ask him to come and inspect it.'

I laughed. 'No, I don't think we should push our luck with him at the moment, do you? We'll have to hope he comes in to buy some flowers.'

'I'd settle for anyone buying flowers today,' Nina said, surveying the display of blooms we had on offer.

'While we have a quiet moment, let's talk customers.' I took out my notebook. 'Who can we sell to who doesn't currently come into the shop? And how can we sell more to those who do?'

She blinked at me. 'If I knew the answer to that, I'd have done it long ago. Ooh, hold on, customer.'

The door opened and two women dressed in brightly coloured raincoats and shielded by an umbrella blew in, showering the floor with raindrops.

'Delphine and Maria!' said Nina, darting to the door to help them with their things. 'Come in!'

'*Grazie, grazie*. What a terrible day!' exclaimed one in a heavy Italian accent. I recognised her from the wedding, it was Rosie's grandmother. She unzipped her yellow waterproof coat and flapped it, sending a second shower in Nina's direction.

'But good for the garden,' said the other, stoutly. She threw back her hood and beamed at us both. 'Hello, dears.'

She had an elegant white bob, pink lipstick and a dolphin brooch pinned to a purple scarf poking from her pink mac.

'*Humph*. Not good for me. My body need sun, like poor lemon trees outside café.'

'Perhaps you've got that thing – *SAD*?' said her friend studying her as she peeled off leather gloves.

Maria looked affronted. 'I not sad, I very happy, just wet. I was born in Sorrento, I like my water in the sea, not falling from sky.'

'Well, you're inside now and it's lovely to see you,' Nina butted in. 'Come and meet my new team, Fearne and Scamp!'

At the mention of his name, Scamp got to his paws, stretched and pootled over sedately to say hello.

'We meet already,' said Maria, pulling me in and kissing both my cheeks. 'You do a beautiful job for my Rosanna's wedding in the big tent. And I bring you this to say *grazie*.'

She produced a plastic box from her handbag and lifted the lid. '*Biscotti alle mandorle*. You like nuts?'

The box was full of slices of biscotti, golden on the outside and packed with chunks of almond. The smell was making my mouth water.

'I do. Thank you so much,' I gasped, touched by her gesture. 'You've made these?'

'Of course,' Maria said proudly and tucked an escaped curl back into her bun. 'Try with a little glass of Vin Santo. *Perfetto!*'

I promised I would, although it was far more likely that Nina and I would tuck into them as soon as the ladies had left.

'And we've not met but I've heard a lot about you,' said Delphine. She didn't kiss me, but took my hand in hers and patted it.

'Delphine lives at The Evergreens, the big Victorian house up on the hill, beautiful gardens with all sorts of flowers,' said Nina.

'I know it,' I said smiling at the old lady. 'Scamp and I walked up that way last week. The garden in front of the little cottage was brimming with spring colour.'

Delphine's eyes softened. 'I'm very lucky to call it home.'

'Well, I'm lucky too, ladies,' Nina said excitedly. She put her arm around my shoulders. 'Because as of today, Fearne is my new business partner. She's going to help me revolutionise the shop.'

'Oh, delightful!' said Delphine. 'So nice for you to have a partner; having someone to share life's trials and tribulations with is such a bonus.'

'I happy for you, *cara*.' Maria patted Nina's cheek. 'Now you not have to fight that Hoggy dicky head on your own.'

'You know our landlord?' I said, surprised.

'Oh yes.' She pulled the corners of her mouth down in disgust. 'He try and screw me for more every year.'

'More rent,' Nina explained. 'Maria used to own the Lemon Tree Café, before Rosie and her sister Lia took over.'

'He has a nice boy working for him now, *molto sexy*, eh, Delphine?' Maria said with a dirty laugh.

Delphine tutted fondly. 'I haven't noticed, dear. And you shouldn't be looking at your age.'

144

'I might be old, but my eyes still know what they like, eh?' She winked at me.

'I've already met the man you mean,' I said, enjoying their banter. This would be Laura and me when we were their age; it was a warming thought.

'Oh!' Maria hooted with laughter. 'You also think he sexy, your face go red like roses.'

'Anyway,' I said swiftly, willing my cheeks to calm down. 'As Nina said, I'm her new partner. I'm new to floristry, but I've loved flowers since my grandmother taught me how to make a daisy chain and I'm looking forward to getting to know everyone's favourite flower. What's yours?'

'Jasmine. The perfume on a hot day in Italy is like heaven on earth.' Maria kissed her fingertips, adding darkly, 'No point growing it here.'

'And mine is violets,' said Delphine dreamily and Maria patted her arm. 'I adore them. But I haven't come to buy today, I need your help, I'm afraid.'

She reached into a voluminous shopping bag and produced a jug of sprigs of battered lilac, interspersed with woody stems of waxy variegated leaves.

I buried my nose in the frothy flowers. 'Mmm, divine.'

'Yes but they keep flopping over.' Delphine frowned.

I was confused. 'And how can we help?'

'She need your help,' said Maria, folding her arms. 'She fiddle with it all morning. I tell her to put more in, but it still looks like a doggy dinner.'

I gave Nina a bemused look; had she really brought her own flowers into a florist to be arranged for free?

'I'll just, er, leave you to get to know one another.' Nina picked up my notepad and pen and disappeared through the arch.

'So then I took them out again,' Delphine continued. 'But whatever I do, they don't look right. I added the euonymus in to pad it out but that didn't help either.'

'Ah, I see.' I blinked at her.

She gave a tinkling laugh. 'I was just as bad with the tulips I picked. Nina made a splendid job of arranging those.'

I had to smile. The reason for the business's failings were becoming more and more apparent with every passing day. Nina ran her business as an extension of herself. She was kind but completely uncommercial. She did what she loved and turned a blind eye to the bits she didn't. Freddie would have adored her.

'Let me see what I can do,' I said, taking the jug from her. 'Ah, I think I see the problem. I'd suggest a jug with a narrower neck.'

'I tell her that,' Maria put in.

'Oh, shush,' said Delphine. 'This one matches my bedroom.'

'In that case, let's try this.' I took a piece of flower foam from under the counter and cut it to size.

'I never use foam,' she said, leaning in. 'I've always been a bit scared of it.'

I soaked it in water, fitted it into the jug and quickly arranged the flowers in it.

'*Santo cielo!*' Maria said, clapping her hands. 'You come up trumpets again.'

'Yes well done,' Delphine agreed.

'You're welcome,' I said, helping her to put the flowers back into her bag without damaging the flower heads.

Delphine might not have spent any money, but I had made an old lady happy and as Nina had already set a precedent, I could hardly have refused to help her out. Besides, perhaps she couldn't afford to buy flowers every week.

'Right,' said Delphine putting her hood back up. 'How about treating ourselves to a slice of cake and a cappuccino next door before braving the wind and rain again, Maria?'

'I always say yes to cake,' Maria answered, zipping her coat back up. '*Ciao*, Nina, *ciao* Fearne!'

I smiled cheerfully as I waved them off. I didn't know how much they'd spend at the café, but I was pretty sure it would be more than one of my new bouquets.

'Nina?' I called sternly, once the two of them had gone.

She appeared with her hands up in surrender. 'I know, I know. I shouldn't have started doing people's flowers for free.'

I gaped at her. 'You mean it's not just Delphine?'

She chewed her lip. 'The perfume of home-grown flowers is always so wonderful. I can't resist helping people get the best out of them.'

'Getting you to focus on making a profit is going to be like herding cats,' I said sternly.

Her eyes lit up. 'Oh, that sounds like fun.'

I groaned.

'Don't be sad. I think we should celebrate,' she said, tweaking a twenty-pound note out of the till. 'An official business partners' lunch.'

I pinched it from her and put it back. 'I've brought ham sandwiches to share and we've got Maria's biscotti. We can celebrate when we see the bank account go back up again.'

'This partnership business isn't half as fun as I thought it was going to be,' she grumbled, taking the lid off my plastic sandwich box.

Scamp scooted straight over and eyed the box hopefully.

'It will be fun,' I assured her. 'Just think how happy you'll be if we can turn the flower shop's fortunes around and start making a profit.'

'I suppose I just kept hoping that one day things would change and the shop would start being more successful.' She picked up a sandwich and bit into it.

'In my experience, it's no good hoping that things are going to change,' I said firmly. 'You've got to make it change.'

I had a flashback then to that day last month when I'd read Freddie's letter. That had been my catalyst for change. Was it egotistical of me to hope that I could be the catalyst to help Nina change, or at least change the fortunes of the florist's? Because I couldn't think of anything which would make me happier.

'You're right,' said Nina decisively, feeding a bit of crust to Scamp, and then laughed. 'I hope you're not already regretting throwing your lot in with mine?'

Just then someone arrived outside the front door. Whoever it was had a large striped golf umbrella over their head. But as it lowered I found myself looking directly into the deep blue eyes of Sam Diamond. As Maria would say, *molto sexy*.

'No,' I said, a wide smile crossing my face. 'Not at all.'

Chapter Fifteen

'Oh balls,' Nina grumbled, following my gaze. She scrabbled to put the lid on the sandwich box and slid it under the counter. 'What does he want now?'

Sam turned away from the door, shaking the drops off his umbrella into the street and refolding it neatly.

'Calm down. He's not chasing money today,' I said, trying to smooth my hair down without being noticed. 'We can perhaps build bridges instead, improve communications, rather than do a runner.'

'Ooh, that's true,' she said, wide-eyed. 'Which must mean he's chasing something or *someone* else.'

My heart gave a little skip. He probably wasn't; he probably wanted flowers for his girlfriend.

'By the way, you've got crumbs on your chin,' Nina said as the door opened and Sam stepped in.

'Hello,' he said, closing the door gently behind him. I brushed my face quickly while his back was turned.

'Hello again,' I said, casually, secretly pleased to see him. His visits here might be something which Nina dreaded, but he was only doing his job, and the way he'd apologised on his way out last time was enough to convince me that he wasn't all bad. Nina, on the other hand, bristled as he approached the counter.

'What do you want?' She folded her arms and stuck her chin out. 'You only ever visit when the rent is due.'

'No I don't,' he replied, looking for somewhere to rest his dripping umbrella. 'I visit when it's *over*due. Which is every time.'

'It has been paid,' she said indignantly. 'Didn't you get the memo?'

'What Nina means to say,' I said smoothly, 'is that she regrets the late payments and that we are looking at ways to streamline the business to ensure it doesn't happen again.'

Sam raised his eyebrows. 'The landlord will be pleased.'

I took the umbrella from him and put it in a bucket to drip-dry.

'So you won't have to visit again,' Nina put in.

Scamp, having woken up and realised who was here, positioned himself in front of Sam and sniffed hopefully at his pocket.

'At least someone's pleased to see me,' said Sam, catching my eye and giving me a wink.

I smiled at him, grateful that he had a sense of humour. I thought he looked tired. There were dark shadows under his eyes and his hair looked ruffled as if he'd been raking his hands through it.

'Of course we're pleased to see you,' I said. Nina snorted softly. I gave her a stern look. 'Customers are always welcome, especially *paying* customers.'

She tutted beside me. 'That's a marketing tactic. Half the battle in sales is getting people through the door, and when they do, I try and build a rapport with them, no matter what they come in for. Unless it's him.' She jerked her head towards Sam.

'Sorry.' I mouthed to him when she wasn't looking. He shrugged lightly as if to show that it was water off a duck's back and fed Scamp a treat. The greedy mutt was staring at him adoringly, watching his every move. I was going to have to monitor that dog's diet or he'd be obese before long.

'If it's any consolation, chasing small business owners for money is my least favourite job.'

'You can't possibly hate your visits as much as I do,' said Nina, drily.

'You get a rent bill every three months, you know it's coming,' Sam said evenly. 'It would really help if you planned for it.'

'Oh yeah, like it's that simple,' Nina scoffed.

I suppressed a sigh; so much for building bridges. Her diplomacy skills may need some work, as well as her so-called marketing tactics. Thankfully Freddie's old iPad beeped from its stand on the counter, where it now resided.

'That'll be an order. So I'll leave you in Fearne's capable hands,' Nina said and flashed me an encouraging look before taking the iPad into the back of the shop. I cringed; she had all the subtlety of a sledgehammer.

'Don't you like your job?' I twirled a lock of my hair around my fingers until I caught sight of myself in the mirror. I looked like I was flirting. I started pulling flowers from the display instead as if I had a bouquet to make up. I'd have to put them all back afterwards, but I needed something to do to stop me staring at him inanely.

'Um.' Sam let out a long breath. 'It pays the bills, I suppose.'

Nina reappeared and selected my twenty-pound bouquet. 'Sold! I'm going to take this to the primary school. One of the teachers has won an award and they want a quick gift. I can take Scamp with me, if you like?'

At the sound of his name, Scamp flicked a whiskery glance at Nina only to return to watching Sam just in case of further biscuit enticements.

'Please do,' said Sam, holding his empty hands out to the dog. 'I feel like I'm under interrogation.'

'Yeah? Now you know how I feel.' Nina quirked a sardonic eyebrow, wrapping the ends of the dripping flowers in paper. She looked at him again and did a double take. 'Hey! Your beard's gone.'

'Oh, yes!' I stared at his smooth face. 'I knew there was something different about you.'

He still had a handsome profile and the dimple in his cheek was more visible, but he looked more vulnerable somehow.

Sam touched his chin, a faint flush spreading over his face. 'Had to be done, I'm afraid. I had my orders.'

'Shame,' Nina said blithely, pulling on her waterproof jacket. 'Fearne was only saying earlier how much she liked it.'

'Beards *generally*,' I said with a stutter. 'Not yours. I mean, not specifically yours. I liked yours as well, of course. But I just like a bearded man. In general.' I delved into my bag to fetch Scamp's lead, before my mouth got me into any more trouble.

'Got it,' said Sam, clearly amused. 'Thank you. In general.'

Nina stepped forward to study his face more closely. 'And I see what you mean about the chiselled jaw. Very manly.'

I shot her a murderous look. At this rate our partnership might be very short lived.

'Take a poo bag with you, won't you,' I said, clipping on Scamp's lead. 'In fact two to be on the safe side.'

Nina's nose crinkled up. 'Ew, maybe I shouldn't—'

'Thanks so much.' I helped her make up her mind by opening the door. Scamp, spotting his chance, charged through it.

'Fine.' She sighed and as a parting shot winked at me. 'Behave yourself.'

'So, Sam,' I said, surreptitiously pressing a cool hand to my cheek. 'What can we do for you?'

'I need to buy some flowers and they need to be really special.' He walked slowly around the shop, peering at the buckets of flowers.

He leaned forward to smell a peony which wouldn't smell of much. If I thought I'd get away with it without him noticing, I'd take his photo to show Laura. *I've met a man I quite like*, I'd tell her and we'd giggle like teenagers about it.

'Then you are definitely in the right place. That peony, for example is perfect. It's a plump bud today, but tomorrow it will burst forth, masses of pink and frilly-edged petals and hugely romantic.'

'Sounds good.' He chewed the inside of his cheek.

My heart sank slightly. 'So is it romantic you're after?'

'Well.' He exhaled and ran his hand through his hair. 'Yes. I think. It's a bit complicated.'

'Romance often is.' I pasted on a smile. *So there you have it, Fearne. He's taken. The flirting stops right now.*

He was so close I could smell his scent. He smelled fresh and citrusy and earthy and the overall effect was like an early morning walk in the woods. The feeling I had the first time we met a week ago returned; this man was having such a strong effect on me that I was tempted to flip the sign on the door to closed to make sure nothing could spoil the moment.

Get a grip, Lovage.

'You might be interested in our new line.' I waved my arm with a flourish towards the remaining bouquets priced between ten and twenty-five pounds. 'There are peonies in those.'

He squatted down to take a closer look. I was quite proud of my efforts. They were jam-packed with flowers and foliage and even the cheapest one looked impressive wrapped in layers of pink tissue and brown paper and finished with raffia ribbon.

Sam inspected the twenty-five-pound bouquet. I held my breath. This was what I was hoping would happen: that people would be tempted to spend a little more. 'Increasing basket size' as the supermarkets would say. If I could sell a few of these every day, the coffers would soon begin to swell.

'These are great but, she doesn't often get flowers.' He stood up and smiled apologetically. 'So I want something very special. And they need to make up for the last time, because things didn't go to plan.'

My interest was piqued. Could he be referring to me, or Nina? I'd told him that *florists* don't often get flowers. And his last visit to us was definitely tense. Being in Sam's company was making me think that maybe I was ready for dating again. Was it terribly pathetic to hope that they were for me?

'Oh, don't worry, I'm sure it wasn't as bad as you think,' I said.

'Well.' He stroked his chin and pretended to think about it. 'I ended up homeless and almost jobless, so . . . that counts as fairly bad.'

'Really?' I gasped, dumbfounded; no wonder he hated his job! His boss sounded dreadful, a proper dicky head as Maria had called him. It took all my self-restraint not to give him a comforting hug. 'That's terrible.'

He gave me a lopsided smile. 'Anyway, I'm not giving up yet so, let's splash out on the flowers. Say forty pounds?'

'In that case,' I said, delighted at the prospect of my biggest sale yet, 'I suggest you buy individual stems and I can make something up for you. And if you don't know what the lady likes, we can . . .'

'Oh I know what she likes, all right,' he laughed without humour. 'And what she *doesn't* like. She's not shy when it comes to getting what she wants.'

Ah. I had a creeping feeling that the flowers were for someone he knew rather better than Nina or me. 'And who is the lucky lady?'

He looked down at his feet. 'My wife, Pandora.'

'Your wife,' I repeated flatly. He was married. Of course he was. All the good ones were. Although Hamish wasn't, at least not yet. And Freddie hadn't been. He'd got as far as being engaged but his girlfriend, Gemma, who I'd really liked, had asked him to give up riding a bike when they were married. And that was the end of that. *If only you'd listened to her, you idiot.*

'Technically, my *ex*-wife,' he said, pulling his phone out to check the screen. He frowned and put it back in his jacket pocket. 'She asked me to leave the family home last autumn and we've been separated ever since.'

Thank goodness I hadn't done anything more than gaze at him like a love-struck puppy. Dignity just about still intact, I leapt into professional mode. 'So let's start with what she doesn't like?'

'Garage forecourt flowers,' he said with a grimace. 'She said, and I quote, giving her a bunch of half-dead, bargain basement flowers I'd picked up while buying petrol was the final nail in the coffin of our marriage. Apparently garage flowers say "afterthought".'

'Well . . .' I sucked in air; I did have to agree slightly with Pandora on that point.

'But you have to put it into context,' he protested. He took a step back and leaned against the counter. 'It was just an ordinary Friday night and I'd bought us all something. Dark chocolate for me, some sweets for the kids . . .'

'Oh.' *Kids*. As if married wasn't enough, he had kids. Plural. Cutest man I'd met for ages and with three simple words 'wife and kids' he'd slipped from eligible bachelor to Baron von Trapp.

'Yeah, I know,' he said with a shrug, misunderstanding my reaction. 'I regret it now, but I knew she wouldn't eat junk food, she's very figure-conscious, and I didn't want to go home empty-handed. It was either that or a Thermos travel mug.'

Our eyes met then and we both bit our lips to stop ourselves from laughing.

'Buying garage flowers in those circumstances is entirely acceptable,' I said. 'I think you were very thoughtful.'

Sam smiled. 'Thanks. Anyway, I won't make the same mistake twice. These flowers have got to say a lot more. Pandora might have said our marriage was dead, but I'm holding out for a resurrection.' He checked over his shoulder to make sure no one was about to walk in. 'I miss the children so much. I want us to be a family again. So I'm going to try harder to be the man she wants me to be. She says she wants to be wooed, worshipped like a princess, so that's what I'm going to do.'

I felt a spike of malice towards Pandora. If I ever married, I'd want to be treated with love and respect and kindness, but as an equal, not as someone whose every whim needed to be pandered to like a spoiled princess.

'And is that what you want?' I said, unable to keep the note of cynicism from my voice.

He stared at me for so long that I had to look away.

'I hardly see the kids at the moment,' he said finally. 'I'm missing them growing up, I even miss watching them

156

while they're asleep. Annabel sleeps on her back, arms out, like a little starfish as if she's addressing a crowd and Will curls up, one arm clutching his teddy bear, thumb in his mouth. And I miss being woken up by their boundless energy in the morning. Pandora and me, we've had our share of problems, but the kids are worth setting them aside for.'

His words came from the heart and made mine squeeze with warmth. I bet he was a great dad. I wasn't sure how I felt about staying together for the kids. After all, I'd been there and Freddie and I had turned out OK. But I was his florist, not his marriage counsellor.

'In that case, you're going to give Pandora an absolutely unique bouquet,' I said determinedly.

'Great.' He pulled up a stool to perch on.

'Uh-uh,' I said pulling him up to his feet. 'It's better to stand while you arrange flowers.'

'Me?' He looked horrified. 'Forty quid and I have to do it myself?'

'Forty pounds and,' I counted on my fingers, 'you'll get the best flowers in Derbyshire. One to one tuition from a *professional* and I can almost guarantee a place in Pandora's good books.' Although the jury was out as to whether I was a professional, and as to whether she deserved it, I couldn't possibly comment.

'When you put it like that,' he said with a grin, 'it's a bargain.'

I told him to take his jacket off and roll his sleeves up while I made room on the counter, selected plenty of flowers and foliage and put them in a bucket of water.

'We'll both do a hand-tied gift bouquet, you can copy mine and give it to Pandora and mine can be for the next suitable phone order.'

'Deal.' He looked at the bucket of flowers I'd selected and exhaled. 'So where do we start?'

I gathered together three stems: a bushy piece of ruskus, some white spray roses and a huge peach peony, and showed him how to grasp them in his left hand, keeping his thumb free. It took a few goes for him to get the grip right but once he did, he was quite pleased with himself.

'Look at that! I think I'm a natural,' he said in surprise, inspecting the flowers from all angles.

'And modest with it,' I teased, enjoying his success as much as he did.

I lined up the next few stems for him.

'Open up the thumb, place your new stem between your thumb and first finger and slide it behind the others, keeping it at an angle.' I demonstrated with a sprig of gypsophilia. 'Next some foliage.'

He nodded, dragging his eyes from his hand for a split second to see what I'd chosen and then picked the same. We repeated it twice more before I showed him how to give the bunch a quarter turn.

'Now we add more. Can you see that the stems below your hand are forming a nice spiral?'

He looked at his and then mine and frowned. 'Why does yours look better than mine?'

I laughed. 'Because you're uptight. Relax, drop your shoulders and loosen your grip on your precious flowers or they'll end up bruised.'

'I am tense, you're right.' Sam blew out a sharp breath and circled his shoulders. 'You sound like our cricket coach.'

A sportsman; that explained the broad shoulders and toned arms. Something Ethel once said came back to me from nowhere: if you find a young man who plays sport, hang on to him. Not enough youngsters *do* anything these days, they're all armchair experts. I smiled at the memory until I remembered that Sam wasn't mine to hang on to; he was Pandora's. Or trying to be. The woman must be barmy.

'You said earlier that you ended up homeless and almost lost your job?' I put my flowers down for a second and adjusted the two delphiniums which Sam had added into his bouquet and which now protruded like horns. 'Seems an extreme punishment for giving your wife substandard flowers?'

'My marriage and my job come as a package. Pandora's dad is Duncan Hogg who owns the company. He and my mother-in-law Sybil moved to the Canaries a few years ago, but he still calls the shots. The vague plan was that I'd eventually take over the business, but I can't see him ever giving up his position of power. Not sure I want the company, to be honest. Anyway, Pandora phoned her parents in floods of tears to tell them *I'd* left *her* and they both jumped on a plane and flew home. Sybil moved into our house for a week to look after the children while Pandora refused to get out of bed and Duncan hauled me over the coals under the illusion that if she'd thrown me out, I must have been unfaithful to his daughter.'

'They sound very . . . involved,' I said tactfully.

'They're very protective of their only child, but after I'd given my side of the story, Duncan apologised for jumping to conclusions. All the same, I've been "strongly advised" to make a go of my marriage if I know what's good for me.'

I wondered if Pandora had been given the same advice. I wasn't naïve; there were two sides to every story, but it takes two to tango.

'If I were you I'd—' I stopped in my tracks and snapped my mouth shut.

'You'd . . .?' He looked at me, deep blue eyes focusing on mine. 'Go on?'

Look for another job.

I swallowed my words. We'd only met twice; it wasn't for me to make that sort of comment. We *had* only met twice and yet I felt a real connection between us. I wondered if he felt the same. I gave myself a shake.

'I'd extend my arm,' I said plucking something from the air. 'So you can see the flowers from a distance, spot any gaps or over-crowding.'

'Oh, right.' His gaze lingered for a second and then he did as I suggested. 'Like this?'

'Perfect. What do your friends and family say about your situation?' I stopped myself with a gasp. 'Oops, ignore me, it's completely none of my business.'

Sam chuckled. 'I don't mind. The majority verdict is that I'm crazy.'

But it was all right for them, he pointed out, the younger ones had none of his responsibilities and the older ones were happy to dole out advice that they wouldn't have dreamed of taking themselves. And then there was his job. It wasn't perfect, but he liked not being tied to an office, and there were benefits to having a boss who was out of sight for ninety per cent of the year.

It was quite soporific listening to Sam's deep gentle voice while my hands were busy, creating and tweaking, weaving flowers into a perfect combination. I noticed that his grip had softened, his posture was less rigid and he was inserting each flower into his bouquet with care.

He looked up suddenly and laughed. 'Fearne, I'm so sorry. You're so easy to talk to that I got carried away. You must be bored rigid!'

'That's the magic of flowers,' I said simply, flattered that he felt comfortable with me. 'Therapy for the soul. And you haven't bored me at all.'

'Counselling with an added side of flower arranging . . .' He pretended to shudder. 'That's my street-cred completely wiped out. Worth it though. This bouquet would win prizes at my mum's gardening club.'

'Hmm.' I pretended to scrutinise it. 'Not bad for a beginner, I suppose.'

I thought back to last month when I'd turned up at the Wisteria Cottage Flower School worried that I wouldn't be able to keep up with the others on the course. And here I was, a partner in a florist's, teaching someone else how to do it.

Life had been a whirlwind since finding Freddie's letter. Maybe I'd rushed into handing over the money to Nina, maybe I would lose it all but the flip side was that it was an adventure. One which Freddie had made possible.

'You're smiling to yourself.' Sam's words jolted me from my thoughts. 'A penny for them?'

'I'm doing a job that makes me happy, that's all,' I said, turning my smile to him.

Like Freddie had and Ethel too, who'd decided to be happy in the care home even though it must have been such a wrench to give up her independence. Emotion rushed up inside me and I allowed myself a moment of pride.

'I'm quite envious,' said Sam.

'What would your dream job be, if you could do anything?'

'Something food-related. I'm a geek when it comes to food. I can lose hours in the kitchen, working out flavour combinations, creating my own recipes.' He spoke rapidly, his face becoming animated. 'And if I'm not in the kitchen, I'm visiting farmers' markets, collecting artisan products or experimenting with herbs and spices for marinades and stuff. I love it.'

'Then that's what you should do,' I said. 'I'm a firm believer in doing what makes you happy.'

He blew out a breath, and frowned. 'Pandora wouldn't agree. When she met me cooking was my hobby, but by day, or night, I suppose, I was the manager of a bistro. She loved it at first, sitting at the bar, sipping cocktails and telling anyone who asked that the manager was her boyfriend.'

'Who wouldn't,' I murmured. I bet she didn't have to pay for the cocktails either. If it were left to me, I'd give her a bunch of nettles.

'My dream had been to set up by myself. But once we were married, Pandora wanted me to park the restaurant idea and get a "proper" job with sociable hours and a pension. Duncan had already approached me several times with an offer to be his second in command but I'd turned him down. Then she got pregnant with Annabel and everything changed. We were only young and neither of us was ready to settle down, I can see that now with the benefit of hindsight. But at the time I needed stability, so I took the job.'

I prised the flowers out of his hands. 'Let's get these tied before you crush them completely.'

He scratched his face absentmindedly. 'Yeah, sorry, got a bit tense again there.'

'Take it out on the stems,' I said, pointing him in the direction of some sharp scissors.

Between us we cut the bouquet down to size, tied it with string, wrapped it in layers of pretty paper and finished it off with a cardboard box and some ribbon.

Sam looked at the final thing and whistled. 'This is amazing. She'll never believe I made it myself.'

I whipped out my phone and took a picture.

'There,' I said, showing it to him. 'We should have taken some action shots, but it's better than nothing. Give me your number and I'll send it to you.'

'Sure, thanks.' He reeled off his number, I tapped it into mine and sent him the photo.

His phone beeped and he checked the display. 'Got it.'

He noticed the time and groaned. 'I've got to go. I'm supposed to be meeting a client at a hotel in ten minutes. I lost track of time, I'm going to be so late.'

'Time flies when you're having fun,' I said with a grin.

'It does.' He paused, running the backs of his fingers along his jaw. 'Fearne.'

'Yes?'

'Thanks. For everything.'

'Just doing my job,' I shrugged casually but my pulse had quickened under his gaze.

The moment hung between us. He was leaving, going back to work and then off home to patch up his marriage. The intimacy we'd shared would be gone. She was bound to take him back; she'd be mad not to. Then she'd be his wife again and not his ex . . . Which was as it should be. Obviously.

Sam cleared his throat. 'Have you got a business card? I can leave it at the hotel reception, next time they need flowers they might give you a call.'

'Sure.' I found a dog-eared card under the counter and handed it to him. It had Nina's name on it and a mobile number which she'd crossed out and written a new one in smudged ink squashed into a corner.

He inspected it, amused. 'Very . . . *Nina*.'

'I'm getting some new ones printed.' Another job for the list.

'I'll pop in next week and pick some up if you like?' he offered. 'I can leave them with all our managed properties as I visit: hotels, offices, hairdressers.'

There it was: the way to attract a new customer base.

'Oh my goodness!' I laughed in surprise. 'That's it! That's what the flower shop is missing. Sam, you're a genius.'

'Business cards?' he said, confused.

'A corporate clientele! I can't believe I didn't think of it myself. Even the company I used to work for had a weekly delivery of flowers. There must be loads of places we could target.'

'Oh, there are,' Sam smiled. 'Most of our clients. We even have a funeral director on our books. I can give you a list if you like.'

'I *do* like, thanks!' I grabbed hold of him and as if it was the most natural thing in the world, I placed a smacker of a kiss to his cheek. 'You're bloomin' brilliant!'

'Wow.' Sam looked stunned. 'I'll email it to you.'

Selling the flower shop's services to other prospective businesses would be a piece of cake; it was essentially the same as I'd been doing in my old career for the last ten years. I could phone, or email, or better still, invite them to the shop . . .

'Well!' I turned to see Nina and Scamp in the doorway. 'Looks like you two have had more fun than me.'

'Probably.' Sam nodded towards the full poo bag in Nina's hand.

'*Humph*,' said Nina, letting Scamp off the lead. 'Not only did I have to double-bag his offering, but he forced me into Biddy's Pet Shop and wouldn't leave until he'd been given a chunk of something which reeked of old fish.'

I winced with apology. Scamp loved it in there. I'd booked the doggy pedicure which Biddy had given me a discount voucher last week. here. Scamp quivered with fear at the sight of the clippers and Biddy had had to feed him dried liver to coax him round. Since then he never missed the opportunity to drag me in there when he could and he and Churchill had become good friends.

'That'll be forty pounds please.' I held my hand out to him, my eyes still shining.

'Good luck,' said Sam, handing over the money. 'And thanks for the flowers and the chat.'

'You're welcome.' My heart tweaked.

He collected his umbrella and looked down at the flowers. 'These don't say afterthought, do they?'

'No,' I promised, shaking my head slowly, 'they say "I'm a very lucky girl".'

Nina stepped aside to let Sam out.

'So?' she demanded, wide eyed with curiosity. 'Have you got yourself a date?'

'He's married, so sadly not,' I sighed as Sam crossed the road to his car, placed the flowers carefully on the back seat and drove away.

'Balls.' She gave my arm a sympathetic pat.

'However, he did give me an idea to help the business. So I was thinking: what do you say to having a party?'

'I say YES!' She grabbed hold of my hands and danced us both around the shop. 'I take it back about this not being fun. I love parties.'

I grinned at my new business partner and for the second time in as many minutes I delivered a big kiss to an unsuspecting face. 'I thought you might.'

Chapter Sixteen

Nibbles, check, sparkling wine, check, price list, check . . .
My eye roamed the shop as I mentally ticked off everything
on my list. Everywhere and everything looked perfect.
The shop floor was swept, the windows were smear-free
and sparkling and every single bloom on display was at its
freshest and most fragrant best.

'I think we're ready, Scamp.' I bent down to his bed and
stroked his head. His tail thumped companionably against
my leg. 'Everything, I'm pleased to say, is under control.'

The only thing missing at the moment from Nina's
Flowers was Nina herself. But I wasn't concerned, she'd
phoned yesterday morning and told me not to worry but
that something unexpected had come up and she'd had to
go to London urgently. She'd promised faithfully that she'd
be here before the party this afternoon at three. Strictly
speaking, it was an open day to drum up new business, but
as long as she was here, I didn't mind what she called it.

As promised, Sam had emailed me a list of companies
who might order flowers and we'd invited over a hundred
businesses to come and see what we had to offer. We
hadn't had many responses, but I knew from experience
that business people often made attendance decisions late
in the day, depending on their other priorities.

Nina hadn't been as enthusiastic as I was about my
attempt to attract a corporate clientele.

'Corporate flowers are just a chore to be ticked off by some faceless person with a to-do list. When I make up a bouquet for someone, the best bit is seeing the pleasure on their faces. Create a big centrepiece for a hotel reception and the person who ordered it simply looks over and tells you where to put it. There's no emotion involved.'

'Possibly not,' I'd agreed, 'but we can't choose our customers based on those who'll show the most appreciation, can we?'

The side eye Nina gave me implied that she thought we could.

'I suppose not,' she'd admitted. 'But it's just not what I saw my shop doing, that's all.'

'And crawling out of the back door, commando style to avoid the landlord is?' I'd asked.

'Fair point,' she'd conceded, breaking into a smile. 'OK, I'm in, but I'm in charge of ordering refreshments for the party.'

I gave Scamp one last tickle and stood up, catching sight of myself in the shop mirror. Not bad: the up-do I'd wrangled my hair into this morning was largely still intact, thank goodness. I turned left and right, checking my outfit. Not jeans for once but a long maxi dress and ankle boots: practical and professional.

There was a fizz of excitement in my stomach. The sort I used to have just before a big presentation to my paper industry clients. It was a sensation I hadn't felt in months and I welcomed its return.

Just then I heard the rumble of Nina's van in the courtyard behind the shop and moments later she came flying through the door and into the front of the shop. Scamp leapt up, turned a few circles and barked, pleased to see her.

'Fear not, for I am with you!' Nina dropped her bags and stared around the shop. 'Bloody hellfire, Fearne. This all looks amazing!'

I followed her gaze, pleased with our efforts. 'It does, doesn't it.'

The area towards the back of the shop which had always been under-used was now our new workshop space. Lucas had helped us source a big chunky table from one of his suppliers and this took centre stage. On it were piles of floristry supplies including sprigs of fern and thorn-free roses in every hue, which Nina would be making into button-holes to give away to our guests. A trestle table held glasses, soft drinks and bowls of crisps and olives, a crate of fizz was chilling in the cold store and on the counter was a display featuring glossy pictures of floral arrangements which Nina had done previously.

'It all looks so . . .' she sounded choked up '. . . impressive.'

'Teamwork makes the dream work,' I said lightly.

'No, this is you, this is *your* work.' She gave a sudden laugh. 'You don't need me at all. I don't know what I was worried about.'

'What do you mean?'

'Oh, nothing.' She picked a piece of stray leaf from her sleeve. 'I suppose I thought no one would care about the shop as much as I do.'

'Don't talk daft,' I gave her a shove with my shoulder. 'And of course, I need you. Look at all those gorgeous flowers in the photos. You did them.'

She opened her mouth as if to argue but changed her mind. 'Oh, I almost forgot: I bought you something.'

She rifled in one of the carrier bags and pulled out a parcel beautifully wrapped in tissue and tied in raffia.

'I thought it was about time you had your own special set.'

I tore off the wrapping. Inside was a matching set of floristry scissors and secateurs in their own leather holster. 'I love them, thank you,' I said, genuinely moved.

Nina took a deep breath. 'And thank *you*. From the moment you rocked up here pressing your nose to the glass on the day of Rosie and Gabe's wedding you've done nothing but help me. I don't know what I've done to deserve you. But from the bottom of my heart thanks. For everything.'

'You're welcome.'

We looked at each other for a moment, grinning like loons until Nina's eyes slid sideways towards the cold store where she knew I'd stashed the booze.

She chewed her lip. 'I know that you said we weren't allowed to celebrate until we'd started making a profit, but . . .'

'Yes. Definitely. Let's get this party started.'

An hour later the shop was buzzing. I hadn't taken any orders yet, but seeing the shop so busy was a great start.

There was the owner of a hair salon who was deep in discussion with Nina about the pros and cons of having a fringe, a couple of hotel people enjoying the free drinks, two office managers who'd paid scant attention to the flowers but seemed quite interested in each other and a group of beauticians who took a lot of selfies with the flowers as their backdrop. There was a manager of a care home, a dental receptionist and even, to my great delight, someone from Enchanted Spa where I'd taken Laura back in March . . . all here to see what we could offer them.

We played to our strengths: Nina demonstrating her floristry skills and delighting each guest by making them up an individual complimentary buttonhole, just as she'd done at her London flower stall, and me gathering information, talking to people, finding out their needs, their budget and their current supplier, working out how we could provide them with a little extra to tempt them to give us a try.

I'd assumed guests would pop in, collect some information and go, but half an hour later, the shop was getting busier and busier. And a lot of the newest arrivals were people I'd seen in Barnaby.

'Did you invite all of these people?' I said to Nina, nodding to where a group of mums were giggling over glasses of prosecco while their offspring sat on the floor with Scamp and persuaded him to roll over in return for a smoky bacon crisp. He did, of course, repeatedly.

She nodded sheepishly. 'You did say party. And it was a back-up plan in case none of Sam's contacts showed up.'

But they had, thank goodness, unlike Sam himself, I thought with a pang of sadness. Still, there was time yet.

'Let's hope we don't run out of bubbly,' I said, leaning back as someone popped the cork on another bottle.

'Don't stress.' Nina nudged me with her elbow. 'I can always nip out for more. It's worth spending a bit of money on your customers now and again.'

'Providing they *are* customers,' I said, reminding her.

'They're *potential* customers,' she pointed out. 'All of them. We're in this for the long haul.'

'True,' I said. 'Although technically I'm only here for another three months.'

We'd discussed this when we'd agreed my investment in the business. I'd continue as her sleeping partner indefinitely, but I hadn't been prepared to commit to longer than the end of summer as a member of staff.

'Well anyway,' said Nina briskly, turning away. 'I'm glad to have the opportunity to thank everyone for their support over the last five years.'

'You make it sound as if we're closing down, not trying to grow,' I laughed, rebuking her.

We didn't have a chance to talk any longer; Rosie and her sister, Lia arrived and I resumed my welcoming duties. They didn't look like sisters, Lia had blonde curls and pink cheeks while Rosie had traditional Italian colouring: dark hair and olive skin which was still tanned from her honeymoon.

'I feel a bit guilty for accepting the invitation,' said Lia, sipping a glass of sparkling wine. 'We haven't bought flowers for the café for ages.'

'Since we took on the pizza cabin at the garden centre down the road it's become pricey to do it at both places,' Rosie apologised.

'It's our margins,' Lia said, ruffling her hair to cool down her neck. 'Everything has increased but our prices. So we had to make a choice: go easy on the pizza toppings, or lose the flowers.'

'And there'd have been uproar if we'd skimped on the food,' said Rosie. 'Not least from Nonna.'

Lia inhaled deeply and sighed. 'But it does smell amazing in here.'

'Agreed,' said Rosie. 'And you did single-handedly save my wedding.'

I held my breath as the pair looked at each other.

'Maybe we could stretch to a small monthly budget?' Lia suggested.

My first order of the day.

'Yay! Thank you! I'll sort out the perfect thing,' I said, scribbling a note on my order pad. 'Something long-lasting, with impact and good value. Leave it with me.'

Business talk complete, Lia topped up her glass and went to watch Nina make a buttonhole while Rosie sat on a chair near the door, fanning herself with a price sheet.

'You look as if pregnancy is suiting you,' I said, handing her a drink.

Her baby bump had grown since the last time I'd seen her and her face had a golden serenity to it which made her look like nothing could possibly mar her happiness.

'Happy mummy and hopefully a happy baby,' she said. She smoothed her dress over her stomach fondly. 'Plus getting married to a fabulous man, followed by two weeks in my grandmother's home town of Sorrento helped. Thank you for helping out with the flowers by the way. Poor Nina. I had no idea about all the stress she'd been under trying to cope on her own.'

'I should be the one thanking you.' I waved my arm around. 'It was doing the flowers for you that led me to working here.'

'Nonna is still raving about that spring meadow table runner you did a month later,' she laughed.

'She was very complimentary at the time,' I told her. 'And she brought me some biscotti to thank me after I'd started working here.'

Rosie shook her head fondly. 'She got so caught up on my wedding preparations, I really hoped she'd put Stanley out of his misery and set a date.'

'Why won't she?'

She pulled a face. 'She's scared of losing him like she lost the first love of her life. Stanley had a heart attack a few years ago, she's worried that too much excitement would finish him off.'

I nodded in sympathy. 'Poor Maria, I know how it feels to be scared of losing loved ones.'

I remembered earlier this year, the sheer terror of finding Ethel collapsed on the bedroom floor. She might be ninety-four but I wasn't ready to lose her yet. I wasn't ready to lose *anyone* else ever.

'They both seem very happy together, married or not,' I said. 'And very much in love.'

'Oh they are. Take my advice: don't ask Nonna about their love life.'

'Why not? Not that I was planning to.'

'Because she'll tell you!' she said with a snort. 'Pass me some more crisps, will you, I've fully embraced the concept of eating for two. And then you can tell me how you persuaded Nina to try and drum up business. I've been on at her for ages to do something like this but she'd never listen.'

'Confidentially,' I whispered, pulling up a chair and handing her a bowl of crisps, 'the shop needs to make more money.'

'I know,' she said sympathetically. 'Nina's very open about her inability to make a profit.'

'What I don't understand,' I said, frowning, 'is why people are happy to spend a fiver on a coffee and a slice of cake . . .'

'More than that,' she corrected.

'Which is gone in a couple of minutes. Whereas for the same money, they could take home a big bunch of tulips which would bring a smile to their faces for a whole week.'

'Ah,' said Rosie sagely. 'But it's not just food and drink they get in the Lemon Tree Café, it's company, escapism and a little bit of Italian sunshine thrown in.'

I nodded. 'That's very true. So I need to make buying flowers more than just about buying flowers?'

'Worth a shot. Anyway, great party but I need to get back to the café.' She stood up and handed me back an empty crisp bowl. 'Gosh, now I'm standing up I need the loo. Sorry. You didn't need to know that. I'm just glad Nina's got you to help her. It would have been awful if she'd just abandoned the shop and left the country as she planned. You obviously managed to persuade her to stay and soldier on.'

'I don't think she was serious about going abroad, really.' I smiled, remembering Nina's throwaway comment about New Zealand. 'She was probably just having a bad day.'

Rosie blinked at me. 'Oh she was. Deadly serious. Oh look, here come Nonna and Stanley now, I might have known she wouldn't miss out on a free drink. *Ciao*, Fearne. Thanks again, and let me have some costs for flowers when you can.'

'Rosie wait,' I begged, 'tell me more about Nina!'

She winced. 'Sorry, I really do have to go. My bladder is the size of a walnut at the moment. Ask her yourself, it's not a secret.'

I watched her leave and then sought out Nina across the room. As if by a sixth sense, Nina turned her head towards me and smiled.

'You OK?' I mouthed.

She beamed and stuck both thumbs up in return.

I breathed a sigh of relief. Everything was fine, I had nothing to worry about. Nina and I were partners now and if there was anything I needed to know, she'd tell me. Wouldn't she?

Chapter Seventeen

A few minutes later I'd been cornered by Maria and her fiancé, Stanley.

'Usually the café is the place for parties in Barnaby,' said Maria, a glass of fizz in her hand. 'This is good idea. Good for community spirits.'

'Then the afternoon is a success,' I said, ignoring the number of empty bottles stacked up at the back door compared with the skimpy pile of orders on the counter.

'I must say,' said Stanley, sipping a glass of fruit juice, 'it's quite a selection of *flora* you've got here. My late wife used to favour dried flowers. She was allergic to pollen.'

'Full of dust,' said Maria shuddering. 'First thing I do when I move in. Put them in the bin.'

'Yes, well.' Stanley took off his glasses and polished them on his handkerchief. 'It's hard to let go of the life you had with a loved one.'

His words touched my heart; I knew exactly how that felt.

Maria's gaze softened. 'I know, *caro*. But if you're lucky enough to find love again, like us, you have to make the most of every day. No regrets.'

'Hear, hear.' Stanley reached for the crisps but Maria swiped the dish out of his grasp.

'Not for you. Dicky heart,' she whispered loudly to me.

Stanley took her hand and placed it on his chest. 'Feel how strongly it beats for you, my dear. Just say the word and I'll waltz you down the aisle quicker than you can say *limoncello gelato.*'

Then he drew her close and began to dance her around in a circle, crooning into her ear about a moon hitting your eye while she whooped with shock and delight.

I couldn't help but laugh along with them. Married or not, that's what was important in life at the end of the day: someone to laugh with, someone to love. If you were brave enough to give them your heart, that is.

'Stanley Pigeon,' cried Maria, fluttering her eyelashes at him. 'You a dicky head, but you my dicky head.'

'*That's amore,*' Stanley sang loudly.

I left them to their smooching and did the rounds again, topping up glasses and attempting to bring the conversation around to people's flower-buying habits. The group of women who had brought their children with them had plenty to say on the matter.

'I used to get flowers on birthdays and Valentine's from my other half,' said one. 'Before he buggered off with that tart from his office.'

'You should buy yourself flowers then, Tina,' said her friend, the most glamorous member of the group. 'Treat yourself.'

Tina looked around timidly. 'I'd never be brave enough to walk in and buy something from here. Easier to just pick out a bunch at the supermarket where no one's watching you.'

Another woman nodded. 'Same here. You walk in and there's buckets of this and buckets of that. No offence.' She looked at me. 'And I don't know whether I should mix and match or stick with one flower. And you never know how much it's going to end up costing.'

The glamorous one nodded. 'Then when you get them home you can never find the right vase. I'm Paige, by the way.' She shook my hand and then introduced the others:

Tina, Vicky and Kirsty. 'I've literally got hundreds of vases, but never one that suits the flowers I've got.'

'I got a flower subscription for Christmas last year,' said Kirsty. 'A delivery every month for three months and it came with a picture, so even though I can't arrange flowers for toffee, I could just copy. Like paint by numbers only with flowers.'

I made a mental note; no reason why we couldn't offer something like that.

'That would suit me.' Vicky laughed. 'I need a set of instructions when I buy flowers.'

Instructions: another good idea.

'This is all so useful, ladies, thank you.' I smiled and topped up their glasses, telling them as I did so about the pre-made bouquets I'd recently introduced. We hadn't had a chance to make any up today, but it was good to know I was on the right lines.

'Really?' Kirsty gave me a cynical look. 'Us giving you one hundred and one reasons why we don't buy flowers?'

'Definitely! Now I know what the barriers are, I can do something about it. But in the meantime, follow me.' I quickly plucked some flowers that would suit any colour scheme, found a basic urn-shaped vase which most people were likely to own and led them to the table. 'I'm going to show you how to do something very simple.'

Working at the opposite end of the table to Nina, I showed the friends how to create a stylish arrangement with one large green chrysanthemum, some white lisianthus, three delicate ivory roses and fronds of frilly fern.

'There,' I said, pivoting the vase so they could see it from every angle. 'It's as simple as that.'

'That *did* look simple,' agreed Paige. 'But I doubt I could recreate it at home.'

'Then try it here.' I took the flowers from the vase, laid them on the table and separated them out so she couldn't just put them straight back in as they were. 'Have a play. All of you. There is no wrong way to do it. And if you did want to buy a similar bunch to this, I'll do you a special deal.'

My challenge was met with great enthusiasm and I stepped back to let them each take a turn.

'Nicely done,' said an amused voice. 'If that tactic doesn't sell four decent bunches of flowers, nothing will.'

I turned and smiled at the tall dark haired woman dressed in black beside me who must have just arrived.

'Apparently people are intimidated and don't know what to ask for when they come in,' I said, offering her a drink. 'I'm hoping that a bit of DIY messing about will break down some of those barriers.'

She gave a wry smile. 'Try being an undertaker. My customers don't even want to be there, let alone part with any cash. Mind you, I think I'll draw the line at DIY embalming though. Could get a bit out of hand. I'm Wendy from A.J. Mallet Funeral Directors.'

Funeral flowers weren't something that Nina had actively promoted and to be honest, I had my reservations. Even though I felt as if I was coping better with the loss of Freddie, I wasn't sure I was ready to face the new raw grief of anyone else yet. Having said that, we couldn't afford to turn business away.

'Good of you to come,' I said, shaking her hand. 'How's business for you at the moment? Brisk I hope?'

Wendy arched an eyebrow. 'We're somewhat reticent when it comes to trumpeting our sales as it inevitably goes hand in hand with someone's demise.'

I winced. 'Of course, I should have thought.'

'But our reputation precedes us and we get a lot of repeat business,' Wendy admitted proudly.

I was confused. 'Surely it's a once in a lifetime event?'

'It's a bit like having a family solicitor,' she explained. 'Once you get one person through the door, their relatives tend to follow.'

'We also have regulars,' I said wryly. 'But Nina is so generous that many of them leave without parting with any cash.'

Wendy chuckled. 'We don't have that problem. In fact, a lot of people want to pay silly amounts for a funeral. The more bells and whistles the better, to show their respect. I have to rein them back in half the time, remind them of their Dear Departed's wishes.'

'Providing they've left wishes,' I said, remembering the stress of organising Freddie's funeral. How many people his age had even considered what sort of funeral they wanted, let alone shared their wishes with others? I certainly hadn't.

Wendy nodded solemnly. 'The funeral is the last thing they can do for their loved one and there's a lot of pressure on them to get it right. That's where our experience comes in. We help them do the best they can. It needs to strike the balance between what the deceased would have wanted and what the bereaved need; it has to be both a sad goodbye and a joyful celebration.'

'That's a lovely way of putting it.' I swallowed the lump which threatened to constrict my throat. I hadn't been able to celebrate Freddie's life at the time: for me his funeral had been nothing less than gut-wrenching sadness. 'We could help people hit the right note with flowers, if you'll consider us?'

'I might.' She tilted her head. 'Show me what you've got.'

I led her towards the counter and flicked through our portfolio.

She stopped me when I reached the photos of Rosie's wedding.

'These are good,' she said, taking a closer look. 'We're getting more calls for natural looking flowers these days. We did one the other day in the woods. The trip hazards we had to overcome just to set the cardboard coffin down in one piece, you wouldn't believe. So this sort of more informal stuff. Yeah, I can see it working.'

I was flattered that she'd chosen the only design of mine in our portfolio. The florist they used at the moment was very good, Wendy explained, but didn't believe in unstructured floral tributes for sombre occasions.

'They've done all sorts for us over the years,' said Wendy. 'Flags, dogs' faces, football club emblems. Last month one family requested a motorbike. A floral tribute in the shape of the thing that killed their dad. Imagine that?'

Heat rose to my face. One thing was for sure: a floral tribute in the shape of a motorbike was something I could never do. I hated bikes with a passion which invaded every nerve in my body.

'No.' My voice came out as a croak. 'I can't.'

I pressed a hand to my forehead, suddenly aware that I was getting over-heated. And dizzy. I needed air. Why was there no air in here? All these people, standing around with drinks in their hand. The smell of the lilies and . . .

'You OK?' Wendy looked alarmed. 'You've gone an odd colour.'

'No.' A wave of nausea made me sway on the spot. 'Actually, please excuse me.'

I pushed past her, grabbed hold of Scamp and fled outside before I fainted.

Imagine that? Wendy had said.

An image flashed up of Freddie's bike, being rescued from a ditch. Twisted wheels, mangled metal . . . it hadn't even looked like a bike. *No*, I thought, I couldn't understand anyone wanting to be reminded of that.

I'd blocked the details of Freddie's accident immediately. I'd packed the horrific details away in a part of my memory which I never wanted to revisit. I didn't want to go over and over his accident in my head, wondering why someone as experienced and careful would take such a notorious route in the dark, in wet weather. Because it tore me apart. It didn't make sense. Nothing about the accident would ever make sense. In my mind, motorbikes were synonymous with danger and death. And I wanted to remember Freddie full of life. But Wendy's words had dredged the details up and I couldn't unsee the images.

We ran across the road and headed to the green, Scamp tugging at his lead, assuming that this was a game, eager as ever to plunge his nose into every delicious smell.

'Be good and no jumping in the stream.' I unclipped him and let him run off to play with other dogs. And then I sank down on a bench and squeezed my eyes shut.

'Oh Freddie,' I whispered under my breath. 'I miss you, you stupid great idiot.'

Grief washed over me and I let the tears fall.

I hadn't cried for ages. I still thought about Freddie every day of course. I missed him being part of my life. I could tell myself a million times that Freddie would be proud of me, that Freddie would want me to be happy, etcetera, but sometimes that wasn't enough. Every day that passed, I was leaving him behind.

'Take this, dear,' came a soft voice from beside me.

I blinked my tears away and saw Delphine, Maria's friend. She was holding out a handkerchief to me.

'Thank you.'

Delphine sat down on the bench and patted my back softly, her silver bracelets tinkling at her wrist. She said nothing until my tears stopped and I got my breathing back under control.

'I was just on my way to your party,' she said, eventually. 'But you don't look as if you're enjoying yourself very much. Is there anything I can do?'

I managed a watery smile. 'You could catch my dog.'

Scamp was splashing up and down the stream and woofing to his heart's content. Delphine looked down at her white loafers. She was very stylish, I thought through a fog of tears. 'I'd rather not, but I'll cheer from the bank if you climb in after him,' she offered.

'I'd better.' I sighed and got to my feet. 'He's obsessed with the ducks. He'd freak out if he ever actually got close enough to catch one, I think that's why he barks so much: to make sure they can get away.'

'All bark and no bite,' said Delphine wistfully. 'My Violet was just like that. She died last autumn. I used to tease her for being grumpy, now I'd give anything to hear her bark her orders just one more time.'

Violet. Her favourite flower, I remembered.

'Same with my big brother. He died in an accident last year. He used to leave his great big trainers in our hall for me to trip over. Now the hall is clear and I miss having to avoid them.'

Delphine patted my arm. 'I know.'

'I should be getting back; Nina will be wondering where I am.' I cupped my hands around my mouth. 'SCAMP!'

Thankfully the dog bounded back towards us without argument.

'I imagine they can manage for a few minutes more without you.' Delphine stepped out of the way as Scamp shook his coat to get rid of the water.

'You look like you're coping with grief a lot better than I am.' I put Scamp back on the lead and the three of us took a gentle stroll across the green in the general direction of the shop, Scamp slowing us down to sniff at every leaf in our path.

'I have my moments,' she said. 'The early days were completely impossible to navigate; even buoyed up with the love of my friends, I felt all at sea. We were going to grow old together, Violet and I. Without her, life seemed pointless for a while.'

'It was different for me and Freddie, we shared a childhood, a broken home, the same awful taste in jokes. And he was always there for me, cheering me on.'

'He'll still be there, doing the same.'

We drew level with the pet shop on the other side of the road. Churchill was sitting in the doorway and both dogs wagged their tails at each other which brought a smile to my face.

I turned to Delphine. 'I know, and most of the time I can accept that. But it's the unpredictability of grief I find so hard. One minute you're having fun and then up pops a sudden memory, or you hear a song on the radio and it all comes back as sharp as ever. It's like being shot with an arrow.'

'The arrow eventually loses its sharpness,' she said. 'Or at least that's what I'm told. And until then I'm keeping busy.'

'So am I.' I held out my arm for her to take. 'On that note, would you care to accompany me to a party?'

Delphine beamed. 'I'd be delighted.'

Back inside the shop, Scamp retreated to his bed to dry off while I poured Delphine a drink and left her chatting to Maria and Stanley. I hoped to apologise to Wendy for abandoning her but she was nowhere to be seen. I was disappointed; the most interested of all our corporate guests today and I'd blown it by doing a disappearing act. I hadn't even given her any prices, let alone arrange a follow-up meeting.

'Cooee! Fearne, can we buy these?' called a voice, breaking into my thoughts.

Standing next to the till were the four ladies whom I'd left practising their own arrangements. They'd each got a bunch of the flowers which I'd used in my demonstration.

'You said you might do us a deal,' said Paige.

I did a rough calculation; there was about fifteen pounds' worth of flowers there. 'Shall we call it ten pounds?'

'This has been really good fun,' said Tina, handing over a note. 'I've learned something and had a laugh with my friends.'

'Yeah, count us in if you do this again,' said Kirsty.

'Oh yes, do one at Christmas!' said Vicky.

'I might do that. Thank you ladies, goodbye!'

I waved them off, thinking what a good idea that was. A Christmas wreath workshop, perhaps. We couldn't do it for free, but perhaps if people got mulled wine and a mince pie and went home with a fresh homemade wreath, they wouldn't mind paying. I'd suggest it to Nina. My happy list might still only have one thing on it, but what did that matter if I was making a good job of it, I thought.

Chapter Eighteen

By five o'clock everyone had gone. Nina had dashed out to deliver a last-minute order and I was tidying up when Lucas arrived.

'So sorry, darling, I couldn't get away! Is all the champers gone?' He looked around hopefully. 'The shop looks gorgeous and I've seen all the comings and goings and followed it on Twitter.'

'It was on Twitter?' I said, surprised, fetching a half-full bottle from the fridge. I shared it between us.

'Oh yes, Rosie is a social media whizz. She took pictures and tweeted them. Bottoms up,' he said, raising his glass.

'The afternoon was a success,' I said, chinking my glass against his. 'Nina said she enjoyed it and I think she's even coming round to accepting that offering a service to businesses could work.'

'Good for you!' Lucas settled onto a stool at the counter. 'So glad you came along when you did. You saved her bacon and so nice that you were able to have this celebration together. You're a safe pair of hands, anyone can see that.'

I shook my head, embarrassed. 'I haven't done anything except prop up the cash flow temporarily, I'm not exactly the Lord Sugar of the floral world.'

'It's a perfect arrangement though: you get to pursue your dream which means she gets to pursue hers. And about time too.'

I nodded. 'I agree. Together we can get this business running more profitably. We both love flowers and we both want to be happy.'

'Exactly! Career ambitions are all well and good but they don't keep you warm at night, do they?' he said with a wink.

'Well, no,' I laughed uncertainly, not sure what he meant.

'Take me,' he said, waving his glass in the air. 'Prime example. Shop was doing well but I was lonely.'

Ah, now I understood what he meant. I smiled softly, recalling the moment when Nina had dropped her head in her hands and said that she was lonely working by herself..

'Then I met my partner, Tyrone. Landscape gardener, dirty hands, huge feet and the very last person I expected to fall for. But then happiness found its way into my life by stealth until one day I realised that I'd found my soulmate.' He sighed dreamily. 'Everyone deserves that, don't they, or at least the chance to go looking.'

'Absolutely,' I agreed. But was he saying I was Nina's Tyrone? Surely not?

'And now, even though the bed practically oscillates with his adenoidal breathing, I wouldn't be without him for all the sheep in New Zealand.' He nudged me and laughed. 'Get it? Sheep? New Zealand?'

'No!' I said with a giggle. 'I don't get it, I'm completely lost.'

'You do!' Lucas gave a bark of laughter and pushed me playfully. '*The Kiwi Wants a Wife.*'

'Lucas, I adore you but I have literally no idea what you're on about,' I protested.

There was a movement behind me and I turned to see Nina, her face as white as snow.

'What's happened?' I said, alarmed.

'Fearne.' She swallowed. 'I'm so sorry. I should have told you sooner.'

'You mean you haven't already?' Lucas squeaked. 'Lordy, lordy, lordy, I'm so sorry.'

He pressed both hands to his mouth as if he was scared of anything else escaping.

Nina shook her head. 'It's OK, Lucas. This is my fault, not yours.'

I looked at them both, bewildered. 'Told me what? Honestly, I feel like I'm speaking a different language.'

Lucas gave my arm a comforting squeeze and got to his feet. 'I'll be in the gift shop if anyone needs me.'

He fled from the shop, leaving me and Nina facing each other. The atmosphere couldn't have been more prickly with tension if we'd both been holding cacti.

'What's going on?' I asked, worriedly. 'What does Lucas mean?'

She crept closer and sat on the stool Lucas had just vacated. 'Remember I said I'd wanted a farmer, not a flower shop?'

'When you left London?' I nodded. 'Yes, sure.'

'Well, I may have got a second chance.' Her voice trembled nervously. 'How would you feel if I left you in charge and went to New Zealand?'

Suddenly all the little hints she'd dropped into our conversation started to add up. The references she'd made to me not needing her, that I could run this place single-handedly. And Rosie, adamant that Nina had been serious about leaving the country. And now Lucas: *The Kiwi Wants a Wife*. Whatever that meant.

My jaw dropped. 'Tell me everything.'

Chapter Nineteen

'*The Kiwi Wants a Wife!*' Ethel had repeated it several times, hooting with mirth. 'She's got gumption; I'll give her that. Flying to New Zealand to be on a TV dating show! Whatever will they think of next?'

Nina did have gumption and guts. Whatever else I might feel about the bombshell she'd dropped on me earlier, I couldn't help but admire her bravery.

'She has dreamed of marrying a farmer her whole life,' I explained. 'She's dying to do some travelling and when the opportunity came to meet a panel of farmers on the other side of the world, all looking for love, she thought it was too good to be true. And the fact that she's basically getting a free holiday thrown into the bargain made it irresistible.'

My head had been reeling after the events and revelations of the day. So instead of going back to Pineapple Road straight away, I'd wrapped up a bunch of roses for Ethel and called into her care home. It was a warm sunny evening and we were taking a gentle stroll in the grounds, heading vaguely in the direction of the lake. As before, Ethel had shunned the wheelchair we'd been offered and was using her walking frame. It was slow going but I didn't mind; I needed Ethel's company far more than I needed the exercise.

Scamp, normally one to take off at speed at the first sight of water, was plodding along between us, gazing up adoringly at Ethel every few seconds. It seemed that, like me, he was prepared to compromise his normal pace just to be near her.

'Sounds like a peculiar sort of television programme to me,' she said. 'Shipping in women from another continent. Still, it's all in the name of love, I suppose.'

'Or TV ratings,' I said sceptically. 'Apparently the contestants have to undergo a variety of rural challenges to see who's cut out for an isolated life with one man and ten thousand sheep.'

Once Lucas had slipped away, Nina had closed the shop and the two of us had sat in the back to talk. She was fluttery and nervous, bursting with excitement about her news, but scared to death about my reaction to it and she so wanted me to be OK with it.

It had been Lucas who'd spotted it on Twitter and had pointed it out to her half-jokingly. A TV researcher had posted a request for women who wanted a date with a difference. After a couple of glasses of wine, they'd tweeted the researcher back and got some more information. Lucas had egged her on to apply immediately.

'To put this into context, Fearne,' Nina had said, solemnly. 'My love life was and still is barely alive at all, I couldn't see how I could ever make the shop pay, I was overworked, underpaid and lonely and I just wanted to run away from everything.'

When the invoice came from the landlord for the next quarter's rent it was the final straw. She filled in the online application form and sent it off to be a contestant on *The Kiwi Wants a Wife*. It was to be filmed this summer, which would be winter in New Zealand. She figured that even if she didn't get matched with a farmer, it would be a way to get some time to herself and figure out what to do next with her life. The deadline came and went and she heard nothing, so assumed she'd been unsuccessful. It felt like her escape plan had failed and she felt worse than ever.

'Then Kelly got a new job and left me and I had to do the flowers for Rosie's wedding on my own. I was on the verge of a breakdown.' She paused and smiled. 'I told myself if I could just get through the wedding, I'd come in the following Monday and prepare the shop for sale. And then who should turn up but Fearne, my fairy godmother, with her big kind heart and positive attitude that made me believe in myself again.'

'Oh.' I'd stared at her stunned that that was the impression I'd made. 'That's the nicest thing anyone's ever said to me.'

She squeezed my arm. 'I couldn't believe my luck; I'd got another chance to get the business back on track and met someone who not only listened and cared, but rolled up her sleeves and got stuck in.'

Her words had made my chest swell with pride. She'd gone on to tell me that out of the blue she'd received a phone call from the production company last week and had been asked to attend an audition in London yesterday. It had gone well and before she'd even made it back to Derbyshire on the train, she got a call to say she'd been successful. She had forty-eight hours to confirm her place in the show and if she accepted, she'd be leaving Barnaby for New Zealand in two weeks.

'I'd never have accepted a loan from you if I'd known this was going to happen, and I'll pay back every penny of it, I promise.'

I'd dismissed her concerns. 'I'm not worried about that. I'm more worried about running a florist's on my own when I've barely been in the business for a month.'

Nina hadn't pleaded exactly, she'd merely asked me to consider it, but her body language would have put a starving puppy to shame.

There was a bench just ahead and Ethel guided us to it now, sinking down with an *ooph*.

'What happened to meeting a nice young man at the local dancehall?' she asked me, baffled.

'Different times,' I said wistfully, thinking how nice it would be to do just that. 'Nowadays, farmers in small communities struggle to meet partners, apparently.'

'They never seem to have that problem in *The Archers*,' said Ethel.

'Because they ship new characters in to spice things up,' I laughed. 'But I guess if you grow up in a small farming community, you all know each other from childhood so there's none of the spark you get when you first meet someone. And if there's no spark, there'll never be a flame.'

My mind slipped back to the first time I'd seen Sam. There'd been a tiny spark then, on my side at least, which had lit me up from the inside right until he'd snuffed it out with the mention of a wife.

'Tommyrot,' said Ethel. 'There wasn't a spark between George and me to begin with. He was the quiet boy in my class at school, quietly lovely, I used to think. For a long time, I didn't pay him any attention.'

Quietly lovely. Like Sam, I thought with a pang. I had to stop thinking about this man who was a husband and a father. And besides, my heart was still too fragile at the moment to start a new relationship. The old adage of better to have loved and lost than never to have loved at all didn't work for me. The fear of losing someone else from my life was far greater than my need to fall in love.

'Don't tell me you went for the bad boys?' I pretended to be shocked.

Ethel's eyes twinkled. 'Not bad exactly, just a few years older and more worldly-wise.'

Laura and I had once vowed that we'd never go out with any boys from our year at school because whether they admitted it or not, they'd always remember us with spots, or braces or those dodgy few weeks when we didn't wash our hair because someone told us it would make it really shiny but what actually happened was that we stank and no one would sit by us in assembly.

'When did you change how you felt about George?' I asked.

Her hand felt automatically for Scamp's head. He leaned into her and a look of contentment spread across both of their faces.

'He always seemed to be there just when I needed him, with a clean hanky, or an umbrella in a sudden shower, or spare money for chips when I was starving.' She smiled, no doubt remembering George as a young man, herself as a girl on the cusp of womanhood. 'Patient, kind and completely reliable. Then one day something just clicked into place and I saw him for the wonderful man he was. I knew without a second doubt he was my future. And even better, my intuition told me that he felt the same way.'

I loved the way Ethel's face softened until her wrinkles almost disappeared when she spoke about her late husband. I reached for her hand.

'Your story is more romantic than a Nicholas Spark book.'

She shot me a mischievous look. 'That's not one of those rude ones, is it?'

'No,' I laughed. 'It's a bit like *Gone with the Wind* but with more kissing in the rain.'

'I grew up in Manchester, there was a lot of rain.'

'What about kissing?'

'A lady never tells,' she said primly. 'Now that's enough prattling from me. What happens if Nina falls in love with one of these farmers, what then?'

'I hope she does and that the feeling is mutual. But where does that leave the flower shop? And me?'

Ethel twirled her worn gold wedding ring around her finger. 'Fearne's Flowers has a nice ring to it.'

'It does, doesn't it?' I said eagerly. 'The problem with using a name is that it's limiting if you want to sell it. Something more general works better; like Say It With Flowers. Not that I've given it much thought, obviously.'

'Obviously,' Ethel chuckled.

'But taking over the running of Nina's shop which lurches from overdraft to overdraft each month isn't what I signed up for,' I mused. 'I'm still a beginner.'

She squinted as if wracking her brains. 'Remind me about that work trip to Tokyo you went on last year.'

'I did a project about managing growth in a changing market for the Japanese forestry bods.'

She gave me a reproving look. 'Then I hardly think you'll have a problem getting one small floristry business in Derbyshire back on track. On the other hand, if she's putting a lot of pressure on you to take over then that's unfair.'

'She's quietly hopeful I'll say yes. I've said I'll think about it overnight.'

'And if you say no?'

'Plan B is to shut the shop for a month. But I can't let that happen. We're just beginning to make headway. All the work, all the leads I've been working on would come to nothing and the shop would be back to square one.'

'You've made quite a new life for yourself there in a short time, haven't you,' said Ethel proudly.

'I do like it,' I admitted. 'But the whole point of me taking this sabbatical from my job in market research was to be free to do things that make me happy, to be more adventurous and make Freddie proud.'

'And aren't you doing all those things?' she questioned. 'Top of your happy list: flowers? Before I had my fall I remember watching you pull up in your car after work and just sit there, as if you didn't even have the energy to get out and walk into the house. Now look at you; you've come a long way since then, young lady.'

'I worry that I've walked straight into a new job and within days I'm back to analysing the local market, competition, customer trends, gaps in the market. This feels like a cop-out. You don't think I've settled for the first thing that came along?'

Ethel rolled her eyes. 'Do you ever think you might be overthinking things?'

'All the time,' I admitted, laughing.

'Nina will be gone for a few weeks. Blink and it'll be over. And this is still an adventure.'

'*Adventure* is taking a step into the unknown,' I argued. 'It's waking up every morning not knowing where your journey will take you, it's doing things that scare you. Taking risks. It's not running a flower shop.'

'For heaven's sake. Adventures come in all shapes and sizes,' said Ethel tetchily. 'You've given up a steady career, put your own money into a failing business and now in all likelihood you're taking responsibility for it while the owner swans off to the other side of the world. If that's not taking risks, I don't know what is.'

'All right,' I nudged her, 'keep your hair on.'

'Think about it,' she urged. 'With Nina not there, you'll have plenty of freedom to put your own stamp on the shop. Do things your way.'

I felt something flutter in my stomach. I was going to do this and if I made the odd mistake, who cared?

'I guess it would be nice to make a few changes without worrying that I was treading on her toes,' I admitted. 'I'd get our flowers delivered for a start, there's no way I fancy trawling through markets for stock. Then I want to follow up all the leads Sam gave us.'

'Who's Sam, another florist?'

'Sam is . . . a friend, he's really nice.' I felt myself blushing. 'Well, he's the landlord's son-in-law, so I suppose it's in his interests to help us out.'

He hadn't come to our event this afternoon even though I'd made sure he'd known when it was. In fact, he hadn't been back to the shop at all since he'd bought that bouquet for his wife and I was dying to know what her reaction had been.

'I'm *sure* it is,' said Ethel, raising an eyebrow. 'A young attractive woman like you.'

'Stop it,' I warned, feeling even more flustered. 'I helped him get back with his wife, our friendship is completely above board. Anyway, Nina's six weeks off: I'm going to do it; you've twisted my arm.'

Ethel let out a peal of laughter. 'You were going to do it anyway. But I'm honoured to have been your sounding board.'

I put my arms around her. 'You're much more than that.'

We sat for a moment, each with our own thoughts, looking out over the lake. Scamp's eyes scanned around for any wildlife. The surface rippled and shimmered in the evening sun.

She patted my arm. 'You were like an injured bird after Freddie died. But now look at you; ready to spread your wings and fly high. You're going to be fine, Fearne.' She paused and took a deep breath. 'Which is why I know you'll cope when I leave you.'

'What do you mean? You're scaring me.' I pulled back, looking at her in alarm.

'Sorry, dear, I didn't mean to.' She patted my knee. 'I'm moving north, to live with my daughter, Carole.'

I blew out a breath of relief. 'Thank god. For a moment I thought . . .'

Ethel harrumphed. 'Nothing wrong with me. Got the heart and lungs of an eighty-year-old apparently, which means I could be driving my poor family barmy for years yet.'

'But why go? I thought you were happy here?'

She shook her head. 'It's not about me now. It's about what I can do to smooth life's wrinkles for other people. Staying here will use up every penny of mine and George's money and that was supposed to be our legacy to the family. And now I'm feeling stronger, I don't need to be nursed. I miss home comforts and I miss setting my own meal times. It's hard on Carole to come and visit me here and she's got plenty of room now that her children have flown the nest. So I'm off.'

I swallowed a lump in my throat. 'When do you go?'

'Not for a while yet. Carole wants to redecorate a bedroom for me.' She gave me a bright smile. 'I shall be happy there. With my family.'

I was filled with admiration for her. She'd decided to be happy, just as she'd done when she moved into The Beeches. So I'd do the same, I wouldn't let my disappointment show. But I was losing her as well as Nina and my heart felt leaden.

'Scamp and I will miss you.'

'And I you.' She turned away, pretending to look to her right and wiped a stray tear from her cheek.

I blinked my own tears back. 'Will you come and visit the shop before you leave?'

She brightened. 'I'd like that.'

'We'll arrange it then,' I said, squeezing her soft hand. 'I think it's a good decision, moving to Carole's.'

'I'm not giving up, you know,' she said, with a flash of her old feistiness.

'Of course you're not,' I agreed. 'You're just embarking on the next part of life's adventure. Like me.'

I helped her up from the bench and together we went back inside in companionable silence. I was thinking about the challenges ahead and I had a feeling she was doing the same.

Chapter Twenty

The next two weeks flew by and soon it was Nina's last day. The shop had been like Piccadilly Circus since we opened. Nina had become quite the celebrity in Barnaby after word had got around of her trip and people had been dropping by or calling up to wish her luck finding a Kiwi farmer, giving her their top travel tips for places to visit in New Zealand and asking for signed photos of Molly Wilson, the famous TV presenter who'd be hosting the series.

'I feel quite overcome,' Nina said, after waving off Maria and Stanley. She was still clutching a bottle of Maria's homemade limoncello they'd brought her as a farewell gift. 'I didn't think people cared so much for their local florist. It almost feels a shame to leave.'

'Yeah, right.' I looked up from preparing a birthday bouquet for someone's auntie.

Nina acknowledged my sarcasm with a grin. 'I said almost. There's no going back now. For a start I'd have to give this limoncello back.'

She'd been like a grasshopper on speed for the last two weeks. Jumping around from one thing to the next. But on the plus side, she'd torn through the shop like a whirlwind, getting rid of old clutter which had probably been hanging around for years. The accounts were up to date and she'd left me list upon list of important contacts, dos and don'ts for every possible scenario from what to do if the shop got flooded to how to deal with the outside tap if it froze. At which point I'd drawn a line and reminded her that she was only going for a month.

Despite her constant level of panic, she looked radiant and glowing. She'd been on a crash diet, which she hadn't needed, she'd performed two hundred sit-ups a day in the shop which had given the postman quite a shock when he'd dropped off her travel money and found her flat out on the floor and gasping for breath. She'd plucked, preened and pruned every hair on her body (I took her word for that), had had a manicure and pedicure and had treated herself to a spray tan and a whole new wardrobe.

I was going to miss her a lot I realised now as she dashed outside onto the pavement to fling her arms around Rosie, who was attempting to wipe tables in front of the café. She was a joy to work with and although we were very different in many ways, her talent with flowers was something I could only aspire to.

A phone call came in and Nina pulled her mobile out of her pocket, but I got there first on Freddie's iPad. She was leaving her mobile with me because it had been the shop's number for so long and had bought herself a new one, but I'd yet to prise it off her.

'Nina's Flowers?' I answered brightly, expecting another well-wisher for Nina. 'Fearne speaking.'

'It's Marcia from the Claybourne Hotel here.'

I almost gasped; a corporate client? I'd almost given up hope. We'd had lots of thank-you messages following our new business party, but next to no *actual* business. Even Wendy from the funeral parlour hadn't returned my calls; surely I couldn't have really annoyed her by running away?

'Oh, hello! We met at the open day. It's good to hear from you,' I said.

Nina walked back in at that moment and I pointed at the phone and stuck my thumb up.

'We've got an event coming up at the hotel and I thought you might be interested in doing the flowers for it. It's for a client called Edelweiss.'

'An event at the hotel? Definitely!' I said loudly for Nina's benefit, before she had a chance to go any further. 'Thank you for thinking of us.'

Marcia laughed down the phone. 'I had a feeling you might say that, let me give you the details . . .'

Nina gave me a squeeze and a smile and wandered off to top up the flower buckets with water, while I resisted jumping up and down on the spot.

The Claybourne had been asked to take on a booking as a favour for a large hotel in Chesterfield who'd had to cancel after finding themselves double-booked. The event was to be held at the beginning of June and the client was a Swiss pharmaceutical company. Apparently the brand was all about purity and the beauty products contained ethical ingredients and floral extracts.

'Sounds wonderful!' I made a note to google them later.

'I know! I hope they bring lots of samples,' said Marcia, sounding excited. 'The hotel manager wanted our usual florist to provide the flowers but I remembered how unfussy and natural your flowers were and I thought you might fit the bill better.'

'I'm flattered!' I said, just about keeping the squeak out of my voice. 'And I'll make sure we don't let you down.'

My feet were already doing a celebratory dance. This would be a brilliant addition to our portfolio, not to mention our bank balance.

I made some notes while Marcia gave me all the details. Edelweiss was new to the UK and looking for an exclusive number of franchisees to introduce their beauty products to the British public. They wanted their potential partners to be wowed with flowers when they stepped into the hotel to recreate the brand's ethos. We were to invoice Edelweiss directly for our work, but the hotel manager had agreed to pay us an initial deposit on their behalf to secure the booking.

'When you say "wowed with flowers" does Edelweiss have a budget in mind?' I asked.

Marcia named a sum which made me drop my pen. I thanked her profusely, arranged to visit the hotel for a look round and ended the call.

'How much?' Nina's eyes were out on stalks when I showed her the budget. 'Bloody hell, well done!'

'Thanks, but I can't take all the credit,' I beamed with pride. 'I seem to remember it was you she talked to most at the party.'

'You'll be the one fulfilling it though,' she pointed out. 'And that's the biggest order the shop has ever had, bigger than any wedding. It'll take heaps of flowers to fill that hotel; it'll be a lot of work.'

'Gosh, I suppose it will.' I bit my lip, feeling a flutter of nerves. Then I put my shoulders back and took a deep breath. 'But I wanted corporate clients so I can't back out at the first sign of difficulty. I'm going to do the best job I can and bring a big fat fee home for the shop. I might even enjoy it.'

She shook her head fondly. 'A head for business and a heart of gold. They broke the mould when they made you.'

'You're not so bad yourself,' I said, giving her a hug.

The phone rang again, interrupting our mutual appreciation society and this time Nina answered it.

'Nina's Flowers?' She listened to the voice on the other end. 'Hold the line please.'

She covered the phone with her hand. 'Fearne, can you squeeze in another delivery today?'

'Sure.'

'Yes, we can do that,' she replied to the customer. 'What was it you had in mind? Two dozen red roses? Yes of course we have them in stock. They're two pounds fifty per stem.'

She held the phone away from her ear. I could hear a man's outraged voice from across the shop. The customer had obviously just done the maths and realised what a tidy sum he was about to spend.

'These are the best roses you'll find in Derbyshire,' said Nina, haughtily. 'They smell divine and make a very romantic statement to whoever is lucky enough to receive them. Of course, if you'd rather nip into the supermarket . . .? No? Excellent. A good choice.'

She winked and I nodded my approval; nicely played.

Our roses were perfect: fragrant, beautiful and would last for ages. But as a romantic gesture, red roses were a little clichéd. For the same money I'd choose a mix of flowers and foliage which spoke of holding hands, and sun-kissed skin and smiling eyes and romantic walks . . .

I dragged myself out of my reverie to select the twenty-four red roses as Nina asked for the customer's credit card details.

'That's gone through for you. Any message with them?'

She held her pen poised over the paper, ready for the person on the other end to dictate.

'To my darling Pandora . . .'

My ears pricked up. How many Pandoras could there be in the area? It had to be Sam's wife. In which case, the sender had to be Sam. My first thought was one of annoyance; why hadn't he come in personally to choose something? Had I taught him nothing? He hadn't been in the shop since he bought her the last bunch, but if he was buying her more, that answered my question: their reunion date had obviously gone well.

Nina was still dictating the message. 'Thank you for a great night last night, you were incredible. Lots of love, your sexy tiger. PS can't wait to play with my kitty cat again next week, kiss, kiss.'

Ew. Make that very well indeed.

We caught each other's eye; I grimaced and Nina pretended to put her fingers down her throat.

I wished I hadn't heard that. I was glad they were back together, of course I was, but there was something nauseating about other people's nicknames for each other.

'That must be Sam. Can I speak to him before you hang up?' I whispered, holding out my hand for the phone. I wanted to tell him about the Claybourne order.

She shook her head and leaned away from me. 'And can I take the name on the front of your card, please?'

I looked over her shoulder as she wrote in capitals: GARETH WEAVER.

Oh, I thought, surprised; Pandora was clearly a more common name than I realised.

'Thank you, Mr Weaver, we'll get those delivered for you this afternoon. Goodbye.' Nina ended the call and selected a gift card to go with the roses. 'Well, well, well, nothing like a peek into someone else's sex life to make you feel nauseous. Why did you think it was Sam?'

'My mistake,' I said, dismissively. 'His wife has the same name as Mr Weaver's kitty cat, that's all.'

'Unless . . .' Nina paused for dramatic impact, widening her eyes, '. . . Sam's wife was playing big cat, little cat with another man last night.'

'If you don't mind, I'd rather pretend we're simply delivering flowers from sexy tiger to kitty cat and it's got absolutely nothing to do with Sam.' I wrapped the flowers in cellophane while Nina wrote the card out. For his sake, I hoped that Sam was happily back with his family, just as he hoped he'd be.

'Either way it's none of our business. What happens in the florist, stays in the florist,' said Nina, solemnly. 'We are the keeper of many secrets.'

'Ooh, secrets? Sounds like I've arrived just in time, darlings.' Lucas sprang up between us, startling us both. 'Tell your uncle Lucas. I want all the juicy details.'

'How do you creep in so silently?' I said, pressing a hand to my chest. 'Not even Scamp woke up.'

Scamp rolled over and presented his undercarriage to our visitor but didn't deign to get up. Lucas, from his experience, rarely carried treats.

'I'm light on my feet,' said Lucas, primly inspecting his nails. 'I could have been a ballet dancer. I swear, Billy Elliot's *arrières* had nothing on mine at one time. Anyway don't change the subject, what secrets?'

'Oh, nothing exciting,' I said hurriedly, doing a terrible job of hiding my discomfort. I fetched some raffia to tie around the mysterious Pandora's roses.

Lucas cocked an eyebrow.

'Fearne's being modest; it's very exciting,' Nina piped up, expertly changing the subject. 'We've won a massive contract with a hotel.'

'Oh. Well done.' Lucas looked disappointed for a second before producing a parcel from inside his jacket. 'I came round to give you this. A going away gift from me.'

Nina tore the paper off to reveal a teal blue silk scarf printed with tiny white flowers. She gasped with delight, put it on and gave him a twirl. 'It's gorgeous, I love it! Thank you. I'm really going to miss you.'

She kissed him and he dabbed tears from his eyes.

'Now,' he said with a sniff. 'I want you to get on that plane and don't give the shop, or us a second thought.'

'I think Fearne might have something to say about that,' she replied, her own voice sounding a bit wobbly. 'But thanks.'

Lucas winked at me. 'Don't worry about Fearne, Barnaby is a friendly place, we'll all take her under our wing. Any problems, and we'll be here in two shakes of a lamb's booty.'

'Thanks, Lucas, I might hold you to that,' I said, thinking of the Edelweiss job. 'Are you any good at flower arranging?'

'Look at these dextrous fingers!' He waggled his hands. 'I'd be ace at it, I'm sure. And as for you, Nina, be careful with those farmers, they might want a wife, but there's no need to go that far if you don't want to. Next thing you know the wife will want a child and if I remember the words to the song correctly it ends with a bone that won't stand. Disaster.' He pulled a comical face and Nina and I laughed.

'I promise I won't come back pregnant, or married,' she said. 'I'm ready for an adventure and thanks to Fearne, I can have one and still have a business to return to when it's over.'

'You're welcome,' I said. 'But I expect plenty of updates.'

'Yes, I'm up for that!' he agreed. 'We need photos of the farmers. Only of the sexy ones. Not the munters.'

'Oi,' she said with a snort of laughter, 'those are my potential husbands you're talking about, have some respect.'

'Ooh, talking of sexy ones, isn't that your landlord?' Lucas nodded his head to the window and we all looked out. My heart gave a leap when I saw who it was. Lucas kissed Nina and said his last farewell, passing Sam on his way out.

'Hello, ladies,' he cried, bounding in.

'Sam!' I exclaimed, taken aback by his exuberance.

He had a laptop case in one hand and a small gift bag in the other. He looked good. I took a deep breath. Really good. Full of smiles and with a healthy glow which suggested time well spent in the sunshine. He wasn't wearing a jacket today and his shirt fitted snugly over his chest and arms. I bet he was strong. I bet he was the sort who could pick you up and carry you off . . .

'Whoops, better hide that,' muttered Nina. She picked up sexy tiger's card and slid it under the counter.

I was still holding the red roses. But they clearly weren't destined for his wife, I thought with relief. Sam was far too happy for a man whose marriage was over.

'Nice flowers,' he said, with a grin.

'Very nice. Bit predictable though,' I said, wrinkling my nose. 'The flowers you gave your Pandora were much nicer.'

He laughed. '*My* Pandora, how many others do you know?'

'Er . . .' I blinked at him. 'A couple.'

'She's still swooning over how romantic you were, making that big bouquet for your wife,' said Nina, coming to my rescue. She whipped the roses away and put them in water next to the other deliveries. 'But whoever gets these will be over the moon, I'm sure.'

'Two dozen red roses.' He set the champagne down on the counter and leaned on it with his arms. 'What's not to love.'

'So, I haven't seen you for ages, how are things between you and your wife?' I held my breath.

A broad smile lit up his face. 'Pandora and me, well, we're taking it slowly but it looks like we could be a family again soon.'

Nina and I exchanged relieved glances.

'I'm delighted for you,' I said, from the bottom of my heart. Just because I hadn't liked what I'd heard about her didn't mean I didn't want him to be happy.

'I'm sure it was the flowers from here that did it,' he marvelled. 'She took some convincing that I'd done them myself. But she loved them. Then I took her out, treated her like a princess, just as she likes it and afterwards . . . Well, let's just say there was a second date. I brought you this to say thank you.'

He handed me the gift bag and placed the lightest of kisses on my cheek.

'I'm very happy for you,' I said, trying to ignore the sensations rippling through me at his touch. 'And there was no need for this, it was my pleasure.'

I opened the bag and took out the contents. It was a set of three little jars of flavoured honey: lavender, wildflower and heather.

'Wow! Sam, these look delicious.' I took the lid off one of the jars and inhaled the aroma. The sweet smell took me straight back to breakfasts at Granny's. I remembered that no matter how much honey Freddie and I had spooned over our porridge, we never got told off. It became a bit of a challenge. Happy times.

'How cute!' Nina exclaimed, reading the labels over my shoulder.

Sam picked one up. 'Aren't they! I was at a fantastic Derbyshire food market last weekend, amazing cheese and bread and flavoured oils. Anyway I got chatting to the producer of this English honey,' he said animatedly, pointing to the jars. 'Look, this one is heather honey made by bees on the Yorkshire moors, and this one is wildflower honey. The flavour is so distinctive and you can really taste the difference between the flowers. I thought with you being a florist, you'd like them.'

'I do like them.' I smiled at him. 'Very much.'

Was it wrong of me to be glad that he'd been thinking about me at the weekend? I loved that he'd chosen me such a thoughtful gift, but most of all I loved seeing how his whole body came alive when he talked about something he cared about.

I was staring at Sam, my insides fluttering. Nina cleared her throat and shot me a warning glance.

'So, you went on a second date,' she prompted.

'Yep. And since then we've been seeing a lot of each other. Well,' he waggled his head from side to side, 'mostly I've seen the kids. But it's nice to be in my home with them. I've been living with my mum since we split up and it's not the same, having them over there.'

'Looks like you've spent time outside as well,' I said. 'You've got quite a tan.'

It suited him. His eyes looked an even more startling shade of blue, and his hair had lightened in the sun.

'I like cooking outside in weather like this. Typical bloke.' He laughed. 'We were outside until the sun went down last night. I did us a cracking barbecue: steak, halloumi, chicken wings and then we played cricket. The kids loved it.'

'And Pandora?' I asked innocently.

The phone rang, interrupting our conversation but for once I didn't make a move to answer it. I was still gazing at Sam.

'I'll get it, shall I?' said Nina drily.

'No. She wasn't in last night.' He ran his fingers against his chin. I heard the rasp of the hint of stubble. It was such a masculine sound that my pulse quickened, reminding me how long it had been since I last felt a man's arms around me. 'She's started a weekly evening course in yoga. She's going to train to be an instructor. And it's only fair. I play cricket once a week, tonight actually, this way we both get a night off.'

Yoga? My mouth opened and closed as I floundered for something to say other than *are you sure?*

Nina ended the call and shut my mouth with the tip of her finger. 'Excuse my colleague,' she said to Sam. 'That's a yoga pose. Called the fish. Good for Pandora, don't you agree?'

'Yes.' I smiled weakly. 'Good for her.'

'That call was from Wendy at A.J. Mallet funeral directors,' said Nina. 'She wants to see you next week.'

Sam's ears pricked up. 'Are you doing business with them? That's great.'

'Not yet,' Nina replied. 'But she's asked Fearne to go and see her, which is a good sign. And the Claybourne Hotel also wants us to get involved with an event. Fearne will tell you all about it, my taxi will be here soon and I've got some bits to finish off.'

She retreated into the back of the shop, leaving the two of us together. I arranged the pots of honey into a line and told him about the Edelweiss beauty launch.

'So this could be the beginnings of a regular corporate clientele,' I said. 'And I've you to thank. We couldn't have done it without your contacts.'

Sam shoved his hands in his pockets and grinned. 'That was nothing, business acquaintances should always help each other out when they can.'

Not friends, I noted, glumly.

'Fearne!' Nina reappeared looking pink. 'My taxi is on its way. Help!'

'I'll leave you to it. Best of luck, Nina,' said Sam, reaching to shake her hand.

'Aw, I'm sure you'll miss me like a stone in your shoe,' she said with a wink and then pulled him into a hug.

'Enjoy the honey,' he said, giving me a wave before turning away

'Wait.' I cried as he got to the door. 'There are some lilies in the cold store which we really need to sell tonight. Give me Pandora's address and I can deliver them to her. It's the least we can do, considering you've helped us get some new business.'

'Great idea!' said Nina, cottoning on straight away.

Sam looked embarrassed. 'There's no need, really.'

'I insist.' I picked up a pen and held it out to him.

Sam came back and scribbled his address down. There was a harsh tooting of a car horn and Nina let out a little scream.

'This is it! I'm off! Arrghhh! Wish me luck!'

Sam slipped away quietly while Nina collected all her belongings. Scamp and I went outside to see her off and suddenly the pavement was brimming with people. Rosie and Lia from the café and their staff and customers who'd come out to see what was happening. Ken from the mini mart, Biddy from the pet shop, Lucas of course. All cheering her on her way.

'Good luck!' I called, holding on to Scamp with one hand and waving madly with the other. 'Have fun!'

'I plan to,' she shouted from the back of the taxi through the open window.

I watched as the car circled the village green and vanished from sight and I turned to look at the shop. The window displays were summery and bright. The plant rack outside selling pots of osteospermum and geraniums and herbs looked fresh and inviting and the fragrance of English summer roses wafted through the door; I felt my spirits lift with anticipation at the weeks ahead.

The future of the flower shop looked as bright as it could possibly be and I had every intention of making a success of my solo stint while Nina was away. I felt a stirring inside me: passion and determination. Ethel was right; this was an adventure and it was mine for the taking.

There was just one tiny thing worrying me. Back inside the shop, I picked up the piece of paper Sam had written on and compared it with the one written beside the order from Gareth Weaver.

They were identical. My skin prickled with goosebumps.

'Oh Sam,' I murmured. 'I'm so, so sorry.'

So there was only one Pandora after all and what I'd discovered would break Sam's heart. Should I tell him, or should I stay out of their business? A knot of worry twisted in my stomach. I knew what Nina would say: what happens in the florist, stays in the florist.

Could I really stand by and watch him get hurt? I guessed only time would tell.

Part Three

Chapter Twenty-one

The Claybourne Hotel finally came into view as Laura and I made our way up the long approach from the road. It was stunning. Festooned in frothy lilac wisteria, the Edwardian building stood proudly at the head of the drive amid pristine gardens. The façade was like something a child would draw; it had four rows of pretty white sash windows set into soft grey stone walls, steps leading up to a wide front door and two bay trees either side adorned with pale lilac bows. Directly in front of the house was a circular water feature with a fountain at its centre and terraced flower beds, bursting with colour, flanked each side.

'Wow,' said Laura and I at the same time.

We were into June and it was my first Monday without Nina and I was wasting no time in getting the week off to a positive start. I'd asked Laura to accompany me to visit the Claybourne Hotel for a bit of moral support and she'd been happy to oblige.

We grinned at each other in excitement and Laura whistled.

'Fearne! Can we just acknowledge just how goddamn well you're doing at this floristry lark to get a gig like this?'

I laughed and headed to the car park behind the hotel. 'Getting the gig was the easy bit, now I need to work out how to deliver it.'

She flapped a hand. 'You'll find a way.'

I laughed. 'Says someone who struggles to display a single rose.'

'I've got Hamish trained now.' Her eyes twinkled. 'He buys the ones which are already arranged.'

'He's a keeper then?'

She didn't have to reply; everything about her glowed: her skin, her eyes, her smile. Being in love suited her.

I pulled Nina's van into a space and we both stared at the hotel.

'This would be an amazing venue for a wedding.' I nudged her. 'You'll have to bear it in mind for if Hamish pops the question.'

She gave me a look of rebuke as we got out of the van. 'It's the twenty-first century, Fearne, these days, we can ask men out on dates, say I love you first, pop our own questions.'

'I suppose.' I said and then sighed wistfully.

Laura raised her eyebrows, missing nothing. She had watched me sabotage my last relationship. I had shut Steve out. There'd been nothing malicious about my actions, Freddie's death had left me numb to the needs of other people and a layer of ice had grown around my heart. And now the ice was beginning to thaw. I'd taken my work life in a new direction, maybe it was time for my heart to do the same.

She must have read my mind. 'Do you think you might be ready to start dating again?'

'Maybe,' I said, taking her arm. 'Come on, let's go and do a recce on this place, I need to get back to the shop. I've left Scamp with Biddy and he misses me when I'm away.'

'OK,' she said, shouldering her handbag. 'But don't think you can change the subject that easily. I'm on a mission to find you a man. And I don't mean one with a waggy tail and four legs.'

★

Inside, the hotel foyer was every bit as elegant as the exterior. Polished wooden floors gleamed, crystal chandeliers sparkled in the sunlight and a pair of receptionists beamed at us from behind a long mahogany desk. The overall effect was a welcoming blend of good taste, glamour and laid-back comfort.

I gave my name and asked for Marcia and while we waited for her, Laura and I were directed to a pair of wing-backed armchairs with a view out onto the terrace and the gardens beyond.

'It's like being in the home of a wealthy old aunt,' I whispered to Laura, sitting down.

There was a small table between us on which sat a vase of old-fashioned roses, just like the ones which used to smother the trellis outside Granny's back door. I leaned forward to sniff them and it took me straight back to my childhood and being taught to bash the stems of cut roses with a rolling pin to help them take up water.

A tray of coffee and biscuits was set in front of us and Laura's eyes lit up.

'The last time we were somewhere as grand as this was on our spa day,' she said, pouring us both a drink.

I winced. 'I was a bundle of laughs that day. I'm surprised you're still willing to go out with me.'

'Of course! You nut job.' She slid a cup and saucer towards me. 'Anyway you've come a long way since then. We both have. I think that crystal healer would be proud of us.'

'You mean Maureen Sinclair?' I said reaching for my bag. I pulled out the crystal she'd given me.

'Ha snap!' Laura found hers and we chinked them together.

'Do you remember what she said about them?' I asked, taking her crystal from her. Whereas mine was a smooth egg-shaped stone, hers was irregular, shaped like a little bird, golden threads within it catching the light.

Laura nodded, her gaze soft. 'That mine would help me work on my communication skills.'

'It didn't take long to take effect, did it?' I teased. 'We'd barely left the studio and you spilled *all* the beans.'

'That was one of the most difficult things I've ever done,' she admitted. 'But then I plucked up the courage to suggest Hamish and I moved in together.'

'That was your suggestion?' I said surprised.

'Yep. Losing Freddie . . .' She lifted her shoulder. 'Well, it puts life into perspective. I knew I loved Hamish and I didn't want to waste time not being with him. So I told him.'

'I love that you two are so happy,' I said. 'And Maureen's advice to me was to be kind to myself. So on that note . . .'

I helped myself to a delicious chocolate biscuit from the plate. Laura joined me and we crunched away for a few moments. Maureen had said more than that of course, she'd asked me if I'd forgotten what made me happy. She'd hit the nail on the head, but now with Freddie's help, I felt like I was getting there. Here I was in a beautiful setting, with my best friend, about to discuss the biggest order Nina's Flowers will have ever taken. Life was good. Except for one thing: Sam . . .

'Despite what I said about it being the twenty-first century,' Laura said out of the blue, breaking into my thoughts, 'I would prefer it if Hamish were to propose to me rather than the other way around. And I don't think I'd have the reception here.'

'Oh?' I took another biscuit. 'I like it.'

'It's a bit fancy for me.' She wrinkled her nose. 'I'd just go for something simple. Or just escape to a white sandy beach and do it in secret.'

I looked alarmed. 'I hope the maid of honour will still get an invitation?'

She pretended to think about it and I poked my tongue out at her.

'Of course you will,' she laughed. 'I don't mean entirely in secret. I won't have my mum there to see me get married but I couldn't do it without Dad.'

'I'm so happy for you.' I took a deep breath and blinked away the prickle of tears in my eyes. 'My best friend and Freddie's best friend. There's a circular beauty to it that just feels right somehow.'

Laura smiled, misty-eyed. 'Thank you.' She cleared her throat. 'Perhaps we need to keep the circle going and find you someone from Hamish's list of Facebook friends.'

'Um.' I brushed the crumbs from my lap. 'I have made a friend since I've been in Barnaby. Sam. He works for the landlord. The one I said came around to chase Nina for money.'

She looked surprised. 'Isn't he supposed to be the baddie?'

A picture of Sam's handsome face appeared in my mind and the look of concentration in his eyes when he was trying to twist the stems for Pandora's bouquet.

I shook my head. 'Sam only wanted the rent which was overdue, he's hardly a loan shark threatening to send the heavies round. He's nice and kind and it was he who helped me get a foot in the door here.'

Laura stared at me amused. 'You really do like him, don't you!'

I felt the beginning of a blush. 'No. Possibly. But it doesn't matter either way because he's just got back with his ex-wife. And I helped him.'

'Sounds complicated.' She arched an eyebrow. 'Trust you.'

'I know.' I smiled ruefully. 'And in theory, of course I want him to live happily ever after with his wife and children, but I'm not sure his wife feels the same.'

Laura ploughed through the rest of the biscuits while I told her I'd discovered that Pandora might be having an affair.

'I was hoping to see her for myself when I delivered two lots of flowers to her house, but a cute little boy answered.'

It had had to have been Sam's son, Will. The one who slept curled up with his thumb in his mouth. My heart fluttered as I remembered the look of adoration on Sam's face when he'd told me about his children. I hope Will hadn't read the note from Sexy Tiger which had accompanied the roses. I gave a shudder.

Laura shook her head. 'Poor kid. Sounds like Sam might not be married for much longer.'

'I hate knowing something about his wife that he doesn't know,' I screwed up my face. 'It feels underhand.'

'Hmm,' she said thoughtfully. 'Do you know him well enough to tell him?'

I shook my head. 'Nina has a motto: what happens in the florist, stays in the florist. It would be unethical; Gareth Weaver, or should I say Sexy Tiger, deserves our trust.'

'And what about Sam's trust?' Laura said doubtfully. 'What about the children? It's not fair on them.'

'I know.' I'd thought about nothing else all weekend and I still didn't have a good answer. 'But if I say something, he'll hate me for spoiling his marriage and it'll be me who ends up being the baddie.'

Laura looked at me solemnly. 'For the record, if you ever find out something like this about a relationship I'm in, I'd want to know.'

'Oh god,' I groaned. 'Now I don't know whether I'm being a better friend by not telling him, or a worse one.'

Her lips twitched. 'Are you sure that's all he is? A friend?'

Sam Diamond was on my mind more than a casual friend should be. And I needed to put a stop to it. He belonged to someone else, even if Pandora didn't feel the same way. Besides my heart was still delicate. It couldn't take any further loss and a man with as much baggage as Sam was a risk I didn't dare to take. I blew out a breath and met Laura's inquisitive gaze.

'He's just a friend,' I confirmed. 'That's all he can ever be.'

Laura looked as if she had more to say on the matter but right on cue I noticed a familiar face heading our way.

'Brush the crumbs off your chin,' I said with a grin. 'Here comes Marcia to show us around the hotel.'

An hour later, Laura and I were back on the road. I was negotiating the sharp bends and steep hills which led us back to Barnaby and Laura had her elbow hanging out of the window while singing along with great enthusiasm to the nineties hits on our favourite radio station.

'Rather you than me,' said Laura during a lull in the music. 'That hotel ballroom is huge, I wouldn't know where to start.'

'Well once I managed to tune your dreadful singing out, I've been thinking about it and I've got loads of ideas.'

'Rude,' said Laura, picking up Scamp's bag of doggie chocolate buttons.

I stopped her just before she tipped them into her mouth. 'Although I'm sure they're edible.'

'I'll pass.' She folded her arms. 'Go on, hit me with your ideas, it'll take my mind off my rumbling stomach.'

'OK. I'm going to do a moongate at the entrance to the ballroom. That's a big metal hoop which you cover in flowers,' I added, noting her blank expression. 'Then once inside the ballroom, I'm going to get some wooden trellis panels and put them either side of the entrance so it feels like you're walking into a secret garden. I'm going to do a pathway of flowers . . .'

I stopped, feeling Laura's eyes on me. 'What's the matter?'

'I hope Nina knows how lucky she is to have you,' she said fondly.

I shrugged. 'I'm the lucky one. I'm really enjoying this and if it goes well, we could get other conference work. People seem to have elastic budgets when it comes to special events.'

'Good for you. I'm proud of you.' She reached across and squeezed my leg. 'As long as you've got a watertight contract for all your outlay, that's the main thing.'

A dart of nerves pierced my happiness for a second but I quickly dismissed it. I hadn't got a contract yet, but there was plenty of time for all that.

Laura groaned at my hesitation. '*Fearne!*'

'Oh, stop worrying.' I laughed as she squeezed the sides of her face with her hands. 'I'm putting my heart and soul into this, it can't possibly go wrong.'

And with the windows down, the breeze in my hair and my best friend by my side, I sang along to the radio feeling on top of the world. Nothing, but nothing was going to spoil my good mood.

Chapter Twenty-two

The next morning, there was a sharp rap on the door of the shop shortly before seven thirty.

I looked up from the counter where I was working on my laptop. There was a short barrel-shaped man with wild grey hair sticking out from under a blue cap staring at me through the glass. Outside was a huge lorry with 'Sunshine Flowers' along the length of it.

I opened the door, Scamp at my heels.

'Mr Sunshine?' I offered him my hand to shake and he pumped it up and down a couple of times. 'Thanks for coming to see me.'

'Morning. You can call me Victor. You the new girl then?' His voice had a musical Welsh lilt to it.

'Correct. I'm Fearne Lovage.'

'That other girl given up, has she?' He looked mildly amused. 'Not surprised. Bloody city girls. Doing their escape to the country bit, thinking it'll all be cream teas and village fetes. Ridiculous.'

'If you mean Nina, the proprietor, no she hasn't given up,' I said evenly. 'She's away . . . on a research trip.' No need to mention she was researching New Zealand farmers for possible husbands, I had a feeling Victor would find that even more ridiculous.

He stood in the middle of the shop, hands on hips and looked around. He was wearing a navy Guernsey jumper despite the building warmth of the June morning and wouldn't have looked out of place mending lobster pots on the Cornish coast while singing sea shanties.

Scamp sat neatly at his feet waiting to be admired. Victor rewarded him by bending down and scratching him behind his ears.

Sourcing a flower supplier who'd make deliveries to the shop was a priority. I didn't fancy making crack of dawn trips to the market as Nina had been doing. I'd gone with her once but we'd had to leave Scamp locked in the van and he'd been barking his head off when we'd returned. Now I never left him alone for more than a couple of minutes if I could help it. Nina had recommended I chat to Victor because she'd almost taken him on before; she'd omitted to tell me that he was a miserable so-and-so.

'Glad to see you're tech-savvy,' he said, looking at my laptop which I'd set up on the counter next to my iPad.

I was using it to make a customer database by going through old order books and trying to determine a pattern in people's ordering. I hadn't got very far; reading the messages to go on the gift cards which accompanied each bouquet had become my guilty pleasure, it was like reading the best bits of a Mills and Boon novel.

'The last one wasn't,' he grunted, bending down to inspect a bucket of stargazer lilies. 'That's why she didn't order from Sunshine Flowers. Our system is state of the art.'

'Can I offer you a cup of tea,' I said, 'or coffee?'

I was desperate for one myself. The café next door did wonderful coffee and Nina and I had got into the habit of buying cappuccinos every morning at eleven. But in the meantime, a cup of instant would do.

'No time.' Victor straightened up and looked at his watch. Scamp padded back to his bed and lay down with a 'flump' noise. 'Folk will be moaning about the lorry blocking the road shortly. Bloody commuters. So. Down to business. You wanted to start ordering flowers from us?'

'That was the idea, yes,' I said, 'I'll be working on my own for the next few weeks, so anything which can make life easier for me is a win.'

'Easy life.' He shook his head in despair and shoved his hands in his pockets. 'You're in the wrong business if you want an easy life, my girl.'

'I know,' I said tetchily, wondering whether I should cut my losses, ask him to leave and look for another supplier. I'd called Sunshine Flowers because it had reminded me of the thing Harriet on the floristry course had said about flowers being sunshine for the soul. Also, I'd gone back through some of Nina's old business records and found a business card for them. But Victor was about as sunny as a wet weekend in Blackpool.

'Unsociable hours, high risk, low margins,' he warned. 'And of course, your stock is deteriorating from the second you order it. It's a race against time to flog it before it dies.'

'You remind me of my Granny; she used to say the same,' I said. Although she seemed to enjoy the challenge. 'The rewards are high though. As is job satisfaction. Working with such beauty is such a privilege, don't you agree?'

'I can tell you're new to the game,' he said with a smirk. 'Beautiful it might be, but this is a business dictated to by whims and weather and—'

'Whinging?' I said, tongue in cheek.

'Exchange rates,' he ploughed on without seeming to notice my jibe. 'One daft move by the government and the value of roses can drop twenty per cent by the time I've moved them from one side of the Channel to the other. Bloody politicians.'

'Is Sunshine your real name?' I said blackly. I couldn't remember meeting such a killjoy. Ever.

'Oh yes.' He nodded earnestly. 'Sunshine by name, Sunshine by—'

A sarcastic laugh escaped me and I coughed to cover it up. 'Sorry.'

He glanced at me and scratched his chin. 'No. I'm sorry, love. Business is tough at the moment and I've had a few customers go bust owing me money recently. They open up, heavy on enthusiasm and light on experience. And six months later you turn up to empty premises and a 'To Let' board outside. And with Europe the way it is . . .' He winced. 'Sorry. Again.'

'You must love it,' I pointed out. 'Or you'd do something else.'

'This is a family business, I'm the third generation. There's no question of me doing anything else. My grandparents started wholesaling flowers with one small van seventy years ago. They'd drive from Wales to Covent Garden and back again in time for the shops to open. Completely different game now. I don't know what my granddad would make of the giant flower markets in Holland. All computerised. Flowers arriving and leaving from all four corners of the globe. Big digital screens, people all over the world sending in their bids over the internet. Crazy.'

'Snap!' I grinned. 'I'm also third generation. And my granny would be gobsmacked. She never even trusted mobile phones. Plus, guess what, she lived in Wales in a village called Llanidaeron. Had a stall on the market.'

'Good grief! I know it!' Victor laughed in disbelief. 'Not Carrie and Evan? God rest their souls.'

I stared at him in surprise. 'That's them. My mother's parents. Although I never met Granddad.'

'I knew it,' Victor punched the air. 'I knew you had floristry in your blood.'

I hid a smile: a minute ago he'd said he could tell I was new to the business.

'Fancy that!' he said in wonder. 'Well that changes everything. I will have that cup of tea.'

Twenty minutes later Victor and I had almost finished our drinks and discussed the needs of the shop. I'd explained the foray I was making into corporate business and he'd promised to make sure I got the pick of the blooms when I ordered. He'd shown me how to log on to his website, set me up with an account and my own log-in details.

'You've got until two a.m. to place an order for the following day. And once an order is placed there's no going back. And no credit either.' He smiled apologetically. 'Not that I don't trust Carrie's granddaughter but . . .'

'I understand.' I assured him. 'I don't expect special treatment.'

His eyes crinkled as he chuckled. 'Good, because you won't get it. Nice cuppa that.'

He drained his mug and set it down on the counter with an appreciative sigh. 'Right. Better be off or my delphiniums will be drooping.'

He got to the door and turned around. 'I will look after you though, love. Any problems, just ask. I've been in this game long enough to know the solution to most of them.'

'Thanks, Victor,' I said with a rush of warmth towards the gruff little man.

'Oi!' shouted a voice from outside. 'You going to move this lorry sometime today, or what?'

'Sorry mate!' Victor replied with a wave of his hand, muttering under his breath, 'bloody car drivers.'

I laughed. 'Is there anyone you do like?'

Scamp stood up to see what was going on and his tail thumped against Victor's leg.

'Dogs.' He winked on his way out. 'And florists with dogs.'

'That went surprisingly well.' I crouched down and gave Scamp a cuddle. 'Let's hope the next one goes our way too.'

At two o'clock I left Scamp in the back of the shop where it was cool, with a bowl of water and one of Biddy's special marrowbones, locked the doors and set off for my meeting with Wendy to discuss funeral flowers.

A. J. Mallet Funeral Directors was at the end of a run of shops on the outskirts of Chesterfield. It wasn't the most attractive place: an unprepossessing flat-roofed seventies building on the outside, and inside, an excess of pine wooden panelling, with brown and yellow dog-toothed patterned carpet. The receptionist straightened up and greeted me with a warm smile as I entered.

'Wendy is expecting you,' she whispered reverently once I'd signed the visitor's book. 'Go straight through to her office.'

I followed her directions down a corridor to an open door, through which I saw Wendy, dressed in black, sitting at a desk. The office was a large airy room with polished wooden floorboards, white walls and tasteful modern artwork. The décor was a sharp contrast to the reception area. A small sofa and a couple of slouchy armchairs were set around a low coffee table at the opposite end to her desk. She slipped the reading glasses she was wearing onto the top of her head and stood to greet me. We settled into the armchairs.

'I do appreciate you inviting me to come over,' I said, smiling at her. 'Especially after abandoning you at our new business event. I'm so sorry about that.'

She waved away my apology and unbuttoned her jacket. 'As I said, our florist is experienced, but she's very conservative. She's never point blank refused to do something, but she has very fixed views on what she deems to be sacrilegious ceremonies and we're getting more and more unusual requests all the time.'

I chewed my lip. 'I must be honest, I'm not experienced at all. But I'm willing to learn.'

'I appreciate your honesty,' said Wendy with a soft laugh. 'I can talk you through what our requirements are. Can I get you a drink?'

I asked for some water. No sooner had she poured us a glass each than an elderly golden retriever pattered casually into the room, tail wagging rhythmically and tongue hanging out.

'You bring your dog to work like me,' I said, stroking the soft fur on the animal's head.

Wendy nodded. 'This is Florence, after Florence Nightingale because she's always been such a brilliant nurse. There's a cat called Charlie around somewhere as well. Animals reduce anxiety and we get a lot of that in here. Both of them seem to have a sixth sense, knowing when they're needed. People tend to arrive here in a state of bewilderment without a clue what they want for their loved ones.'

I felt a lump in my throat. It was the anniversary of Freddie's death next month; a whole year would have passed. But the memory of sitting in a room similar to this one, forced to choose between mahogany and pine when all I really wanted to do was scream that this must all be a giant wind-up was as fresh and raw as if it had happened yesterday.

'Charlie will curl up into a ball on someone's lap and within minutes, the client is calmer and able to make some decisions.'

Florence lowered her chin onto my knee and gazed up at me with heart-melting chocolate brown eyes.

'And Florence does that,' said Wendy with a smile.

I swallowed. 'They're magic, aren't they, animals? Scamp came into my life just when I needed him. He gave me something to get out of bed for, someone to smile for every morning. And gradually I found I didn't have to fake my smile any more.'

'You've lost someone recently?' said Wendy.

I nodded. 'My brother. We were very close. We even bought a house together. Life lost its meaning for a while.'

'Sorry to hear that.' Wendy nudged the box of tissues on the table in front of us towards me.

'He had a motorbike accident.' I took a deep breath but managed to stave off the tears. 'Yet he was the safest rider I knew. His friends even called him Steady Freddie.'

Wendy groaned. 'And I made a stupid comment about a floral tribute in the shape of a bike. I'm so sorry, no wonder you made a swift exit.'

'It's fine. Really,' I assured her. 'In a way I'm glad it happened. It made me realise that getting over a bereavement isn't a linear process, it's a journey that can circle back and forwards at any time. And I don't want to *not* talk about Freddie. He was a big ray of sunshine in my life and it isn't right to shut out that light. He deserves better than that.'

Wendy nodded. 'He sounds like my type of guy. I always go for bikers.'

I laughed softly. 'I used to. But not any more. It's four wheels or nothing now.'

There was a gentle knock at the door; the receptionist appeared, chewing her lip. 'Sorry to intrude but Mr Benton-Ridley is here early. He's brought his sister with him.'

Wendy checked her watch and frowned. 'Right. Offer them a drink and I'll be out shortly.'

The receptionist nodded and left.

'You're busy. I'll leave you to it,' I said, levering Florence's head from my knee so I could stand up.

'Wait a sec,' said Wendy, going to her desk and picking up a leaflet. 'This is what we give to our clients who want a traditional funeral. Can you do something similar for more modern arrangements? I'd like to give people some idea of the alternative to the norm.'

I flicked through it quickly. 'Of course I can.'

'And just a thought, but would you like to sit in on this meeting? I've spoken to Mr Benton-Ridley on the phone already. His wife's death was expected. That doesn't lessen the grief, obviously, but I got the impression that he wouldn't be a weeper. It might help you to see the sort of details which go into organising a funeral.'

I felt a flutter of unease at being in the presence of someone else's grief, but I spread my hands. 'If the client doesn't mind, then yes please, that'd be useful.'

Wendy excused herself to double check that everyone would be happy with that. She returned almost immediately with a man in his late fifties with fatigue etched into his face and a small woman who shared the same hazel eyes and auburn hair. Both of them carrying drinks.

'Our florist, Fearne Lovage,' said Wendy, making the introductions and showing her clients to the sofa. 'And this is Mr Benton-Ridley and his sister . . .?'

'Annette,' supplied the woman. She paused to blow on her drink and then sipped it. Florence stood up politely to sniff the new arrivals. 'Gorgeous dog. We're dog lovers aren't we, Nigel? Brought up with dogs. I've got three shih–tzus myself. Val, his wife never wanted one though, did she?'

'No, she was allergic,' said Mr Benton-Ridley quietly. His cup wobbled in its saucer as he sat down and he set it carefully on the coffee table. 'Please call me Nigel.'

'I'm very sorry for your loss,' I said as we shook hands.

'Thank you,' he said, inclining his head. 'My wife had Alzheimers. I began losing her four years ago. It has been a long and painful goodbye.'

My heart went out to him. He looked shattered and bewildered.

Annette squeezed his arm. 'You were a saint to that woman, Nigel. An absolute saint. No one could have done more.' She gave me a sideways glance and lowered her voice. 'Not that she deserved it.'

Nigel flushed. 'She wasn't herself at the end.'

Annette harrumphed. 'True. I almost liked her by then.'

Wendy cleared her throat. 'Shall we discuss what you had in mind for your wife's funeral? I believe you've already got a date arranged with your local church?'

'Yes, I have.' Nigel looked relieved. He produced a small notebook from the inside of his jacket pocket. 'I've made a list of questions. Val didn't have much in the way of family, or close friends.'

Annette folded her arms. 'No surprises there.'

'So it'll be a select gathering, but nonetheless it needs to be done properly, as she'd have wanted it. A top quality coffin, funeral car, flowers, pall bearers . . .' I listened carefully as Wendy expertly guided Nigel through the very last job that he could do for his wife to make it an event which she'd approve of. She was discreet and respectful while at the same time managing his sister's obvious dislike for the deceased.

'We can do flowers from both of us, can't we,' said Annette, draining the last dregs from her cup. 'No point in wasting money on two wreaths.'

A weary smile passed across Nigel's face. 'No, I suppose not.'

She turned to me. 'Lilies. A big spray of lilies for the top of the coffin.'

'Something like this?' I passed her the leaflet from the other florist, not sure whether Wendy would want her original florist to handle the order.

Nigel shook his head. 'Lilies made her sneeze.'

'Not any more they won't,' Annette muttered.

'What did your wife like?' I asked.

He gazed into the middle distance. 'Her garden shed. And vegetables. She didn't like flowers, said they were a waste of space. Over the years the lawn has got smaller and the veg patch bigger.'

I didn't think I'd ever met anyone who didn't like flowers. Wendy gave me a look which implied that nothing surprised her.

A sudden image popped into my head of something I'd seen on a website for the wedding of a couple who owned a greengrocery store. I took my phone out of my bag and searched online until I found it.

'How about this?' I showed Nigel and Annette the quirky arrangement.

It was similar in shape to the coffin sprays they were looking at but that was the only traditional thing about it. Bunches of radishes sat like rubies amid broccoli crowns, glossy aubergines shone between bunches of bright orange carrots with feathery tops, and sunshine yellow courgette flowers peeked through a lacy veil of delicate pea shoots. Not a flower in sight but nevertheless brimming with colour and interest.

'Fruit and veg?' Annette spluttered. 'I've seen it all now.'

Then a smile spread across Nigel's face and he began to nod. 'Perfect. Val would love it. Could you make us one like that please?'

'I'd be honoured,' I replied.

'What will everyone think?' Annette said, red-faced.

'I've spent years worrying about what everyone else will think. And I've come to the conclusion that I've been wasting my time.' Nigel gave his sister a defiant look. 'Life's too short to worry about what others think.'

Annette evidently couldn't think of a response to that, so I used the opportunity to say my goodbyes. I was feeling pretty pleased with myself as I headed back to Barnaby. It was only week one without Nina, and I'd already got my first corporate event and first funeral order under my belt.

Business was beginning to boom.

Chapter Twenty-three

'You're not helping, you know,' I said sternly, tripping over Scamp's rubber bone for the umpteenth time. I gave it a kick out of the way.

It was the day after my trip to the funeral directors and I was in the shop early again, which seemed to be my new normal, and despite his advanced age, Scamp was having his daily mad half hour. This mostly entailed him dropping one of his toys at my feet and staring at it, nose close to the ground, bottom in the air and paws ready to pounce. Then as soon as I tried to pick it up to throw for him, he'd steal it back and charge around the shop growling triumphantly. Most of the time this was fine, but when I was trying to manoeuvre the cumbersome metal plant racks through the shop, not so much. I was lucky really, at least I could leave the door to the shop open safe in the knowledge he wouldn't dash out and across the road. Biddy had no end of problems with Churchill popping over to the green to flirt with his favourite bitches.

And right now the door was open as I attempted to get the front merchandise attractively ready for the early coffee trade which the Lemon Tree Café attracted.

Scamp squeezed in front of me, pranced on the spot and dropped the bone again.

'Nooo,' I moaned in despair and reversed back into

the shop, lowering the stand to the floor. 'That's it. I'm phoning Battersea Dogs' Home. You'll have to go.'

The sound of warm laughter made me spin around; Sam was leaning in the doorway, sunlight in his hair, his blue eyes twinkling with humour. He was all in black: smart trousers and shirt rolled up at his wrists to reveal his tanned forearms. My heart gave a little leap.

Rubber bone forgotten in an instant, Scamp greeted him enthusiastically, jumping up and sniffing his pockets for possible treasure.

'Don't listen, Scamp,' he said, covering the dog's ears and pressing a kiss to his head. 'She loves you really.'

Lucky dog.

'That's debatable,' I said, sternly. 'It's tough going on my own as it is without him throwing obstacles in my path.'

'Here, let me help.' Sam picked up two of the racks at once and set them down outside.

'With pleasure.' I followed behind with trays of plants and between us we got the job done in a fraction of the time it would have taken me.

'Thanks,' I said, brushing loose soil from the sleeve of his shirt. 'Not that I'm a feeble female who can't cope without a man.'

We were standing at the front of the shop in a patch of sunshine. Scamp was lying in the doorway, chin on paws, watching us.

'I know that.' He gave me a lopsided smile. 'But some things are better with two.'

'Agreed.'

He held my gaze and my heart thumped. I returned his smile, thinking of several things which could fall into that category, but I gave myself a shake. Sam was taken, he was married to Pandora. Even if she didn't deserve him.

Sam yawned and clapped a hand over his mouth, mortified. 'I'm so sorry. How rude of me. I didn't get much sleep last night.'

'No worries,' I said, not wanting to dwell on why that might have been. 'Same here. I was up until the small hours planning a flower scheme for the Claybourne Hotel.'

'Your meeting went well then?' Sam's face split into a smile. 'That's great news!'

'At this rate, I'll need an assistant before Nina gets back. I'm shattered already and she's been gone less than a week.'

'I was up late as well, decorating.' He showed me his hands. There was paint ingrained under his fingernails. 'I'd forgotten what a taskmaster Pandora is.'

I raised my eyebrows. 'So you've moved back in?'

He shook his head, scraping at the dried paint with his fingernail. 'Not yet. Pandora thinks it'll unsettle the kids. She's probably right.'

There was something about his tone that made me think he wasn't one hundred per cent convinced about Pandora's strategy. Or maybe he was just keen to be living under the same roof as them all again. I wondered what she'd said to him about the flowers she'd received from her admirer. And most importantly, what was she playing at, pretending to be at yoga when she had someone as kind and caring as Sam waiting at home for her?

Sam yawned again and we both laughed.

'Perhaps we should both get an early night tonight,' I suggested.

'I appreciate the offer but . . .' He quirked an eyebrow.

'No, no, I didn't mean it like that!' My hands flew to my face and I laughed, embarrassed.

'I'm only teasing you.' He smiled and squeezed my arm gently.

I knew he was only being friendly, but my heart still quickened at the sensation of his fingers on my skin. This was ridiculous; I had to get my feelings under control. It was either that or avoid his company completely and I didn't want to lose him as a friend.

Just then the door to the café opened and Rosie appeared wearing a T-shirt stretched over her bump and carrying a cloth and a towel. Sam dropped his hand from my arm casually and put his hands in his pockets. Scamp padded over to her.

'Morning! Another hot one, I reckon.' Rosie's tummy was getting so big that she struggled to bend and stroke Scamp's head. 'You look pink already, Fearne.'

'It's thirsty work setting up for the day.' I could feel my face burning, but it had absolutely nothing to do with the weather. 'Have you got the coffee on yet?'

'Patience, patience! I need to dry the morning dew off the tables and chairs first.' She leaned on the back of one of the chairs and puffed her cheeks out. 'And then I'll probably need another sit down.'

'Sit down now,' said Sam, pulling a chair out for her. 'We'll dry the tables.'

'I'm perfectly capable of doing it myself,' she protested but I took her cloths and Sam gently persuaded her to sit. She sank down with a sigh. 'Oh all right then, thank you.'

Sam began drying the tables and I dried the chairs.

'While I've got you,' she said, lifting her feet up onto the chair I'd just dried, 'what do you think of baby showers – cheesy or cute?'

I wrinkled my nose. 'I've never been to one, isn't it just like a hen party but without the booze?'

'I suppose.' She smoothed her hands over her stomach. 'Although I was sober at my hen party and my wedding and last Christmas. So I'm getting used to it.'

'Pandora had baby showers for both of her pregnancies,' said Sam. 'She held them in the hotel we got married in and neither of them were sober affairs, or cheap.'

Another strike against Sam's wife; it would be so much easier to put him out of my mind if I thought she was a wonderful woman. Then I could resign myself to simply being a friend. But as it was, I'd probably always carry an unrequited torch for him. It was so unfair. I groaned aloud.

'Broke a nail,' I said vaguely as Sam and Rosie looked at me.

'I don't want a posh do,' Rosie continued, inspecting her own nails, 'and I don't want people spending money on me; but I thought maybe a few friends at home would be fun.'

'Or you could have it here in the café,' I suggested. 'That way there'll be no tidying up to do afterwards.'

She grinned. 'I like your style.'

'And involve the grandmothers-to-be,' said Sam, drying the last table. 'They love all that stuff, feeling part of it. It's important.'

His lips pressed into a line and I just knew that Pandora hadn't invited her mother-in-law to either of her baby showers. I hid a smile; I was doing it again – demonising her. Poor woman, if I ever met her I'd be expecting her to have horns and a red tail. She couldn't be that bad, not if Sam loved her.

'Good thinking. The baby will be here next month; I can't wait, obviously, but a part of me thinks it would be nice to be made a fuss over one last time before he or she arrives and steals the limelight for the rest of my life. Right, that's settled then.' Rosie heaved herself off the chair. 'Thanks for the advice. I'm going to go and invite everyone. You'll come I hope, Fearne?'

'I'd love to,' I said, amused. 'I'll be in in a minute for my coffee.'

'Two coffees coming up. On the house.' She collected the damp towels.

Sam and I looked at each other after she'd gone in and laughed.

'I get the feeling she'd already made that decision before asking us,' I said.

'Story of my life,' Sam muttered under his breath. He looked at his watch. 'Crikey, look at the time, and I haven't even got around to the reason I came yet. Have you got your diary handy?'

'It's on the counter.' I was intrigued. I clicked my fingers to Scamp and the three of us went back inside.

'That bouquet you helped me make. Could you do it again, do you think?' he asked, raking a hand through his hair.

'You mean help you make something?' I had to hand it to him, he was certainly dedicated to her.

Sam nodded. 'But not just me, the whole cricket team this time.' He grinned. 'Honestly, the stick I took off them for doing some flower arranging. And when Archie suggested getting together for a night out, somehow your name came up and suddenly everyone wants to learn how to make a bouquet.'

I was delighted at the idea; I'd enjoyed teaching Sam and if his team members were anything like him it would be fun – if a little cramped. 'Are they all as broad as you?' I nodded to the space around the work table.

His eyes crinkled with pleasure and he laughed. 'I'll take that as a compliment. But don't worry, we're used to squeezing up. You should see the size of our changing room.'

The thought of eleven men, all as attractive as him in one room delayed my response for a moment and Sam mistook my silence for reluctance.

'And we'd want to pay you for your time and your expertise, not just for the flowers,' he added hurriedly.

Teaching a group wasn't something I'd done before, but this week seemed to be a week of firsts. He stared hopefully at me; how could I resist those blue eyes?

'Would a Saturday night suit you?'

'So you'll do it? Thanks, Fearne.' His eyes shone. 'The lads will be chuffed.'

We flicked through the diary and found a Saturday night which had nothing written on it. If he noticed that actually none of my evenings had any engagements he didn't mention it.

'Obviously I'll be besieged with offers of hot dates between now and then,' I said, airily, 'but don't worry, I'll turn them down.'

'Thank you, you're an absolute star!' He grabbed my shoulders and planted a kiss on my cheek. 'We've got a cricket match the next day, so we'll be able to present them to the ladies as a thank you for always putting on a good spread at the cricket teas.'

How quintessentially quaint. My mind conjured up a summer's day with the ladies cheering on their men before darting off to the pavilion to serve up cucumber sandwiches and bite-sized slices of quiche.

'Even *Pandora*?' The words were out of my mouth before I could stop them. 'Sorry. I mean . . . with you being separated for a while.'

'Even Pandora.' He stroked the side of his face and I got the impression he was hiding a smile. 'Although admittedly our contribution generally comes from a certain upmarket supermarket. The summer is too short to be in the kitchen making your own sausage rolls, she reckons.'

'I'm with her on that one,' I said. Finally, something she and I agreed on. 'Well, the cricket team's floral workshop is in the diary. So it's a date.'

Scamp leapt to his feet with an excited yap and Sam and I turned to find Biddy hovering at the door.

'Ooh,' said Biddy, beaming. 'A romantic liaison? How thrilling.'

'That's right, Biddy,' I grinned. 'I've got a date with an entire cricket team.'

'Ah, those were the days.' She winked at Sam cheekily.

'Biddy, you dark horse!' I exclaimed, introducing them to each other.

'That sounds like a story I should stay and listen to,' he said with a grin. 'But I've got an appointment with another troublesome tenant.'

'*Another* one? I hope you're not lumping me in that category?' I pretended to be affronted.

'Not at all,' he said. 'At least not any more.'

Just then Lucas's excited face appeared at the window before he burst into the shop.

'The most romantic thing *ever* has just happened in the gift shop,' he cried, fanning his face with his hand. 'I've got to tell you or I'll explode.'

Sam laughed. 'Now I *really* want to stay. Fearne, you have all the fun in this place but I must go; please excuse me, everyone.' He bent down to Scamp's bed to say goodbye and walked to the door. 'See you a week on Saturday.'

'Oh, I almost forgot!' He stopped and dug down into his back pocket. 'Remember I told you about that special rub I do?'

'Ooh?' Biddy's eyes twinkled. 'Like bowlers do with their cricket balls?'

Sam threw his head back and laughed. 'No, not quite.'

'Um, no I don't think I do,' I replied, willing my face not to flush under Biddy's curious gaze.

'I don't either but I'm all ears,' Lucas murmured, resting his forearms on the counter.

'For meat cooked on the barbeque?' Sam pulled out a parcel of aluminium foil. His face lit up, just as it had when he'd enthused about the honey. It was clear to see where his passion lay. 'I've been playing about with the flavours and thought you'd like to try some. This has got smoked paprika and ground chipotle chilli flakes in it. Here you go, honest feedback welcome.'

'Thank you, that's so sweet of you.' I took it from him. It was warm and bent where it had moulded itself to the shape of his body and a ripple of longing ran through me as I flattened it between my palms.

'I hope you like it,' he smiled again. 'Bye for now.'

'Goodbye!' Lucas and Biddy chimed.

'Bye, Sam,' I waved a hand as he left the shop and crossed the green towards his car.

Our barbecue hadn't been fired up since last summer. I'd invited the girls from the book club over and Freddie had joined us later and hoovered up everything we hadn't eaten. That had been a good day.

Biddy sighed. 'Goodness me. I wouldn't kick him out of bed for eating crackers.'

'Neither would I,' said Lucas wickedly, momentarily distracted from his story.

'Goodness me, Biddy,' I said pretending to be shocked. 'I thought you only had eyes for your animals.'

I was very fond of the pet shop owner; I'd assumed

she was single because she'd never mentioned anyone else and didn't wear a ring. But she certainly wasn't blind to Sam's charms.

'I've had my moments.' She patted her hair.

'Ooh and talking of moments,' gasped Lucas, 'can I just tell you what happened?'

Biddy bit her lip. 'Actually, I need some flowers and I'm in a bit of a rush; one of my piggies is due any moment. Guinea pig,' she clarified, seeing our blank expressions. 'Pregnant. Gorgeous thing, glossy dark hair and a lot to say for herself. Reminds me a bit of Rosie, perhaps I'll give her one of the babies as a present, tie a pink or blue ribbon around its neck.'

Just what every new mother needs, I thought.

Lucas patted her arm. 'Dear Biddy, you have a heart of gold, but another live creature in the house might not be the best gift for Rosie, although doubtless Noah and Hugo the dog will approve. No, I have a delightful line of Beatrix Potter soft animals, I'll give you a generous discount. Trust me, you can't go wrong with Peter Rabbit and Friends.'

Biddy looked surprised. 'Are you sure?'

'He's right, Biddy,' I said carefully. 'So. Flowers?'

'Yes please. I'm having supper with a friend. And I thought I'd take her some flowers. Nothing complicated . . . you know.' She gazed around the shop. I recognised that look. It was a *where do I start?* look.

I helped her choose some peonies and anemones.

'Let me wrap them,' Lucas insisted, heading for the drawer where we kept the ribbon. 'You'll be amazed at my triple bows.'

While Biddy was counting out the right money, I quickly selected a bunch of sweet-scented stocks.

'And these are for you, to say thank you for looking after Scamp the other day.' I handed them to her.

'Oh gosh. Any time!' She beamed shyly. 'These are divine. It's years since anyone gave me flowers. Used to have a bouquet from here every week. Not a *bunch* you understand, a *bouquet*.'

'So what changed?' I asked.

'Everything.' Biddy frowned and sighed and looked like she was in the middle of an internal battle. 'Oh, sod it. I might as well tell you, it was years ago now and it isn't as if I'd upset anybody by being indiscreet.'

Lucas looked up from curling ribbon with a pair of scissors. 'This story is in danger of outdoing mine. If I ever get the chance to tell it.'

'Ignore him, Biddy and do tell, it won't go any further, I promise.'

Biddy took a deep breath. 'For a while I had a lover. There, I've said it. I had a lover and he bought me flowers and for eighteen months I was the happiest woman in the world.'

Lucas punched the air. 'You go, girl!'

'And then?' I prompted.

'And then it was over,' she said flatly. 'We had it all planned. We were going to be together but disaster struck.'

'Oh no!' Lucas bit his lip. He joined us at the counter and folded his arms.

She leaned forward and I caught the smell of marrow-bone and rawhide dog chews on her clothes. 'Dementia.'

My heart melted for her. 'I'm sorry, Biddy. Did he . . . did he forget you?'

'Never,' she said stoutly. 'We could never forget each other, I'm sure of that. It was his wife who got dementia. She was a horrible bully. He came into my pet shop to see if I knew of anyone selling a kitten. He'd wanted someone to love, he'd said. Poor soul; I've kept chickens all my life and I'd never met anyone as henpecked as Nigel.'

'She sounds awful,' said Lucas crossly.

'I've never told anyone his name. And then whoosh, out it comes.' Biddy slapped a hand over her mouth, looking horrified.

I tapped the side of my nose. 'Don't think any more about it. Florists are the best keepers of secrets. I won't say a word.'

Lucas mimed zipping his lips. 'Ditto.'

Biddy blew out a shaky breath. 'Thank you. I know falling in love with a married man was wrong. It started off innocently enough and it took us both by surprise: I'd been single since a messy divorce and I was lonely and he was in a lonely marriage. We became friends and then one day out of the blue, Nina came round with the most beautiful flowers for me. The card said just 'from an admirer' but I knew it was him. And from then on . . .' She blushed daintily. 'Our romance blossomed. Happiest time of my life. Right up until she got ill.'

'Have you never been tempted to look him up, see how he is?' I asked.

She shook her head fervently. 'No. Wouldn't be fair. We made a clean break. He'd never leave her when she needed him. No matter how hard it was to live with her once she became ill. He'd never have forgiven himself.'

'He sounds like a dreamboat.' Lucas looked misty-eyed.

'He was.' Biddy reached into her pocket and fished out a tissue. 'But he was a *married* dreamboat and we were destined never to be together. Thank you for listening, both of you. But now, I'd better get back to the shop.'

With promises not to breathe a word to anyone, we waved her off and as she reached the door with her two bunches of flowers, Juliet, one of Rosie's staff appeared with two coffees in takeaway cups.

'Oh,' she said, looking at the three of us in disappointment. 'Is that sexy man-mountain of yours not here any more?'

'Sadly not,' I said, donating Sam's coffee to Lucas. 'But then he was never mine in the first place.'

And unless Pandora threw him out again, he was never likely to be either. Like Biddy's admirer, he was a married dreamboat, I thought glumly.

'My turn to tell a story!' Lucas piped up, taking a slurp at the coffee.

'I'd better not stop to listen,' said Juliet, promptly pausing to give Scamp some fuss. 'We're snowed under next door, hence taking so long with the coffees.'

Lucas pouted as Juliet marched back to the café.

I put my arm around his shoulder. 'I'm still listening, go on.'

'OK.' He brightened and gave a little shimmy. 'So this guy comes into the gift shop earlier and buys twelve cards with *I love you* on the front, all different. He's going to write a message to his girlfriend in each one, leaving clues on where to find the next card.'

'Like a treasure hunt?'

'Exactly!' He nodded with enthusiasm. 'And in the final card, he's going to ask her to marry him! How romantic is that?'

'Very,' I agreed.

'I suggested hiding the ring in one of the café's hand-made truffles, they do a heart-shaped one. He's in there now buying them, you'll see him come out in a minute. Oh, there he is!'

I looked out of the shop window to see a man with blond hair tied back in a ponytail and wearing a leather jacket head away from us.

Lucas ran to the door. 'Cooee!'

The man turned around and held up his parcel. 'Thanks for your help!'

'You're welcome, good luck!' Lucas shouted back.

The man pulled on a motorcycle helmet and my stomach gave an involuntary lurch; parked a few metres away at an angle to the kerb was a gleaming black and silver bike.

'Cute isn't he?' Lucas joined me at the window, leaning forward to get a better look.

'Hmm.' I forced myself not to turn away and tried to ignore the waves of fear inside me. 'Good luck to him. I hope she says yes.'

Lucas sighed dreamily. 'How could she refuse?'

There was a black Range Rover parked in front of the bike. Suddenly the red brake lights came on followed by the white reverse lights. My heart began to pound.

'What's that car doing?' I gasped.

The car began to creep backwards towards the motor-bike. The biker waved his arms at the driver. But the driver evidently didn't see anything because the car kept on coming. My heart was in my mouth as I heard the crunch of metal. The car stopped with a screech of brakes. The biker stared in horror at the mangled remains of his bike.

And then I was running. I was outside on the pavement banging on the driver's window.

'What the hell do you think you're doing?' I yelled. 'Don't you look behind you before you reverse?'

The door of the car was flung open and I had to jump out of its way. A blonde woman wearing huge sunglasses looked at me coolly and then brushed past me.

'Are you OK?' she asked the biker, joining him at the back of her car.

He was squatting down looking at his bike in dismay. 'I've had better days.'

'But you're not injured.' The woman sagged with relief, resting her hands on her thighs. She was wearing jeans, a strappy top and high heels.

'No thanks to you,' I yelled. 'If he'd been on that bike, you could have killed him.'

'But thankfully he wasn't,' said Lucas, appearing by my side. He put his arm around my shoulders, trying to console me.

But I'd gone too far to be soothed. All the anger, the terror and the grief inside me bubbled up to the surface and I shook free of him.

'He is about to propose to his girlfriend. His whole life ahead of him and you, you just casually reverse your massive car into him. You could have wiped out that life like that.' I snapped my fingers in her face.

'I'm fine, honestly.' The biker removed his helmet, he was pale and shaky. 'But thanks for your concern.'

'Get a car, please,' I begged him. 'For her, for your girlfriend so she doesn't have to live in fear of you having an accident.'

'I'll bear it in mind,' he said grimly.

'Oh please,' muttered the driver. 'What a drama queen.'

Her flippant tone sent my fury into overdrive.

'You haven't even said sorry,' I spluttered, squaring up to her. 'At least apologise to him.'

She drew herself up tall and whipped her sunglasses off. Fierce brown eyes burned into mine.

'No one has been hurt and quite frankly this is none of your business.' She took a step forward and prodded my chest. 'You are mad.'

'You're right there,' I replied furiously. 'In fact I'm livid. I'm calling the police.'

'Back off, lady,' she hissed.

'You, you . . . monster!' I gasped furiously.

'OK, petal, let's get you inside,' said Lucas firmly, gripping my arm.

Someone else appeared and took my other arm. It was Rosie. Between them they bundled me back into the shop where Scamp was waiting anxiously for me.

Rosie made me hot tea laced with sugar and Lucas stroked my hair.

'Want to talk about it?' he asked once my sobs had subsided.

I shook my head. How could I explain what I didn't even understand myself? I knew it was irrational, this fear I had of motorbikes. I'd always felt safe on the back of Freddie's bike but all my happy memories had been wiped out by the enduring image I had of his last, fatal ride. I hadn't even seen it for myself: I hadn't needed to; my imagination had created it for me and I couldn't envision a time when I'd ever feel any differently.

Chapter Twenty-four

The following week I arranged to speak to Nina on the phone. So far, we'd spoken mostly via text and email because of the eleven-hour time difference between us. But the cost of the flowers I was going to need to fulfil the Edelweiss order was so enormous that I'd wanted Nina's blessing before committing to it. It was morning here, and night where she was. It was lovely to hear her voice and she sounded in very good spirits.

'Just go for it,' she trilled down the phone. 'I trust you wholeheartedly.'

'Are you absolutely sure?' I said, wincing at the amount in the 'total' box on the screen. 'Last chance to back out.'

'Edelweiss have emailed their approval, haven't they?' Nina asked before hiccupping. I'd interrupted her having a drink with her new friends. I suspected it wasn't her first.

'Well, yes.'

'Press confirm and stop worrying about it. As the saying goes: you've got to speculate to accumulate.'

Even from over eleven thousand miles away, I could detect the new lightness to her voice. And not only because of the alcohol. Her time away from the business was definitely doing her good.

'OK, here goes.' I tapped the 'confirm' button, committing us to the largest amount of flowers the shop had ever bought for a single event. 'Let's hope this is the start of our accumulation phase.'

I had butterflies in my stomach; I felt the weight of responsibility passing from Nina to me as I took the company bank card out of the drawer and typed in the number.

I kept thinking about what Nina had said about corporate flowers being for 'faceless' people. Of course Marcia at the Claybourne Hotel was a real person and I had already been paid the deposit. But I hadn't actually spoken to anyone at Edelweiss and although I'd had a prompt response to my email I still felt nervous about it. I tried to explain this to her but she was only half listening; it sounded like someone was topping up her drink in the background.

'Did you always meet your clients face-to-face in your last job before doing a market research project for them?'

'No. You're right,' I admitted. Perhaps I was being over cautious. 'I just want to do a good job for you.'

'*Are you kidding me!*' she shrieked. 'Thanks to you I'm in New Zealand for six weeks while it's business as usual for Nina's Flowers. There's no way any of this could have been possible without you. You've made my dream come true. Well, between you and Freddie. If you hadn't told me about the lovely letter he wrote to you, I'd never have had the balls to actually go ahead with this. I'm finally doing what makes me happy and I'm so proud of myself.'

My heart skipped for her. 'Oh, that reminds me, talking of letters, Biddy was telling me about her romantic past. Can you remember her receiving a weekly bouquet for a while?'

Biddy's story had really stuck with me, so much so that I'd spent the last two evenings going through every single one of Nina's old order books to take a glimpse at the messages he wrote to her for myself. But I hadn't been able to find anything which matched what she'd told me.

'Yes, I do,' she said thoughtfully. 'It was early on, probably during the first year of me opening the florist's. The whole thing was utterly romantic. The first note was something about her bringing sunshine into his life. She cried when she got the first bouquet. And they got steadily more intimate. He told her that he counted down the days until he saw her again, that she'd always own a piece of his heart, that he dreamed of the day he could wake up and the first thing he saw would be her. The loveliest one brought tears to my eyes; it said something like her smile was his sunrise, her eyes his stars, and her heart the centre of his world.'

No wonder Biddy was heartbroken when it ended. Imagine having a love as intense as that and losing it.

'Goodness, I don't think anyone has felt like that about me,' I said.

'Me neither. Anyway, this went on for months. And then one day he wrote that even though they could never be together, he'd never stop loving her. And that was the last I ever heard from him. It nearly broke my heart delivering that final bouquet.'

Poor Biddy. At least the reason the love affair finished was because he'd decided to do the honourable thing and stick by his sick wife.

'What was he like?'

'I never met him. That was the weird thing. He used to drop an envelope of cash through the shop letter box along with a handwritten note. Whoever he was, he was a beautiful letter writer. I used to look forward to getting them to read first and then once I delivered the flowers, just knowing that Biddy had received that romantic message

253

used to make my day. Biddy has never said a word. Not one word of explanation. I've always wondered. Why do you ask?'

'She mentioned it the other day, that was all and I was intrigued.'

So that was why I hadn't found any records, because there weren't any. I'd had some vague notion of somehow trying to track him down via his credit card details. Just as well; it would probably have been breaking a dozen data protection laws anyway.

'What else has been happening in my absence?' Nina wanted to know.

'Besides making a fruit and vegetable-themed coffin spray and planning a flower workshop for a cricket team?' I said airily. 'Not much.'

'A what?'

She snorted with laughter and gasped in delight as I filled her in on what I'd been up to.

One of Wendy's staff had collected the arrangement for Mrs Benton-Ridley's funeral yesterday (from the look on his face he'd never seen anything like it), and Sam had called in again yesterday evening to confirm numbers for the cricket team workshop this coming Saturday night and paid a deposit of twenty-five pounds per head. And then of course, the big event at the Claybourne Hotel.

True to his word, Victor had been really helpful, and yesterday when he made our delivery, I'd gone over my list of requirements with him and he'd made a few suggestions to save me a bit of money. Just as well, because any more and I'd have wiped the bank account out completely.

'And as well as everything else,' I said, 'I'm thinking of doing a customer newsletter.'

She interrupted me with a burp. 'Oh excuse me. We are staying on this apple and pear and cherry orchard farm thing today and they keep giving us cider.'

That explained a lot, I thought fondly. 'Sounds fun. Lucas wants to know whether you've met any hot farmers yet?'

'There are farmers everywhere you look here. Well, one every few acres anyway. The ones on the show are a mixed bunch. My favourite, but not in a sexy way, is Ralph. Massive arms, short legs and grunts a lot. Then there's Pete, who addresses our chests instead of our faces. Then little Scott who trembles and blushes when a woman comes near him, definitely a thirty-five-year-old virgin. I'm going to take him under my wing, help him out.'

I was going to ask what she meant by that but her snort told me all I needed to know.

'Any romance in the air?' I asked.

'Nah, not so far.' She hiccupped again. 'Although Eric the sound man is cute and makes me laugh. But I don't think getting together with a member of the film crew is quite in keeping with the spirit of the show.'

'Maybe not. But I'm glad you're enjoying it enough to stick the whole six weeks.'

'God yes! Easily. I used to think people were mad doing a gap year, living in the same three scruffy outfits, all their belongings stuffed into a fusty-smelling rucksack. But I get it now. Now I'm wondering how they can give it up and return to normal life after a year. I'm not sure I'll be able to.'

My ears pricked up. 'But you *are* coming back, aren't you?'

She gave a high-pitched laugh. 'Yeah, yeah. Don't worry, I'm just talking hyper-theo-pathetically.'

'Easy for you to say.'

'I think I've had enough cider now.' She giggled. 'Being a florist is part retailer, part therapist. It makes a refreshing change to concentrate solely on myself for a while. I'd forgotten what I was like.'

'You're fab. And I miss you,' I said, realising with a jolt just how true that was.

'Aw, thanks. Listen, I'd better go, someone is playing guitar around the campfire and I want to go and join in.'

'Have fun!'

It was only after I ended the call that I noticed that she hadn't said how much she missed me. And that nervous laugh when I mentioned coming back didn't go unnoticed either. Still, I was happy here. If she did extend her stay, the worst that would happen was that I'd have to work on my own for a while longer. I was sure I could manage that.

I didn't have much time to dwell on Nina's intentions, I was too busy keeping the flowery wheels of commerce turning in her absence. For the rest of the morning, I worked solidly, dealing with customers and, in every spare moment, putting together the first customer newsletter to go out to everyone who'd left their email address with us in the past.

At lunchtime, I was about to lock the door and take Scamp for a walk when the phone rang.

'Nina's Flowers, Fearne here, how can I help?' I said, sending Scamp a look of apology as he settled patiently back in his bed.

There was a long pause on the end of the line.

'Did you say Nina's Flowers?' He sounded confused. 'Or Fearne?'

'Both.'

'Gosh.' There was another pause, followed by, 'Good grief. It's been years since. Gracious me.'

'Is everything all right?' I asked.

'Yes, yes.' He cleared his throat. 'Sorry. That took me by surprise for a second. I asked the funeral director for your number to thank you for the flowers – well, garden arrangement – you did for my wife yesterday. Using fruit and vegetables might not be to everyone's taste, but it suited her perfectly.'

'Mr Benton-Ridley!' I said, realising who it was at last.

'Call me Nigel, please.' There was warmth in his voice as he spoke. 'Benton-Ridley is such a mouthful.'

'You're very welcome. It was a privilege to do something so special and personal. I hope the service went . . . well, or as well as it could do.' My voice trailed off.

That was possibly one of the most superfluous pieces of polite conversation in the English language. *You know yesterday when you watched the person you love most in the world disappear from sight forever in a coffin? Did it go well?* I'd hated that sort of comment in the weeks after Freddie died; I should have known better.

'It was a fitting send-off,' said Mr Benton-Ridley, coming to my rescue. 'Just a small gathering. She didn't have any family and she could be a difficult woman, she'd never been one for friends. As her Alzheimers took an ever firmer grip on her mind she lost contact with the few friends she did have. I did my best to keep her happy and calm . . . anyway, she's at peace now.'

I heard the tremor in his voice and my heart went out to him. 'You must be in need of a rest yourself.'

'Looking after Val has taken every spare minute for the last four years, I'm going to try and remember what I used to like doing. Anyway, I've taken enough of your time.

I just wanted to thank you. And I'm sorry if I sounded confused when you answered the phone, the name of the florist's threw me for a moment. A blast from the past.'

He laughed awkwardly and I had a sudden thought. *Nigel.* A wife with Alzheimers. It couldn't be, could it?

'Have you shopped with us before, then?' I thought back to the database. There were hundreds of names on it but I'd have remembered a Benton-Ridley. But then if he always paid in cash, it wouldn't be.

'I . . . Yes.' His voice was barely audible.

My breath caught, goose pimples instantly covering my arms.

'Funny that your name didn't come up on our database.'

He didn't respond straight away and when he did his voice was shaky. 'There used to be a pet shop nearby.'

My heart thumped against my ribs; it was him. 'There still is. Biddy still owns it.'

'I wonder . . .' He hesitated and in that space I could almost feel how torn he was; the guilt and the joy and the hope.

'Yes . . .?' I prompted eagerly.

'Nigel? You on the phone? There's a lady at the door with a casserole,' I heard a female voice in the background. It sounded like his sister who'd been at the undertaker's with him. The one who hadn't seemed overly fond of Nigel's wife.

'Thanks again,' said Nigel, hurriedly.

'Well, you know where we are,' I said quickly as he ended the call.

Had he been on the verge of asking me to give Biddy a message, I wondered, or even better sending her some flowers? I made a note of his number and typed it into the new database. Should I tell Biddy that his wife had passed away, or should I leave Nigel to make his overture towards her in his own time? The latter, I decided; this wasn't my story, it was theirs and if Nigel no longer felt the same way about Biddy, she'd have her hopes raised only to have them dashed again.

At ten o'clock that night I put clean sheets on the bed and dived under the covers, sighing with pleasure at the unique sensation that only fresh bedding can deliver.

Scamp took my sigh as an invitation and scooted up closer until I could feel his hot breath on my arm.

'You do know that sleeping on my bed is only a temporary arrangement, don't you?' I said. I didn't know how he did it, but he seemed to make himself double in length and girth at night-time and he took up far more than fifty per cent of the space.

Scamp opened one eye and gave me a smug look.

I laughed and stroked his ears. 'I guess I'll just have to hope that when I meet the man of my dreams, he likes dogs.'

As I turned out the bedside light and my mind started to quieten, I couldn't help but wonder who exactly was the man of my dreams? An image of someone with golden hair, gentle eyes and a warm laugh popped into my head and I squeezed my eyes shut. Biddy had fallen in love with a man who couldn't be hers and if I wasn't careful, I could end up making the same mistake.

Chapter Twenty-five

I sat on a stool behind the counter hugging my knees happily, watching Sam unload his car. It was the Saturday evening of the cricket club workshop; I didn't think I'd looked forward to anything quite so much for months. All the other shops had closed up for the weekend except for Ken's Mini Mart on the other side of the green, where Sam had just been to stock up.

I'd been hoping for a warm balmy evening so that we could have all the doors open. But despite being mid-June, the temperature had dropped and we'd had rain earlier. Now a brooding sky meant we had to have all the shop lights on. The weather didn't seem to have had any impact on Sam's choice of outfit; a T-shirt and cargo shorts which showed off his toned arms and legs and broad chest and in the dove grey light, his tan looked deeper than ever.

'Have you got enough booze, do you think?' I teased as he carried in a second case of beers from the boot of his car.

He'd already proudly laid out a selection of artisan snacks in the back of the shop, talking me through each one. There was a platter of serrano ham and various different salamis, dishes of olives and cheese and nuts, all very upmarket. It looked like the scene was being set for a party rather than a flower-arranging session.

'I hope so,' he said, pulling a face. 'I'll be in trouble if we haven't. The only drivers are me and Tom. The other eight will put these away and all the food.'

Of the squad of fourteen, only ten could make it this evening, which was probably just as well; it was going to be a squash around the table as it was. Even now when it was just Sam here, I was acutely aware of his maleness; goodness knows how it was going to feel with ten men like him in the shop. Rather nice, probably, I thought, smiling to myself.

'And I thought cricket was all polite clapping and cucumber sandwiches,' I said.

He raised an amused eyebrow. 'Everyone thinks because we look so smart in our whites and we all sit down to tea together nicely with the other side, that we're perfect gentlemen. When in truth, we can drink your average rugby team under the table.'

He set the beer down on the floor and brushed his hair back off his face. I tried not to stare at the little dimple on his cheek or the golden stubble which highlighted his strong jaw, or the way the muscles in his back rippled beneath his shirt when he bent to stroke Scamp. I wondered instead whether Pandora, despite her exploits with 'sexy tiger' knew how lucky she was to have this handsome, capable, full-of-fun man in her life. I hoped so.

'So you're not gentlemen?' I feigned shock. 'I'm spending the evening with a bunch of hooligans? *Now* you tell me!'

'Don't worry, I'll make sure no one gets out of hand.'

The earnest look on his face made my heart squeeze; this man was so caring and thoughtful.

'I'm not in the least bit worried.' I turned away from him in case my expression gave my feelings away and went to the big old wooden chest where we kept supplies. I took out all the scissors and secateurs we had and distributed them along the table. 'They'll have their hands full of flowers so they won't be able to drink much.'

'Flower arranging, who'd have thought it.' Sam grinned and rested his hands on his hips, surveying the room. I watched him take it all in: the flowers set out in containers, the jute bags I'd bought in specially, the ribbon, the tissue paper. 'I've known most of the lads since I was at school. Somehow we've become middle-aged without noticing.'

'What do they all do?'

'Apart from being particularly terrible at cricket? Did I tell you that by the way?' he confessed. 'What we lack in expertise we make up for in enthusiasm.'

'Sounds like my floristry skills.'

'*Now* you tell me,' he said, mimicking my earlier comment.

'Oi.' I flapped a cloth at him.

He jumped back, laughing and lifted his hands in defence. 'Joke! They do all sorts: there are a couple of builders, a gardener, a surveyor, a PE teacher – that's Tom, who's driving them all here in the school minibus – a journalist and a lawyer.'

I blinked at him. 'Gosh. I'm quite nervous now.'

Teaching Sam had been fun but a big group of them was a whole different ball game. Why had I agreed to it? Oh yes, because Sam had asked me and I had a feeling I could never say no to Sam.

'Don't be. They'll love you,' he reassured me. 'None of them can arrange flowers to save their lives, so no matter what you do, you are the expert in their eyes. *Our* eyes. And whatever we produce is guaranteed to impress our ladies.'

I tweaked a guard petal off a rose and folded it between my fingers. 'Is everyone making bouquets for their wife or girlfriend?'

262

He offered me a plump green olive and I took it, savouring the salty sourness. 'I think so. Although Mikey is single, so who knows. Actually, he's the only one you might have to watch after a couple of drinks.'

I smiled. 'Why's that?'

He popped a handful of nuts in his mouth and bent down to give Scamp some fuss. 'Because he goes for the pretty ones.'

'Oh.' My heart skipped a beat and I felt the heat rise to my face but before I could think of a witty reply, a car horn sounded outside and a minibus pulled up alongside the kerb.

'They're here.' Sam reached the door in three long strides, catching hold of Scamp's collar before opening the door. He turned back to me. 'Ready for this?'

I pretended to roll up my sleeves and grinned. 'Let's do it.'

As expected, the evening was loud, messy and a lot of fun and I was enjoying every second of it. As the noise levels had risen steadily so had the temperature in the shop. I propped open the back door and took in lungfuls of cool damp air.

'Getting rowdy, are we?' Tom the PE teacher looked over, concerned. 'Some of these lads are worse than my year nines.'

'Only in a good way,' I replied, reassuring him.

Despite Sam's jokes earlier about heavy drinking, the cricket players behaved impeccably. They alternated between teasing each other, bemoaning their own efforts and secretly getting a kick out of how well they were all doing. Scamp was happy too, mooching about under the table for any dropped morsels.

As well as making his own arrangement, Sam was doing a great job of helping me: clearing up empty beer bottles, sweeping the floor every so often to get rid of the debris from stripped and snipped stems and rushing to get cloths when the inevitable spillages occurred.

So far Mikey was my favourite. He was quiet and earnest and determined to master spiralling the stems properly. I'd spent at least ten minutes helping him to work out where to place the flowers and not once did I get the impression that he was a flirt as Sam had implied. He didn't have a girlfriend, he confided, but his mum always came to watch the cricket matches and she'd volunteered to make the tea tomorrow, so he was going to give the flowers to her.

'Come along if you like?' He had a boyish face, dark curly hair and friendly eyes which crinkled when he smiled.

I'd never been to a cricket match, but the idea of spending Sunday afternoon in a deckchair watching this lot enjoy themselves had a certain appeal and I knew Scamp would enjoy being in the fresh air.

'I might just do that,' I replied. 'But only if the sun shines.'

He made a fist and I bumped mine against his.

'Date,' he said with a grin.

'You're not wasting any time, Mikey,' said Sam, appearing between us. He slapped his friend on his back.

I wondered if Pandora and the children would be at the match. If I saw Sam with his family, as a father and a husband, it might help cement him in my head as purely friend material. It had to be worth a try, I thought, feeling his gaze on me.

'I've just been invited to the cricket tomorrow,' I said brightly. 'What do you think? Shall I come?'

Sam's eyes flicked to Mikey's briefly and he shook his head. 'You'd be bored. And if the weather stays like this, it'll be cold.'

'Oh. Well as I said, I might come, weather permitting,' I said, disappointed. Sam clearly didn't want me there. Perhaps he was simply trying to warn me off Mikey, although he seemed perfectly charming to me.

'Speak for yourself, Diamond!' Tom pretended to be insulted. 'Come along, Fearne, my top spin has to be seen to be believed. Besides, my wife will be there and she'll enjoy having someone new to talk to, to stave off the . . . er . . .'

'Boredom?' Sam finished for him and we all laughed.

This camaraderie was something I missed, I realised. Summer evenings in Pineapple Road had meant parties for Freddie and me. We'd decide late on Saturday afternoon to invite a few people over and before we knew it, a party was in full swing. We had a garden shed that we'd converted into a Tiki bar and even though our garden was tiny, it became known as party central for our friends. Even Ethel had been known to join us for a tipple, with Scamp of course. I had very fond memories of her showing Freddie and Hamish how to do the quickstep to a Foo Fighters track. I thought about that parcel of foil sitting in my fridge with Sam's special barbeque rub in it. It was time to let laughter back into the house . . .

Sam murmured in my ear. 'You OK?'

My eyes were shining with tears. Everyone was looking at me. I ruffled my hair, trying to hide behind it.

'I am actually!' I said, smiling. 'Now, how is everyone doing? Are you ready to tie your bouquets?'

'No!' said Archie plaintively. 'How did you get the surface of yours to be all spherical?'

I made my way around the table, relieved to escape the attention. 'Don't worry, everything is fixable.'

'Except Tom's nose,' Richard sniggered. 'That's past redemption.'

'Hey,' Tom retorted, covering his nose with his hand. To be honest it did look as if it had been in the wars once or twice. 'This is the nose of a multi-discipline sportsman.'

'Yeah,' said Sam, 'there isn't a single sport in which Tom hasn't managed to end up in a crumpled heap.'

Everyone laughed and the mood lifted again.

I focused on Archie's bouquet; it did look a bit ragged, his line flowers sticking out and his focal flowers bunched up together.

'Come here and look at your reflection,' I beckoned him to the mirror.

Someone started singing 'here comes the bride' as Archie posed in front of the mirror, clasping his hands in front of him.

Henry took his phone out and took a photo. 'One for the album.'

'See these rabbit ears?' I touched the matching stems of lisianthus he'd put each side of the arrangement. 'Maybe move one of them to the front. Then space out the big roses a bit more.'

'Got it,' Archie beamed proudly. 'That looks professional now.'

'Watch out, Fearne,' said Henry. 'He'll be after a job next.'

The banter continued for a bit longer until I gave them a five-minute deadline to finish their bouquets which sent them into such a mad flap that I couldn't stop myself from giggling. Then I showed them how to secure the stems with string and trim them to length. Soon the gift boxes were assembled, the flowers wrapped and the cellophane bags filled with water and everyone was choosing cards to write their own personal messages.

'Anyone got a spare pen?' Mikey asked, shaking the one I'd given him which appeared to have dried up.

'There are plenty under the counter.' I strode through the archway to fetch some.

Archie slurped the dregs of his drink. 'And are there any more beers, Sam?'

Sam slapped him on the back. 'Luckily for you, I stashed some emergency tinnies away.'

He headed in my direction just as I bent to look on the shelf under the counter for more pens. I straightened quickly, aware that there wasn't much room behind here.

'Excuse me.' Sam sucked his stomach in, touching my waist as he passed by. The move was ineffectual; he had a flat stomach anyway. I breathed in and caught the scent of him: fresh air and summer rain.

'You smell nice.' The words were out before I could stop them.

'Ditto. You smell of flowers. Even your hair smells of flowers.'

'Funny that.' I smiled, conscious that he hadn't moved past me. We were almost touching, my body so close to his that I could feel his heat. 'You have white paint in your hair.'

'You sure that's not just my natural highlights?' He felt his hair but missed the clump of paint stuck near his temple.

'I'm sure. Here.' I took his hand and placed his fingertips over the dried paint. 'Can you feel it?'

He cast his eyes down to where my shirt brushed against his T-shirt and looked up again, locking eyes with me. 'Yes,' he murmured softly.

I could hardly breathe; I knew this could go nowhere, I knew I shouldn't be feeling this way, but my body was betraying me, every nerve-ending attuned to his presence.

'Good.' I stepped aside, flustered suddenly.

'Wait,' he caught my hand. 'You have something in your hair now.'

I laughed. 'Oh, so *I* have natural highlights.'

'No, it's yellow.' He moved in closer, squinting. 'I think it's pollen.'

'That'll be the lilies. Occupational hazard.' I raised my hand to my hair at the same time as him and our hands touched. I allowed my fingers to brush his, just for a moment, but it was enough to send my pulse racing.

'Here.' He passed me a tissue from the box on the counter.

We both laughed nervously, smiling at each other. We were close, *very* close. *He was married*, I told myself. *He loves Pandora.* I tried to move away, to put some distance between us but I couldn't, I was frozen to the spot. The air around us was charged. Did he feel it too?

Chapter Twenty-six

The moment lengthened between us; my heart thumping so loudly, I could hear it in my ears.

'Where's that beer?' shouted Archie suddenly.

'And my pen?' Mikey added.

A look of disappointment flashed across Sam's face. 'We'd better . . . um.'

'Yes, definitely.' I jolted myself back into action and laughed awkwardly.

Before either of us moved, someone banged on the glass of the shop window, making us both jump.

'Hold on!' I called, pressing up against Sam's chest as I squeezed by. 'I should have put a notice saying *private party* on the door.'

'I CAN SEE YOU IN THERE!' a woman's voice shouted through the glass. There was a blur of movement as whoever it was moved from the window to the shop door.

'Oh rats,' Sam muttered. 'Now I'm in trouble.'

'Why? What's the matter?'

'My wife has turned up,' he said with a sigh. 'That's what. I recognise her dulcet tones.'

I stared at the figure through the glass as I crossed the shop floor. Her hands were shielding her eyes so she could see in. A tight black outfit, blonde hair wound into a bun with sunglasses perched into it. I groaned inwardly and slowed my pace.

It was the woman who'd reversed into the motorbike last week. The one I'd yelled at like a banshee. Sam's wife.

In my head I'd built a picture of a demanding, spoiled princess who twisted her long-suffering husband around her little finger. Now I could add selfish, unapologetic and unobservant to the list.

'Are you going to open this door?' Pandora yelled. 'Or do I have to smash the glass with my shoe.'

'I'm coming!' I raced to the door to unlock it before she started to batter at it with her footwear.

Sam quickly dumped the beers and pens on the work table for his friends, whose heads had all swivelled in our direction.

'Busted, mate,' said someone with a chuckle.

'Yeah,' I heard him mutter, as he made his way back towards me. 'Party could be over for me.'

In my haste, my fingers fumbled but finally I got the door open.

Her dark eyes narrowed. 'You again. Well, well, well.'

'Come in,' I said, trying to keep my voice neutral. I stepped back to let her past.

Pandora stalked in, her jaw set like granite. Her perfume was so strong that it completely overpowered an entire shopful of flowers.

'I was going to introduce you,' said Sam lightly. 'But of course, you two ladies will have met when Fearne delivered your flowers.'

He approached his wife and attempted to kiss her. She side-stepped him, leaning back as if trying to dodge a wasp.

'Er, no, actually.' Pandora wet her lips.

I raised an eyebrow, sending her a silent message: *and which bouquet is he referring to?*

'I think it was your son who answered the door when

I delivered the flowers,' I told Sam, turning away from Pandora, who'd gone a little pale. 'He was very polite.'

'That sounds like Will.' Sam smiled proudly.

Pandora adjusted her sunglasses and pursed her lips.

'*She* and I met on the pavement outside,' she said sourly. 'She screamed her head off at me and caused a scene.'

'Really?' Sam looked at me bemused. 'Why on earth—?'

'I didn't realise you were Sam's wife then,' I said, feeling the heat rise to my face. I was annoyed at the way Pandora uttered 'she' as if somehow I was in the wrong. 'And I'm sorry we got off on the wrong footing but I'm afraid it doesn't alter how I feel. You were at the wheel and not paying attention to where you were going.'

Pandora rolled her eyes. 'I was scarcely moving. I wouldn't have hit the bike at all if that mobile phone holder wasn't so fiddly. I can never get it in properly.'

'You had an accident?' Sam looked horrified. 'Dear God. Was anyone hurt? Were the kids in the car?'

'No, there was hardly a scratch on the car. And stop fussing, Dad has sorted it all out.' Pandora tutted irritably and inspected her fingernails. They were painted a nude colour which matched her lipstick. '*She* blew the whole thing out of proportion.'

'Fearne. My name is Fearne.' I felt my hackles rise but offered to shake her hand. She gave me a withering look and ignored me.

'Anyway, all of that is irrelevant,' she said, folding her arms and glaring at Sam. 'Now that I've discovered your little secret. You and *Fearne*. It all makes sense now.'

My heart skipped a beat. Had she seen us behind the counter, I wondered, standing closer than we should have been? I glanced at Sam who looked so apologetic and awkward I could have hugged him.

Scamp padded over to her, wagging his tail and jumped up at her legs. She pushed him down and wiped her hands on her jeans. I clicked my fingers to tell him to go back to his bed and he wandered off dejectedly.

Sam inhaled a breath. 'Yeah, sorry about that, but it was only a little white lie.'

'Really?' Her laugh was harsh. '*Your mum* is looking good these days.'

The look she gave me could have stripped paint. The cricket team had gone quiet in the back but now Tom joined us in the front of the shop. 'Hey Pandora, looking gorgeous as usual.'

'Thank you.' She shot him an icy smile.

'Want a beer, Panda?' Mikey added, poking his head around the archway.

Pandora bristled. 'No, thank you. And it's Pan*dora*, please.'

Mikey pulled a face. 'Sorry.'

'Look, love, I only told you I was taking Mum out for dinner because this was meant to be a surprise,' Sam gestured behind him where the rest of his team mates sat in front of their flower arrangements. They waved awkwardly. 'We're doing flowers to give the wives and girlfriends at the match tomorrow. To say thank you for supporting us all season.'

She eyed him warily and a faint flush rose to her cheeks. Probably guilt, I thought, remembering what Sam had said about her lack of help with the cricket teas.

'I knew you were lying all along.' She shook her head slowly. 'I knew when you turned up with those flowers that you couldn't have arranged them yourself.'

'I did!' he protested in disbelief. 'I promise. Fearne taught me.'

'It's true,' I confirmed. 'Sam wanted to do something special for you.'

'Oh. I see,' Pandora sneered, folding her arms. A collection of gold bangles tinkled on her wrist. 'A one to one session was it? How . . . romantic.'

'No!' he said crossly. 'Well, yes, but it wasn't like that.'

'It was all perfectly above board,' I explained, not liking the insinuation. 'Sam put the bouquet together for you while the shop was open and I was serving other customers.'

Sort of. But Pandora wasn't listening to me.

'And then I got a second bunch,' she said triumphantly, tilting her chin. 'Guilt, I realised. It had to be. You've gone from giving me crappy petrol-station flowers to two expensive bouquets. So I came up here to see what was so interesting at the florist's all of a sudden. And hey presto, what do I find but the mad woman here, with her road rage and badly manicured fingernails.'

I curled my nails into my fists and not because I was ashamed of them. I wasn't a violent person, but I wasn't sure how much more I could take from Pandora Diamond. The air in the shop was almost quivering with tension. Sam looked furious.

'OK, Pandora, stop.' He held his hands up. 'Fearne *did* help me put a bouquet together. But there was nothing underhand about it. And as for tonight, the rest of the lads fancied having a go themselves so we arranged for Fearne to run a workshop for us all. That's it. I've got nothing to hide.'

He stepped closer to me and leaned on the end of the counter. 'Fearne, I'm sorry you've been caught up in this, you've been nothing but accommodating and kind.'

I shot him a smile. 'It's fine.'

It wasn't fine; I wanted Pandora out of my shop.

His wife harrumphed. 'Dress it up how you like, Sam Diamond, but you lied to me. You knew how much I wanted to go out with the other students on my yoga course tonight.'

'Sam said you were doing a weekly yoga course,' I said slyly. 'That sounds energetic.'

She glared at me suspiciously and carried on. 'But when I asked you to babysit you made up a ridiculous lie about your mother.'

'I'm sorry about that but you only asked today,' Sam explained wearily. 'This was in the diary first. I couldn't cancel my plans.'

'Ha.' She threw her hands up in the air. '*First*. That sums you up. Always putting yourself first.'

I looked from Sam to Pandora. My heart was thumping. I hated this. I couldn't bear to hear them fighting. The years fell away and I was a little girl again, hiding under the dining table holding Freddie's hand, listening to Mum and Dad arguing with each other.

I'd heard people talk about staying together for the sake of the children. But the best thing my parents did for us was to separate; make new lives for themselves. Freddie and I might have lost touch with Dad but Mum had blossomed without having to live in an unhappy home, and so, eventually had we. I looked down at my own hand, wishing Freddie's was curled around it now and a tear pooled in my eye.

'Wow.' Sam gave a low whistle. 'I don't know how you can say that and still keep a straight face.'

She rolled her eyes. 'Oh please, not the Saint Sam speech again.'

I wanted to shout at Pandora, yell that it was she who was the liar, but I couldn't bring myself to do it. *What happens in the florist, stays in the florist*; I could hear Nina's voice as clearly as if she was in the room. But Pandora had crossed the line: not only was she the one in the wrong, but she was trying to turn the tables on Sam.

'Sometimes I think you only wanted to give our marriage another shot because I'm a convenient babysitter.' Sam's face was set like stone.

Pandora gasped. 'Oh my God. Are you saying you resent spending time with your own children?'

He gritted his teeth. 'You're twisting my words. I love them to bits; I've certainly seen more of them than I have of you in the last few weeks.'

She began pacing up and down the shop. 'I've heard it all now. There I am, studying hard, trying to build a career for myself because you're always moaning that you can't afford our lifestyle. We can't afford the kids' school, I can't have a new car. Blah blah blah.'

An idea hit me suddenly: I couldn't say anything, but if Sam *happened to see* the order from another man to his wife, then I wouldn't have done wrong, would I?

I pulled the order book from under the counter, flipping back the pages to the date in question. It was easy to remember because it had been Nina's last day in the florist's. Sam's team mates had abandoned their pretence of not eavesdropping and were hovering, grim-faced in the front half of the shop.

'I'm going to ask you a question now and I want the truth.' Sam caught hold of his wife's hand. 'Do you still love me?'

She glared at him, saying nothing, which to me said everything.

'Perhaps you should take this outside,' Tom said softly to Sam, resting a hand on his shoulder.

'I need to know.' Sam shrugged him off. 'Pandora. Yes or no?'

The silence was oppressive and then she swallowed, looking down at their linked hands.

'We were good for a while, Sam.'

He smiled sadly, letting her hand drop away.

'But you don't love me,' he murmured.

She said nothing, checking the screen on her phone instead.

'So why ask me to come back?' He stared at her, confused and hurt. 'Why let me do all that work around the house, painting, decorating, gardening? Giving me false hope?'

'I thought we could make a go of it for the children. But we can't; we want different things and now of course, there's her.' She nodded in my direction. 'Sorry, I don't buy it; you're clearly having an affair with her. You were all over her when I banged on the window. I want a divorce.'

'For heaven's sake, Pandora.' Sam raised his hands to his face and swore under his breath.

'What?' She pouted. 'You can't expect me to sit back and take it. And look on the bright side; at least the house is ready for sale.'

'Marriage vows are sacred,' I said fiercely. 'Whether they are mine or not I would never break them. *Never*. The bigger question is, would you?'

'You stay out of it,' she spat.

Sam turned to me, lines of sadness etched into his face. 'Fearne, I can't apologise enough.'

My pulse quickening, I grabbed a pen and circled the order showing the address of his family home and nudged the book towards him. His eyes followed my pen but his face didn't register anything.

'I'm sorry, lads,' Sam began, his body language defeated.

I circled the details again, more firmly this time and tapped the pen to attract his attention.

'I think we should probably go home and . . . *what*?' His jaw dropped as his attention was finally caught by the order book. He blinked at the page.

'That's our address. Gareth Weaver, your ex?' he gasped in disbelief. His eyes widened as he read on. 'A great *night*, your sexy tiger . . . Pandora? What the hell? Are you seeing Gareth behind my back?'

His eyes blazed at his wife and she froze, horror-struck. Her mouth flapped open and closed like a suffocating goldfish.

'And you have the nerve to accuse me?' Anger was coming off him in waves.

'Sam,' Pandora stuttered, laughing nervously 'it was just a bit of fun, he—'

'Save it.' His lips curled in disgust. He flipped the book shut without looking at anyone and strode to the door. 'I don't want to know.'

He slammed the door behind him. Pandora yanked it open and ran after him, calling his name but he didn't turn around.

I collapsed onto a stool and tried to catch my breath. My heart was knocking so hard against my ribs that I hardly heard the rest of the cricket team take their flowers and say their goodbyes.

Once the shop was empty I sank down beside Scamp's basket. I breathed out the tension I'd been holding and tried to ignore the trembling in my chest. My dog looked up at me with his gentle brown eyes and let out a little puff of breath as if he was relieved that everyone had gone.

I knew how he felt, but had I done the right thing? Or had I interfered in something that was none of my business?

I'd definitely broken a client's confidence and in so doing, I might also have broken Sam's marriage. I wouldn't be going to the cricket match tomorrow; in fact, it was probably best if I didn't see Sam again for a very long time.

Chapter Twenty-seven

'Long time no see, big brother. I've missed you.'

My voice was low, but it needn't have been; it was nine o' clock on Sunday morning and the cemetery was still deserted. Even at this early hour, the sun was getting warm. The moisture on the grass after yesterday's rain was rising as steam, giving a suitably eerie mistiness to the air.

I traced Freddie's name on the headstone with my fingertips and I felt the pain of his loss like a physical ache in my sternum. I hadn't been to visit his grave since the day after I'd found his letter; it felt good to be here again, connecting with him, as if by sharing my news, he was somehow still part of my life.

I picked up the vase which stood just below his headstone. The flowers I'd left here back in March had long since disappeared and I tipped out dried bits of leaf. I took it to the tap, washed it out and refilled it with clean water, yawning to myself. I'd watched the clock for most of the night, unable to sleep and it was almost a relief when Scamp had insisted on getting up at six to pay a visit out to the back garden. After that I'd made tea and sat outside with him, brooding over the incident with Pandora and Sam in front of his friends.

Before locking up the shop last night, I'd collected some of the leftover flowers from the workshop and gathered them into a posy. And now here I was, arranging them on my brother's grave.

'I'd give anything for a proper chat,' I murmured. 'Just a bit of reassurance that I'm not a terrible person. But you'll just have to listen instead.'

Scamp had settled on the path nearby, his chin resting on his front paws. Poor dog; he wasn't having the best of days either. Ethel's house had been sold and the new occupants, a couple in their twenties with a little girl, had arrived noisily at the crack of dawn. I'd left Scamp inside and gone out to say hello and they told me they'd be here for a few hours taking measurements for curtains and furniture. Poor Scamp had sat and howled at the window, confused by the intruders in his old home.

I knelt down on the damp grass and unwrapped the brown paper from the flowers, spreading them out so I could select each stem easily.

'You'd really like Sam,' I said softly. 'You'd warn me off him, I'm sure, and tell me that married men are off limits, no exceptions. And you'd be right. Don't worry, I haven't done anything to be ashamed of. But I do really like him. The question is, does he still like me? As a friend, I mean. He might really resent me for being the one to spill the beans about Pandora's affair.'

I sighed and popped the flowers into the vase absent-mindedly: gerberas, stocks, roses . . .

'I probably sound like a right misery, full of woe,' I said. 'But until last night, things were going pretty brilliantly. Working at the florist's is making me happy: the village is really friendly, the people are so kind, I'm enjoying being creative and I love sharing my love of flowers with others. I might even be quite good at teaching people how to do it for themselves. Ten cricket players last night. Yes, you heard that right. Your antisocial sister chose to spend the evening in a large group.'

I turned the vase around, automatically checking the display from all angles.

'But I think I've really messed up where Sam's concerned; I've been unprofessional and that's unforgivable. I never ever thought I'd fall for a married man, and I have. At least technically he's still married. And this could be all in my imagination, but there was a moment last night when I thought he might feel the same as me.'

I groaned. 'That's probably wishful thinking on my part. He's too honourable for that. Worse luck,' I added softly.

I sat in silence for a few moments and picked up a handful of the pea gravel which covered the grave, letting it run through my fingers. In the distance, I heard the heavy wrought iron gates to the cemetery clang open and shut again; people were starting to arrive to visit their loved ones, to reminisce about the past and share their new stories just like me.

I didn't want Sam to be part of my past, I realised with a jolt. Which meant putting all thoughts of any sort of relationship other than friendship out of my head. I'd give Sam space, but I'd let him know I was thinking about him, that I could be a friendly ear if he needed one. There was nothing wrong with that, was there?

'I'll send him one text, just one,' I said, getting to my feet. 'What do you reckon? I'll check he's OK and I'll apologise for causing upset. Then I'll leave it. He knows where to find me.'

I called to Scamp and then blew a kiss in the direction of Freddie's headstone.

'Thanks for listening Freddie. I love you.'

★

'I sent him a text yesterday but I haven't had a reply. What if Pandora found it and is using it as evidence of us having an affair. What if I've made matters worse? And then there's Nina. I should probably tell her what I've done.' I reached for the mayonnaise, added an extra squirt to the side of my plate and dipped my chicken into it.

'At least your misplaced anxiety hasn't dented your appetite,' said Laura, watching me tuck into my dinner.

'Very funny,' I mumbled through a mouthful of food. 'And it isn't misplaced.'

It was Monday evening and Hamish, Laura and I were sitting in my suntrap of a garden with Scamp at our feet. The doors to our little Tiki bar were open, the music was on and I'd even dusted down and rehung the bunting in honour of the occasion. The barbeque had been put back on active service and for the last hour, I'd cooked salmon and pesto parcels, lemon chicken kebabs and steak marinated in Sam's special spicy rub. Scamp was in seventh heaven as various titbits found their way onto the patio and despite my continued concerns about Sam, I was pretty pleased with myself. It was the first time in almost a year that I'd cooked for anyone else and it felt like an enormous milestone.

'Not to dismiss your concerns, Fearne, but that steak was fabulous.' Hamish wiped his chin with a napkin and put his knife and fork together neatly. 'What flavours did you use?'

'I didn't,' I said. My face was already hot from the heat of the barbeque but I felt the temperature rise a bit more. 'I used something Sam gave me. He's a real foodie; that's his passion. He loves nothing better than to . . . what?' I stopped in mid-sentence; Laura and Hamish were grinning at me.

'I don't know about you,' said Laura, leaning against Hamish's shoulder, 'but I feel like I know this Sam intimately.'

'You mean Sam with the deep blue eyes and cute dimple.' Hamish wrapped his arm around her.

'On his left cheek,' she added with a snort and the two of them laughed.

'It's not funny,' I said, put out. 'What I've done could be the straw that broke the back of their marriage.'

I popped the last morsel of chicken in my mouth and collected their empty plates. We just had time for a quick bowl of raspberries which Delphine had brought into the shop for me as a thank you for helping her arrange some sweet peas.

'Cream?' I said, handing round the jug.

I say 'quick' because Laura and I couldn't hang around for long; the florist's van was outside loaded with flowers and equipment and as soon as we'd finished eating, we were setting off to do as much work tonight as we could, ready for the Edelweiss event tomorrow. Laura bit into a plump raspberry and sighed with pleasure.

'Let's talk about this rationally,' she said. 'The wife sounds awful, so you could well have done him a favour.'

'That's true,' I agreed. 'Listening to her humiliating Sam like that made me so angry that I couldn't stop myself. Before I knew it, I was interfering.'

'Reading between the lines,' said Hamish, pouring cream into his bowl, 'Pandora may have been using Sam to get the house ready for sale. Perhaps she was planning on divorcing him anyway. At worst, all you've done is escalated things.'

I chewed my lip. 'Those poor children. I feel so sorry for them.'

Hamish nodded. 'How confusing for them: their father moved out, then reappearing and presumably going again.'

'We don't know that for sure, they may have kissed and made up.' I shuddered at the thought. 'Although I doubt that. He knows she doesn't love him, he knows she's been lying to him; even for the sake of his kids, I don't think he'd put up with that.'

'It's enough to put you off marriage for life, isn't it?' Laura glanced at Hamish.

He pulled her into his arms and kissed her. 'No. But if you ever tell me you're starting a yoga course, I might start worrying.'

'Ha, no chance of that,' she giggled. 'I don't know my downward dog from sun salutation.'

A well of affection rose up inside me for these two lovebirds. After witnessing a relationship gone bad, sitting here in the reflected glow of their happiness restored my faith in love.

'Pandora's probably never even been to yoga,' I said crossly. A thought struck me. 'Gareth Weaver is going to be furious when he finds out.'

Hamish topped up my water glass. 'Hmm. Technically it was a breach of confidentiality.'

'*Technically*,' I argued, 'we don't say "don't worry, we won't tell a soul that you're sleeping with someone else's wife".'

He raised a sceptical eyebrow. 'Two words: data protection.'

I wrinkled my nose. 'Yeah, I know, and anyway it's implied that we wouldn't reveal personal information about customers. *Nina* wouldn't.'

'You're overthinking it,' said Laura, stacking our bowls. 'Pandora's lover knew she was married, he knew the risks. He'll have a lot more on his mind than what the local florist's role in this sordid affair was.'

I wasn't convinced. 'Imagine if he sues us? That'll be a nice homecoming present for Nina: here are your shop keys, oh, and by the way, you're due in court next week.'

Nina had phoned this morning and I hadn't mentioned any of this to her. It would only worry her and what could she do about it anyway? However, I had told her how much money we made on Saturday night, and that one of the cricket girlfriends had phoned to book a workshop for her hen party. Nina had been full of praise for me, which made me feel even more guilty.

'Look, it's very unlikely,' said Hamish. 'There's so much more going on here than that one act of yours.'

'Agreed. You were careless,' said Laura, never one to beat about the bush. 'But it wasn't intentional, got it?'

I went bright red. 'Well. I suppose I could have just had the book open at a random page and it was just bad luck that Sam happened to spot the message written to his wife from another man.'

Hamish grinned. 'So just stick to that and you'll be fine. She was having an affair and she lied to her husband about where she was; Pandora is in the wrong, no question. How and why that information about the flower delivery got out is pretty irrelevant in the grand scheme of things.'

Laura sniggered. 'Did he *really* call himself sexy tiger?'

My lips twitched. 'Really.'

Hamish leaned back in his chair and folded his arms. 'While you two are out I might come up with a macho name for myself.'

Laura pouted. 'What's wrong with Mr Snuggle Bunny?'

'Shush!' Hamish laughed.

'And on that note,' I said, getting up from the table swiftly. 'I think we should get going to the Claybourne Hotel before my dinner makes a repeat appearance.'

Half an hour later Laura and I were well on our way to the hotel. Hamish was staying at my house to clear the furniture out of Freddie's old room. All three of us had stood in there earlier trying to decide what I should use the room for. Last winter, I'd contemplated selling up and moving somewhere else because it hadn't felt like home without Freddie. But over the last few months I'd fallen in love with it again; maybe it was because I had Scamp for company, or maybe it was simply because I was starting to make new happy memories, but either way, I'd changed my mind about leaving. So Freddie's room was going to be redecorated and after my stint at the florist, I might investigate taking in a lodger. It felt good making plans for the future again.

'So apart from breaking up marriages,' Laura said, retuning the van's radio to our favourite nineties station, 'it's working out all right being in the shop by yourself?'

I gave her a stink eye. 'Not funny.'

She grinned. 'Sorry, but you need to stop beating yourself up about your role in Sam's break-up. I think you were really restrained given the circumstances.'

'Hmm, I'll stop beating myself up when Sam rings and I know he and I are OK.'

She was quiet for the moment. 'You really like him, don't you?'

I sighed. 'I do, but the next few months are going to be tough for him and his family. The last thing he needs is another woman complicating matters. I'll be a friend if he needs one and nothing more. To answer your question, I'm loving running the shop. It's busy and I feel like it's a constant juggle between making up orders and serving in the shop and making deliveries. I followed your advice about not doing weddings so I'm saying no to those but I do enjoy workshops, so I'm going to try and grow that side of the business.'

'Look after yourself,' she warned. 'It wasn't so long ago that you were wiped out with grief. Don't overdo it.'

I was working long hours and yes, it was tiring, but Nina was only away for a few more weeks so there was no point looking for extra help.

'Thanks for caring.' I smiled at my friend. 'But sleep is overrated and the shop is worth it. You should come for a visit and see for yourself.'

'Ooh yes!' Her eyes sparkled. 'And if you can arrange for Sam to be there at the same time, even better.'

'That's funny, I've got Ethel coming to visit tomorrow afternoon; she said the same thing.'

'Ah, darling Ethel,' Laura sighed wistfully. 'I miss seeing her cheery face at the window next door.'

'Ditto.'

After I got home from visiting Freddie's grave yesterday I'd phoned Ethel to ask if she was up to having a visit from Scamp and me that afternoon. I hadn't seen her much since Nina had gone away because I'd been so manic and I'd been feeling guilty about it. Her move from The Beeches care home where she'd been since spring had been delayed by one thing and another: a room had had needed to be decorated for her, there'd been a family holiday and then a couple of routine hospital appointments which Ethel hadn't wanted to miss, but when she'd answered my call I'd found her buzzing with excitement and far too busy for visitors.

'I'm moving to Carole's!' she'd cried. 'This Tuesday! I'm up to my ears in packing.'

'That's great news!' I'd responded with gusto, brushing away my own sadness at the thought that I'd no longer be able to call in for a dose of Ethel's sage advice when I needed it. It would be comforting for her to be so close to her family in Yorkshire. I'd suggested she drop in to the florist's on her way up north to see us. She'd jumped at the chance.

'I'll check with Carole, but I'd love to.' She paused for a second. 'And it will be nice to say goodbye properly to you. It'll be nice to be able to think of you in the shop when I'm miles away. Do you see much of that chappie? What's his name . . .?'

I made a mental note to make sure there were plenty of tissues in the shop and then one of our favourites came on. Laura turned up the radio and we both launched into an enthusiastic rendition of 'Nine to Five' and all my worries were put on hold for the rest of the journey.

This time when we arrived at the Claybourne Hotel, I drove past the pretty entrance with its canopy of wisteria blooms and headed straight round the back. Marcia had given me instructions to use the service entrance which gave us easy access to the set of function rooms Edelweiss had booked.

Laura and I set about unloading the van. We had all the usual floristry equipment as well as containers, fairy lights, wooden trellis panels, heaps of flowers and the metal moongate I'd managed to borrow from a friend of Nina's. To create the natural summer meadow feel that Edelweiss wanted, I'd have to do a lot of the work early tomorrow morning. But the large pedestal displays would contain plenty of water, so that meant I could get them out of the way tonight.

288

'What is this anyway?' Laura was attempting to bolt together the pieces of the moongate. 'I'm trying to work out if it looks like an instrument of torture, or one of those hoops you see at a circus with an acrobat dangling from it by her teeth.'

'Hopefully it's better than both of those.' I took out my phone and showed her the picture of the one we'd done on our floristry course back in March when spring flowers had been in season. 'It's usually the centrepiece for a wedding but I thought it would fit in here quite well.'

'Wow. That's gorgeous.' She took the phone out of my hand and zoomed in on it, her eyes sparkling. 'Let's do it tonight, I want to see it covered in flowers.'

I suppressed a smile; she'd kill me for pointing it out, but since she'd been with Hamish her romance-ometer had gone off the scales and it warmed my heart to see it.

'No can do, I'm afraid,' I said, sliding my phone back in my pocket. 'It's not something you can water so I'll have to do it first thing in the morning. I'll take lots of photos, I promise.'

'We could keep Scamp overnight, if it helps? It would give Hamish a taste of responsibility.'

I grinned at her. 'Care to expand on that statement?'

'Nope.'

We both laughed. Perhaps they were thinking about what the future might look like as a family. Wasn't that what I wanted for myself one day? Although right now there was more chance of me flying to the moon.

'Thank you for the offer but Biddy from the pet shop has offered to have him for as long as I need.'

'Any news on her and the lover?'

'Nothing to report, but I'll keep you posted,' I promised.

I'd told her about Biddy and her affair with Nigel. We'd agreed I shouldn't do anything for now. But I hadn't forgotten about them; maybe one day when the time was right, I'd get the chance to re-introduce them.

'I wish Dad had found someone new after Mum died. I know he's lonely and I feel guilty that I don't do more with him.' She sighed.

'There's still time, perhaps he just hasn't met the one.'

Laura shook her head sadly. 'For Dad there'll only ever be Mum. Theirs was the perfect marriage, he says nothing could ever beat it.'

'That's so romantic,' I said with a wave of affection for the man who'd been like a dad to me during my teenage years.

She nudged me sharply. 'Look at the two of us: gooey pair. Let's get cracking before we start weeping.'

An hour later, we'd done as much as we could. I'd practised all the displays back at the shop to speed things up and I'd already cut the stems to length to keep this evening's work as quick as possible. We were both yawning as I was finishing off the last bits while Laura was giving everything a spray with water.

'You're bloody brilliant, Fearne Lovage,' she marvelled, looping an arm over my shoulders. 'I come out in a sweat with one vase of flowers to arrange, and you, cool as a cucumber can take on an entire scheme without turning a hair.'

'Hmm,' I said, trying not to picture the moment I'd first met Nina, face down on the counter and sobbing her heart out in a race against time to get ready for Rosie's wedding. Victor would be delivering the rest of the flowers directly to the hotel at the crack of dawn in the morning and I'd be here at six a.m. to get started. 'Let's see if I'm still looking cool this time tomorrow.'

We were about to leave the room when we heard the sound of rapidly approaching footsteps in the corridor outside.

I opened the door as Marcia burst in, red-faced and perspiring.

'You're here!' She marched straight to the window, threw it open and lit a cigarette, her elbow covering up the 'no smoking' sign. 'Thank goodness for that!'

'Um, yes,' I said, confused. Laura and I exchanged worried looks. 'As arranged.'

She took a long drag on her cigarette and blew the smoke out of the window before replying.

'Everything, and I mean *everything*, has gone wrong today. So I wouldn't have been surprised if you hadn't turned up.' She shut her eyes and massaged the bridge of her nose. 'I should have gone home hours ago. I'm just glad it was my boss who took this booking not me. If heads are going to roll at least I should be safe.'

'Which booking?' Laura asked.

Marcia puffed out another cloud of smoke and this time forgot to aim it outside. She flapped her arms to disperse it. 'Edelweiss. It looks great in here, by the way, very rude of me not to mention it straight away. Sorry. I'm a bit stressed.'

My stomach twisted. 'Is there something I should know about?'

'A major confusion over the bedrooms.' Marcia rolled her eyes. 'Major.'

'Oh dear.' I hid my relief; I was sorry for her, but at least it had nothing to do with my side of the event.

'Is it sorted now?' Laura, reading my mind, squeezed my arm.

'Not yet.' She took one more impossibly long drag from her cigarette, stubbed it out on the wall outside and closed the window. 'The guests are saying that the conference fee they've paid to Edelweiss included overnight accommodation. Whereas Edelweiss told us that guests were settling their own bills. Whatever. It'll work out in the end.'

She stood up straight, tugged her tight skirt down over her thighs and smiled at us. 'They're going to be thrilled with this, it looks great.'

'Oh, thanks,' I said distractedly, still thinking about Edelweiss and the mix-up over payment. What if the same happened to me and there was a dispute over who was paying my bill? An uncomfortable shiver ran down my spine.

'Can't you ask an Edelweiss representative about it?' Laura asked.

'You'd think,' said Marcia wryly. 'But they haven't turned up yet. Their flight has been delayed.'

'It's a Swiss company,' I explained to Laura.

'Flying in from . . .?' she wanted to know, getting her phone out. 'I've got an app for live flight information so I know if Hamish is going to be late.'

Marcia shrugged. 'No idea, but they're hiring a car from Manchester airport.'

'Their office is in Geneva,' I said, wishing I'd made more effort to find out their travel arrangements.

Laura shook her head. 'No flights due in. There's one from Zurich.'

'That's probably it,' I said hastily.

She pulled a face and showed me the phone. 'It's already landed. No delays.'

'That's odd,' I frowned.

Marcia flapped a hand and laughed. 'Look at your worried little faces. There'll be a perfectly reasonable explanation.'

'There'd better be,' I murmured, eyeing up all the flowers in the room, not to mention the ballroom next door and the other half of the delivery on its way from Holland as we spoke.

Marcia tucked her cigarette lighter down her bra and checked her phone. 'It'll be fine, it always is. The hotel business is always full of last-minute niggles: things go wrong, we sort them; customers complain, we pacify them. Welcome to my world. Tomorrow will be fantastic, don't worry. I'd better get back to the front line. See you in the morning.'

And with that, she marched out of the room. Laura and I listened to her receding footsteps and pulled worried faces at each other.

'I don't like the sound of this,' said Laura. 'If I'm ever delayed for a business meeting I always make sure I ring ahead and let people know.'

Ditto. It was common courtesy. I felt a bit sick. I daren't tell her that I still didn't have a watertight contract from Edelweiss for the flowers. Besides, I knew from experience that having a written agreement didn't automatically mean that getting paid by a client was problem-free. I remembered my old boss Bernie, tearing his hair out trying to get payment out of a Bulgarian paper mill once. We never did get the money.

'Marcia's right,' I said briskly, 'there could be a hundred and one reasons why they haven't been in touch yet.'

'And said they're delayed. And taken money from guests for their hotel rooms . . .' Laura raised an eyebrow.

I couldn't think of anything positive to say to that so I picked up my bag and chivvied us to the door.

'Just putting it out there,' said Laura, pulling the function-room door closed as we headed into the corridor, 'but can you reduce your flower order for tomorrow?'

I'd been thinking the same, but somehow I doubted it.

'Some of the stock I ordered comes from Colombia,' I said, pushing open the service door and stepping into the night air. 'The cut-off time for cancellation went a long time ago.'

'How much have you spent?'

I fumbled in my bag for the van keys and unlocked it. 'Shush. Tonight you're doing my donkey work, not my accounts.'

The van seats creaked as we both climbed in.

Laura frowned. 'But—'

'Goats butt,' I cut in sternly, starting the engine. 'And donkeys bray. Now let's get you home; Mr Snuggle Bunny awaits.'

Hamish and Laura headed off as soon as we arrived back in Pineapple Road. I went inside with Scamp, feeling shaky with exhaustion and worry. My bed was calling but I couldn't settle straight away. I tried the number I had for Edelweiss, hoping for some reassurances that all was well, but all I got was the automated response telling me that my call couldn't be connected. As a last resort, I called Victor Sunshine on the off-chance that I could reduce my order as Laura had suggested. But it was as I feared; there was nothing he could do at this late stage.

My whole body was stiff with tension; I knew I wasn't in for a good night's sleep. But there was nothing else for it but to go to bed and hope everything would be coming up roses by the morning.

Chapter Twenty-eight

I was wrong about not being able to sleep. When my work phone started ringing I had to drag myself from the depths of slumber to answer it. Normally it was on *do not disturb* at night, but I'd kept it on, on the off-chance that Edelweiss called. They hadn't.

'Nina's Flowers,' I said in a croaky voice. I checked my bedside clock: five a.m.

'This is Tim Sullivan, night manager at the Claybourne Hotel.'

I sat bolt upright. 'What's happened?'

'Thought you'd like to know that you've had a massive delivery.'

I collapsed back against my pillows with relief. 'Thank you. Yes, I was expecting them. I thought for a moment you were ringing with bad news.'

'It *is* bad news; they're blocking up my reception area.'

I got out of bed and went downstairs to make coffee. 'I'll make sure they're out of the way before guests start to emerge.'

'Hmm.'

'Were you on duty when the Edelweiss team arrived last night, have they seen what I've done so far, do you know?'

'They didn't arrive.'

The hairs on the back of my neck stood up. 'Are you sure?'

'Positive. It's a right shit show down here. Oh, *fff* . . . please forget I said shit, I'm on my last warning for swearing.'

I wasn't interested in his language; I was more bothered about the *shit show* part. I switched off the kettle; caffeine would have to wait.

'Balls. I'm on my way.'

The next hour flew by in a blur.

I made myself presentable, took Scamp out for an abbreviated morning walk, dropped him off with Biddy (who was still in her dressing gown and slippers) and reached the hotel just after six o'clock. The Edelweiss itinerary would begin with a choice of herbal infusions and plant-based snacks in the main function room at nine-thirty; I had just over three hours to turn their little part of the Claybourne Hotel into a floral idyll. Assuming, of course, that the event was even still going ahead.

The car park was full, which must mean the hotel was busy. I parked as close as I could to the service entrance and headed inside, intending to check on last night's work first. I tried the doors to the two rooms I was working in but they were both locked. I dashed along the corridor towards reception to find the night manager.

There was a crowd of people standing outside the restaurant already, mostly women. Hotel guests liked an early breakfast, it seemed. In the midst of them was a young woman in the hotel uniform of black waistcoat and white shirt, trying to keep the peace.

'I'm sorry,' she was saying, looking harassed. 'But breakfast can only be served to those who've left credit card details at reception.'

'For the love of God,' snarled a man with a suspiciously orange tan. 'How many times? We have paid Edelweiss already.'

A woman in a voluminous kaftan and a lot of eyeliner took a step forward.

'You must let us in for breakfast,' she barked at the poor girl who was having to guard the entrance to the restaurant with both arms. 'It's a basic human right.'

'I think that's water,' said the woman behind her. 'Not bacon and eggs.'

Kaftan lady glared at her. 'Shut up, Amy, this is all your fault in the first place.'

I squeezed past and continued to reception.

This area was also hectic. A swarm of guests was gathered around the check-in desk and a young male member of staff was pleading with them to not all speak at once. Twelve boxes of flowers were stacked to one side and I winced in horror as a woman with long grey plaits balanced a tie-dye handbag on the top of the pile.

'I was here first,' she said, glaring at her fellow guests. 'And I demand to see the manager.'

The young man pulled at his dark hair until it stuck up in unruly tufts. 'That would be me. Tim Sullivan.'

Oh good; I'd found him.

I moved to the end of the reception desk and waved a hand discreetly, communicating by a series of gestures that I was the florist. Tim shot me a look of recognition, followed by a look which said *help me, please.* Unfortunately, I needed as much help as the others did and I urgently needed answers.

'A *proper* manager,' said the woman, 'who'll sort this mess out.'

'Fair enough,' Tim replied with a shrug. 'If you'd like to take a seat, I'll let him know.'

'I shall be leaving my review on TripAdvisor,' she said, snatching up her bag and flinging it over her shoulder. 'And it won't make for comfortable reading.'

'Tim,' I said quietly. 'Is there somewhere we can talk? I need to know what's going on.'

'As if I know,' he muttered gloomily. 'Yeah, give us a minute.'

Just then a minibus pulled up at the front of the hotel and another twenty or so ladies alighted.

Despite the hour, they were very loud and exuberant, and one of them had a clipboard; Tim's shoulders slumped another couple of inches.

'Which way to the Edelweiss pre-conference breakfast?' demanded the one with the clipboard.

'Excuse me!' A blonde-haired woman leaning against the reception desk looked up from her phone and glared at the new arrivals. 'There is a queue, you know.'

I froze, my heart nearly exploding with shock. I'd recognise that cutting voice anywhere: *Pandora*. What was she doing here?

I took a step backwards out of her eyeline; I had enough to cope with without hearing another tirade from her. Tim turned away from the desk and swore just as a door behind us both opened and a man appeared.

He pointed at Tim. 'Did I just hear you swear?'

The blood drained from Tim's face.

'He was giving me directions,' I said jumping in front of Tim and bending to pick up one of my boxes. 'Flowers off that way. I'm the florist.'

Tim looked pathetically grateful. 'That's right.'

The man scowled at all the boxes. 'Pleased to meet you. I'm Joe Blake, hotel manager. Get this lot moved please, they're a fire hazard.'

'I will,' I said crossly, 'but first I need to know what's happening.'

'Don't we all,' said Joe. He barked at Tim. 'Where the bloody hell is Marcia?'

Tim shrugged. 'How do I fff . . . *flippin'* know?'

Joe gritted his teeth. 'She's supposed to be managing this event.'

Someone started pressing the bell on the reception desk repeatedly. 'Hello! Any chance of being served?'

'Are you the manager?' The woman with the plaits was back. 'I demand some answers.'

Behind her stood a woman in her dressing gown shouting that she'd ordered room service half an hour ago and it still hadn't arrived.

'One second, ladies.' He smiled politely at them, then hissed at Tim. 'Get Marcia on the phone. Now.'

'Marcia was still here when I left late last night,' I pointed out, 'surely she's unlikely to be due in at this hour.'

The hotel manager grunted. 'Her shift starts and ends when the event starts and ends.'

I let out a breath of relief. 'Oh! So it is still on then? Because I need to know whether to finish these flower displays or not.'

Joe jerked his head in the drection of his office and we stepped towards it out of earshot of the guests.

'No one from Edelweiss has turned up. There's been no word from them,' he said grimly. 'Guests are refusing to pay for their rooms and are now demanding food which hasn't been paid for. Until we've had clarification from Edelweiss—'

Tim interrupted his boss, tapping him on the arm.

Joe growled. 'What?'

Tim held out the phone. 'Phone call for you. Says he's a detective.'

A Mexican wave of gasps and whispers rippled over the assembled crowd. Joe grabbed the phone, marched into his office and shut the door.

I glanced across at Pandora, who can't have noticed me because she was talking into her phone, laughing and twirling a lock of hair. Two minutes later Joe emerged, ashen-faced.

'Can I have your attention please, everyone.' His face was weirdly blank as if he'd been hypnotised and he was clutching the phone to his chest. 'I have just taken a call from the police. It appears we've all been scammed. There is no company called Edelweiss. Today's event is cancelled.'

A cold stab of fear stole the air from my lungs; I stared at the boxes of imported flowers. *Expensive* imported flowers.

What the hell was I going to do now?

As the news sank in, the guests swarmed forward angrily, Pandora included. I stepped inside the manager's office to catch my breath. Joe darted in to put the phone back in its cradle.

'Where does this leave me?' I asked, blocking his route back out.

He frowned irritably. 'Superfluous to requirements, I imagine. I suggest you take your flowers and leave.'

'Can I sell them to the hotel?' I stuttered, grasping at straws. 'After all, the order came via you and it would help me out.'

He stared at me as if I was mad. 'And who's going to help us out? The hotel has got the small issue of thousands of pounds of unpaid rooms to resolve.'

I swallowed. 'As a small business—'

He cut me off, holding his hand up. 'We've already paid you a deposit as a gesture of goodwill on behalf of Edelweiss. I'm not sure where we stand on recovering that.'

With that he pushed past me into the sea of demanding guests. It was no good trying to argue with him. The hotel was owed far more money than I was. Right now the best thing I could do was to get the flowers back to the shop, along with all the displays I'd already done and then come up with a plan to recoup my losses.

I picked up as many boxes from reception as I could and staggered back down the corridor towards the function room. The hard corners dug into my arms; they were bulky rather than heavy and I soon had to stop to readjust them. I rested my hip on a windowsill and leaned forward until my forehead met the cool glass.

So much for my grand idea of corporate flowers being the key to the shop's fortunes. I'd be more likely to bankrupt us after this fiasco. Something Nina said came back to me about the lack of joy involved with corporate flowers, that she didn't like it because ordering flowers was simply a chore to be ticked off by some faceless person with a to-do list.

How prophetic that had turned out to be.

The enormity of the situation I'd got myself into hit me head on and my eyes began to burn with tears; it was only flowers and only money, but I'd been gullible and naïve. I felt stupid and lonely and in that moment I'd never missed my brother more. If Freddie were here he'd make light of the situation, make up a silly song for us to sing and annoy me by telling me that one day we'd look back at this and laugh.

But he wasn't here. Nobody was, this was my mess and I was going to have to sort it out by myself.

Come on, Fearne, get your act together.

I'd got Ethel visiting me in the shop this afternoon with her daughter. I'd imagined sitting her down at the workshop table with Scamp by her side and a cup of tea in her hand while I told her of my triumph at today's event. I'd been planning to show her the photos and impress her with my

301

work. Now all I'd have to show for it was a shop full of flowers and an empty cash register. I groaned and blinked away the tears.

Outside, a raised brick bed had been planted with calming shades of purple lavender, verbena and petunias, silvery grasses and shiny-leafed hostas.

The order and symmetry of the display held my gaze and I felt my face soften into a smile; four months on from deciding to write my own happy list and flowers still did it for me.

I straightened up, feeling more positive about the task ahead. Ethel wasn't due until later on, I wasn't going to let this defeat me; by the time she arrived, I had to have turned the situation around. Somehow between now and then, I had to have some sort of adventure. Buoyed with new energy, I was about to step forward when my phone rang. Trying not to drop anything, I reached inside my bag with one hand and grabbed it quickly. The name on the screen made my breath catch.

'Hello?'

'Fearne? It's Sam.' His voice was urgent and anxious.

'Morning,' I said, swallowing hard. I hadn't heard from him since Saturday night when he'd stormed out of the shop. If he was about to shout at me for interfering between him and Pandora, I didn't think I could cope. Not on top of anything else.

'Listen, sorry to call so early, but I've just had a call from a contact of mine. Apparently the Edelweiss company doesn't exist.'

'I've just found out,' I said bitterly. 'I'm at the hotel now.'

'Oh Fearne, I'm so sorry,' he said, his voice laced with gentle concern. 'It's not just the Claybourne that's been caught out. Twelve venues in the UK have been scammed

302

and over a thousand people have already come forward to say they've lost money.'

I gave a little moan under my breath. I was dreading breaking this to Nina. I'd really wanted to be such an asset to her with my market research experience and my new-girl enthusiasm for floristry. First I'd breached data protection rules and now this. I had to be the biggest liability her business had ever encountered.

'Fearne? Are you still there?'

'Yes,' I gave a stilted laugh. 'I'm just working out my next move. But hey, I'll think of something. Thanks for ringing, I appreciate it.'

I heard him take a breath. 'Would you like some help?'

'Really?' My heart skipped with joy. 'That would be amazing.'

'On my way.'

Chapter Twenty-nine

Half an hour later, Sam found me kneeling in the ballroom, unwinding fairy lights and dismantling the wooden trellis panels either side of the moongate that I'd never even had the chance to decorate.

'Hey, there,' he said, approaching me slowly.

'Sam!' I jumped up, startled to see him so soon. I'd had butterflies in my stomach since the phone call and it had been really difficult to focus. 'Thanks for coming.'

I jammed my hands into my apron pocket; it was all I could do not to hurl myself at him. He was as handsome as ever, although it looked like he hadn't shaved or slept much since I'd last seen him. He didn't look dressed for work, either.

'No worries; besides, I don't have any plans for the next few days.' He looked down at his shorts and trainers. 'I'm taking some time off; I've been at my mum's house since Saturday.'

I nodded, understanding the subtext: he hadn't gone back to Pandora. I knew how worried he'd be, thinking about his children and what was next for his family. On top of all that, working for your father-in-law when your marriage was on the rocks couldn't be easy.

'How are you doing, Sam?'

'I'll be fine.' His eyes met mine briefly and then he cleared his throat. He looked around the room at the flower displays and whistled. 'You made all these?'

'Yep.' I stood and stretched. 'I spent all our money on the stock for a client that doesn't exist. And now I have more flowers than I know what to do with. Some of them are already cut so they need to be sold today. And boxes and boxes of others that you'd never normally find in a village florist because either they're expensive, or unusual or simply too flimsy to last in a home arrangement. I've been phenomenally stupid, I've worked ridiculously long hours for the last few days, I'm knackered and—'

'Whoa.' He crossed the room and put his hands on the tops of my arms and turned me around, forcing me to look at my work. 'Just, for one minute, let's put the Edelweiss element out of our minds and stop and enjoy this. What you've achieved is incredible.'

I swallowed a lump in my throat, floored by the deliciousness of his presence. 'They're not even finished.'

'You mean it's possible to get better than this?' He smiled playfully and rested his arm lightly on my shoulder. 'I never really thought about it before but floristry is art. Looking at these flowers and smelling their scent, how could anyone stay down for long?'

'I seem to be managing quite nicely,' I grumbled. 'You know, I got into flowers after my brother died, as a way of bringing happiness into my life. But all I seem to be doing at the moment is wreaking havoc.' I glanced sideways at him. 'And not only mine. I'm so sorry, Sam. About Saturday. About letting you see that flower order for Pandora.'

'Don't be.' He withdrew his arm, picked up the tangle of fairy lights and began winding them in a loop around his hand and his elbow. 'The damage had been done years ago. You have nothing to be sorry about. I'm the one who should be apologising for letting my personal life spoil the end of the workshop for the cricket team. They loved it, by the way. I could write a book about the mistakes I made in my marriage, and, spoiler alert, it won't have a happy ending. There's no way back for her and me this time.'

His smile slipped and my heart ached for him. No matter how angry you were with someone, ending a relationship was sad and exhausting. Sam frowned, setting the lights neatly on the floor and starting on the second set.

'And Annabel and Will, are they OK?'

His eyes lit up. 'You remember their names? I'm impressed'

'Occupational hazard,' I said, laughing. *Actually laughing*. Sam had been here less than five minutes and he'd already lifted my mood. 'I used to work in market research, collecting data on people is what I do.'

He held his hands up and pretended to look scared. 'I'd better watch what I say, then.'

'Probably wise.' I remembered everything he'd told me, every detail. Stick me on a quiz show and Sam Diamond could be my specialist subject. I didn't say that though, because there's healthy interest and then there's being a stalker.

'Sam . . .'

'Fearne . . .'

We spoke at the same time and then laughed. He pointed at me to go first.

'I just wanted to say that I'm so glad you're here,' I said, feeling suddenly exposed under his direct gaze. 'I've been muddling along OK without Nina but this Edelweiss thing has really taken the wind out of my sails. It's nice to have someone to share the load. You're very kind.'

'Just call me the Good *Sam*aritan. Get it? *Sam*?' He gave me a lopsided smile as I groaned at his bad joke. He clapped his hands together. 'So how can I help, what are we going to do with it all?'

'Good question.' I took a deep breath. 'For starters, I guess I should get everything back to the shop, see what I can salvage, then write a letter of resignation to Nina. And for the rest of the day, I might just get drunk and wait for an old friend of mine to arrive for afternoon tea.'

He grinned. 'Why don't I help you with the first one and we can talk about the rest when we get to Barnaby.'

I twisted a lock of my hair around my fingers and counted to ten while I swallowed the lump in my throat. Kindness always did that to me; knocked me off kilter and brought the tears close to the surface.

'Sounds like a plan.' I said gruffly, managing a weak smile. 'And you? What was it you wanted to say?'

'Just that, like you I've been muddling along on my own for a couple of days.' His eyes lost their shine for a moment. 'But it's nice to do something positive and it's good to be useful.'

He ran the back of his fingers along his jaw and the rasping sound caught my attention.

'You've stopped shaving again!'

He grinned sheepishly. 'Apparently some women like bearded men. In general.'

Hearing him quote my words back to me gave me a little thrill but I was careful not to read too much into it. If there was a spark between Sam and me I wanted it to have the best chance of staying alight, which meant taking it slowly.

'But do *you* like it?' I said softly.

He thought about it, scratching his chin. 'I do. It suits my mood. Unkempt and scruffy. Although it's getting to the itchy stage. Feel.'

I stepped closer until I could feel the heat from him. I brought my hand to his face; the rough hair prickled my fingers and woke up all sorts of sensations I hadn't felt for a while.

'It's not unkempt and you're not scruffy.' *You're lovely*.

Sam's hand covered mine and the connection between us sparkled like a million stars. A small part of me worried about what was happening, but the other part was thoroughly enjoying the moment.

A harsh laugh from the doorway made us spring apart. Pandora folded her arms and smirked.

'I'd say *get a room*, but you already have one.'

'Pandora?' Sam's jaw dropped and he glanced at the clock on the wall. My eyes followed suit. It was still only eight o'clock. Today was endless.

'Well, well, well,' she drawled. 'It's like déjà vu. I thought I recognised you earlier in reception, Fearne, I followed the cloying smell of flowers to find you, but I must say, I didn't expect to see you here, Sam.'

Sam exhaled impatiently. 'Your dad owns the lease on the florist business, that's how Fearne and I know each other. There's no déjà vu about it. We had nothing to hide when you saw us together on Saturday and this time . . .' His blue eyes glinted defiantly. 'And this time, it's none of your business what I do.'

'Whatever.' She pursed her lips. 'I came for the Edelweiss thing. More fool me. I thought it sounded like a fab idea: natural beauty products, combined with a yoga studio. Because whether you believe me or not, I am serious about setting up my own wellbeing business.'

Sam planted a hand on his forehead and groaned. 'Great. So we've just lost a grand?'

'A *thousand* pounds?' I gasped. No wonder the guests were so annoyed about being denied their breakfast.

'Someone else who witters about money.' Pandora gave me a withering look. 'You two are a perfect match. Are these flowers going spare?'

'They're for sale,' I corrected her swiftly. 'The large arrangement is seventy-five and—'

'For a few lousy flowers?' she shrieked. 'I'd rather have new shoes.'

'Pandora.' Sam's voice was low. 'The money for Edelweiss: spending that sort of money without consulting me—'

'Oh, stop fussing.' She stalked further into the room, peering at everything sniffily. 'Of course *we* haven't. As if *you* give me enough money to come to something innovative and exciting like this.'

Sam and I exchanged bemused looks. So exciting and innovative that it was actually a scam.

He shook his head in disgust. 'So, your dad paid?'

She stopped strutting and fiddled with a huge rock of a diamond earring (surely that couldn't be real). 'Daddy doesn't know anything about it. Probably best if it stays that way for now. The whole thing is very disappointing and they're being totally unreasonable about the hotel room.'

'What hotel room?' Sam stared at her. 'Are the kids with you?'

'No.' She stiffened and then walked swiftly towards the door. 'They're with my mum.'

'OK,' he relaxed. 'Fine. But please let Sybil know that I'm collecting them from the school bus and taking them to *my* mum's tonight?'

Her make-up couldn't conceal her blushes. 'They're with my mum in Lanzarote. Or at least they will be by lunchtime.'

Sam's jaw dropped; he looked so wounded that my heart melted for him. 'You've sent them away?'

I decided to give them some privacy. I picked up one of the large arrangements.

'I'll start loading up,' I mumbled.

Sam caught my arm as I passed him. 'Sorry. *Again*. I'll be right with you.'

I tried to convey solidarity through my smile. 'It's fine. You take all the time you need.'

I could still hear them when I stepped out into the corridor and despite feeling guilty for eavesdropping, I slowed my pace.

'My children have left the country and you didn't think to let me know?' Sam's voice was low and angry. 'What about school? When will they be back?'

'Next week. Probably,' Pandora replied vaguely. 'I needed some space, OK? I needed to process what happened this weekend. Mum offered to help out.'

'I'd have had them! Jeez, Pandora, you've overstepped the mark this time,' he growled. 'I'm going to apply for custody. I'm not dancing to your tune any more.'

'You think I'm enjoying all this?' Her voice trembled as if she was close to tears. I reached the service door which led to the car park but I didn't open it. It was like when Freddie had begged me to watch a scary film with him; I couldn't bear to watch but I couldn't drag myself away either. 'Us separating is stressful.'

'We're not *separating*. That implies a joint decision. You told me to leave last summer. You told me you wanted to try again. As we both know, you've always called the shots in this marriage. Until now. Goodbye, Pandora.'

He was on his way out. I quickly put down the flowers and opened the door. The doorknob turned easily, I held the door open with my bottom, picked the flowers up and noticed a flash of movement in my peripheral vision. I stood at the door and waited.

Poor Sam. I really felt for him, there was still so much anger and frustration in him towards his wife. *Ex-wife*, I corrected myself.

'Steady, fella!' said a jovial voice.

'What the hell?!' Sam yelled.

There was a series of thumps and some serious swearing and I turned back to see Sam and another tall skinny man with fine blond hair fronting up to each other and several cartons of my flowers in a heap on the floor.

'*Gareth bloody Weaver,*' Sam said with considerable menace. 'I might have known.'

'Please be careful!' I scooted down to them, heart in my mouth, praying that my precious blooms were still intact. If those Columbian roses ended up as a pile of petal confetti it would be the cherry on top of the worst cake ever. Also, shamelessly, I really wanted a closer look at the man Pandora had thrown away her marriage to Sam for. Surely he'd have to be something really special.

'Totally my fault,' said Gareth in such a posh accent I assumed he must be putting it on. He flapped about, all elbows and knees, trying to pick up boxes and making matters much worse. 'Such a clumsy oaf, I'll cover any damages of course.'

'Of course you will.' Sam's face was expressionless. 'A man who can afford to take on Pandora will be used to forking out large sums of money unexpectedly.'

Gareth guffawed until realising Sam wasn't joining in and grimaced. 'Yes, know what you mean. Here, please, I insist.' He pulled what looked to be two fifty-pound notes from his wallet and handed them to me. The offer was tempting, I was considerably down financially after today's non-event, but even so, one hundred pounds just for having my flowers knocked to the floor?

'I, er, well, I'm not sure . . .' I looked quickly at Sam for help; he gave the tiniest nod. I took the notes and tucked them into my pocket. 'Thank you, very decent of you.'

'Well this is awkward, but had to happen sometime.' Gareth smiled tentatively at Sam and held out his hand. 'Let's be gentlemen about this.'

'Gentlemen don't have affairs with married women.' Sam's face was grim. He restacked the flowers and picked them up.

'Married? Hold on just a minute.' Gareth's face turned puce. 'Pandora was separated.'

Pandora emerged from the room in a rush and came to an abrupt halt when she saw both men together. 'Oh.'

'Here she is!' Gareth beamed, holding his arms out to her. 'Right, I've spoken to my solicitor about Edelweiss, we're going to pursue these charlatans, even if it costs me ten times more than we've already spent. I will avenge you!' He thrust his arm into the air like a red-faced, lanky superhero.

I was confused; did the man have no shame, being so open about his relationship in front of Sam?

'Hmm.' She stuck her nose in the air. 'I'll be waiting in the Rolls.'

'Rightio, darling.' Gareth bent down, lips puckered to kiss her, but she flounced past without a second glance. 'Be right there, Kitten.'

Pandora's retreating form made a noise not unlike a cat getting ready for a fight. A burst of laughter escaped from me before I could catch it. I covered it up with a cough.

'I'll do the same,' I said, sending Sam a smile of solidarity. 'Not the Rolls, obviously. The erm, van.'

The corners of Sam's mouth twitched. 'Be right there. After I've put Gareth right on a few things.'

I headed back to the doors to the car park, thinking that Sam had had a lucky escape and actually feeling a bit sorry for Gareth. Although, I reminded myself, he had a Rolls and a wallet stuffed full of cash, so not that sorry.

Chapter Thirty

An hour later we were back in the florist's shop. Sam filled the dog's water bowl while I made us both coffee, each lost in our own thoughts. I'd got back to the shop shortly before him, bought us both breakfast from the Lemon Tree Café and fetched Scamp from Biddy's.

I'd had time to think on the way back from the hotel. I wasn't going to waste any more time moping about my mistakes; I had a lot of stock to sell and as Sam seemed to be in no hurry to go, I decided to rope him in. We made space on the workshop table and sat down to eat hot paninis and drink our coffees.

'Which do you prefer,' I held up the two brown paper bags: 'Portobello mushroom and mascarpone, or smoked bacon and mozzarella?'

'Ooh, tough one.' Sam deliberated. 'Can we have half and half?'

I grinned; this man got more amazing by the second. 'Good call.'

I divvied them up and put a bit of my bacon to one side for Scamp, who was poised between us watching our every move like a tennis fan at Wimbledon.

'Do you ever watch *The Apprentice*?' I said.

'You're fired.' Sam jabbed a finger at me. He winced. 'Actually more like *I'm* fired. Ugh. Forget I said that. I don't want to think about Hogg Property Services today.'

'If you do get fired, which I don't believe for a moment, but if you do, maybe it could be a good thing,' I said gently. 'You could have a change of direction. Like I did coming here. This could be your opportunity to go into catering.'

His eyes lit up. 'You really do remember everything I say, don't you?'

I shrugged nonchalantly. 'Of course.'

Then he screwed his face up. 'I dunno, I think maybe that ship has sailed. But thanks for the encouragement. Why did you ask about *The Apprentice*?'

'OK.' I took a sip of coffee, noting the change of subject. 'You know how there's always a task to make products and then sell them by the end of the day for a profit?'

He swallowed his mouthful, nodding. 'And then the team who makes the most profit wins.'

'Exactly, so . . .' I waggled my eyebrows. 'How do you fancy a challenge?'

'Hmm.' He narrowed his eyes as if sizing me up. 'I fancy it a lot.'

Suddenly the day was looking a hell of a lot better. I felt a frisson of excitement. 'Fantastic! I hope you're not a bad loser because I'll win.'

'That's what you think.' He clapped his hands together with glee. 'I can sell ice to the Eskimos.'

'A-ha! Your first mistake. They don't need ice,' I said triumphantly, slipping Scamp's bacon to him. You could only do that when you'd finished eating, otherwise he'd be on your knee clamouring for more. 'A clever sales person would sell them something they'll really appreciate, like those hand warmers you put in your gloves that get hot when you crack them, or Kendal mint cake to give them energy in the cold. Not something they have by the bucketload. Are you laughing at me?'

Sam was sniggering into his coffee cup. 'No. Well, yes, *a bit*. You're very sweet. I just mean I can convince people to buy things they didn't even know they needed.'

I was sweet. Which was all right, I supposed, but I'd rather be heart-stoppingly gorgeous. Of course, he might think I was gorgeous but not want to say so. On the other hand, he might be reeling from splitting up with his wife and not thinking about me in any other terms than a friend with a lot of flowers to sell. Probably that one.

Sam was still smiling, I smiled back.

'Things they don't know they need – you mean like *flowers*?' I gasped in mock offence. 'Flowers are very important things.'

'You're right, I apologise,' he said softly, holding my gaze. 'Thanks, this is just what I need.'

His hand covered mine and all my nerve endings jumped up and yelled *YES*.

'What, breakfast?' It came out a bit wonky because my mouth had gone dry.

'No, you crazy woman, a day doing something fun.'

'You're welcome.' My heart was clanging against my ribs like the pipe to the bathroom radiator but I thought I'd just about managed to stay cool.

'So what's the prize?' He chewed on his last mouthful of panini.

'Oh, er, I hadn't thought about a prize.' As far as I was concerned I was already the winner: I got to sell all these excess flowers and spend the day with Sam.

'How about . . . I dunno, the loser buys dinner?' he said casually.

There was a beat of silence while I processed this and tried to work out whether there was a subtext here or whether it was simply wishful thinking on my part. But then he went slightly pink.

'I know, sorry.' He held up his hands. 'Forget I said that. Why on earth would you want to spend even more time with a bitter and twisted old misery guts? But how about I promise not to say a single word about Pandora? And a girl has got to eat.'

'True,' I said pretending to think about it. I slipped my hand out from under his and reached for my mobile.

'What are you doing now?'

'Winning.' I twinkled my eyes at him and scrolled until I came to the number for the Wisteria Cottage Flower School. I pressed call. 'Fiona? Hi, Fearne Lovage here, just wondering if you'd be able to use three dozen avalanche roses? Cancelled order. I know. Very annoying. Two dozen? Absolutely. Fantastic! I'll get my driver to bring them over.'

I sorted out the details, negotiated a price which pleased us both and ended the call.

'Your driver?' Sam said, impressed.

I giggled and handed him a piece of paper with Fiona's address on it. 'I'd hurry if I were you, I'm winning already.'

Sam got to his feet, shaking his head in amusement. 'Sneaky, Very sneaky.'

Within a couple of hours my blood pressure had almost returned to normal. I was still knee deep in flowers but the friendly banter I had with Sam all morning had made the situation infinitely more bearable. He hadn't been lying when he said he was good at selling. Even before he set off with the roses to Fiona's flower school, he'd managed to sell two of the biggest arrangements to a football club. He also spread the word about our newly-created buy one bouquet, get a second half-price offer through his contacts which included his cricket team friend, the journalist, who had two thousand followers on twitter. Meanwhile I put in a call to Victor, who kindly managed to resell three boxes of spray roses to another of his customers in Derby.

As soon as Sam had gone, I dismantled some of the other arrangements and repurposed the flowers to make smaller, more saleable ones. Before long the phone was ringing with brand new customers putting their orders in for two bouquets. My heart was singing and even though my back was stiff and my fingers were sore from having them in water on and off for so long, I was euphoric and my cheeks were aching from so much smiling. At noon, I popped Scamp on his lead and took him for a quick leg-stretch on the green.

Scamp spotted a West Highland terrier he knew called Archie and went off to say hello and I took my phone out. I'd texted Laura earlier to tell her about Edelweiss, now I ought to let her know that the day wasn't a disaster at all. My call went to voicemail, I left her a message telling her about mine and Sam's challenge and seconds later a text appeared from her.

Can't talk at the mo, taking Dad to hospital. Glad it worked out. And VERY excited that Sam is helping you. Loser buys dinner? Sounds like you win either way. GO FEARNE! Xx

Oh? Hope he's OK?

Yep. Routine stuff apparently. Tell me more about SAM???

Glad to hear it, give him a kiss from me. Sam is . . . gorgeous *sigh*

I KNEW IT!!

I'm falling for him big time. But the timing is all wrong.

Forget timing, forget soul-searching. Go for it. Life's too short for anything else, honey.

But what about his wife?

EX WIFE. You are overthinking this. Do what makes you happy. Got to go. Will call you later. Big hugs x

My heart gave a little leap when I read this one. Perhaps she was right. Maybe I could just relax and see where it went. As Freddie would say: we get to choose who we love. I had a feeling that my heart had already chosen Sam.

By three o'clock, I realised I'd hardly stopped smiling all day. Somehow, the very worst day had turned into one of the very best and at the heart of it was the fun I'd had working with Sam. Between us we'd created and delivered more flowers today than I imagined the shop had ever done in its five-year history. I'd also learned a valuable lesson about securing payment upfront for large orders – if I even bothered chasing corporate business in the future, that was. Right now, I was revelling in the happiness that our flowers were giving our customers; seeing someone's joy when they buried their face in one of my bouquets was such a good feeling. Nina had been spot on about that.

'I'm winning, aren't I?' Sam was keeping score on a piece of paper. 'Admit it. I am Sir Alan's apprentice.'

'Is Rosie's last-minute order for tonight's baby shower on there?' I hid my smile, knowing it wasn't. 'It's in the cold store waiting for you to deliver when you have a moment.'

Sam muttered under his breath about cheats and then sucked in air. 'OK, fine, you're currently ahead by a whisker.'

'I'm just glad we've sold them. The main thing I was worried about,' I said, tying raffia around some flowers headed for the bistro in Chesterfield where Sam used to work, 'was not having enough money to pay the next rent instalment.'

'Oh, yeah,' he replied straight-faced. 'Having that dreadful Sam Diamond chasing you for money is the pits.'

'The worst,' I agreed with a cheeky smile.

Thanks to Sam's tireless tenacity, we'd almost recouped the shop's investment. Most of the Edelweiss flowers had been resold; I still had a stack of orders to make up but Sam had offered to do the deliveries for me this afternoon which would really help.

'If you don't mind a car with Hogg Property Services on the side of it turning up at customers' houses, that is?'

I looked at him, surprised. ''Course not.'

'Pandora refused to go anywhere in it,' he said with a grimace.

'Even though it's a BMW?' I raised an eyebrow. Then I had a thought. 'Was she a Hogg before she married you?'

He stifled a laugh, nodding. 'When I was trying to propose, she yelled *yes* before I even got to pop the question. Even at the time, I wondered whether she just wanted to get rid of her maiden name.'

Just then my phone rang with another order. I took the details while Sam loaded his car.

'I'll make these deliveries then,' he said, a few minutes later. 'And when I get back, we'll do the final calculation. Loser buys dinner. Agreed?'

'Agreed.' I grinned. 'Hope you've got your credit card with you.'

He laughed at that and picked up his car keys from the counter.

'I might surprise you yet.' He stooped and kissed my cheek and, before I had a chance to react, he left.

You just did, I thought. My hand flew to my face where his lips had brushed my skin.

A few minutes later, I was still reeling from what had just happened when Scamp flew from his bed as if he'd been given an electric shock and leapt up at the shop window, barking loudly, his tail whirling in happy circles.

I joined him and spotted a car which had just pulled up to the kerb immediately outside the shop. The back of the car was packed with boxes and suitcases, and in the front, her white bun only just visible in the passenger seat was my dear friend.

'It's Ethel!' I cried, ruffling Scamp's ears. 'Come on, let's go and meet her.'

The two of us dashed outside. Scamp was trembling with joy, his whole body wagging as he lolloped to the car. The passenger door opened slowly and as soon as the gap was large enough Scamp pushed his nose into the car and onto Ethel's lap where he promptly squeaked with uncontained bliss and licked her face. Meanwhile, Carole got out of the driver's side and joined me on the pavement.

She hugged me warmly. 'Thanks for inviting Mum round, she's so excited to see your shop. Although I think she's a bit overwhelmed with the emotions of the day: leaving Derbyshire after all these years.'

I liked Carole, I'd got to know her better since Ethel's fall in January and thought how capable and calm she always was, whatever life threw at her.

I nodded. 'And a big day for you and your husband, having your mum move in. How are you?'

'Ask me after a few months!' She laughed. 'In all serious-ness, I'll be glad to have Mum close to me. She's a dear old thing and gives the best advice.'

'I know.' I smiled ruefully, 'I shall miss her words of wisdom.'

'Good grief!' Ethel hooted with laughter from inside the car, trying to escape Scamp's attentions. 'What a welcome! Enough now, you silly old thing.'

I opened the car door wide and crouched down, watching Ethel trying to avoid Scamp's tongue. My heart twisted suddenly; now that she was out of the care home, would she want him back? She was within her rights, of course, he was her dog really not mine, but . . . I gave a shudder.

'Come on now, Scamp,' I said, patting his rump. 'My turn for a kiss, out you get.'

Scamp jumped out of the car but danced around my feet anxiously in case the door shut again and I held my hand out to Ethel.

'Long time no see, it is so lovely to see you,' I beamed, thrilled to have her here.

'Hello dear.' Ethel's bright eyes twinkled. 'What a charming village! And such a pretty flower shop, no wonder there's a sparkle in your eye.'

I laughed and automatically raised my fingers to the spot Sam had kissed. 'That could well be residual adrenaline after the day I've had.'

She grasped my hand in hers and after shuffling her feet out of the car took a big breath before pushing herself upright. Beside me she was tiny; I reckoned she must have shrunk a couple of centimetres this year.

I pressed a kiss to her soft cheek.

'Goodness me, dear!' She looked up at me, tongue in cheek. 'I think you've grown.'

'Yep. Thirty-four and I'm having a growth spurt,' I laughed, teasingly. 'Come on in and I'll put the kettle on.'

'Do you want your walking frame, Mum?' Carole asked, shutting Ethel's door.

'Me?' Ethel looked affronted. 'Not on your nelly, I could run around this village green if I had time.'

I raised an eyebrow at Carole who rolled her eyes fondly.

'Talking of time, if it's all the same to you,' she said, checking her watch, 'I won't come in, I spotted a garden centre on the way into the village and I've run out of tomato food. I won't be long.'

Ethel and I waved her off in the direction of Garden Warehouse and went inside.

'Delightful,' she declared after I'd given her a tour of the shop.

Scamp hadn't left her side for a second and now she was seated at the work table he pressed his body against her and stared adoringly up at her.

'I love all the little details: the props which add character to the displays, and the smell is heavenly.'

'Those are Nina's touches,' I said proudly, from the kitchenette where I pulled out coffee, milk and a china cup and saucer I'd brought in from home especially for Ethel's visit. 'She's very arty, I'm better at the business side.'

I paused and pulled a face. 'Although after today, that's debatable.'

'Oh?' Ethel raised her eyebrows, as astute as ever. 'Sounds like you're having adventures just as I'd hoped.'

'Oh, I am, don't worry,' I laughed drily. 'Plenty of those.'

Although investing all the business's money in flowers for an order that was never formally confirmed was probably not quite what she meant by being adventurous.

'How's that man, the landlord? Sam, isn't it?'

'You don't forget a thing, do you.' I chuckled, pouring water into her cup and my usual mug.

'My legs might be dodgy but my brain still works. It's the quiz shows; I knew they'd come in handy for keeping the old grey matter alive. Ask me any capital city and I bet I can get it.'

'OK, what's the capital of Uzbekistan?'

'Never heard of it. Anyway, stop changing the subject, I want to hear more about this young man.'

I laughed as I set her cup down. 'I've missed you so much.'

'Ooh, real china?' Her face lit up. 'And I've missed you, but I'm here now so get on with it. Sam. All the details please.'

I put my mug down beside hers. 'Are you sitting comfortably?'

She ruffled Scamp's fur and her eyes shone. 'Indeed I am.'

I told her everything. About how Sam had come in to buy some flowers for his wife, which led to them getting back together. I told her about the order we'd had to make up for her from her fancy man Gareth and how treacherous Nina and I had felt delivering flowers to Pandora behind Sam's back. I told her about the events of Saturday night with the cricket team. Finally, I told her about the fiasco at the Claybourne Hotel and how Pandora had got caught in the same scam, but that Sam had been helping me all day.

'Poor lad,' Ethel tutted when I finished. 'That flibberti-gibbet has really put him through the mill. He's far better off without her.'

'I think so.'

She eyed me shrewdly. 'Sounds like he's quite fond of you.'

I couldn't help the smile which broke out on my face.

323

'And me him. But I can't help feeling that I should hold myself back, when his love life – in fact his whole life – is in chaos.'

'Or.' Ethel sipped her tea. 'You could allow yourself to be happy about having this person in your life, instead of feeling guilty about it?'

'He's not free to be in my life, not while he's still in someone else's,' I pointed out.

She was quiet for a moment. 'You're right, love. And you're very sensible.'

'Sensible would be putting him out of my mind completely.' I leaned forward at the table, resting my chin in my hand. 'If any of my friends were in this situation, I'd advise them to avoid him like the plague until he's ready to move on. Everyone knows you shouldn't go from one relationship straight to another.'

'This happened to some of our friends in the forties after the war, you know. Husbands sometimes didn't come home and sometimes they did but the war had changed them so much that they couldn't settle back into the life they'd left. There were lots of young women left on their own who started courting as soon as they could, wanting to feel a man's arms around them again. But even under those circumstances, I always advised my friends to take it slow. I'd say the same to you.'

I felt a rush of warmth for my dear old friend and I covered her hand in mine. The skin was warm and papery thin. It was easy to think that affairs of the heart were the preserve of the young. But Ethel's heart had decades more experience at loving and being loved than mine.

'You're right,' I agreed. 'Although he kissed my cheek earlier and if he does that again, I might find it almost impossible to take it slow.'

She chuckled. 'I'd like to have met the man who's put the colour back in my Fearne's cheeks. He'll need a good friend like you in the coming months. Someone who'll be unconditionally on his side, someone to listen. It sounds like he's got a lot to be angry about.'

'I can be his friend,' I said, meaning it. 'I'd rather be just a friend to him than nothing at all.'

'I'm sure you would, dear,' she warned. 'But you've had your own share of sorrow this past year. You deserve to be someone's significant other, not to just be a shoulder to cry on.'

'I'll remember. Scamp likes him by the way.'

She chuckled. 'Then that's all I need to know he's a good 'un.'

'Thank you, Ethel.' I patted her hand. 'What would I do without your advice?'

'Thank *you*, dear.' Ethel smiled faintly and felt in her handbag for a tissue to blow her nose. 'You don't know how much it means to me to hear that. Thank you for making me feel like me again. Most days I'm in the way. I'm on this earth just taking up room. It's nice to feel useful for a change. Even just having Scamp to look after gave me something to do.'

At the mention of his name, the dog turned to look up at Ethel, resting his chin on her leg and she stroked his nose and smoothed back his wiry eyebrows. A lump had formed in my throat, tears threatened to fall and for a moment I couldn't speak.

'Hello, old friend,' she murmured. 'Yes, I'm talking about you.'

I knew what I had to do; I had to let him go. It was the right thing to do. Ethel had only agreed to give him up for good when she'd thought she'd be staying in the care home for the rest of her days. But now things had changed.

Through the archway, I saw Carole's car pull up again. She got out of the car, collected her handbag from the back seat and marched purposefully towards us.

I dropped onto the floor and buried my face in Scamp's fur, hugging his neck and kissing his face again and again.

'What a wonderful variety of flowers you have!' Carole exclaimed, joining us at the back of the shop.

I sprang up, quickly brushing any stray tears from my face. 'Thank you.'

'Fearne is a very talented girl,' said Ethel struggling to get to her feet. 'And I think she's found her happy place.' She bent down to the dog. 'And so has my faithful friend.'

'Oh yes, the dog,' said Carole slipping her arm through her mother's. 'We were talking about Scamp coming up to Yorkshire, weren't we, Mum?'

Ethel nodded. 'If that suits you? It's just I can't bear to think that I might never see him again.'

'Of course, I completely understand.' I tried to smile but my mouth wouldn't bend into a line. I wasn't sure how I could bear it either. 'He's been yours since he was a bundle of fluff, it's only fair that you take him to Yorkshire with you.'

I turned away, pretending to look for a bag to put his things in. I'd got his lead and his bed here, his water bowl and one or two of his toys. The rest I supposed I could send in the post.

Carole gave a strangled laugh. 'No, no, not now!'

'We mean if you go on holiday,' Ethel said quickly, 'and didn't want to put him into a kennel, he could come to us.'

'We can't really accommodate a dog,' Carole explained.

'Oh.' I blinked at them both. I felt dizzy with relief. 'I thought . . . I thought you meant . . .'

'It's not fair to uproot him at his age,' Ethel said, brusquely. And yet she was uprooting herself, I thought, marvelling at my old friend's eternally optimistic spirit. 'And you love him. He belongs with you now. So that's that.'

I hugged her close. 'I'll look after him, I promise. And yes, coming to you for a holiday is a brilliant idea.'

I helped Carole tuck Ethel safely into the passenger seat and stood back to give her some privacy while she clutched Scamp to her for a final hug and I pretended not to see the tears run down her face.

'Are you belted up, Mum?' Carole asked, putting the keys in the ignition. Ethel confirmed that she was and I lifted Scamp out of the car.

'Let's talk again soon,' I said, kissing her cheek.

'I'd like that.' She hesitated. 'Keep having those adventures, Fearne.'

'I will if you will,' I replied.

'Lord help us,' I heard Carole mutter as I shut the door.

Scamp and I stayed on the pavement, me waving and him whimpering softly until they were out of sight. And then we turned and went back inside where I sat on the floor and cuddled my dog, a tear of gratitude and relief slipping down my face.

By the time Sam arrived back I'd pulled myself together, sold half a dozen posies to the customers sitting outside the Lemon Tree Café and hurriedly made a bouquet for Sam to give to his mum.

He walked in as I was tying raffia around the stems.

'Bad news,' I said, grinning at him. 'Unless you've managed to sell a miraculous number of flowers while you've been gone, I'm declaring myself the winner. But to show I'm a gracious winner, these are for you, or your mum anyway. With my compliments.'

I held them out to him and he took them from me.

'That's very thoughtful of you,' he said flatly.

He didn't return my smile; in fact, now I looked properly at him, he'd gone a ghostly shade of grey.

'Sam?' I demanded, 'what is it?'

'More bad news, I'm afraid. Come and sit down.' He took my hand and led me to a stool at the counter and numbly I did as I was told. 'I've just taken a phone call from my father-in-law, Duncan Hogg.'

I gasped, worried for him. 'What's happened? Is it the children?'

He smiled grimly. 'It's not the kids, but it's kind of you to think of them. No, the bad news involves you and this shop.'

My heart was in my mouth as I stared at him, waiting for him to elaborate.

He raked a hand wearily through his hair. 'There's no easy way to say this but Duncan's decided to terminate your lease.'

'No!' I clamped a hand over my mouth. 'Can he do that?'

He nodded. 'As long as he gives you adequate notice, he can do what he likes.'

I leaned towards him, resting my head against his chest, Sam put his arms around me.

'This is all my fault,' I murmured. 'Poor Nina, she's going to wish she'd never got involved with me.'

'It's my fault, not yours.' His touch on my back was gentle, but his voice was as hard as stone. 'I'm absolutely livid. Pandora will have spun him some lies about you and me and he's acting out of spite. The sooner I'm out of this family the better. I'll do my best to talk him out of it, but to be honest that might make things worse. My best bet is appealing to Pandora's better nature.'

Then we're doomed, I thought to myself.

'Thank you, it's got to be worth a try. I suppose I'd better tell Nina,' I murmured, conscious that it would probably spoil the rest of her New Zealand adventure.

I sat up straight again and we smiled at each other sadly; it was such a rubbish end to a happy day.

'I'm going to find Pandora now and have a few things out with her.' Sam shoved his hands in his pockets looking very glum. 'I guess this means we'll have to take a rain check on that dinner.'

'Probably for the best.' I swallowed down my disappointment.

'Chin up,' he said, kissing the top of my head chastely. 'I'm not giving up yet. And I'm glad I'm the loser, because now there's no getting out of having dinner with me.'

A laugh bubbled up inside me; he'd done it again: managed to make me happy even when times were hard.

'Every cloud has a silver lining,' I said with a grin. 'See you soon.'

He laughed and headed out to his car with the bouquet for his mum.

As soon as Sam's car had vanished from view, I made a snap decision to close the shop early. I needed some fresh air and some time to work out what I was going to say to Nina. I quickly tidied up the shop, topped up the water in the flower buckets and flipped the shop sign from open to closed.

Scamp and I got into the van and I wound down the windows to let in some cool air. I'd just strapped us both in when my mobile rang again. I smiled with relief when I saw Laura's name flash up.

'Boy, am I glad to hear from you,' I said, relaxing back in my seat. 'You wouldn't believe everything that's happened to me today.'

Laura laughed shakily. 'Ditto.'

Scamp settled down on the seat, sensing he could be here some time and I fondled his ears, a renewed sense of relief washing over me that he was still here and not halfway to Yorkshire with Ethel and Carole.

'So what's up?' I asked.

'I don't know where to begin.' She let out a long breath. 'There's good news and there's bad.'

I frowned, not liking the vibes I was getting from her down the line. 'Laura, are you sure you want to do this over the phone? I can drive over if you like.'

'No, not today, tomorrow maybe, but I . . . we . . . just not tonight. Thanks,' she added as an afterthought. She sounded high-pitched and panicky.

'OK' I said softly. 'Tomorrow, that's no problem. I'm here for you whenever.'

She groaned. 'I'm sorry, I'm all over the place. Right, here goes: I know I told you not to do any more wedding flowers, but will you make an exception for me and Hamish?'

'Of course! You know I will.' I held my breath, wondering what was really going on here.

'Thank you,' she said in a wobbly voice. 'He's just proposed and I said yes.'

'OH MY WORD, this is so exciting!' I squealed. 'Congratulations. Tell me everything: how did he propose? Have you set a date? And who's going to be maid of honour? Oh, Laura, I am so thrilled for you!'

My reaction to this wonderful news was so exuberant that it took me a while to pick up on the fact that Laura didn't seem to be laughing with me.

'Hamish proposed to me in the garden at Dad's, under the rose arbour. He was wonderful, he told me that I made his life complete and if I'd be his wife he'd make it his mission to make me the happiest woman on earth.'

'That's so romantic!' I exclaimed, but my brain was sounding the alarm, something didn't fit.

'And I'm hoping that as well as being my florist, you'll also be my maid of honour.'

'I'd be delighted,' I said, aware that she still hadn't mentioned the bad news.

Laura continued as if I hadn't spoken. 'Hamish is already on his way to start the ball rolling. We're going for the first date possible. It takes a minimum of twenty-eight days to do the legal bit, so I'm hoping we can do it about thirty days from now.'

My eyes widened. 'So you and Hamish are hoping to get married in July?'

'It's Dad, you see,' Laura blurted out, her voice finally cracking. 'He's ill. Properly, seriously ill. Hamish and I have been with him all day today. And if we don't get married in a hurry, he might never get the chance to walk me up the aisle. I'm losing him, Fearne and he's the only family I have left.'

'Oh, darling, I'm so sorry, your poor dad,' I said, my own voice wavering. My heart ached bitterly for her. Just when she and Hamish were enjoying their life together.

She blew her nose. 'I feel so helpless. He's known for a while but wanted to deal with it by himself, not wanting to make a fuss. But now he's been told he's only got weeks.'

'I think you're amazing,' I said stoutly. 'You and Hamish, I'm so proud of you.' Holding back the tears, I added, 'You just concentrate on your dad and leave everything to me. Every tiny thing.'

'Really?' she gasped. 'That would be so helpful. I want to make the wedding as special as it can be but I just don't think I have the energy to do that and look after Dad.'

'I give you my word,' I said solemnly. 'Your wedding day will be magical and memorable and the happiest day of your life.'

Laura sobbed. 'Oh Fearne, you don't know how much that means to me.'

'You're my best friend,' I said. 'And you were there for me. Now it's my turn to be there for you.'

'It's so good to have you back, Fearne.'

Laura was right; the old me was back, I realised. I was done with keeping people at arm's length, I'd had enough of letting my grief get the better of me. Forcing myself out of my comfort zone and accepting the job with Nina had helped beyond doubt, but choosing to be happy, taking risks and letting others see what was written in my heart had also worked wonders. Life was exhilarating and fraught with ups and downs, but whatever the future threw my way, I knew I could deal with it.

I smiled through my tears. 'It's good to be back.'

I drove back home, my head whirling with ideas and plans, sadness and pain and my hand stealing across to comfort Scamp as often as I could. The day had been such a roller coaster and a few months ago, all this would have sent me into freefall, I'd have shut myself off, hidden from my grief. But I'd learned a lot since then.

This time I wasn't going to run away. The pain of loss might be strong, but my love for life was stronger. I had a business to save before Nina came back, an emergency wedding to organise and as for Sam, could I hide my feelings and be the true friend he needed right now? The next month was going to be the most challenging of my life. *So what*, I thought, as I pulled up outside my house.

Bring it on.

Part Four

Chapter Thirty-one

It felt like somebody had turned Britain's thermostat up to max and Barnaby was in full-on heatwave mode. Shorts, sundresses and sunglasses were *de rigeur* and the smell of suncream and barbecues filled the air. On the village green, freckled children caught silvery fish in the stream with their nets while parents flopped on blankets.

I was a big fan of summer; give me some good music and a cold drink and I could happily lie on a sun lounger for the entire day. Although possibly not right now; I had too much on my mind to enjoy the warm weather this week. I had a last-minute wedding to organise and before I could get properly stuck into that I needed to speak to Nina about the news Sam had delivered two days ago.

Unfortunately, she was proving very tricky to get hold of. She'd warned me this might happen, that on some days she'd be on a farm in the middle of nowhere with no access to the outside world. It was one of the things she'd been most looking forward to. But as I was left holding the baby, it was giving me sleepless nights.

I left her another text message letting her know that I'd agreed to do Laura's unexpected wedding and that I couldn't wait to hear from her, which was the most urgent I could be without worrying her, and crouched down by Scamp to check he wasn't overheating in the shop window.

'You daft thing,' I laughed softly. 'There's a big cool patch of floor back there and you're lying in the hottest place in the shop.'

Scamp panted in reply, his tongue twice as long as usual. I stood up and refilled his bowl with cold water, glancing at the calendar on the wall on my way to the tap.

Two months. That's all we had. Two short months from the first of July to relocate Nina's Flowers. It didn't seem right to me that Hogg Property Services could give us such little notice, but Sam had confirmed that they could and would. By September, Nina and I would no longer be looking out over buckets of hydrangeas and roses and lilies onto this idyllic little corner of England; we'd be goodness knows where.

Still, there was no use moping about it, I had a country-garden-inspired wreath to prepare for a funeral which I instinctively knew Granny would have adored and Wendy would be sending her driver to collect it in half an hour. I buried myself in work and the morning flew by.

By twelve o'clock there'd still been no word from Nina. I was just considering closing the shop and popping over to Ken's Mini Mart for an ice cream when Stanley came in.

'Good grief,' he said, dabbing a crisp white handkerchief to his brow. 'I've only walked for ten minutes and I'm at melting point.'

I poured him a glass of water and directed him to a chair. I had a soft spot for Stanley; he was such a gentleman with his old-fashioned manners and I loved the way his quietly spoken ways complemented those of his feisty fiancé, Maria.

'Not enjoying the sunshine, then?'

'This isn't sunshine; this is an inferno. I can't sleep a wink at night,' said Stanley. 'And Maria's no better, huffing and puffing all night, wrestling with her rucked-up nightie.'

'You'll have to tell her to sleep in the buff, Stanley,' I suggested. 'That might help.'

He chuckled. 'I did propose that and I got a clip around the ear. What she really wants is a room with air-conditioning.'

'Then whisk her away for a night. The Claybourne Hotel has some good offers on.'

Stanley polished his glasses thoughtfully. 'Now that's not a bad idea. I believe the Claybourne is licensed for weddings, so maybe I can tempt her to set a date while we're there. I'll take her some flowers to get into her good books first and then bring up the subject. Thank you, Fearne.'

I helped him choose a bunch of exotic orange calla lilies and was waving him on his way when Nina called.

'Hello, stranger!' I said, relieved to hear from her.

'Sorry you couldn't get hold of me,' she gushed. 'I've just had the most amazing couple of days of my entire life! Guess what I've been doing. No don't bother, you'll never get it. I helped deliver a foal! In the snow! It was just breathtaking and bloody freezing. The mother was so strong and brave and then her baby appeared and . . . oh God, it was the most gorgeous sight. I cried. I'm crying now! I love it here. Absolutely love it. Being filmed all the time was weird at first but now I'm quite enjoying it. I know I've said it a million times, but I owe you so much for holding the fort so I can have this adventure. And no, before you ask, I haven't fallen in love yet.'

She paused to laugh and her joy warmed my heart; all the stresses and strains of running a struggling business blown away under a giant antipodean winter sky.

My chest was getting tighter and tighter as she rambled; I hated that I was just about to burst her bubble. But it had to be done.

'Anyway, how are things in little old Barnaby?' She paused for breath. 'Any more matches, hatches or despatches I should know about? And I've heard how hot it is! Bloody typical. First decent summer we've had in years and I'm eleven thousand miles away freezing my tits off.'

I swallowed. 'Funny you should mention it; things have been getting a little hot under the collar this week.'

'Oh, yes, you've had that Edelweiss thing! I knew that would be a tough one, how did it go?'

'Cancelled.'

Nina gasped. 'Balls! All those flowers! Nightmare!'

'Don't worry, we managed to sell most of them. So we ended up even by the end of the day.'

In fact, by the end of the day, we'd ended up facing eviction, but I was building up to that.

'There were some left over so I made a bouquet of pink, yellow and blue blooms and gave them to Rosie for her baby shower.'

'Which I missed,' she said.

'So did I in the end,' I said. After the events of that day, I hadn't felt up to joining Rosie and her friends to celebrate at the café.

'Wait,' said Nina excitedly. 'I've just realised what you said. You said 'we' managed to sell the flowers. Who's we?'

'Me and Sam.'

'You and *Sam*?' I held the phone at arm's length while she squealed in delight. 'YESSS! I'm so happy for you. So he came back, I knew he would.'

The last time I'd updated her it was to tell her about the Saturday night when Pandora had turned up during the cricket players' workshop and Sam had found out about Gareth and stormed out.

'He's been brilliant,' I said. 'We made a great team.'

'And yet I'm sensing all is not paradise in the garden. What's up?'

'It's not Sam, it's me,' I groaned. 'I'm so sorry, I've made a mess of everything.'

'Hey, you've brought nothing but good stuff to Nina's Flowers, I've got a couple of minutes before the next task, tell all, it can't be that bad.'

'I'm afraid it can,' I said and proceeded to prove it by bringing her up to speed.

'Jeez! By September? The absolute shitbag!' she spluttered. 'How pathetic and spiteful and un-bloody-necessary.'

I felt wretched. I leaned my elbow on the counter, resting my head in my hand. 'We haven't had it in writing yet, but I'm expecting it any day now.'

'And this is all because Pandora has gone crying to Daddy about Sam's relationship with you?'

'I think so. I can't prove it, but it's a bit of a coincidence, isn't it? And the annoying thing is, Sam and I have done nothing wrong. In fact, we've done nothing full stop. Unlike her.'

Nina was quiet except for her breathing which sounded like the snort of a bull getting ready to lower his horns and charge.

'I'm sorry. I feel totally responsible,' I began, feeling the weight of the silence. 'So I thought perhaps—'

'Oh shit, look I've got to go, I'm wanted again,' she said abruptly. 'I'll call back later.'

'Later today or later—' I stopped, realising the line had gone dead. 'Well done, Fearne, you handled that brilliantly.'

'Talking to yourself?' came a familiar voice from the door. 'Sounds like I came in the nick of time.'

I lifted my head and there was Sam: golden and gorgeous, the sunlight behind him creating a halo effect around his hair. *Just friends*, I reminded my heart which had automatically started to thump at the sight of him. Not that I was ruling anything else out in the future, but Ethel's advice was to give him space to extract himself from his feelings for Pandora, and that was what I needed to do.

'Hello, Sam,' I managed to say casually. 'Your timing's perfect. I'm just making tea.'

Scamp was off his bed in a flash and sat down at Sam's feet to gaze up adoringly at him. Sam patted his pockets and produced a Tic Tac.

'It's all I've got. I don't suppose he can eat mints?' He gave me a lopsided smile.

I nodded. 'He loves them. In fact, you'll be doing a public service; he had salmon for breakfast.'

I watched the two of them having a cuddle and tried not to feel jealous.

'So how are you?' we both said at the same time and then laughed awkwardly.

'You first,' said Sam.

'On edge. I've just given Nina the news about the lease and she was called away before we had chance to talk it through properly.'

He sucked his cheeks in. 'I can guess how well that went down.'

'Hmm,' I gave him a knowing look. 'I'd really like to find a solution quickly so it doesn't ruin the rest of her trip. I've been looking online for new premises, but no joy yet.'

I allowed myself a small sigh of exasperation and headed into the shop's tiny kitchen.

He followed me and caught hold of my hand gently. 'Fearne, come here, you look like you need a hug.'

I smiled. 'I'm fine, honestly.'

But he folded me into his arms anyway and I didn't resist. I closed my eyes and felt his heart beating through his T-shirt. How did he always manage to turn up just at the right moment?

'I've already put the word out to my contacts; if any suitable shops come up for rent, I'll be the first to know. You'll be the second.'

'Thanks.' I pulled back from his arms and smiled. 'I can't deny that it's a blow but I'm determined not to let it get me down. Besides, I haven't got time to be worried; my best friend is getting married next month and I've offered to organise the wedding for her.'

I put the kettle on and Sam leaned back against the sink, watching me.

He grinned. 'Nina hightails it to the other side of the world and you take over her business, now you're doing the same for your friend's wedding. You're quite an inspiration, Fearne Lovage.'

'Nonsense,' I said dismissively, secretly proud. I brushed aside the doubts which had bobbed in and out of my head over the last few days. I did have a lot on my plate, but I'd been good at juggling deadlines in my old job and besides I had no intention of letting Laura and Hamish down. 'Now your turn, how are you?'

He didn't reply straight away and then gave a surprised smile. 'To be honest, I'm OK. Yes. I'm really OK.'

'And Pandora?'

'When I left here on Tuesday I went straight to our house. *Her* house. Gareth was there but he made himself scarce pretty quickly after apologising to me. Pandora hadn't told him we were trying again. Poor chap. I almost felt sorry for him.' He paused, running a thumb along his lower lip.

He had lovely lips, I noticed; I couldn't drag my eyes from him. I turned away to make the tea to stop myself from staring at him.

'Anyway I made her sit down and talk to me properly. I think we've both accepted we want different things. Our marriage is over for good.'

'I'm sorry,' I said, meaning it. Whatever I thought of Pandora and however much my own selfish heart was fizzing with future possibilities, she and Sam were parents, they had history, children and the breakdown of any relationship was never without stresses and strains.

He shot me a smile of thanks. 'We've made some decisions and for the first time in months we've actually made some progress.'

He crossed his ankles and smiled. His whole demeanour seemed to have changed in the last two days: the creases between his eyebrows had gone, his eyes shone and even though he was leaning back against the sink, I could see he was holding himself straighter.

'Well done, you should be proud of yourself.' I handed him a mug and his fingers brushed mine as he thanked me. My insides quivered and I took a step back.

'We've made some rules about the kids. I'm going to find somewhere to live so they can have their own rooms and as soon as they're back from Lanzarote, she and I will share their care.'

'Joint custody?'

'Yep.' His face lit up when he talked about his children; I was so pleased it was working out for him. 'I know it's not ideal for the kids, but if Pandora and I work at it, we can make sure the kids have the best of both worlds.'

I squeezed his arm. 'That's brilliant.'

'I think so, I can't believe my luck.' He grinned. 'She doesn't want her dad to know about her affair with Gareth. So in return for my discretion, she's promised to play fair.'

I crossed my fingers and held them up. 'Does this mean the shop is safe?'

A flash of annoyance crossed his face. 'Not yet, I'm still working on it. I spent two hours on the phone to Duncan arguing your case but I can't get him to move on it. Once he's made a decision about something it's virtually impossible to get him to retract it. It's where Pandora gets her stubborn streak from. I'm not giving up, though.'

'Oh well.' I shrugged. 'Thanks for trying.'

'I've got an official letter for you.' He winced as he pulled a white envelope from his back pocket and handed it to me. 'It's the termination notice. I hope you know how bad I feel about this.'

I nodded and stared at the envelope in my hands.

'I came to work here because flowers were top of my happiness list. I wanted to make myself happy.' I tapped the envelope against my palm. 'I hope my happiness hasn't come at the expense of Nina's.'

He caught hold of my fingers. 'Do you regret it?'

I didn't answer straight away. I remembered what had set me on this journey: the decision to live a life that I'd chosen, one filled with happy moments, one that I'd look back on and have zero regrets about. I thought about the happiness that I'd experienced over the last few months and how happy Nina was to be finally doing the travelling she'd always dreamed of. A smile broke out slowly on my face until I was beaming at him.

'What?' He smiled. 'What have I said?'

'Exactly the right thing,' I said, barely able to contain my exuberance. 'I have absolutely no regrets, none at all. Isn't that amazing!'

He laughed at me. 'It is amazing. So amazing that I think we should go out and celebrate on Sunday. I owe you dinner, remember?'

My stomach fluttered; I couldn't think of anything I'd rather do.

'I'd love that,' I said shyly.

'Then it's a date.'

We sorted out the time and place – Sam was going to pick me up from my house – and then he had to go.

'Until Sunday, then.' His face flushed. 'Blimey, I haven't been on a date for a long time. Not that it is one!'

'No, of course not.' I shook my head rapidly.

'Unless . . .?' He cocked an eyebrow and we both laughed.

After a moment's hesitation he pulled me into his arms and we laughed some more and I knew that whatever happened I'd always look back at this moment with this man and my heart would smile. I was living the life I'd hoped for and I had a feeling that with Sam by my side, I could carry on that way for a long time to come.

Chapter Thirty-two

Sam had only been gone a few minutes when I had a visitor to the shop whom I'd not met before, although I'd seen her from a distance.

'Oh these flippin' wheels!' she muttered from the doorway. 'They all insist on going in different directions.'

She was trying to manoeuvre a double buggy over the threshold. It was long rather than wide and contained two sleeping children. She was breathless and red-faced, her pale pink hair escaping from a ponytail.

'Let me help.' I went to her assistance, guiding the front end in.

'I'm so unfit. You must be Fearne!' She beamed at me and thrust a hand in my direction, still panting. 'I'm Gina. I was hoping to meet you at Rosie's baby shower. I saw your flowers though. Really gorgeous.'

'Thank you.' I shook her hand. 'Nice to meet you, finally.'

She pulled a face. 'I know. Sorry, I don't buy flowers much at this time of year. We've got such a big garden that I can usually find enough to stuff in a vase or two. But despite the garden growing like topsy, as Bing would say, I haven't got what I need for today's emergency.'

'You're in the right place, I'm an expert at emergencies.' I set the envelope with the Hogg Property Services logo down on the counter and gave her my full attention. 'How can I help?'

She peered at the two little ones to check they were still asleep, which they were, and then pulled a couple of vases out of a bag she'd got hooked over the handles of the buggy. 'Massive cheek, but Delphine said you were very kind and wouldn't mind helping me? I'm afraid I'm in a terrible rush.'

'You're a friend of Delphine's?' I smiled, remembering that she'd been one of the first customers through the door on my very first day, bringing her own flowers with her.

Gina nodded. 'We all live together at The Evergreens. There's me, Dexter, my boyfriend, and then our older residents, Delphine, Bing and Una, plus half a million children in the daytime.'

It sounded the most unusual living arrangement I'd ever heard; I wondered what the emergency could be.

'I can deliver them this afternoon if you like,' I offered, thinking that I'd quite like a peek inside The Evergreens.

'Under normal circumstances, that would be great,' she said, wrinkling her nose. 'But I've got some . . . er . . . unexpected visitors arriving in half an hour. I've left my friend supervising nap time, Dexter and Delphine tidying inside and Bing and Una titivating the garden. I had to bring Tabitha and Harris with me because they wouldn't sleep. I've got twenty minutes, tops.'

'Gosh, you really are in a rush.' I looked at the big vases. 'How about I make bouquets to fit those with their own water pouch, then you can just pop them in vases when you get home.'

She shot me a look of gratitude. 'Oh, please. And can I leave the buggy here while I nip into the café and pick up a Victoria sponge?'

I said she could. She was only gone for five minutes and thankfully neither child had stirred, despite Scamp stealing a soggy biscuit out of the hand of the little boy in the front. I picked big bold blooms which would quickly fill the vase to save time and filled the gaps with foliage.

'That's so impressive,' said Gina, whistling through her teeth as she watched me make a cellophane bag for the first bouquet and fill it with water. 'If today's meeting goes well, we'll be in the market for flowers regularly. This sort of thing will look amazing in the hall.'

'You'll have to be quick.' I nudged the envelope in her direction and invited her to read it. 'Our landlord wants us out. Goodness knows where we'll be come September.'

Gina frowned as she skimmed over the letter. 'You have my sympathy. This exact thing happened to me with my business. So unsettling.'

Just then the little girl sitting in the back of the buggy woke up and began kicking her legs. Gina scooped her up and cuddled her while she told me how she had come to buy The Evergreens last year. The owner, Violet had passed away and the relatives who had inherited it decided to sell. Gina had been renting the small gatekeeper's cottage at the time while Delphine and Bing had lived with Violet in the big house.

'I couldn't bear the thought of my friends being made homeless, so I decided to try and buy the property myself. It was quite an eye-opener to find that I had the courage to do it. I'd never really fought for anything in my life before.'

'So what changed?' I smiled at the little girl and handed her a flower to hold. She gasped and waved it about like a wand.

'I just knew that The Evergreens was my future and I couldn't bear the alternative. It had so much potential and I wanted to see it full of love. It also helped that the person who was trying to evict me was the most gorgeous man I'd ever met.' She sighed dreamily.

'Is he now your boyfriend?'

Gina grinned. 'Dexter, yes.'

'What a coincidence.'

'Do you know him?' she asked, surprised.

'No,' I laughed. 'It's just that the person evicting us is also pretty gorgeous.'

'Then you must fight for it like I did!' she declared, passionately. 'It wasn't plain sailing, mind you. And at one point I thought I'd completely cocked it up. But things have a way of working out. I hope they do for you.'

'So do I.' I finished the second bouquet while Gina strapped Tabitha back in the buggy and handed the little girl a beaker.

I helped her back outside with the buggy and said goodbye, my mind fizzing with questions. I could try and fight this eviction for Nina, but was the florist's shop *my* future? I wasn't sure if I'd like working here in the depths of winter, although I did love doing the workshops and sharing my love of flowers with others. Was there some way I could focus on that? And what about Nina? She'd thought about closing the business before, perhaps this would be the tipping point for her to walk away completely. I needed to know where she stood as soon as possible. And Sam . . . I bit my lip; I had good intentions about staying friends, but today, the moment he'd mentioned a date, I was putty in his hands. Should I listen to my head or my heart? I groaned aloud and Scamp cocked his head anxiously. I flipped the sign from open to closed and fetched his lead.

'Let's go down to the river.' I clicked my fingers to my ever eager dog. 'I've got some serious thinking to do.'

I made it along the towpath as far as the Riverside Hotel and was just casting my mind back to the day I'd finished off the flowers for Rosie's wedding when Nina rang me back.

'Sorry I had to cut you off earlier,' she said breezily.

'That's OK. It was a shock. I'm sorry that I had to deliver such upsetting news, I'm not surprised you hung up.'

'What are you on about, you daft thing?' she cried. 'I had to go because it was all kicking off. Anya is threatening to walk after a massive row with Pete after he called her a heifer; to be fair I don't think he even thought it was an insult, that's the level of chivalry we're dealing with here, and two of the farmers had an actual fight because they've both got the hots for Lindsey. The production team of *The Kiwi Wants a Wife* are having kittens.'

'Oh.' I smiled with relief. 'Actual kittens or . . .?'

She snorted with laughter. 'No, although you can't take anything for granted here. Joe had an entire family of ferrets down his trousers yesterday.'

I cleared my throat, conscious that we needed to get down to business in case she was called away again. 'Listen, I was talking to Gina about how she fought to save The Evergreens.'

'Yep. I remember it well. No one thought she'd be able to raise the money to buy it on her own. But she was determined not to let it slip from her grasp.'

'Maybe that's what we should do: challenge Sam's father-in-law?' I said.

'Um . . . we *could*. I suppose.' Nina huffed and puffed and I could hear the frustration in her voice. Finally, she said, 'What do you think?'

'Remember I told you that after Freddie died, reading his letter made me appreciate that although his life had been too short, it had been well lived but I couldn't say the same for myself?' I began.

'Yes, of course I do, I remember that letter almost word for word, it's one of the most profound things I'd ever heard,' she replied.

'Ah, thanks.' My heart pinged with warmth for her. 'Well, now that's my goal: to look back at my life with no regrets and be proud of what I've done. And I guess you're in the same position. You've seen another side to the world and the question is, will coming back to Barnaby to carry on running Nina's Flowers make you happy?'

There was a deadly silence on the other end of the line.

'Think about it,' I said, gently. 'There's no need to rush into a decision.'

She took a deep breath. 'I don't need to think about it. I know Nina's Flowers is my company and I should want to save it but . . . well, I don't think I do.'

I blinked. 'Really?'

'Really,' she said firmly. 'There, I've said it. Bloody hell, I feel better already!'

I listened while she told me that Pandora had unwittingly done her a favour. Since she'd been in New Zealand, she had become increasingly certain that her future didn't lie in floristry any more.

'I guess the thing is,' she said shyly, 'I've fallen in love.'

I squealed down the phone. 'Who? Eric, the sound man? Or one of the actual farmers? I know, it's the virgin, what's his name?'

'If you mean Scott,' she said with a giggle. 'No, he's great and so is Joe when he isn't carrying ferrets about his person, but not them. In fact, not any of them. It sounds silly, but I've fallen in love with life, *this* life, with *myself*. Being free, having no responsibilities, doing what suits me.

I know I still have the shop at the moment and a mortgage and bills to pay. But being away from home has made me realise that I don't really need all that. I want to see more of the world. I want to travel, maybe work my way round waitressing or fruit picking. Or anything.'

'You sound so happy,' I laughed softly. 'In fact, you sound like my brother.'

'I am *so* happy. It's because of him and you that I've dared to let these feelings in. For three of the five years I've run the flower shop, I've dreamed of getting out of it, but I didn't want to admit defeat or be seen as a failure. Freddie's letter pointed out that we get to choose: what we do, where we go, who we love. So that's what I'm doing.'

I felt a pang for my brother then; I'd always miss him and I'd always be bewildered about the fact that an experienced biker like him had lost his life in a stupid accident, but I was full of pride that he'd managed to inspire both Nina and me after his death.

'So,' Nina continued, 'I vote we shut the shop when the lease runs out and from now until then, all the shop's profits go straight to you to pay back the loan you gave me. How does that sound?'

I smiled with surprise. 'It sounds like a very simple solution.'

'Simple is best in my opinion,' she said airily. 'So is that a plan?'

I told her it was fine with me. We talked for a few more minutes about shop matters and I explained the rush behind Laura and Hamish's wedding.

'If it's OK with you, I'm going to stay on another couple of weeks after the end of the show and do a bit of travelling, but I'll be back to help with the wedding, seeing as you helped me with the last one. It can be our last hurrah. Right, I'd better go. I'm going to take a leaf out of your book and write a happy list.'

Scamp and I took a slow walk back to the shop. I'd never added anything other than flowers to mine. Perhaps it was about time I did.

Chapter Thirty-three

'So what do you think of my domain?' I asked Laura as soon as she arrived at the florist the following Saturday morning.

'I think it suits you perfectly!' she exclaimed brightly, although there was no disguising the new smudges of tiredness beneath her eyes. She stood just inside the door, inhaling deeply. 'And it smells gorgeous: all fresh and cool and full of life. And everywhere I look there's something lovely.'

'And now you're here, there's something even lovelier.' I pulled her in for a hug; she seemed insubstantial in my arms as if she'd already lost weight since she'd received her dad's devastating prognosis a few days ago.

I put on a brave smile, determined to make sure she enjoyed her visit to Barnaby today. It was noon, exactly twenty-four hours until my date with Sam, which was my current reference point for time. The sun was blistering hot outside and along with Scamp and all our flowers, I was wilting in the heat. I'd brought in a fan from home and he and I were sharing the breeze, which helped slightly. It had been a quiet morning – people just weren't buying flowers today – but it had given me a chance to make sure everywhere looked perfect for Laura's first visit and get on with writing a to-do list for her wedding.

'You sweet talker,' she said with a quiet laugh. 'Thanks for suggesting I come over today, it's doing me good just having a couple of hours out of Dad's house.'

I'd popped in to see Laura and her dad, Terry last night. Laura had moved back in with her dad temporarily and the three of us spent an emotional couple of hours in the garden looking at Laura's parents' wedding album. The talk inevitably turned to Laura and Hamish's wedding and my stomach had swooped with nerves; so far I'd made virtually no progress except for enlisting Lucas next door to help decorate the venue – when I finally found one. And it turned out that nothing could be done until the venue was booked, so the twenty-eight-day notice period hadn't even started yet. No pressure . . .

At one point Laura had gone back inside to fetch us drinks and Terry squeezed my hand and thanked me for helping her.

'Listen, Hamish has offered to pay for their wedding but she's my only daughter, I want to pay for it all, no arguments,' Terry had said. His voice was weak but there was no mistaking the strength of determination in his eyes. 'Whatever she wants, she can have. Horse and carriage, sit-down dinner for two hundred, thirty bridesmaids, don't even think about the money, it's hers. She's my world.'

I'd nodded and promised I'd make sure he got his wish somehow. The easiest place to start was with the flowers, hence inviting Laura in to see me today.

'Come and see me any time, or call me and I'll be there,' I said now, meaning it and then I tapped my shoulder. 'See this: anytime you need to lean on it, it's yours.'

'Thanks, Fearne, you're already helping more than you realise. For a start off, you're the first to see this.' She waggled her hand in front of my face and a gold ring set with diamonds caught my eye.

I grabbed her fingers and gasped. 'Your engagement ring! When did you have time to choose this?'

Her eyes were sparkling with tears when she smiled at me. 'Hamish had bought it a few weeks ago, he'd been planning to take me to Paris and propose on the Pont Alexandre III, but then with Dad . . .'

Her voice faded out and I nodded, understanding what she didn't want to put into words.

'He's a keeper, that Hamish,' I said, catching hold of her hand. 'And you can go to Paris anytime.'

'The fact that he already had the ring is romantic enough,' she said softly. 'It means that he wanted to marry me before all this happened. At least I know it wasn't a spur-of-the-moment idea.'

I smiled wistfully. Unlike his best friend, Freddie, who'd proposed to his girlfriend at the stroke of midnight one New Year's Eve because he'd been carried away with the moment.

'Oh and my dress!' she exclaimed. 'I've fallen in love with one. Hold on, I've brought the magazine I found it in.'

She fished into her bag and pulled it out and we spent the next few minutes oohing and ahhing over lace and tulle and I jotted down ideas for colour schemes and flowers and invitations.

'Just so you know,' I said, 'we might be pulling this wedding together in a hurry, but it'll be no less awesome for that.'

'I have every faith in you,' she said, smoothing her coppery hair behind her ears. 'And the most important thing about my wedding day is that Dad is there. Hamish and I have the rest of our lives together to celebrate our relationship. I want a simple day, short and sweet, no pomp and ceremony.'

'Understood,' I confirmed. 'And Terry has asked to settle all the bills, *no arguments*.'

She gave a rueful smile. 'I can hear him say that. It was his standard phrase at bedtime when I begged to be allowed to stay up and watch *Big Brother* on a school night.'

'He'll always be with you, you know,' I murmured. 'In thousands of little memories which pop up when you least expect it.'

'Just as long as my wedding day memories include him,' she said worriedly. 'That's the most important thing.'

And we both had a little cry.

Later on Maria came in to the shop as I was working through a list of phone numbers for possible venues. We needed to find somewhere which could host the marriage ceremony and the wedding reception so that Terry wouldn't have to be transported from one place to another. So far I was drawing a blank and I was glad of the break.

'*Buon giorno, Scampito,*' she cooed at the dog, who was so hot, his only reaction was a limp flap of his tail.

I beamed at her. 'Hello, Maria, you look like a glorious butterfly today.'

'*Grazie, cara!*' She chuckled and gave me a twirl in her loose-fitting purple and orange kaftan and sandals. 'This my coolest dress. It is hot enough to cook pizza on the pavement today. Poor Stanley is as pink as porn.'

I stifled a giggle and hoped she meant a prawn.

'What can I get you?' I waved an arm over my flowers. 'Are you shopping for yourself or someone else?'

Maria produced a Spanish-style fan from a pocket in her kaftan and wafted it over her face. 'I not buying, I come to say thank you for telling Stanley about the Claybourne Hotel.'

Go Stanley, I thought to myself. 'You went! I'm so pleased. Was the bedroom nice and cool?'

'It was perfect. I feel like princess and Stanley is my prince.' She fluttered her eyelashes. 'Very romantic.'

'And what about the hotel?' I prompted, wondering if Stanley had brought up the subject of a wedding date. 'Was that romantic?'

'The hotel is beautiful but . . .' Her voice drifted off and she shrugged. 'I don't know.'

'I'm trying to find a wedding venue for my best friend and I tried there but they're booked solid for the next four months.'

'Ah.' She nodded wisely. 'A gunshot wedding, I understand.'

I smothered a smile and explained about Terry's illness. 'It's forced them to think about marriage sooner than they would have done, but Laura would regret it if she didn't have her father there to give her away.'

Maria sat down heavily on a stool I used to reach the high display shelf and slipped her fan into her pocket. 'Regret is a terrible thing. Stanley want us to marry soon, but I so happy now. I don't want to lose this feeling.'

'How long have you been engaged?'

'Two years.' Her gaze drifted off into the middle distance, her fingers twisting a slim diamond ring on her left hand. 'We out there on village green and he get down on his knee and tell me he want me to be Mrs Pigeon.'

'And do *you* want to be Mrs Pigeon?'

'Oh yes.' She sighed. 'But it risky business. I only have three men in my life. In Italy, Lorenzo, he died, and Marco, he my husband, but he such a dicky head, I run away from him to England with my baby in my arms. Then no one until Stanley. With him by my side, my life is good. What if it go wrong again?'

'Love is risky,' I agreed. 'But then *life* is risky. We never know how much time we have.'

'*Dio mio,*' she tutted, shaking her head. 'This is true.'

I swallowed a lump in my throat, thinking how life can be as still as a mill pond one minute and then just one pebble can change everything, sending ripples throughout every part of your world. Losing Freddie was my pebble, and Terry's sudden illness was Laura's.

'Stanley adores you Maria, but . . .' I hesitated, unsure whether I should interfere or not.

She lifted her palms impatiently. 'But what? Kitty got your tongue, eh? I am big girl, just say the truth.'

I laughed. 'All right, I think he'd feel complete if you were his wife. Perhaps to Stanley, you being only engaged is a job half done.'

She thought about that, chewing her thumb nail.

'He is very neat and tidy man. Once he was very ill, his heart was all blocked up and I thought I would lose him. It would break my heart if I didn't make him as happy as he could be.'

'This is about both of you,' I reminded her. 'Getting married needs to be a decision which makes you happy too.'

'But I no want fuss, we old people, I no want a big, big party like Rosie and Gabe. If we can have a wedding, just quiet, just me and my Stanley, then I say yes. You are right. I do it to make him happy.'

'There was something my mum used to say about happiness,' I said, surprising myself by remembering it. '*Happiness is like perfume: you can't pour it on others without getting some on yourself.*'

She used to say it every time I asked for some of her Estée Lauder perfume and she dropped some onto my wrist, showing me how to dab them together. It hadn't really registered with teenage-me at the time just what a poignant saying it was; I hadn't thought about it in years.

But it was such a nice sentiment. It brought back that story from Freddie's letter about how happy that young boy had been when Freddie had given him a pair of old trainers, and the subsequent joy Freddie had got from making that simple gesture.

Her dark eyes lit up. 'That is it! Stanley is my perfume, he make me so happy. Unless he eat pittle eggs, then he smell like trump.' She got to her feet, shuddering in disgust.

'Thank you, *cara*.' She kissed my cheek. 'You make me remember what is important. I go and talk to Stanley now.

I was still laughing about his 'pittle eggs' as she got her fan out and left the shop. I assumed she meant *pickled*; I wasn't so sure about the 'trump' reference.

An hour later I decided to close up and began clearing the display area on the pavement outside the shop. All I'd sold all day was a couple of pots of herbs, a bunch of roses to the pub landlord and I'd taken an order over the phone for some flowers for someone's mum's birthday which I'd be able to drop off on my way home. But it wasn't the meagre takings I was worried about; it was the lack of venue for Laura's wedding. I couldn't do much else until that was sorted and so far, I'd drawn a blank.

'Cooee, Fearne!' came a wavery voice.

I looked across the pavement to the tables which, tucked under the café's awning, looked lovely and shady. There was a family tucking in to ice creams and beyond them, Delphine was sitting with another woman of a similar age. Both of them were piling jam and cream on to scones from a cake stand bursting with afternoon tea goodies.

She waved to me. 'Come and meet my friend.'

I did as I was told, closely followed by Scamp, ever the opportunist where café crumbs were concerned, and Delphine introduced me to Una who also lived at The Evergreens.

'And aren't you a dote!' Una declared in a broad Irish accent. 'Such pretty hair. I had blonde locks like yours once. Before it turned into white wire wool. So there's something to look forward to for you.' She gave me a mischievous wink.

'You two look so glamorous,' I said, smiling at Delphine in a floaty pink chiffon dress and Una in a white linen shift, both of them wearing matching wide-brimmed hats. 'I feel a proper scruff beside you.'

'You are a dear!' Delphine looked delighted. 'My best friend Violet and I went to Royal Ascot a few years ago and this was the dress I bought for the occasion. I saw it hanging in the wardrobe today and decided to put it on. I'd been saving it for best, which is ridiculous at my age.'

'And this is the only thing I can fit into at the moment,' Una laughed uproariously and patted her round tummy. 'Mind you, if I had pins like yours I'd be in shorts in weather like this. Unfortunately, my legs look like an ordnance survey map of the Himalayas, thanks to my varicose veins.'

Out of the corner of my eye I saw Delphine slip Scamp a piece of ham under the table.

'We're being decadent,' she said, giggling girlishly. 'We'd planned a walk in the Dales today but it's too hot for that sort of nonsense.'

'Besides, we've worked our fingers to the bone this week,' said Una, holding out her hands. She had stubby fingers with rings stacked up on the ring fingers, the backs of her hands freckled with age. 'So we deserve a treat.'

'I heard from Gina that you'd been busy getting the house ready for visitors,' I said. 'How did it go?'

'Pretty well, I think,' said Delphine vaguely, pulling out a chair. 'Have a seat for a minute.'

'Yes, do. Then you can help us eat some of this food, we've been going half an hour already and we've barely made a dent in it,' said Una.

'That's very kind, I don't mind if I do.' I sat down gratefully. The shop was still open, but as virtually no one had been in all day, it was unlikely to be burgled.

'And then we need some flowers from you to fill this jug.' Delphine pulled a beautiful glazed jug in deep blues and purples from her shopping bag.

'My granny used to have one of those and I loved it so much!' I gasped. 'I remembered asking her with all the non-existent subtlety of a child if I could have it when she died.'

'And I bet she said yes?' Una smiled indulgently. 'I can never refuse my grandchildren anything.'

I nodded. 'Unfortunately, my brother got obsessed with the Karate Kid films and used to leap around Gran's living room wearing his pyjamas with Granddad's black tie around his waist, and he kicked the jug off the dresser.' I laughed at the memory. Gran had been cross but Freddie was so proud of his highest-ever kick that the telling-off he received was like water off a duck's back.

'Then you shall have this one,' Delphine declared, putting it in my hands. 'We've hundreds of others which will do just as well.'

I started to protest but Delphine insisted.

'Please accept it. It would make me so happy to give it to you. I shall think of you enjoying it and remembering your granny every time you fill it with flowers.'

My heart pinged with affection for the old lady. I kissed her soft cheek.

'Then I'd be honoured to accept it in exchange for a bouquet of your choice. What would you like?'

Delphine and Una exchanged looks and both spoke at once. 'Roses, please.'

'Dexter and Gina have been working so hard all week that we've decided to do a special romantic dinner for two tonight in Welcome Cottage for them,' Una explained.

'That's the cottage at the top of the drive to The Evergreens,' said Delphine, 'Gina used to rent it before she bought The Evergreens and then Dexter moved in and now he's moved into the main house with her.'

'So it's going to be kitted out as the honeymoon . . . ouch!' Una clapped her hand over her mouth as Delphine prodded her with a fork.

My ears pricked up. 'Honeymoon *suite*?'

'That's top secret,' Delphine hissed at her.

'Sorry,' Una mumbled.

My mind whirred. If there was a honeymoon suite at The Evergreens, it followed that there might be a wedding venue too.

I leaned forward conspiratorially. 'Listen ladies, I won't breathe a word to anyone, but I'm desperately seeking somewhere to hold a wedding and if there's any chance of you helping me I'd be very grateful.'

Una blinked at me like a child caught with a hand in the biscuit tin, clearly not daring to say another word.

Delphine took a bright pink lipstick from her bag and applied it precisely without using a mirror.

'Give Gina a call on Monday,' she said mysteriously. 'That's all I'm saying.'

'Thank you, I will,' I said, intrigued. 'Thanks again for the jug, and the tea. I'll go and choose you some roses.'

I clicked my fingers to Scamp and we headed inside the florist's. This could well be the answer to my prayers.

Chapter Thirty-four

Sunday finally came around and despite the fact I'd been awake at six, I still managed to be drying my hair when the doorbell rang at ten minutes to noon. I'd have missed the sound altogether if it hadn't been for Scamp barking his head off from his lookout post in the front room. I switched off the hairdryer and tried not to sprint to open the door. My room looked like the proverbial bomb had hit it; I'd tried on every item of clothing I possessed in a quest to find the outfit which struck the right balance between lunch with a friend and lunch with a man I'd dreamed about last night and woken up all of a quiver. The mess could wait, I decided, closing the door on it.

'Coming!' I called as I reached the bottom of the stairs.

I caught sight of my reflection in the hall mirror and nearly died; that was the last time I dried my hair upside down for speed. I looked like a witch. Even Scamp had reduced his tail action to an unsure slow wag at the sight of me.

I grabbed a baseball cap from the peg over the shoe rack and crammed it on over my puffy hair, laughing at myself. I'd be lucky if Sam didn't get straight back in his car.

I flung open the door. 'Now don't be alarmed . . .'

The words died on my lips as I took in the sight in front of me; a tall bear of a man filled my vision, his shoulders wide thanks to a padded leather jacket, his entire head hidden inside a motorcycle helmet with a visor pulled down over his face. He held up a gloved hand in greeting.

My legs trembled. 'Freddie?' I gasped.

'Ready for your adventure?' Sam flipped up the visor, grinning, and produced a second helmet from behind his back.

There was a scream, followed by a sudden movement, the front door slammed and I found myself back inside, my head spinning.

Sam was a biker? How did I not know this? In all the conversations we'd had over the past couple of months, how had this never come up?

'Fearne?' Sam knocked on the door softly. 'Are you OK?'

My heart was beating so fast that it was hard enough to catch my breath, let alone speak. Scamp pattered a little way down the hall uncertainly and I leaned back against the door.

The letter flap squeaked open and I stepped to one side. Even in the state I was in there was no need to give the poor man a view of my bum squished against the opening.

'I handled that badly,' he said, his voice loaded with regret. 'I'm such an idiot for not realising how frightening opening the door to a masked man would be. I'm so sorry I made you scream.'

'It's not *that* I'm scared of,' I managed to reply.

How could I tell him that it was the ghost of my brother which had caused my world to spin?

There was a pause before he spoke again.

'Oh, I see. It's me.' The disappointment in his tone melted my heart. 'If you've changed your mind, that's fine but at least open the door and talk to me.'

'It's not you, it's your motorbike,' I replied. 'I don't do motorbikes.'

'Ahh, right. I thought you were always up for an adventure, but that's no problem.'

I could hear the smile in Sam's voice, the relief that it wasn't personal. Except it *was* personal. Freddie had lost his life because of a stupid bike ride. The baggage Sam would be bringing from his recent break-up I could cope with, but a motorbike? That was a deal-breaker.

'Riding a motorbike isn't an adventure, it's dangerous and it's selfish,' I felt a sob rising in my throat.

'I'm safe, I promise!' he pleaded, his voice dancing with humour. 'I've never had an accident, never even gone over the speed limit and I had the very best motorcycle instructor.'

'Doesn't mean a thing.' I shook my head as a tear ran down my face. 'Doesn't matter how experienced you are, or careful, or slow. Accidents can still happen.'

'Open the door, sweetheart. Please. Let me put this right.'

Sweetheart. My heart twisted; he'd never called me that before. I wanted to see him, I wanted to hold his face in my hands and feel his warmth. I took a deep breath and opened the door. His jacket and both helmets were on the ground. Scamp jumped up at Sam's legs and whined with pleasure to see him.

'Jeez.' Sam ruffled his hair. He looked baffled and nervous. 'My first date in ten years and I've made her cry before she even leaves the house.'

My lips twitched into a smile and I couldn't help feeling sorry for him.

'Sam, I'm afraid this is something you can never put right. My brother thought he was safe, and *he was* a motorcycle instructor. He was the most careful rider I knew. He'd never been in an accident either until the one which killed him.'

'You mentioned a brother but I never realised . . . Oh, Fearne.'

A second later I was wrapped in his arms, my head buried in his chest. His chin resting lightly on my head. I felt my body melt into his; it felt so good to be held.

'I lost him, Sam and it broke my heart,' I said, my voice muffled against his shirt. 'I still struggle to understand how it could have happened, his nickname was even Steady because he never speeded.'

'*Steady*?' Sam pulled away from me sharply, his eyes boring into mine. 'You're Steady's sister?'

I nodded, alarmed by the strength of his reaction. 'You knew him?'

'Yes, I did,' he stared at me in disbelief. 'He was my motorbike instructor.'

For the next half an hour, we sat out in the garden with cold drinks, filling in the gaps in both of our stories, side by side at the patio table.

'You're always in the car with the Hogg Property Services logo on the side,' I said, stretching my bare legs out in the sun. 'You've never mentioned that you had a bike.'

'I don't use it very often. The bike is my way of letting off steam. And today I thought it would be a good surprise.' He winced. 'How wrong can a man be. You've talked to me about your brother before, but it just didn't click that you and Steady were related.'

'You weren't at his funeral, were you?' I remembered the crowd of bikers who'd come to mourn. I hadn't been able to look at them, let alone speak to them, as though they were somehow jointly responsible for what had happened.

He shook his head. 'Sadly not. We were staying with Pandora's parents in Lanzarote last summer when I heard the news about Steady. It rocked the biker community. I think we all moderated our speed after his accident. I even thought about him as I rode over here, thinking that he'd approve of biking on a day like today when the sun is cracking the flags.'

I gave him a reluctant smile. 'That's true. He'd have been up and off at dawn for a ride to the coast somewhere.'

'And you?' Sam studied my face. 'Would you have gone with him?'

I blew out a breath. I'd avoided this sort of question for almost a year. The truth was that even though I'd never been tempted to have my own bike, I'd loved riding pillion on Freddie's. I'd trusted Freddie all my life, I'd trusted him *with* my life, but now he was gone.

'Probably.' I admitted. 'But bikes are synonymous with danger for me now. I don't know what possessed him to ride along a road renowned for accidents in the wet. It was such an uncharacteristically stupid decision on his part.'

Sam's eyes softened. 'In hindsight, yes, but I guess at the time he thought the risk was worth it given the urgency.'

For a moment I was so shocked that I couldn't speak.

'What urgency?' I said, wide-eyed. 'Do you know where he was going or where he'd been?'

Sam stared at me and an expression passed over his face that I couldn't read. 'Well . . . yes, I do.'

My heart began to pound; was I finally going to hear the truth?

'Where? Who was he seeing?'

'OK. But, Fearne . . .' He took my hands in his and held them tight. 'I need you to know that this story doesn't have a happy ending.'

'Tell me,' I stammered, 'whatever it is, I need to know.'

He took in a sharp breath before speaking.

'When I was taking my bike test, last spring, there was another guy doing it at the same time called Rav. We got on really well. He'd recently been declared cancer-free after having treatment for lumps in his oesophagus and he and his girlfriend were expecting their first baby. So he'd decided to buy a bike to celebrate both life events. We both passed our test within days of each other.'

'What a relief for him to get the all-clear.'

'It was.' Sam nodded, stroking the backs of my hands lightly. 'But the next thing I heard was via a text from Yasmin to say that the cancer was back and Rav was terminally ill. They were both hoping he'd be alive to welcome his baby into the world. But in the meantime she was organising some last things that he wanted to do.'

'Oh, that poor man.' My heart ached for them. 'And what was it he wanted to do?'

Sam shot me a cautious look. 'He wanted to ride his bike one last time but he wasn't strong enough to go by himself. Time was running out, Rav was getting weaker. So Yasmin called Freddie and asked him to come straight away.'

I gasped. My mind raced ahead, filling in the gaps. 'And he did.'

Sam stroked my hair while he told me the rest. How Freddie had made it to Rav's house and given him his last ride on a bike before delivering him safely back home to Yasmin. How Rav had died the following day, and his baby girl was born prematurely a week later.

The story made me cry. I cried for Freddie, I cried for Rav and I cried for Yasmin who must have gone through so much in the weeks and months after the birth of her child.

'All this time, I've thought Freddie was selfish and thoughtless to have ridden his bike along that dangerous road,' I said, pulling another tissue from the box Sam had found in the kitchen. 'But I should have trusted him. He'd been the exact opposite. He'd have been so happy to be able to do that one last thing for Rav. He'd lived the life he set out to live to the letter, right until his very last breath. I'm so proud of him.'

Sam brushed away my tears with his fingertips. 'So you should be. He made Rav's last day on earth a happy one.'

'I want to show you something.' I blew my nose and went inside to fetch Freddie's letter for Sam to read.

'That's incredible,' Sam said, sniffing, after he'd finished it. 'Bloody hell, even I'm crying.'

'Freddie was an amazing man,' I said, and then I had a thought. 'I'd like to meet Yasmin; do you think she'd be OK with that?'

He looked at me thoughtfully for a long moment. 'Yasmin has been suffering with guilt over texting Freddie ever since that day. I'm sure she would.'

'The poor girl,' I said, trying to put myself in her shoes. I shuddered; it didn't bear thinking about. I had a sudden urge to wrap my arms around her and tell her to let go of that guilt. 'Why don't we go now?'

'*Now* now?' Sam laughed in surprise.

I nodded. Hearing about Yasmin and Rav had answered some of the questions which had had me perplexed for nearly a year. Now I wanted to know more; I *had* to know more. This was the closure I'd been searching for and if Yasmin had feelings of guilt, perhaps meeting me would be cathartic for her too.

'You won't be needing those.' I pointed to his helmet and leathers. 'Because I'll drive.'

'Understood. I hope that one day you'll trust me enough to take you out on my bike, but I'll wait for you to be ready.'

We were still sitting in the garden side by side and I rested my head against his shoulder.

'Thank you,' I said.

I didn't know if I'd ever be ready for that but the thought that there might be other days like this, the two of us – three including Scamp – having adventures made my heart soar. I'd been adamant that I'd never let anyone close to me again for fear of losing them, but now I wasn't so sure.

'I'll call Yasmin first,' he said sensibly. 'This is going to be a shock for her.'

He was right, but I knew how easy it was to turn people down on the phone. In the first six months after Freddie's death I rebuffed everybody's attempts to come and visit. I thought I was better hiding myself away and dealing with my grief alone. If Yasmin didn't want to see us, she could turn us away when we got there, but at least we'd have tried.

'Wait,' I said, as he took his phone out. I got to my feet. 'Let's go on spec. You can knock on the door and warn her before I crawl out of the woodwork and if she's out, or she'd rather not, you can buy me lunch instead.'

He sat there for a moment looking up at me, a gooey smile on his face. 'Deal.'

'Come on then, slowcoach.' I held a hand out to him and he stood up.

'You're full of surprises,' he said, kissing my fingers.

'Says the man who turned up in biker gear *and* knew my brother!' I shook my head, still taking it all in.

'Fearne,' he whispered huskily. He lowered his head towards mine and I stepped closer, holding my breath. 'Would it be OK if I . . .'

I don't know who made the final move to cross the gap between us, but one minute my heart was fluttering and the next it took flight. His kiss, when it came, lit me up from inside like sunshine. His arms slipped around my waist, drawing me to him, my hands in his hair, touching the soft part of his neck. I'd dreamed about his kiss and the feel of his skin underneath my hands and the pressure of his body against mine; it was everything I'd hoped it would be and more. And all at once I didn't care that he was a biker or he had an ex-wife or that this could either be the start of something wonderful or the end of a friendship. Because in that moment everything felt like it was slotting into place.

It was another half an hour before we stopped kissing and made it into the car.

'It's not quite the romantic date I had planned,' said Sam, in a muffled voice.

My heart skipped at the word romantic but when I looked across at the passenger seat I burst out laughing. Scamp was pressed up to Sam as tightly as the seat belt, his tongue out and hanging perilously close to Sam's lips.

'He's not used to sharing,' I chuckled.

Sam raised an eyebrow. 'Sharing *you* or sharing the front seat?'

'Neither.'

'He'll get used to it,' said Sam, firmly, tickling the dog's wiry ears.

I couldn't speak for Scamp, but I'd happily get used to it, I thought as our little trio departed from Pineapple Road.

Yasmin lived just outside the centre of Sheffield. It took us longer to get there than it should have done because the quickest route would have taken us over the winding road where Freddie's accident had happened. I wasn't sure how long it would be before I was brave enough to drive that way, but even with Sam by my side it wasn't going to be today.

Sam directed me to Yasmin's address and we parked on the opposite side of the street. I waited in the car with Scamp with the windows wound down while Sam got out and knocked on the door.

So this was where Freddie had been that day. This time, the twist of guilt I felt for doubting him was mixed with a wave of pride. Right until his last moments he'd lived his life according to the plan he'd set out for himself when he'd written that letter to me in India. Every day, in every way, I thought, feeling a prick of tears, Freddie continued to inspire me and fill me with pride.

The front door opened and a woman in denim shorts and a vest top appeared on the doorstep. She had dark skin and a soft cloud of black hair and greeted Sam with a one-armed hug. Her other arm was wrapped around a chubby baby who was balanced on her hip, wearing only a nappy. Despite straining to listen, I couldn't hear what they were saying but my pulse raced as Yasmin pressed a hand over her mouth and Sam squeezed her shoulder. They both looked in my direction as Sam pointed to my car. I was holding my breath, nervous about what her reaction would be.

The next second, Yasmin was crossing the road towards me; there was a smile on her face, but her eyes mirrored my own nervousness. She tightened her grip on the baby as she leaned down to my open window.

'Hello,' she said, shyly. 'Please, come in, I'm so happy to meet you.'

'This is Inca, my daughter,' said Yasmin, proudly, pressing a kiss into the baby's soft curls. 'She's into everything. I don't think it'll be long until she's walking.'

We were sitting under a huge sunshade which took up most of Yasmin's tiny back garden. There was a jug of iced water on the table along with a plate of fruit which Yasmin had hurriedly pulled together. After sniffing every corner of the garden, Scamp flopped in the shade under my chair.

'She's beautiful.' I held out a finger to the little girl. She grabbed onto it and beamed at me, revealing four perfect white teeth.

'She's the image of her dad,' Yasmin smiled. 'And has his sense of adventure, unfortunately.'

She had been through such a lot over the last year and yet she had the sunniest smile; I warmed to her instantly.

'I've told Fearne how Rav and I met,' said Sam. 'We didn't spend an awful lot of time together, but he was great fun to be around and he loved that motorbike.'

Yasmin rolled her eyes fondly. 'And I hated it with as much passion as he loved it, but it's good to know it brought him happiness.'

Inca struggled against her mum's arms to be set free and Sam asked if he could have her. He walked her around the garden, bouncing her in his arms and pointing out things to capture her interest. The sight of the little girl nestling in his broad arms sent my hormones into overdrive; how did he manage to look so sexy and yet so adorable at the same time?

'He's great with babies,' Yasmin said with a note of amusement, watching me.

'He's had two already,' I said, gulping my ice cold water. 'So I guess he knows what he's doing. Unlike me. You seem like you're enjoying being a mum?'

'I love it,' she said, gazing at her daughter. 'Although we had a rocky start, she and I. It was hard to see past my grief for a while.'

'That's understandable.' None of my close friends had had children, but I could imagine how acclimatising to motherhood would be difficult enough without trying to deal with grief at the same time.

'How are you coping,' she asked, 'after losing your brother?'

'It doesn't get easier,' I replied, 'but I'm getting used to it. I still burst into tears randomly, but less than I did.'

Yasmin nodded. 'Freddie was so kind and gentle with Rav that day. By then everything hurt, his bones, his joints . . . everything. My heart was in my mouth when Freddie started up the bike. I hardly dared breathe while they were gone. But when they came back I knew it had been the right thing to do. Experiencing that rush of speed again had made Rav feel alive.'

'There's no feeling like it,' said Sam. He was holding on to Inca's hands now, supporting her while she explored the grass with her bare feet.

I smiled, remembering the sensation for myself; it was exhilarating.

'Rav and Freddie were both emotional when they got back and Freddie helped Rav climb off the bike. We all knew it was Rav's last ride. After Freddie left . . .' She paused, a look of anguish crossing her gentle face, 'Rav was buzzing for the rest of the night. We had no idea that Freddie didn't make it home. I'll never forgive myself for that.'

'You must,' I insisted. 'Because there's nothing to feel guilty about. Freddie would have enjoyed being with Rav, he'd have had no regrets.'

'Thank you,' she said, swallowing. 'Kindness must be a family trait.'

'And I was on holiday completely oblivious to any of this,' Sam grimaced. 'I hadn't heard that Rav's illness had deteriorated to that degree and I didn't know about Freddie until after the funeral.'

'The day after Freddie came to visit, my world turned upside down,' Yasmin said, blotting a tear from her face. 'Anything that wasn't about Rav or the baby didn't exist for me for the next few months.'

She poured us more water and filled us in with the details of what had happened. Rav had woken up the next morning in such pain that he couldn't even manage to get out of bed. When a doctor came to see him he'd said that it was only a matter of time and that all she could do for Rav was to keep him comfortable and love him. He died that evening and for Yasmin, that was only the start of the nightmare. Even though she'd known that Rav wouldn't be with her for long, she hadn't been prepared to watch him go. The shock made her ill and a week later, concerned for the health of the baby, Yasmin's midwife arranged for an emergency Caesarean section. Rav and Yasmin's daughter was born a month early into a world of grief and sorrow.

'For a while I couldn't bond with her, I couldn't even decide what to call her. I didn't know whether to name her for her father or whether that would be a constant reminder of him. I even considered calling her Freddie at one point.'

'Inca is a beautiful name, I think you chose wisely.' I looked at the little girl, sitting on the grass, concentrating on a daisy which Sam had picked for her.

Yasmin smiled. 'Thank you. But at the time I couldn't connect with anything. My mum took over the funeral arrangements, Rav had already chosen what he wanted: no fuss, no flowers, no wake, just the briefest service. It had been one of the few times we argued, I'd thought his friends and family should be allowed a space to mourn. But as it turned out, even the quiet, private send-off we gave him broke my heart because I didn't want to say goodbye, I wanted him with me.'

'My mum did the same, Freddie hadn't left instructions so I let her make all the decisions. She said it helped her, but to me it was all so surreal,' I said, shuddering at the memory. 'Afterwards I shut myself off from everyone, too angry with life to be bothered with the outside world.'

'Same here,' said Yasmin.

We exchanged a look of solidarity. Even though we'd both suffered, there was something therapeutic about sharing our experiences.

'Rav's friends had heard about Freddie's accident but they decided I had enough to deal with so they didn't tell me. It was a month until I found out. By then I was a single mother who felt alienated from her own child. I almost considered giving her up, I thought she deserved better. It was another month before I admitted that I needed help.'

I squeezed her hand. 'Oh Yasmin, I wish I'd known all this, I wish I could have helped.'

'I feel awful,' said Sam gruffly. 'I was caught up in my own marital problems. When I texted you and you said you were fine, I should have known you were bluffing.'

Yasmin held her arms out to Inca and Sam handed her over.

'You're both good people,' she said. 'But I had to get there in my own time. My job as Inca's sole parent is a privilege and I'm trying to bring her up the way we would have done if Rav and I were sharing the responsibility of parenthood. Every time I catch her looking solemn I wonder if those first two months when we were strangers to one another will have done any lasting damage. But then she smiles and her father's loving eyes shine back at me and I know it's going to be OK.'

Inca pressed chubby hands to her mum's face and made loud kissing noises and we all laughed.

'It's obvious you're a good team now,' I said, tickling Inca's soft foot.

Yasmin smoothed her hand over Inca's hair. 'I'm glad you and Sam came to see me today, it does me good to talk about Rav. And Freddie. But I still know that it's my fault that Freddie died, if I hadn't asked him to visit Rav that day—'

I shushed her with my hand. 'An accident is just that. Unfortunate, unforeseen and unfair. Until Sam had told me about you and Rav and Inca I'd been holding on to my anger. I'd never understood why an experienced rider like him had taken risks in bad weather. I should have known him better; I should have trusted his judgement. He did the only thing he could in the circumstances, I understand that now.'

Yasmin stared at me uncertainly. 'Even though he's no longer—'

'I want you to have this,' I interrupted her, pulling out a copy of his letter I'd made on my printer at home before Sam and I had set off. 'Freddie wrote it to me when he was twenty-one. He spent his life in the pursuit of happiness, both for himself and others. He'd have no regrets about his life. And you mustn't either. That last act of kindness, arranging to take Rav out would have made Freddie just as happy as Rav. You can be sure of that.'

As she read through the letter, I watched a thousand emotions flash across her face until finally she looked at me, her eyes sparkling with happiness.

'Thank you,' she said, her voice raw.

'Thank *you*,' I replied. 'Today has helped me in ways you'll never know.'

Sam and I drove back home in easy silence, finding excuses to touch each other when the traffic stopped. Scamp, thankfully, conceded defeat and sprawled out along the back seat.

'You promised me an adventure and you certainly delivered,' I said, jingling my keys once we were back outside my house in Pineapple Road.

He looked at me, full of concern. 'Are you glad you know about Rav and Yasmin?'

I opened the front door and let Scamp run inside and then turned back to him.

'I've been so angry: with Freddie, with fate. But now I feel like a weight has been lifted off me,' I reached for him and he stepped closer. 'Meeting her and Inca has changed everything. I can't thank you enough.'

He brushed the hair back from my face, a smile playing on his lips.

'Yes you can,' he said and kissed me again.

Sunday lunch was forgotten, but he stayed for supper. And breakfast.

Chapter Thirty-five

The next morning, breakfast consisted of coffee and kisses and was completely and utterly delicious.

I drove to Barnaby wreathed in smiles; the weather was lovely, the fields and trees and flowers were lovely, the Monday morning traffic was lovely, even the pigeons who'd woken me up at the crack of dawn were lovely because they'd given me a chance to gaze unashamedly at the beautiful man in my bed.

I'd forgotten how good it was to wake up next to someone who didn't chase rabbits in his dreams or circle repeatedly on top of the duvet until he found the perfect position to sleep in. Early morning coffee had been for two instead of one and when I'd talked I'd actually got a reply in English and not just in tail-wags and face-licks.

It had been bittersweet to kiss Sam goodbye and watch him roar away on his bike. But it was nothing compared to the shock of his arrival, seeing him in leathers and a bike helmet; I never wanted to get that sort of surprise again. And when he'd finally vanished from view, I realised that my hatred of motorbikes had lessened a little since meeting Yasmin and Inca. With grief came anger, just as Yasmin had experienced, and whereas she had had the cancer which had stolen her partner from her to rail against, I had pinned my anger on Freddie's bike. I'd never stop missing him, but the moments between the sadness were getting longer and a new life without him in it was beginning to emerge.

My heart skipped a beat as I thought about Sam and the night we'd spent together. We'd sat outside under the stars and talked about our families, our past loves and our hopes and dreams for the future. A future which had flickered that little bit brighter for me when I'd invited him to stay over and he'd said he'd thought I'd never ask.

I checked the time as I pulled up into a parking space outside the florist's. Sam would be on his way to the airport by now. He'd arranged with Pandora to go and collect the children from their grandparents and prepare them for the fact that Mummy and Daddy definitely wouldn't be getting back together again. I'd see him again tomorrow or possibly Wednesday and hopefully by then I'd have set a date and venue for Laura and Hamish's wedding.

Lucas was unlocking the gift shop as I clipped on Scamp's lead and let him drag me onto the green.

'Morning, darling!' he called. 'What news from New Zealand?'

'She's in love!' I shouted back.

'No way! The little minx hasn't been returning my messages! Now I know why.' Lucas yelped with excitement and scampered over the road onto the grass to grill me for all the details.

'But not with a man,' I said, laughing at his shocked expression. 'With life.'

'You tease,' he said, smacking my arm playfully. 'Although I'm deliriously happy for her.'

'She's coming back here for a month and then who knows, the world is her oyster.'

'Imagine that freedom.' He sighed dreamily and then clapped his hands. 'Anyway, now that Nina doesn't need my dating advice any more, I'm all yours.'

'I don't need it either,' I said blithely.

'You're blushing.' Lucas gasped and touched a finger to my cheek. 'No you're not; you're glowing. I recognise that glow!'

'All right,' I said laughing, pushing his hand away. 'Announce my love life to the world, why don't you.'

'Who?' Lucas scoffed, looking around. 'I can only see Biddy and I can't imagine she's going to be interested in your new sleeping arrangements.'

'Shush,' I protested, just as Biddy and Churchill joined us.

Scamp barked happily at the arrival of his friend and the two old boys began to chase each other at a sedate pace through the dew-laden grass.

'Fearne got lucky last night,' said Lucas, wickedly.

'Oh good girl,' she cried, ruffling my hair as if I was a dog. 'I think the last time I got lucky, Brexit hadn't been invented.'

'Ugh.' Lucas rolled his eyes. 'The good old days.'

'Exactly,' said Biddy drily. 'Still, it's my birthday next week, you never know, perhaps fifty-eight will be my lucky age.'

'Perhaps it might,' I said, with a secret smile as a rough plan formed in the depths of my brain.

We rounded up our dogs and opened up our respective shops and an hour later, I dropped Scamp at the pet shop with Biddy so that I could visit The Evergreens alone.

By the time I reached the top of the long drive and parked on the gravel in front of the house, I was already a bit in love with it; the whole place was breathtakingly stunning. The tiny gatekeeper's lodge at the entrance to the estate looked like Hansel and Gretel's cottage and the main house was a Victorian confection of mullion-paned windows and higgledy piggledy chimney stacks, its many gables and rooflines edged with frilly white weatherboards. If there was any chance of holding Laura's wedding here I would leap at it, she and Hamish would both adore it.

Delphine met me at the front door and kissed me on both cheeks. She was flushed with excitement. 'Sorry for all the subterfuge last week, dear, only this is all very new and I didn't know if I was allowed to speak about it or not.'

'Speak about what?' I said bemused. 'Can you tell me now?'

'Gina is in the garden with the children,' she replied, refusing to be drawn. 'Come on in.'

She showed me into the hall and I whistled in admiration. Sunlight through the coloured fanlight above the door caught the crystal chandelier above our heads, sending shafts of light over the walls. With the grandfather clock ticking solemnly in the corner and the wooden panelling around the lower half of the room it felt like I'd stepped out of the modern world and straight onto the set of *Downton Abbey*.

'It's so elegant,' I murmured.

She giggled. 'No need to whisper.'

'I can't help it,' I whispered.

The garden was every bit as wonderful as the house. Gina and Paige, whom I recognised from our open day were sitting under a huge parasol with six or seven little ones. They were tucking in to a pile of toast and singing 'The Wheels on the Bus'.

I waited until they'd reached the end of the song before approaching them. 'Fantastic singing, everybody!'

'This, believe it or not, is our quiet hour: after the school run and before music group in the church hall,' said Gina, with a twinkle in her eye.

'Want toast?' asked a little girl with what looked like Marmite around her mouth, as she offered me her half-eaten triangle.

'It looks delicious but no, thank you,' I replied with considerable restraint. I hadn't had time to eat this morning and my stomach was rumbling.

'Coffee?' Gina asked.

I agreed to that and once she'd wiped a couple of chins, she led me back indoors.

The kitchen was a riot of colour and styles: an ancient wooden dresser, a well-loved Aga and warm quarry tiled floor, a retro-style fridge covered in children's artwork and pretty floral bunting fluttering in the breeze from the open French doors.

'I've got kitchen envy,' I said with a sigh.

She laughed. 'I used to say the same; it's still my favourite room. The heart of the home, I always think.'

'I'm not really sure why I'm here,' I admitted, once she'd put the kettle on, 'except that I mentioned to Delphine last week that I've got a wedding to organise and she thought I should talk to you. I need a venue, catering, photographer – the lot, and all within a month.'

'Ah, good old Delphine, letting the cat out of the bag.' Gina laughed. She handed me a cup of coffee and we sat at the kitchen table.

I was intrigued.

'We have just been approved to hold marriage ceremonies here,' Gina confided. 'We had our final inspection last week and we passed.'

I raised an eyebrow. 'The unexpected visitors.'

'Exactly.' She beamed. 'The flowers must have swung it for us. Biscuit?'

She pushed a tin of shortbread in my direction and I delved in happily. It was melt-in-the-mouth delicious: buttery, crumbly, with a hint of lavender.

'Una makes them, not me,' she said when I complimented

her. 'She and Bing, our other residents, are out in the garden somewhere.'

'I've met Una, I knew she lived here, but what do you mean by *residents*?' I asked, confused.

Gina smiled. 'Walk this way and I'll explain what we do here.'

She led me through the house: a large sunny room kitted out with toys and books and brightly coloured bean bags, a formal dining room and a large room with a piano in the corner and a beautiful stone fireplace. Gina explained that while she ran her childminding business from here, she also had several octogenarian tenants and the multi-generational house had become home for all of them.

'Bing and Una have the top floor, and Delphine, Dexter and I live on the first floor. And at the moment Welcome Cottage, which you passed at the top of the drive, is Dexter's writing studio, he's working on a film script,' she added proudly. 'But it's bigger than he needs really and we've been wondering how we could use the space.'

We returned to the kitchen and sat down at the table.

'Una mentioned something about a honeymoon suite?'

Gina rolled her eyes and laughed. 'Keeping a secret in this place is impossible. But yes, she's right. We're planning on doing a few very special weddings a year.'

'Tell me more.' I was all ears; as far as I was concerned none was more special than Laura and Hamish's.

Gina scooped up her hair and knotted it in a messy bun, while checking the time.

'It was a chance conversation I had with Delphine at the beginning of the year about getting married later in life. She said that finding somewhere to host a wedding when you're not in the first flush of youth isn't that straightforward. Weddings are marketed to the young, or at most to couples in their forties and fifties: the venues, the food, even the wedding cars. But where do you go if you're eighty? Where do you go if your dream wedding can't involve many stairs, or if you don't want incessant background music or staff young enough to be your great grandchildren?'

I nodded in sympathy, thinking that Terry probably wouldn't be able to manage stairs either. 'And wedding vows are no less important just because you might not have to keep them for so long.'

'Oh, that's an excellent way of putting it. You're right!' she agreed. 'And whether the older couple is a bride and groom, or two grooms or two brides, they deserve a dignified service designed to suit their particular needs. So from January next year, that's where The Evergreens wedding package comes in.'

'But that's five months away,' I said, crestfallen. 'Laura and Hamish don't have that long. I've got a friend who needs my help . . .'

Gina chewed her lip while I explained the situation.

'So with Terry so ill, I'm really looking for somewhere they can get married as soon as legally possible.'

'Gosh, that is so sad.' Gina sighed. 'The thing is, we're not ready.'

'Please say yes!' I begged. 'All I need is a licensed venue; I can do the rest. The Evergreens is perfect. I've got a young couple in love, a sick father of the bride and a deadline of thirty days.'

'Sounds like a premise for a film,' said a deep voice from the doorway.

A man with dark wavy hair and friendly brown eyes crossed the kitchen, kissed Gina's head and dropped his laptop casually on the kitchen table.

He looked vaguely familiar, I thought, as Gina introduced me to her boyfriend.

'Dexter, this is Fearne the florist.'

'Pleased to meet you, Dexter.'

He grinned as he shook my hand. 'We've met before. And I'm pretty sure you told me you weren't a florist then.'

'Of course!' I laughed, realising where I'd seen him before: at the church on my first day in Barnaby when I'd been looking at the flowers over the lychgate. 'You were the photographer!'

'Technically, I'm a writer,' he corrected me.

'Rosie and Gabe didn't want a formal photographer doing stilted shots,' Gina explained, 'Dex is pretty handy with a camera so he offered to do it.'

My ears pricked up. 'I need a photographer for my wedding. Can I tempt you?'

'Gina!' Paige called from the garden. 'We should go.'

'Arrghh!' Gina yelped, jumping to her feet. 'Music club. The woman in charge is a right harridan if you're late.'

'Of course,' I said, trying not to show my disappointment.

'I think we should go for it, Gina,' said Dexter, pinching a biscuit. 'this could be a good way of doing a dry run. Especially if Fearne is going to organise everything.'

'Good point. Yes, very good point,' Gina said thoughtfully. 'And it'll be a simple, minimum fuss wedding?'

'Absolutely minimum fuss.' I held my breath and kept everything crossed.

Dexter and Gina regarded each other for a moment and a slow smile crept over Dexter's face.

'Oh sod it,' said Gina, laughing. 'Why not.'

'Thank you!' I leapt up and kissed them both. 'And can I put you down as photographer?'

'Sure,' Dexter laughed. 'I'll have to take it up professionally at this rate.'

Twenty minutes later I was back at Nina's Flowers, having collected Scamp from Biddy.

I took out my phone and sent Laura a text.

I'm delighted to announce that on the last Saturday in July you and Hamish will be getting married in the stunning setting of The Evergreens in Barnaby. You are going to love it xxx

You STAR! I love you Fearne, sooo much. I'll start texting all the guests. And I'll tell Hamish – obvs – no backing out now! xxx

I heaved a sigh of relief; it was all starting to come together nicely. Just the catering, venue decorations, music, cake, bridesmaid's dress for me and flowers to go.

My head spun just thinking about it. Minimum fuss, I'd promised Gina. Even doing it simply carried a fair few complications. It was only when I wrote the details down in the diary that I realised that the day after the wedding would be the first anniversary of Freddie's death.

It was a day I'd been dreading, but now, the next few weeks would be filled with the joy of organising a wedding for the people he and I loved most in the world. I smiled to myself and a sense of peace settled over me. I had the distinct feeling that wherever my brother was, he'd be smiling with me.

Chapter Thirty-six

It was Thursday afternoon and the after-school rush had hit our little corner of Barnaby. Parents were buying their children ice cream from Ken's Mini Mart or the café depending on their budget. Lucas was selling water pistols and was offering to fill them up for free and on the opposite side of the green, people were sipping pints of cold beer outside the pub. I'd adapted to the weather conditions too, on Victor's advice.

'Orchids,' he had said briskly. 'That's what you want this weather. A lot more forgiving than they look.'

And so I'd gone with his recommendation, and so far, his advice was paying off, I thought, wrapping the last order of the day in paper. Once I was finished I stood in front of the oscillating fan, legs akimbo and lifted my arms up, my eyes closed as the draught moved from side to side.

'Hello, stranger,' said an amused voice from the doorway.

My eyes sprang open to find Sam walking towards me.

'Hello, what a gorgeous surprise!' I beamed at him.

Absence, I decided, definitely did make the heart grow fonder. I hadn't seen him since Monday and we hadn't spoken in that time either other than a text earlier to say he was back from Lanzarote.

I held my arms out to him, ready for a hug but all of a sudden, he stopped dead, as if he'd changed his mind.

'Nice to see you,' he said formally. 'The kids are with me, so . . .'

'What? *Your* kids?' My arms were still wide when two children wandered in behind him carrying pots of lavender and marguerite. I shot him a look of panic and not knowing what to do with my flailing limbs, decided to swing them from side to side like a pendulum.

I was flummoxed. Did Sam know nothing about introducing a new partner to his children: the boundaries, the permission from their mother, the talking and preparation that should be done for a recommended three months before actually meeting me? Not that I'd googled it or anything.

'We've chosen, Dad,' said an angelic-faced girl with piercing blue eyes. There was no question who her father was; their mouths and noses were identical. She even had his golden hair which hung in a smooth shiny curtain almost to her waist.

'No we haven't,' said a much younger boy crossly. 'I don't want pots; I want proper flowers. Dad, tell her.'

'This is Will and this is Annabel,' said Sam, in a stilted voice. He looked mortified. 'Kids, this is Fearne, she, er . . .'

I drew in a deep breath, trying to put an image of their immaculately groomed mother out of my head. I was conscious of sweat patches on my T-shirt and wished I'd bothered to do my ponytail; last time I'd looked I had more hair out of it than in.

'She works for Nina,' he scratched his nose. 'And Granddad Duncan owns this shop. So Fearne is a tenant.'

Ouch. That stung. Probably the best approach under the circumstances, given how recently the children's living arrangements had been under discussion. But couldn't I at least have been a friend?

'Hi!' I blurted out. I did a double jazz-hands wave, complete with a comedy clown-face grin. *What the hell was I doing?*

Will tilted his head to one side curiously, obviously wondering the same. 'What is she doing?'

He had the complexion of a peach and with his mother's pale blond colouring and long eyelashes, was going to break many a heart when he was older.

'Stretching!' I said, grinning in what I hoped was a friendly and welcoming way. 'Releases tension in the muscles. This one's called windmill.'

I circled my arms like a complete loon. I swear Sam laughed but he had the good sense to turn it into a cough.

'I do yoga with Mummy,' said Annabel, regarding me suspiciously. 'And I've never seen that one.'

'It's not yoga,' I said, changing the direction of my arms to a backstroke. 'It's Flexercise, much more fun.'

'O-*kay*,' said Annabel slowly, giving her father a look which clearly said *fruit-loop*.

'How have you been?' I asked Sam with as much warmth as I dared, hoping to communicate with my eyes how pleased I was to see him and how I couldn't wait for us to have a moment alone.

'Good. Busy. Lot to sort out, you know,' he said stiffly. He pressed his lips together non-committally and ruffled his son's hair.

'Right. You must have. Good,' I said, automatically mirroring his staccato responses.

It was simply the presence of his children which was affecting his behaviour, I told myself. Only natural, nothing to worry about. I shot him an encouraging smile but his attention was caught by his son.

'A dog!' Will said breathily, spotting Scamp who was so hot this afternoon he couldn't even be bothered to say hello to Sam. The little boy dived across the floor like a goalie saving a ball and ended up with Scamp in his bed.

Scamp obliged by presenting his tummy to the little boy for immediate tickling.

'That's Scamp. Give him one of these, he loves them,' said Sam, producing a packet of polo mints from his pocket. My heart tweaked with hope; this was more like the Sam I knew.

Annabel thumped the potted plants she was carrying down onto the counter with an impatient huff.

'Did you want to buy those?' I asked, sweeping the loose compost she'd spilled into my hand.

'Not especially.' She wrinkled her nose and cast a look around the rest of the shop. 'But I suppose we'll have to.'

'It's Nanny's birthday and I wanted to get her some flowers,' said Will. He had his arm around Scamp's neck and giggled when Scamp tried to lick his ear.

'My mum,' Sam explained. 'Will insisted on coming here because he liked the flowers I got for Pandora.'

'How thoughtful,' I said brightly, trying to ignore the message that it hadn't been Sam's idea to come. 'My mum loves lavender so I'm sure your nanny will.'

An image popped up of Mum rubbing lavender flowers between her fingers and holding them up for me to smell. It brought a wave of love for her. We didn't have many flowers in our house when I was growing up. Too expensive, Mum had said. It was Granny I usually associated with flowers, not Mum.

'I hate flowers. Sorry.' Annabel flicked her hair over her shoulder, not looking in the least bit sorry.

I was bemused. 'I don't think I've met anyone who hates flowers before.'

Sam laughed at his daughter and placed a casual arm around her slim shoulders. 'Since when? You spend hours in Nanny's garden.'

She held up a hand. 'OK, fine, I don't actually hate the flowers themselves. It's what they represent.'

'You mean like saying "I love you" with a bunch of flowers?' I said.

'Ugh, no.' She curled her top lip in disgust. 'If I wanted to say "I love you" I'd—'

'You'd just look in the mirror, 'cos you only love yourself,' Will spluttered, rolling around at his own joke.

I turned away swiftly to hide my mirth under the guise of selecting a nice gift bag.

'Don't be rude, Will,' said Sam in a strangled voice that I recognised as trying not to laugh.

'Buying flowers is a waste,' said Annabel, folding her arms.

'Annabel,' Sam warned. 'You're not too old to be told off for rudeness either.'

'Sorry,' she muttered.

'I haven't been a florist for very long,' I told her, 'but I see how happy people are when they are given flowers. I don't think making people happy is a waste, do you?'

She didn't answer straight away and then she wafted an arm around the shop, taking in the flowers on display. 'It's not sustainable though, is it?'

'Pardon?' I said, taken aback.

She bent down to read the writing on one of the delivery boxes which Victor had dropped off this morning. 'I mean *Ecuador*,' she said in disgust. 'Seriously? You can't find anything closer to this country.'

'Where's Ecuador?' Will wanted to know.

'South America,' said Sam.

'It's the best place for heliconia,' I said defensively.

Annabel gave me a pitying look. 'If the flowers come from the other side of the world, that's a lot of carbon.'

'Good point,' I said, chastised. 'I'll have a word with my wholesaler.'

'Annabel is worried about the environment,' Sam pointed out apologetically.

'I'm not just worried, I'm a campaigner,' she corrected him. 'I'm going to do everything I can to protect the environment. And so should everyone else.'

I studied her with admiration; she was feisty and independent and passionate – all the qualities I'd be proud of in a daughter. Whatever I thought about Pandora, she'd done a great job with her. 'Thank you. We need people like you to make some changes.'

'I know you do. The air miles to fly to visit my grandparents is bad enough, but flying *flowers*,' she lifted her shoulders. 'There must be flowers in England you could sell.'

'I'll look into it,' I promised.

'Good,' she said sternly.

Annabel had given me a thought: Laura would love the idea of having all British flowers in her bouquet. I'd definitely look into it.

'Can we get a puppy, Dad?' Will asked. By now he was flat on his back in the dog bed with Scamp lying on his chest.

Sam looked at his son and shook his head. 'Sorry, Will, it's not a good time for us to get a pet.'

Us? I stiffened. Surely he and Pandora weren't a couple again? He certainly hadn't behaved like a married man on Sunday night when he was at my house.

'And if we were going to get a pet,' said Annabel, 'there are loads of dogs' rescue places full of dogs who've been abandoned and need homes. Getting a puppy is selfish.'

'Shut up, Saint Annabel!' Will buried his head underneath Scamp.

She bristled. 'At least I'm making the world better, not like you, you posy little choirboy.'

'Dad, tell her!' said Will, plaintively.

Annabel pulled a water pistol out of a little rucksack she was carrying, stood over her brother and squirted him in the face. Scamp, thinking it was a game, began snapping at the water and wagging his tail. Soon both children were laughing and despite Sam's warning yells to be careful the three of them began chasing around the shop.

Sam shook his head and groaned. 'Sorry for the chaos.'

'Don't apologise, it's nice to meet them, and it's lovely to see you.' I bit my lip and lowered my voice. 'Are we OK, you seem a bit . . . preoccupied?'

'Um.' He glanced over his shoulder at his children. 'We should probably talk when we're alone.'

'Of course.' My face flushed; the last thing I wanted to do was make things awkward for him.

'Sorry, sweetheart.' He frowned and stroked my arm lightly. 'It's been a tough couple of days with my in-laws.'

My heart lifted a bit; *sweetheart*. We must be OK then. I stared at him, willing him to elaborate, but Will bounded up and looked at my notebook on the counter.

'What are you drawing?' he panted, breathlessly. His hair was messed up and it took all my willpower not brush it out of his eyes.

'This?' I said, turning the page around so he could see. 'It's some ideas for wedding flowers for my best friend.'

'Wedding flowers?' Annabel said, scathingly.

'Just 'cos no one will ever marry you,' Will guffawed and then quickly dodged a punch.

'Wedding flowers are a massive waste,' she announced, nonetheless taking the notebook and flicking through it.

'Oh, darling,' Sam chuckled and wrapping his arms

around her, he pressed a kiss to the top of her head. 'Lighten up, you don't have to have a crusade against everything.'

'It's true though, Dad,' she protested. 'All that effort for two people on one day.'

'Now, I have to disagree with you there,' I said lightly, 'because flowers are one of the most memorable things at a wedding. They can make even the plainest venue very special.'

'Hmm.' Annabel looked unconvinced.

'Did Mummy have flowers when you got married?' Will wanted to know.

Sam checked his phone, avoiding everyone's gaze. 'Yep,' he said crisply, 'red ones.'

'We learn about reduce, recycle, reuse in school,' said Annabel. 'And wedding flowers sounds like the opposite of that.'

'Well the bride and groom usually give the wedding flowers away after the party,' I said, pleased with my comeback. 'So they're not thrown away.'

Annabel frowned. 'But what about the stuff in churches and on tables and all the garlands and the extra bits. What happens to those? I think you should be able to get at least two weddings out of them.'

'They get taken down and er, put somewhere.' I shrugged my shoulders helplessly. 'But you're right, it is a shame to dismantle everything at the end of the day.'

Sam was looking at me, a smile playing on his lips. He was no help whatsoever.

Annabel's jaw was set firmly. 'I knew it. Cutting flowers from plants is wasteful. If you need flowers, use plants.'

Will grabbed the pot of lavender from the counter and started goose-stepping from one side of the shop to the other singing, 'Here Comes the Bride'.

Sam caught my eye and we both smothered a giggle.

'All right then, maybe not pots,' Annabel said, flicking her hair over her shoulder again. 'Just have the wedding in the garden and the flowers will already be there. Growing naturally. I saw a wedding like that on the TV. It was really cool.'

I blinked at her. That could actually work. The garden at The Evergreens was more than big enough. We could hire a marquee . . .

'She got that idea off *Say Yes to the Dress*,' said Will, propping his elbows on the counter and resting his chin in his hands. 'She watches it all the time.'

Annabel snorted with derision. 'Better than sitting on Mum's swivel chair and pretending to be on *The Voice*.'

Her brother glared at her.

'Do you fancy helping me organise this wedding?' I asked Annabel. 'You've got some really good ideas, I'd pay you. If your dad says you can, that is.'

'Really?' Annabel went red. 'Can I, Dad?'

We both looked at Sam.

Sam scratched his chin. 'Don't see why not.'

I half expected him to add that she'd have to check with her mum first but he didn't.

'Yay! Thanks Dad.' His daughter threw her arms around his neck and I had to fight the urge to join in.

'What can I do?' Will popped his bottom lip out.

'Are you really in a choir?' I asked, looking at Sam for confirmation.

Sam nodded proudly. 'Soloist.'

'Right little show-off,' Annabel muttered.

'Yeah, I am in a choir,' said Will. 'But I don't like all the church stuff. I like Ed Sheeran and Michael Bublé.'

His sister pretended to be sick and then put her arm around his neck. 'Your taste in music sucks, but your voice is brilliant, Will,' she admitted.

'You're both brilliant.' Sam grinned at his offspring proudly.

'Would you like to sing at my friend's wedding?' I asked. Although how their mother was going to react at me roping both her kids in, I had no idea. But it was up to Sam to smooth that over with her, not me.

Will looked at Sam, who nodded his consent.

'As long as you pay him a fair wage,' Annabel demanded.

'Of course,' I promised.

'Da-ad,' Will clasped his stomach. 'I'm starving.'

'If you give me some money, I'll take him to the shop,' said Annabel, with a small sigh to indicate that she was doing Sam a great favour.

'I could do with your help choosing a wedding cake,' I said, lifting the lid of a large plastic box. Rosie had brought some samples round earlier. 'If you like cake, that is?'

'I love cake,' said Annabel, shooting me a sly grin. 'Even wedding cake. High five.'

We slapped each other's hands and I felt ridiculously honoured.

The kids swooped down on it like gannets and Sam sent them to eat it on the pavement to minimise mess in the shop. There wouldn't have been any mess because Scamp would have caught the crumbs before they hit the floor but I kept quiet because I was dying to get Sam on his own.

'I've missed you,' I whispered, as soon as they were out of earshot, stepping as close as I dared.

Sam looked down at his feet. 'And I've missed you. Look, what happened on Sunday . . .'

I grinned cheekily. 'Don't tell me you've forgotten already. Here, let me remind you.'

I stood on my tiptoes to whisper in his ear but he leapt back as if I'd stuck a pin in him.

'The kids!' He laughed awkwardly. 'They could be back in any second.'

'Yes, of course, sorry,' I said, feeling slightly ashamed. I jammed my hands in my back pockets to force myself not to touch him again.

'I really enjoyed Sunday,' he began again.

'Snap,' I said feeling a surge of hope; silly me, I'd been overthinking things, he was only being stand-offish because of his children which was entirely the right thing to do. 'Perhaps we could make it a weekly thing.'

'Actually, it's my turn to have the kids next weekend, so . . .'

'Of course!' I said, firmly. 'Absolutely and according to an article I read, we should wait to introduce the children to the idea of you and someone new. So, slowly, slowly.'

'You are sweet.' Sam groaned. 'This is difficult. Fearne, what I'm trying to say is I think we should probably slow things down a bit.'

'Oh.' I blinked at him, feeling utterly deflated. 'You didn't think that on Sunday. So why the sudden change of heart?'

He trailed a finger down my bare arm and this time it was me who pulled away. 'I really like you, Fearne . . .'

'*But*,' I supplied for him. I plastered on a smile. 'There's a "but". And if it's all the same to you, I don't want to hear it. So let's leave it there. Job done. It's OK, no hearts broken.'

He looked over his shoulder to where Annabel and Will were sitting on the pavement swapping lumps of cake. 'It's all happened so fast. I'm trying to find a divorce lawyer, and somewhere to live and now a new job.'

I stared at him in disbelief. 'Have you been fired?'

My mind flashed back to the fun we'd had pretending to be on *The Apprentice* and doing impressions of Sir Alan and I shook them away.

Sam smiled ruefully. 'I gave Duncan an ultimatum: either he withdrew the termination notice on this property, or I walked. I was banking on him wanting me to stay. Turns out I'm not indispensable. So I'm officially unemployed.'

'You did that for us?' I clapped a hand over my mouth, horror-struck.

'I did.' He straightened up. 'It was a matter of principle. I know I didn't get you the result you needed but at least I did my best. I've been under Duncan's thumb for years. It feels quite good actually. I got a decent pay-off and I'm going to put some thought into my next move.'

'But Nina doesn't want to stay in these premises,' I blurted out.

He blinked at me. 'Seriously?'

I bit my lip, nodding. 'It doesn't make her happy any more, and it was only ever a temporary job for me. As soon as Laura and Hamish's wedding is over, we're closing the shop. We're not even going to stay until the end of the lease.'

He began pacing the floor, a hand pushed into his hair. 'You mean I went through all that confrontation for nothing?'

'I feel awful,' I whispered, feeling sick with guilt. 'I was going to tell you on Sunday and then when you turned up on your bike, work just slipped out of my head.'

Suddenly he started to laugh. 'Do you know what, I don't regret it at all. I hated working there and now I'll be forced to find something I really love.'

My shoulders sagged with relief. 'Thank goodness for that. I'm so sorry, Sam.'

'And me.'

He reached out for my hand and I didn't move away this time. It felt like a goodbye and my throat burned with all the words I didn't dare to say.

'Oh, William! You idiot!' came a disgruntled cry from outside.

'Now what?' Sam released my hand and sighed. 'I love them but, honestly, the bickering.'

I smiled. 'I can't say anything, Freddie and I were just the same as kids.'

Annabel marched back in, tugging her brother behind her. 'Dad, we've got to go. Will's just remembered he's got a singing lesson at five o'clock.'

'Oh Christ,' Sam mumbled, pulling some money out of his wallet for the potted plants. 'We'll never make it.'

'Bye, kids!' I called after them, 'goodbye Sam. I'll ring you about the wedding.'

'Sure.' He smiled, but it didn't quite reach his eyes. 'Thanks again.'

I kept looking at him right until the car was nothing but a blur in the distance, just in case he'd waved or looked at me at the last second, but he hadn't.

So that was that apparently. Our relationship had ground to a halt before it had even got going.

I should have listened to Ethel; I'd let things escalate between us and now I was facing the consequences. I groaned so loudly that Scamp's ears pricked up in alarm.

'Right, that's enough moping,' I said aloud, clearing my throat. I was going to have to push thoughts of him to the back of my mind. 'Sam is now officially a friend again and we're just going to have to get used to it. Now, Scamp, where was I?'

At least I sounded convincing even if I didn't feel it . . .

I pulled my notebook in front of me and read through my to-do list and thought about local flowers and how to incorporate Annabel's ideas about using the plants which were already growing in the garden. After a few minutes,

I noticed I'd doodled a rose bower with a happy couple underneath it.

Laura had said hundreds of times that there was no lovelier place to be than the English countryside in the sunshine. Laura and Hamish would love to get married under a rose bower. Let's face it, who wouldn't? Simple, beautiful and fuss-free.

Someone else had said something similar to me recently. I ran over those words trying to remember when I'd last heard them. Oh yes! I knew who it was. *I wonder . . .*

I scanned through the customer database until I found what I was looking for and called the number. To my delight, the phone was answered after the third ring.

'Hello, it's Fearne from the florist, I've had an idea. Can you meet me at the shop tomorrow morning for a chat?'

The call succeeded in lifting my spirits. My own love life might be going off the boil, but if my plan came off, things might just be hotting up for someone else.

Chapter Thirty-seven

It was closing time. I was looking forward to going home, sitting in the garden with a nice cold drink and ringing Ethel for a chat. She was already settled into her new room at her daughter's house and was enjoying hearing about the wedding preparations. Last night I'd told her all about the invitations Lucas had found for us and this evening I wanted to get her input on the music.

I wiped the perspiration from my brow and looked around the shop. The floor was swept, the flowers were watered, all I had to do was put the dustbins out for collection in the morning and I was done.

'Two minutes and we can go,' I told Scamp.

He had a bad habit of barking at dustbins to I tried to sneak out the back door without him noticing. But as soon as I put one foot outside he started to howl.

'Shush, you silly boy, it's just a bin!' I said, poking my head back in for a second. Scamp fell silent, although I could hear the scrabbling of his paws.

'*Help!*' came a timid voice. 'HELP!'

I dashed back into the shop to find Pandora backed up against the counter, clutching her handbag. Scamp was sitting at her feet making a low growling noise.

Bloody hell; this was all I needed. I could see the headline already: *Shop Horror!: Florist's Dog attacks Lover's Ex-wife*.

'Scamp, in your bed,' I said sharply in the voice he knew not to mess with.

'Thank you,' Pandora said with a rush of breath as my cheeky dog slunk off and flopped down, keeping a strict eye on her.

'Sorry about that, he's normally so placid. What can I do for you?' I said coolly.

I looked at her properly and did a double take. She was still beautiful, but devoid of make-up, in a pair of flip-flops and plain cotton sundress, her hair scrunched up loosely, she looked younger and infinitely more vulnerable. Was it a ploy for sympathy, I wondered?

'Can we talk?' she said with a sideways glance at Scamp.

'Actually I'm very busy.' I folded my arms and then made myself unfold them again. 'But, yes, sure.'

'My husband.'

'No we can't.' I marched to the door, opened it and gestured for her to leave. I'd already had Sam in here giving me the cold shoulder; getting a second slap in the face was the last thing I needed.

But she didn't move. Instead she dropped her head. 'I've made such a mess of things. I thought I could have it all. I've been greedy and selfish and I took Sam for granted.'

Yep. All those things.

'It's not me you should be talking to,' I said tightly.

'Yes I know,' she said, looking at me from under her lashes. They shimmered with tears. I could see how men would fall for her. But it wasn't going to work on me. 'I've let my father down, myself down but worst of all I've let Sam and the children down.'

'OK, I'm listening.' I shut the door, flipped the sign to closed and fetched her a tissue from a box under the counter.

'Thank you.' She wiped her eyes, refolded the tissue and held it back out to me. 'Do you have a bin?'

'Look, Pandora,' I said warily, ignoring the sodden offering. 'It's never too late to change. You can make a fresh start. Be the person you want to be. Sam's a good man, I'm sure he's not going to want there to be bad feeling between you.'

'You're right.' She smiled, revealing dazzling white teeth and reached out a hand as if to touch me. From his bed, Scamp let out half a growl. She quickly withdrew her hand. 'We need to find a new way to get along. I'm going to try very hard from now on.'

'Yes, well. Good luck.' I needed her to go now. Being so close to her was making me itch; she was so smarmy and the longer she was here, the more convinced I was that she was acting the penitent wife.

'We'll need you to do your part, of course,' she gazed at me with such sincerity it was all I could do not to laugh.

'Me? What have I got to do with it?'

'Give us the time and space to work it out.'

I was puzzled. 'I don't understand what you mean.'

'I mean stay away from my husband. I realise it's a temptation, he's a handsome man after all. But at least it will get easier once you've moved from these premises.' She tilted her head, pityingly. 'I must admit I was surprised you let him stay the night on Sunday. Quite forward of you.'

'How did you know about . . .' My cheeks burned with embarrassment.

'Our phones are linked.' She said smugly. 'When he wasn't answering my calls I used the *find my iPhone* function. Imagine my shock when I found he'd been in the same location all night.' She looked me up and down, her lips pursed in repulsion.

'I imagine it was very much like Sam's shock when he realised you and Gareth had stayed the night at the Claybourne Hotel the other week.'

A flash of irritation passed across her face but she covered it quickly and managed to look wounded. 'The children would be devastated to know that Daddy had someone new in his life.'

I folded my arms. 'Won't they be devastated about Gareth?'

'Forget about bloody Gareth!' she said, gritting her teeth.

'Whoops, sorry,' I said, not even bothering to sound in the least bit apologetic.

I wasn't going to admit it in front of Pandora, but I did care about upsetting the children. I'd have to be especially careful now that they were both helping me out at the wedding.

'I've said my piece.' She rearranged her handbag on her shoulder and strutted to the door. 'And you said you were busy so I'll let you get on. I think you were doing the dustbins?' She gave me a sly smile.

'Thanks,' I said. 'Your kids are wonderful, by the way.'

She stiffened. 'You've met them?'

'Earlier today. Will wanted some flowers for his grand-mother's birthday.'

'Shit.' She pressed a hand to her forehead. 'I'd forgotten that was today. Can you deliver her some flowers from me? Something extravagant to make up for arriving so late in the day.'

She took a credit card out of her purse and held it out to me. It had the name Mr S. Diamond across it. A knot of anger lodged in my stomach. After every-thing she'd just said, she was still prepared to spend an extravagant amount of money on her mother-in-law's birthday, at Sam's expense, Sam, who, because of me, was out of a job.

'Sorry,' I said with satisfaction. 'We don't deliver that far away.'

She blew out a sharp breath through her nostrils and slammed the door on her way out. I flopped over the counter, feeling like my heart had been put through the blender.

If Sam's visit earlier had made me wobbly, then Pandora's had completely tipped me overboard. There'd be no more flirting from me, no more touching, or suggestive looks. When, and if, Sam was ready to move on from Pandora, I'd be there, but in the meantime, I wouldn't be offering anything other than a friendly ear.

And that, I vowed, as we drove home a few minutes later, laden with the flower orders I had to drop off on the way, was a promise.

Chapter Thirty-eight

A week later, that promise had remained unbroken.

It hadn't even been hard to keep because apart from confirming via text that he was happy for me to contact Annabel directly about the wedding and sending me her number, I hadn't heard a dicky bird from him. I couldn't deny I was hurt, but I'd learned my lesson, and fortunately, I was too busy to dwell on affairs of the heart; well, my own, at least.

I'd spoken to Laura every evening, either on the phone or in person in an attempt to keep her calm and reassure her that everything was under control. Her employer had been brilliant and had let her take a month off to be with her dad and she was doing her utmost to care for him in his own home with the help of a community nurse. Her wedding dress had arrived and looked gorgeous and we'd managed to find a quirky boutique which opened on a Sunday and I'd chosen a beautiful bridesmaid's dress.

During the day, I was running the florist's single-handedly, project managing what was turning into a much bigger wedding than Laura had initially wanted (Hamish had accidently invited a cousin and once you'd invited one, you had to invite them all), and fielding enquiries for workshops (someone had even requested a Christmas wreath session) so I had plenty to keep me from mooning about over Sam.

There was so much going on and so many people who'd stepped forward and offered help that this evening I was hosting a wedding meeting at The Evergreens to check that everything was running to plan.

That was in an hour from now, but I still had something I wanted to do before leaving the florist. Sitting in the cold store was the most perfect bouquet of pink stargazer lilies, pale pink roses and white lisianthus. It had been on my list of jobs since the morning but every time I'd picked up the phone I got an attack of nerves and chickened out.

I stared at the phone on the counter and nibbled my lip, daring myself to do it. Would this be an unwelcome interference, was he ready to be thinking about another woman? It was so hard to judge. The last bit of meddling I'd done had panned out really well. It had started with an idea from Annabel and now it looked as if it might actually be happening. It had given me an enormous boost: I was making two people happy and in so doing, I also was making myself happy. Just like the perfume analogy. I smiled contentedly and was about to pluck up the courage and call him when there was a knock at the open shop door.

'Cooee, Dolly Dream Boat!' Lucas gave me a twinkly wave from the doorway. He was wearing a buttoned-up short-sleeved shirt and tailored shorts and with his mirrored sunglasses looked like he belonged in Barcelona and not Barnaby. 'You look miles away.'

I blinked at him. 'I'm about to meddle in someone's love life. It could change lives. Literally.'

He was at my side in a flash, his eyes sparkling at the prospect of romance. 'Who? Darling! I must know. Oh, this is so exciting. I only popped in to see if you wanted an ice cream from Ken's.'

'I do want an ice cream,' I groaned longingly.

Scamp woofed and pawed Lucas's leg.

'Ouch,' Lucas rubbed his bare skin. 'Someone needs another pedi at Biddy's.'

'If this goes well, we can go round and book him in. With some flowers.'

Lucas gasped. 'Are you talking about *Biddy's* love life?'

'It's her birthday today.' I gave him a secret smile. 'Buy me a mint chocolate cone and I'll tell all.'

He virtually sprinted out of the shop and over the road to Ken's and while he was gone I quickly got to work. I didn't mind telling Lucas when he got back but I'd feel better about having this conversation without him eavesdropping.

I called the number I had on file.

'Hello?' said a voice I recognised. Phew, so far so good.

'Nigel, this is Fearne, the florist.'

'Oh, yes, hello?'

'It's almost the end of the day and I have a perfect bouquet in my shop which might go to waste if it doesn't find a home today.' I crossed my fingers.

He chuckled. 'Goodness me, how sweet of you to think of me! But I'm sure you can find someone more deserving?'

'I was thinking more of someone who has a birthday today, perhaps?' I held my breath. I was certain he'd know it was Biddy's birthday; the question was would he want to acknowledge it with flowers?

'Well, I don't think I . . . at least I'm not sure if . . .' His voice faded.

He'd remembered. I kept quiet, tense with nerves. On the other end of the phone I heard him rifle through papers. Perhaps he was checking his diary.

He cleared his throat. 'Um. What colour are the flowers.'

409

I crossed my fingers. 'Pink.'

'It was her favourite colour,' he murmured.

It still was, I thought excitedly.

'I wonder . . .' He hesitated and in that space I could feel how torn he was: the guilt and the joy and the hope. After all, his wife had only passed away a few weeks ago. It was only natural that he'd think twice before contacting his old love.

'As luck would have it, I do know someone,' he said with a smile in his voice. 'I'd like to buy them please. And I'd like them delivered to Biddy at the pet shop.'

'Of course,' I said, trying not to squeal with joy. 'Any message to go with it?'

'Oh crikey,' he muttered. 'Give me a minute.'

It took several goes for Nigel to come up with the right message but when he did it was perfect.

My darling girl, I deserve nothing, I expect nothing,
but know that even while we have been apart all
these years, your heart has remained the centre of
my world.
Happy Birthday,
Ever yours
Nigel xxx

I was taking down his credit card details when Lucas came back in with our ice creams.

'She's going to be thrilled,' I said, shoving the note under Lucas's nose to read. 'She's had her eye on the orchids for ages.'

'Oh my giddy aunt, he has just melted my heart!' Lucas gasped, pulling a swoony face.

'I can't quite believe I'm doing it,' Nigel said.

'Well,' I said, teasingly. 'You only live once.'

'I used to think that but now I know different,' Nigel replied. 'We only *die* once, we *live* every single day,' he said. 'We owe it to ourselves to get the best out of that life while we have it.'

'That is a great way to think about it, thank you, Nigel.' I smiled down the phone. 'I'll remember that.'

Nigel coughed. 'Will you, er, put my number on the back of the card, in case she should want to talk to me?'

'Of course.'

After I put the phone down, I high-fived Lucas and hoovered up my ice cream.

'You were *a-ma-zing*,' said Lucas, wide-eyed. 'Now I reckon we've just got time to deliver them before we go and plan the wedding of the century.'

I locked up, fetched the bouquet and tucked Nigel's note in the top.

'If floristry doesn't work out for me,' I said, wiping a smear of melted chocolate from my chin, 'I think I might become a fairy godmother. I can see my website now: Fairy Fearne – making dreams come true, one person at a time.'

And if I felt slightly glum about the lack of my own dreams coming true, I think I just about managed to conceal it.

An hour later, I'd assembled my wedding team under the shade of an oak tree in the enormous garden at The Evergreens. Dexter had kindly set up a picnic table for us and from where we were sitting, we could see the spot Annabel and I had identified as being where the ceremony would take place in front of a rambling rhododendron bush covered with pink flowers. There wasn't a rose bower but Annabel had suggested making a willow arch from branches in the garden. So far, my decision to employ her as my assistant was paying off.

I felt a thrill every time I looked up at the house. There was a comfortable elegance to The Evergreens. It would be a gorgeous setting for the wedding: the old stone glowed in the sun and the gardens, although not manicured to within an inch of their lives, were welcoming and pretty and provided plenty of photo opportunities and ample room for the marquee. It was divided into sections so it would be easy to keep the food area hidden from the spot where the ceremony would be held and there were lots of little hideaways for those who wanted a bit of privacy.

Hamish was delighted with it and had already taken loads of photos. Laura wasn't here yet; Terry had had a hospital appointment which had overrun and she would be joining us as soon as she could. I couldn't wait for her to see it.

Una brought out a tray of homemade lemonade for us all. Her partner, Bing, a sprightly old chap with a neatly trimmed white beard, placed a gigantic bowl of freshly picked raspberries on the table while I passed round agendas and thanked everyone for coming.

'This all looks very formal,' I said, 'but it helps to know who's in charge of what and I hope nobody minds but I've included everyone's mobile number. Except Annabel's and Will's.'

'I've got an iPhone,' Annabel said crossly.

'It's just a child protection issue,' I explained. 'I didn't want to give your number out.'

Her eyes narrowed and I realised my mistake instantly.

'Because Will is only seven,' I added.

'You mean in case there are any paedos round the table.' Annabel studied each person in turn and sat back apparently satisfied. 'I don't think there are, we've been trained in spotting that sort of thing.'

'Well, that's a relief,' I said brightly as Hamish smothered a snort.

I hadn't really needed her this evening but she'd wanted to come to make sure I didn't forget anything. Also, shamelessly, I'd hoped to catch a glimpse of Sam, but Pandora had dropped her off. There was still hope, he might pick her up . . .

'Darling, do you mind if I start measuring up for the bunting?' said Lucas, playing with his tape measure. 'I want to get the order in tomorrow.'

'I'll hold the end for you,' Bing offered, getting to his feet.

'Now there's an offer I can't refuse.' Lucas winked at him saucily and Una let out a peal of laughter as Bing blushed the same colour as the raspberries.

'I'm taking notes for the registrar and the DJ,' said Gina.

'I'll do you a playlist,' said Annabel helpfully. 'Because old people don't know what's happening in the music scene.'

Hamish cleared his throat. 'Our first dance will be to our favourite Fleetwood Mac song.'

Annabel wrinkled her nose. 'Who?'

Everyone laughed. Hamish broke the news to her that she wouldn't be getting a say in the music and she looked mortally offended.

Rosie smoothed a hand over her round tummy. She'd be eight and a half months pregnant by the wedding date and it was already impossible to imagine the bump getting any bigger. 'What I need to know is who's in charge of first aid?'

'Don't worry, chum.' Gina topped up everyone's glasses. 'I'm a qualified first aider and I'll be on the lookout for anyone who seems in danger of getting sunstroke.'

The weather experts were predicting a continuation of the heatwave, which was great in that we were definitely going to be able to conduct the service outside. But Gina was right, the sun brought its own risks. I added 'factor 50 sunscreen and spare sunhats' to my list. I gave her a grateful smile and thanked my lucky stars for the umpteenth time that she'd agreed to let us use The Evergreens as the venue.

'And what about delivering babies?' Dexter flopped down in an empty seat and pointed at Rosie's belly. 'Anyone got any experience there?'

'I've watched a documentary about young mothers in Costa Rica,' Annabel offered. 'It was quite graphic. So count me in.'

I felt a surge of affection for Sam's daughter; I hadn't had half as much of her self-confidence at her age. Nothing seemed to faze her, she had an opinion on everything and she was whip-smart. Although right now, Rosie was looking a bit queasy.

'Let's not even joke about it,' she groaned. 'But don't worry, I checked with my mum. Lia and I were both late arrivals. And first babies are always late, it's the law.'

'Let's hope so,' I said. 'I think The Evergreens has enough of a challenge coping with its first wedding, I'd rather not add a birth into the mix.'

'Ditto,' said Rosie emphatically. 'Can we move catering to the top of the agenda please, Fearne. Because as we speak, Gabe is topping up Noah's paddling pool with ice cubes ready for me and I can't wait to go home.'

'Sure.' I looked at her, alarmed. Her poor feet were so swollen even the flip-flops she was wearing were cutting into her feet. 'Let's make the final choices for the menu.'

We decided to keep it simple: a barbecue, salads and a couple of different desserts, plus of course wedding cake.

Lucas and Bing finished their measuring job; Bing sat back down beside Una but Lucas kissed my cheek and dashed off to a prior engagement.

'We should consider a vegan menu,' said Annabel, throwing raspberries into her mouth like popcorn. 'It's better for the environment.'

Hamish pulled a face. 'We don't know any vegans.'

Bing looked horrified. 'You won't catch me eating that toffee stuff.'

'Same here,' said Una. 'I'm meat and two veg every day of the week.'

Bing waggled his bushy eyebrows suggestively and Una smacked his leg.

'Tof*u* not toffee,' Annabel corrected. 'Did you know that it only takes about two hundred gallons of water to produce one pound of tofu compared with two thousand gallons of water to produce one pound of beef.'

'Oh Annabel, I'm so sorry,' I said, mortified. 'I didn't realise you were vegan; that wedding cake I gave you last week had dairy in it.'

She shrugged. 'I'm flexitarian.'

Bing scratched his beard. 'I'm lost.'

So was I, but I made a note to look it up for future reference. Not that I'd probably see her much after the wedding, more's the pity. The more time that passed, the more I realised that once the wedding was over, the florist's shop would close and my time in Barnaby would be at an end. I quickly pushed the thought aside and for the next few minutes, we managed to come to an agreement about the menu. At thirty guests, Rosie was satisfied that she would be able to cope with the catering on her own and everyone offered to step in and help out on the day.

'And drinks?' Rosie looked at Hamish. 'What does Laura like?'

Hamish and I grinned at each other; Laura was most likely to be seen nursing a pint of real ale in a pub.

'Champagne,' said Hamish. 'Already in hand. A gift from a client.'

He named a footballer whom even I had heard of because he was regularly spread across the tabloids displaying his impressive six-pack.

Gina gasped. 'Is he coming to the wedding?'

Hamish shook his head. 'He's on holiday with David Beckham that week.'

Annabel's jaw dropped.

Just then Maria and Delphine stepped out onto the terrace via the kitchen doors. They hugged and Delphine went back in.

'Nonna!' Rosie called. 'Over here, come and join us!'

But Maria simply waved a hand briefly and scurried off through the side gate and away from us.

'Oh, shame.' Rosie frowned. 'She's been very shifty just recently. It feels like she's avoiding me.'

Annabel smirked and I shot her a warning look. She caught my eye and mimed zipping her lips.

'It's probably the heat,' I reassured Rosie. 'Perhaps she wants to get home and cool down.'

'Hmm,' said Rosie, unconvinced, staring after her grandmother. 'As long as she's not ill and hiding anything from us. Oh, look, here comes the bride!'

We all turned to see Laura walking slowly across the lawn towards us, turning her head left and right to take everything in. Hamish stood and held his arms open and she walked straight into them and burst into tears.

'Thank you all so much,' she sobbed, pulling away from his chest to speak. 'This is all so beautiful, it's perfect.'

She buried her head in Hamish's chest again.

He and I exchanged worried looks. I'd expected an emotional response to the location of her wedding, but not this.

'Laura? Is everything all right?' I murmured.

She shook her head. 'Dad's being moved into a hospice tomorrow. Turns out he's been in a lot more pain than he's admitted because he didn't want to worry me. All of his friends and ex-colleagues are ringing up wanting to come and visit. Plus, distant family members he hasn't seen for years.'

Everyone mumbled how sorry they were. It was just over three weeks to go until the wedding. Would Terry make it, everyone was wondering? Even Annabel sat silently, her little face taut with concern.

'I know what you're thinking,' said Laura with a watery smile, 'But Dad says he's not going anywhere until he's given me away. He's already discussed it with the hospital: if it comes to it, we'll pay for a private ambulance to get him here.'

It would break Laura's heart if her dad didn't make it. But I knew Terry; he and his daughter had had an impenetrable bond since her mum died.

'He'll be there, I just know it,' I said.

Laura moved from Hamish's arms to give me a hug. 'Thanks, Fearne, and thanks for all the work you've done so far, it's far more beautiful than I could possibly have imagined.'

'You know what I'm thinking?' Hamish began cautiously. 'The Evergreens is big enough to hold a lot more guests than thirty. How about we extend the numbers? That way we could invite all your dad's friends.'

'He'd love that.' Laura's eyes sparkled at her fiancé and she turned to me. 'But is it doable at this late stage?'

I looked at Gina, whose eyes, shining with tears, were locked on Dexter's. They smiled at each other.

'It's fine with us,' Dexter confirmed.

'It's your day,' I reminded Laura. 'You have to do what makes you happy.'

She wrapped her arm around Hamish's waist. 'If Dad's happy, we're happy.'

'And if you're happy, I'm happy.' And I meant it; in the grand scheme of things, doubling or even trebling the number of guests wasn't out of the question. The major decisions had been made; we'd just need more of everything.

'Hog!' Annabel piped up suddenly.

My first thought was her family. I glanced towards the side gate expecting to see a tribe of Hoggs on the approach.

'This is top secret but Dad's talking to a man about a hog-roast business,' she said in a stage whisper. 'Easier than a barbeque.'

'Oh?' I felt a pang of sadness that Sam hadn't told me this himself, but it was great news, both for him and potentially for us.

'Having tasted Sam's special rub, I think getting him to do a hog roast sounds a great idea.'

'Seconded.' Rosie sighed happily. 'I was imagining flipping burgers for crowds in this heat. If we could hand over that part to someone else, it would be amazing.'

Annabel hugged herself. 'He's going to love this.'

'I hope so, Annabel, but I'll talk to Sam about it. I think it will be more professional coming from me,' I said casually, trying to conceal my thrill at having a legitimate excuse to get in touch.

Laura and Hamish winked at me; I don't think I managed it.

Chapter Thirty-nine

The next three weeks flew by. I'd never been so busy yet felt so fulfilled in my life. I'd organised a big sale in the shop to sell off all the little trinket-y items we had on display. Rosie had helped me push it on social media and although the shelves were looking a bit bare, the bank account looked healthier than ever. Wendy had come up trumps as well and I had as many funeral tributes as I could handle. So although it was bittersweet to think that the florist's would soon be closed, we were going out on a high and Nina had been thrilled with all the updates I'd been sending her.

Annabel had been right about Sam: he was indeed considering investing in a hog-roast oven and after a bit of gentle persuasion he'd agreed to borrow the equipment from the man who was selling his business and do the catering for Laura and Hamish's larger-than-planned wedding. Sam had been into the shop a couple of times, ostensibly about the termination of the lease and checking when we actually intended to vacate the premises. I can't lie; I lived for those moments. I missed the closeness we'd shared that weekend, I missed his kisses and the feel of his body against mine. But I'd kept my promise to myself and not offered anything other than a friendly ear, despite sometimes catching a look in his eye which made me wonder as if there was another subtext to his visits that he couldn't or wouldn't put into words. He'd hovered at the shop door the other day for so long that I almost asked him if he wanted to talk about it, but I decided against it. I'd promised Pandora I'd keep my distance, and I was proud of my willpower to stand by my word. If he wanted to talk, my door was always open, but it was up to him to make the first move.

I hadn't seen Pandora either, other than from a distance. Thank goodness.

'You're doing absolutely the right thing,' Ethel had assured me over the phone, when I'd told her how our relationship had fizzled out after only one date. 'You don't want to be courting a man who can't give you his full attention.'

As usual, I mused, Ethel was right.

She was busy, she'd informed me. She'd joined a club for over-nineties run by a jolly ex-bus driver who came to collect her every Friday. Yesterday she'd had a picnic at Castle Howard. She said living with Carole and her husband Ivan had made her feel ten years younger and had invited Scamp and me to visit for her ninety-fifth birthday in October. I'd promised we would.

And now it was noon on Laura and Hamish's wedding day and we had three hours to go before the big moment. I'd barely had time to blink, let alone sleep in the last twenty-four hours. But Biddy had offered to have Scamp and I'd been at The Evergreens since six o'clock this morning.

There'd been some ups and downs; only last week Terry had caught an infection and Laura had kept an overnight vigil at his bedside. He was weak, but he'd recovered and miraculously, as of this morning, the news was that he'd be coming in an ambulance. He'd be using a wheelchair and we were playing it by ear as to whether Laura and he would simply walk up our flower-strewn aisle arm in arm or whether he'd need one of us to push him.

In other news, Biddy had met up with Nigel. Early days, but the sparkle in Biddy's eyes was unmissable and I was keeping everything crossed for a happy ending for them.

And Nina was back, irreverent, irrepressible Nina. I'd had my heart in my mouth for ten hours when she'd overslept and almost missed her flight home, but she'd been here for two days now and it was such a relief to have her help in putting the final touches to the wedding flowers. She'd become leaner while she was away; she looked fit and strong after completing all those tasks on the various farms she'd visited and although not tanned like we all were after the mad weather of the last few weeks, she glowed with health and happiness.

This morning, I'd been dipping in and out of Welcome Cottage, checking up on Laura who was having her hair and make-up done in there and now Nina and I were working together to do the last few flowers.

'Oh balls, snapped another one.' Nina tutted good-naturedly. 'I mean sweet peas in a bridal bouquet? Talk about fiddly, they bruise as soon as you touch them.'

'But they smell divine,' I argued, snipping some more off Bing's wigwam of bamboo canes. 'They're quintessentially British, they come with zero carbon miles. And they're free.'

She blew her fringe out of her eyes. 'Good point, well made.'

I was sounding more and more like Annabel every day.

The wedding flowers, much to my young assistant's satisfaction, were all British. We'd raided everyone's gardens and borrowed assorted terracotta pots brimming with geraniums, petunias and fuchsias. There was one at the end of every row of seats. Annabel and two of her best friends had made two willow arches as promised and I'd left her to poke in sunflowers at various intervals around them. Victor, bless his cotton socks and clumpy sandals, had come up trumps and had found us specialist growers around the country who'd been able to supply us with everything else we needed.

'I've missed you so much.' I stopped winding the last few cornflowers around Laura's flower crown to give Nina a hug. 'The shop hasn't been the same without you.'

'How have you had time to miss me?' she laughed. 'I'm the one who went off to have an adventure, and yet you seem to be the one with the most stories to tell.'

'It certainly hasn't been dull.' I smiled ruefully, watching her nimble fingers add sweet peas while still maintaining the tightness of the posy. I'd told her all about Sam and me. At least I'd admitted some of it; I'd stopped at the part where I invited him to stay the night. She thought he was an idiot for throwing away a chance to be happy and said she planned to tell him as much. I'd persuaded her not to; at least I hoped I had.

I finished the flower crown and set it in the shade; Laura would love it. I'd take it over there in a minute, but first I wanted to double-check the to-do list. I picked up my clipboard and scanned it.

'Batteries!' I exclaimed. 'For the outdoor fairy lights.'

Lucas had got dozens of them on charge inside. Someone needed to fit them now, otherwise they'd get forgotten.

Nina looked at me over the top of her sunglasses. 'You do know that at some point you're going to have to put that to-do list away and go and do your other job, don't you?'

I shrugged. 'It'll only take me five minutes to get ready.'

'Ew.' She wrinkled her nose. 'You know what they say about sweaty bridesmaids?'

'No,' I laughed. 'I don't think I've heard that well-known phrase.'

'They say the hog-roast man won't kiss them behind the bushes.'

'Yeah, well, I don't think we need to worry about that. I could bathe in ass's milk and douse myself in Chanel and I don't think I'll be getting any bush action. That was a one-off.' I clapped my hand over my mouth. 'Damn, I didn't mean to say that.'

She gasped, her eyes dancing with triumph. 'You dark horse.'

I pressed my hands to my burning face. 'Shush, I don't want to think about it, not while his children are around here somewhere.'

'Well that settles it; I'm definitely going to give him a nudge in the right direction now. You two are perfect for each other.'

Privately I agreed, but I'd rather wait until the time was right for us both.

'You mustn't say anything,' I pleaded. 'Pandora and Sam need space. There are the kids to think about. Adding new people into the mix is too much too soon.'

'You're ace,' she said, her face serious for once. 'I don't think I've met anyone as unselfish as you. I want you to be happy.'

I simply smiled. 'I *am*.'

'Hmm, if you say so.' She pursed her lips. 'Well I really am happy. I was going to tell you later but I've booked a two-month trip to South America. I leave next Sunday.'

I was incredulous. 'What about your house, I thought you were going to rent it out?'

'Funny you should ask.'

Just then Annabel skipped over and whipped my clipboard away. 'Have you told her the good news yet?' she asked Nina and then continued without waiting for a reply, 'We're renting Nina's house while she's away. My idea.'

I blinked at Nina. 'Really?'

She grinned. 'Good, isn't it?'

'It's brilliant!' I said, thrilled for everyone concerned. 'And if you come back from your travels and need somewhere to stay, I have plenty of space.'

Freddie's room was now a spare room. Soft dove walls, big double bed and new white bedlinen. It was fresh and inviting; so much so that when I sent her a photo, Mum had booked herself in for a week. The musty shrine to my brother was no more. I planned to fill it with life, friends, family and maybe in time a lodger, who knew.

'And such a relief to be out of Nanny's house,' Annabel continued, rolling her eyes. 'I love her, but now Dad and Mum are sharing custody, we need more bedrooms. And he needs his privacy, if you know what I mean?'

She gave me a knowing look far beyond her years.

'The batteries need doing,' I blurted out to change the subject.

'Already done them. Good job I'm not a bridesmaid after all,' she said pushing her sunglasses up into her hair to study the list. 'Because you'd never have coped without me.'

Nina and I grinned at each other. Annabel had dropped hints the size of polar bears to all and sundry that she'd never been a bridesmaid and would really like the job, but Laura had only wanted me. We'd compromised and agreed that she would deputise for me as chief organiser while I fulfilled my duties as maid of honour. I had a feeling I'd have to wrestle that clipboard off her if I ever wanted it back. She squinted in the sun and pretended to read it.

'Check on the hog-roast man.' She looked at me. 'You can do that.'

'That's not even on the list,' I said, feeling my face growing inexplicably warm.

'Yeah, well, I'm in charge now,' she said pertly. 'And it's about time someone took control over you two.'

'What do you mean?' Nina asked innocently.

She rolled her eyes. 'Fearne and Dad were talking and now they're not. And it's making him grumpy.'

'We are talking,' I protested. 'We've spoken today.'

Annabel sighed pityingly. 'I mean proper talking with smiles and eye contact.'

Nina snorted.

'I think the world of you, Annabel,' I said calmly, 'but you've gone too far.'

She raised her eyebrows and for a split second it was like looking at Pandora: scary. 'And you, Fearne, you haven't gone far enough.'

Nina exploded with laughter and gave Annabel a high-five.

'Fine.' I tugged my sunhat down to hide my pink cheeks and they both giggled conspiratorially as I marched off to find Sam.

I could have found my way to the hog roast blindfolded, it was already beginning to smell amazing. I made a mental note to keep a steady eye on Scamp when he arrived later. Biddy had arranged to have him bathed and groomed before the wedding. I had a feeling he wouldn't be straying very far from Sam all day. Lucky dog.

Sam was rearranging white hot charcoals with a long pair of tongs as I approached.

'Hi. I'm just going to get ready,' I said, trying to make

eye contact as instructed, 'but wanted to check everything was OK?'

Even before he opened his mouth I could tell he was having the time of his life. He was animated and energetic, his head nodding to music being played by Will who was sitting behind the hog-roast oven in the shade.

Will raised his eyes briefly to acknowledge me before going back to his tablet.

'What do you think?' Sam spread his arms proudly.

'Looks great!' I nodded enthusiastically. 'This could be the career in food you've always dreamed of.'

Actually the sight of a whole pig suspended over a layer of hot coals was fairly disgusting. However, I forced myself to look at it; I loved pork cooked this way and it was hypocritical of me not to acknowledge the process. Goodness knows what Annabel thought about her father's potential new venture.

'It's bringing out the caveman in me. I've got an urge to rip my shirt off and beat my chest.'

'Don't mind me,' I said evenly.

I tried not to think about Sam's bare chest. How I'd spent the night snuggled up against it, how the muscles in his shoulders had rippled as we'd made love. It might have only been one night, but for me it *had* been love.

I felt my heart beat faster as I looked at him. *It still was love.* Shame it was unrequited.

'Fearne.' He lowered his voice and looked at me with such intensity that I couldn't have dragged myself away if I'd wanted to. 'Can I talk to you later?'

'Sure. What about?' I held my breath. Maybe it wasn't unrequited after all.

He lifted his pork pie hat and scratched his head. 'Oh, you know, this.' He gestured vaguely with a hand. 'Everything.'

I nodded, trying to hide my disappointment. So he didn't want to talk about 'us'. Of course he didn't, because there was no 'us'. He probably just wanted to pick my brains about doing some boring market research for the hog-roasting oven market.

'Yep,' I said, turning to go. 'I should have a window about seven o'clock. See you then.'

'A window?' I heard Will say. 'Why has she got a window?'

'Son,' said Sam. 'As Sean Connery says: "I like women. I don't understand them, but I like them."'

I couldn't help giggling as I strode away. *And this woman can't help liking you too.*

It was almost time. The guests were in their seats, including Hamish's parents whom I'd last seen at Freddie's funeral almost a year ago, and some of mine and Laura's old friends from uni. It promised to be quite a party later if the mood already was anything to go by. Gina and Rosie, plus her husband Gabe, who insisted on coming to check she didn't overdo it, were handing out water and sparkling elderflower cordial to everyone to ensure no one got dehydrated.

Laura and I were in the little private garden at Welcome Cottage with Dexter who was taking a last few photographs. Hamish had already come to the door to collect Scamp and all we were waiting for now was for Terry to arrive and the wedding would begin.

'Straighten your arms and hold the bouquet in front of you,' Dexter instructed.

I had to keep turning away from Laura; I'd never seen her look so beautiful and the make-up lady said she couldn't keep re-doing my mascara forever. Her wedding dress looked even more stunning on her than it had done on the page in the magazine. It was a sleeveless ivory lace sheath with a wide boat neck at the front which showed her slender collarbones and dipped into a low curve at the back. Her copper hair was short and feathered prettily around her face and the crown dotted with cornflowers finished the look perfectly.

'Like this?' Laura did as she was told.

'Perfect.' Dexter focused the lens and took the shot.

I started fanning her again while Dexter put her bouquet on the grass, arranged the ribbon streamers artistically and did some close-ups.

I'd taken Nina's advice and had a shower at Welcome Cottage before having my hair and make-up done. I'd requested a minimum amount of make-up because it was all going to slide off anyway, but the nude colours she'd used on my eyelids and lips plus a slick of mascara and a generous dusting of powder had done my confidence a power of good. My hairstyle was simple and exactly what I'd wanted: a dainty plait either side into which tiny meadow flowers had been tucked. I was totally in love with my dress: it was blush pink, strapless and straight and fell to below my knee. It was made of the softest cotton, as light as gossamer. I might never take it off again.

'Oh, that's nice,' Laura said closing her eyes as I wafted air over her. 'If I ever get married again—'

'Which you won't,' I put in.

'*Which I won't*, but if I did, it's going to be in Iceland, in the Ice Hotel, if there is such a thing.'

'There isn't,' I said with a giggle, 'but I know what you mean.'

'And now one of the two of you together, holding hands and facing the house,' said Dexter.

He was taking his role as official photographer very seriously and we patiently posed for picture after picture until he dashed off to get some reportage shots of the wedding guests.

We went to wait for Terry's arrival under the porch in a sliver of shade. The ambulance was five minutes late and I could sense that Laura was starting to get the jitters.

'He'll be here,' I said softly.

She nodded. 'He has to be. I couldn't do this with both parents missing.'

'Your mum would be so proud of you,' I said to my dearest friend.

She smiled her thanks. 'And Freddie would be so proud of you.'

'I wish . . .' I swallowed, conscious that if I mentioned Freddie's name the tears would fall and there would be no chance of stopping them.

'I know,' she said squeezing my arm. 'I wish he was here too.'

'But I suppose they both are here,' I said softly. 'Because they'll always be with us.'

We leaned towards each other so our heads were touching for a moment until there was a crunch of tyres on the gravel drive and the private ambulance tooted its horn.

Once we'd all hugged, it only took a couple of minutes to transfer Terry into a wheelchair. The ambulance driver, whose name was Craig, said he'd never done a wedding before and pushed Terry effortlessly across the grass and we were soon in position under the first of the willow arches.

Laura gasped in delight when she saw the sunflowers. 'Look, Dad, Mum's favourites.'

'Good grief.' Terry's face lit up. 'Sunflowers! We had those at our wedding.'

My heart melted as Laura threw her arms around his neck and told her dad how much she loved him.

Terry patted her back. 'If you and Hamish can be half as happy as your mother and I were, I shall die a happy man.'

'Not on my watch,' Craig said with a sniff. 'Now, Terry, what's it to be, how are you feeling?'

'Like the proudest father in England. I think I shall walk on air up that aisle.'

My heart was in my mouth as Terry gripped the arms of the wheelchair and struggled to his feet. He was so frail and thin, the slightest breath of air would have blown him over.

Craig unhooked a walking stick from the back of the chair and placed it in Terry's hand.

'Thanks, lad,' said Terry.

Annabel, who was in charge of starting the music, was watching me for a signal; I nodded and she pressed play on the music system.

The first few bars of piano music started up and in front of us, Hamish stepped into view. He caught sight of his bride and the look of love on his face almost undid me. Next to appear, one step behind as ever was my faithful dog, looking so handsome with a pink ribbon matching my dress around his neck from which hung two gold rings.

'What's this music?' Terry wheezed as his daughter took her place beside him and Craig quickly whizzed the chair around the side to be waiting for him at the front.

'"A Thousand Years" by Christina Perri,' she whispered back.

'Bloody hell,' he chuckled. 'It better not take me that long to get you up there.'

Behind Hamish the registrar, a friendly lady called Barbara, approached the podium and invited the guests to stand.

As one, the crowd stood and turned, and then, to applause and smiles and cameras held aloft, Laura, on her father's arm, began to walk away from one life and towards the man she'd chosen to spend her future with.

And as I stood beside *my* best friend, watching her marrying *Freddie's* best friend, as I listened to them make their promises to love each other forever, my heart was bursting with happiness. Dexter took a million photographs, Annabel was one step ahead with every detail and Will sang such a beautiful version of 'Everything' by Michael Bublé that even the registrar had to get a tissue out from up her sleeve.

It was perfect.

Freddie would have been so proud of me, and, I realised, I was proud of me too.

Chapter Forty

As soon as the service was over, Sam announced that the hog roast was ready.

There was almost a stampede. The smell of it wafting over us had been so tempting that I'd heard one or two stomachs rumbling during the vows.

Gabe, having sent Rosie for a lie-down, was helping Will and Sam serve up. I hadn't spoken to Sam for hours, I hadn't even had a chance to eat anything, but I saw how much he was enjoying himself. Gina, Bing and Una were wandering round with trays of champagne flutes and I did allow myself one of those.

There were seating areas set up all over the gardens as well as the marquee which, as it turned out to be the hottest place, was almost deserted. Dexter was still taking candid shots: Annabel, I noticed, had commandeered him for the longest; she needed Instagram-worthy pictures and rejected almost every one he took.

In the middle of everything were Laura and Hamish. They were having a ball, introducing each other to friends and family that their new spouse hadn't met yet, never, even for a second, letting go of each other.

Craig kept a strict eye on Terry, forcing him out of the sun and checking he'd taken his medication. He was obviously tiring, but tucked under a large parasol, chatting to all the most important people in his life was probably the best medicine he could have.

The DJ had set a great playlist to run during the wedding breakfast: uplifting, romantic and happy. Annabel hated it. I was humming along to Taylor Swift when she appeared by my side.

'Do you really like this music?' She curled her lip.

'I do,' I beamed at her and risked giving her a hug. 'You've been brilliant today. Thanks for your help.'

'OK, you can let me go now.' She pretended to look horrified but she didn't fool me, her lips twitched with pride. 'Is it time for *you know what*?'

I checked the time and nodded. 'Action stations.'

She raced off to the podium and I headed into the house. Barbara, the registrar, was having a cup of tea at the kitchen table with Delphine. Barbara had been recommended to me by Kelly, whom I'd met on my first day in Barnaby at the Riverside Hotel. She was new to the job and had been very receptive to all our requests. Gina had already asked her to officiate for them at The Evergreens when the time came.

'This is a first for me,' Barbara said, her eyes mischievous behind her dark-rimmed glasses. Her red lipstick had transferred itself to the rim of her cup.

'Same here,' I said. 'Delphine, could you go and let the bride and groom know we're ready for them, please?'

Delphine looked stunning in a pale blue silk dress sprigged with lily of the valley, designed and made by herself. The woman was a marvel.

'Oh, this is so romantic,' she cried, her hands fluttering to the pearls around her neck as she danced out of the kitchen, her sprightly gait belying her age by several decades.

I'd left two bouquets of flowers in the sink earlier. I took them out now and dried the stems thoroughly.

Barbara finished her tea and wandered off nonchalantly so as not to attract attention and as soon as she was out of sight, Stanley and Bing slunk in.

'You two look gorgeous!' I squealed, laughing as the two old men did twirls. Both of them were in pale grey suits and coral pink cravats.

Stanley kissed my cheek. 'And you, my dear, are gorgeous, inside and out.'

'I'll second that,' said Bing, also muscling in for a kiss.

'Eh, dicky heads!' came a sharp voice from the hallway. 'You already taken.'

'Go, go,' I said to the men, ushering them out. 'And stay unobtrusive.'

The men slunk off and as soon as they'd gone Delphine, Maria and Una stepped into the kitchen.

'Absolutely beautiful.' I beamed at the three dear ladies. 'Ready?'

Maria looked at her two friends. 'Come on girls, we knock 'em dead.'

I led the women slowly through the garden, keeping to the opposite side of the lawn away from the food area which was to the far side of the house. We reached the first willow arch and I stepped back. At the podium, Barbara smiled and gestured for Bing and Stanley to take their places. I nodded at Annabel who'd been patiently waiting to do her bit. She pressed play and the hypnotic sound of Etta James singing 'At Last' echoed softly through the trees. Maria, arm-in-arm with her best friends, walked down the aisle towards Stanley who stood waiting for his bride, tears running unashamedly down his cheeks.

Ten minutes later Mr and Mrs Pigeon shared their first married kiss.

Simple, fuss-free and with the meadow flowers she'd

told me she wanted, Maria had got her dream wedding and made Stanley the happiest man in the world.

Annabel turned to me and gave me the thumbs-up and I did it back. The two of us tiptoed away, leaving them to enjoy the moment with their closest friends and once we were out of sight, we flopped down on the nearest seat.

'Phew,' I said letting my head fall back and closing my eyes. 'I don't know about you, but I am shattered.'

'I don't know about you but I could do with a glass of champagne.'

'You are definitely only eleven, aren't you?' I laughed.

'Ugh. Don't remind me,' she growled. 'Everyone thinks that because I'm only eleven, I don't understand what's going on with Mum and Dad. But of course I do.'

Suddenly we appeared to be having a serious conversation. I hesitated before answering. This was important, I didn't want to say the wrong thing. Freddie was always so much better at this sort of thing than I was. 'I'm sure they know how clever you are.'

Annabel continued with a sigh. 'The thing is that I'm the only one who really sees both sides. I love them both, but Jeez, seriously, they are so much better apart.'

I suppressed a smile; she had sounded exactly like Sam then.

'Well, it's good that you think that way,' I said carefully.

'When Mum's with us, she's such fun. She watches what we're watching on TV, even if it's stupid boy stuff with Will. And she watches all my Netflix documentaries even though I know for a fact she isn't really interested. The other day we watched a programme on forced prison labour in China where they have to peel raw garlic cloves.' She paused to frown and shake her head. 'Although how anybody can watch that and *not* sign my petition, I don't know.'

I managed not to register my amusement; her passion for causes was so adorable and admirable.

'Nor me, send me the link, I'll sign it.'

'Thanks,' she said absentmindedly. 'But there's apart and there's lonely, you know?'

'I know,' I said heavily. I'd had the busiest few weeks of my life, it was ridiculous that I'd felt lonely, but I did.

'Mum's scared of being lonely and I think that's why she hooked up with Gareth.'

'Do you like Gareth?' I asked.

'I feel sorry for him,' she smirked. 'But that's not the same thing. I've tried to give him some advice, but you know what adults are like.'

I nodded solemnly. 'I do.'

'He spoils her and that's not going to work. Gran and Grandpa spoiled Mum all her life, she needs someone who she can respect.'

I bristled. And she couldn't respect Sam? 'That sounds very sensible,' I said evenly.

'Mum and Dad were so young when they got together. Like, twenty or something. They grew up together. You grow out of things, you know? Like I used to like the Foo Fighters but now I'm into more indie stuff.'

I stared at her in wonder. 'I'll never be as cool as you, as long as I live.'

She smiled kindly at me. 'That's because you're old.'

'You'll be OK, you know,' I said bumping my shoulder against hers.

She nodded. 'I'll be OK because I'm mature enough to understand that it's not the end of the world if your parents split up. It's not like anyone died.'

She clapped a hand over her mouth. 'Your brother died and I just said died. I'm sooo sorry.'

I laughed. 'Don't worry. It took me a long time to accept that he was really gone, but I'm OK now. Life has to move forward. Things change and we have to adapt to those changes whether we like it or not.'

She exhaled. 'Good, because you might not be cool, but you are kind and I like that. Anyway,' she moved on swiftly as if she'd let herself down by showing a softer side. 'It's Will I'm worried about. He's still so little.'

I smiled at her; she had to be the most amazing, big-hearted and perceptive girl on the planet. 'He'll be OK. I guarantee it.'

Annabel blinked at me and all at once I saw that she was still a little girl who needed reassurance now and again. 'How can you be so sure?'

I closed my eyes for a second and let my mind wander. Two kids, a big brother, a little sister, laughing, arguing, shining torches after lights-out, playing 'Operation' on the church altar, fighting over the last roast potato, but always, *always* together.

'Because he has you,' I said simply. 'Whether you're with Mum or Dad, or with your grandparents, you'll always have each other and that, I promise you, is really special.'

She was quiet for a moment, kicking her heels up while she thought about things.

'Thanks, Fearne.' Her mouth twisted into a smile. 'You're actually alright for an old person.'

'You're welcome, I think. Ooh, I nearly forgot,' I said, taking out the thirty pounds I'd tucked into my bra for her. 'Your wages. I'll give them to you now in case I forget.'

'I wouldn't have forgotten. Pleasure doing business.' She jumped to her feet. 'See you later. I'm going to see if Dad's got any of that pork left.'

I pretended to be shocked. 'I thought you were a flexitarian.'

She gave me an exaggerated wink. 'Clue's in the title. I'm being flexible. Today pork, tomorrow tofu.'

She disappeared in the direction of the food and I sat there for a moment laughing to myself.

There was a rustle from behind me and I turned to see Pandora standing there between the trees, dressed in a white linen dress and espadrilles.

'Pandora! Good grief.' I clutched my chest in shock. 'How long have you been there?'

'Long enough.' She stepped towards me through the long grass. 'I heard what you said.'

I ran back over the conversation to try and identify anything that would have raised a red flag but I could feel myself getting flustered already.

'I just . . .' I stuttered. 'I just tried to be honest with her.'

She nodded curtly. 'I know. Well done.'

A compliment? I narrowed my eyes suspiciously. 'Thanks.'

'You and Sam.' She faltered and fiddled with her bracelet.

'There is no me and Sam,' I assured her.

'Well there should be. You'd be good for him. And for the kids. You're a better match than he and I ever were.'

And then she turned and went back the way she came, leaving me speechless, but just a tiny bit elated.

After she left, I sat there on the bench, just thinking what to do next. I was hot and thirsty and slightly sweaty in this fitted dress but I couldn't move. I'd spent the last month so absorbed in the preparations for Laura and Hamish's wedding and then Maria and Stanley's that I'd pushed my own needs to the back of my mind.

Could it be my turn? To do what I wanted, to search for my own happy ending? A stirring of excitement fizzed inside me. I thought it just might be.

Pandora had as good as given me her stamp of approval. Weird but good. And according to his daughter, Sam was lonely and she seemed to think Sam was grumpy without me. So in theory, there was nothing standing in my way. Other than me.

I remembered that line in Freddie's letter: *what do you want, Fearne Lovage?*

'Sam,' I said aloud, startling myself.

I wanted Sam. Sam who had so quickly become the person I thought about when I woke up and the person whose face was there in my dreams. The man whose body I longed to caress, whose lips I wanted to feel against mine again.

'You called?' came a familiar voice.

I gasped. Sam was standing in the exact spot where Pandora had crept up on me only minutes ago. He took a few steps forward and I sprang to my feet to face him, the beautiful man who'd found his way into my heart even though I'd done my hardest to keep him out, for both our sakes.

'Yes . . . no, I mean, I was just talking to myself and—' I shut myself up with a groan. I sounded like an idiot. I *was* an idiot. How could I ever have thought I'd be able to just remain friends.

'I'm sorry,' he said, his eyes smiling with warmth. 'I seem to make a habit of turning up and frightening you to death.'

'I don't mind. You can frighten me more often if you like. No, I don't mean that. I don't know what I mean,' I pressed my hands to my face, feeling dizzy and over-whelmed. 'Only that I have missed you so much since . . .' I stopped. *Since the day I fell in love with you.*

'Since I took you to Sheffield.' Sam winced.

'I took *you* actually,' I pointed out.

'I stand corrected.' He laughed softly. 'And I've missed you too.'

His words were like warm honey and I allowed them to sink in, I wanted to savour them.

'Fearne, I've behaved really badly. I introduced you to Yasmin and Inca, knowing how important that meeting would be to you and since then I haven't been there for you. I wanted to be but—' he broke off, looking mired in guilt.

'I didn't mind you leaving to fetch the children,' I said, meaning it. 'I love you more for putting them first.'

His beautiful eyes widened. But I didn't care that I'd said *love* because I meant it. The florist's was closing soon, I'd be leaving Barnaby and if I didn't tell him how I felt now, I might not get another chance.

'But I can't pretend I wasn't hurt when you came to see me in the shop.' I took a deep breath and held his gaze. 'You slept with me and then told me you wanted to slow things down. It was such an about-turn.'

He squeezed his eyes shut briefly and then nodded. 'I'm sorry, I got spooked. Because I realised that I loved you and I didn't know how to handle it.'

My heart began to pound. 'What did you just say?'

'I love you.' His face softened into a smile and he stepped closer.

'You do?' I blinked at him.

'I do.' His eyes burned with intensity. I wanted to believe him, but I also didn't want to get hurt again.

'We had one fantastic date, one wonderful night together and then nothing?' I asked softly. 'That's not love.'

He ran a hand through his hair. 'When I came into the shop with the kids to get flowers, as soon as I saw you my heart started thumping like a drum. I realised how quickly

440

I was falling for you. Big time. And I was scared of those feelings. I hadn't even extricated myself from a broken marriage and I was already falling in love with someone else. I panicked, that's all.'

I nodded. 'I know how you feel; I'm scared too.'

Sam took another step forward, until his fingers were in touching distance. 'But it's different for you. You make everyone happy. I've failed at my job, my family, my marriage. I didn't want to fail with you.'

'Oh, Sam.' My heart melted with love for him. I took his hands and pressed them to my chest. 'You haven't failed. Not at anything. You're a brilliant father. And although it's over for you and Pandora, you managed to create two wonderful kids, so you can't possibly call that a failure. And as for your job . . .' I shrugged. 'No one has to stay in the same job for life. Especially when they don't have the heart for it any more. Look at me, I don't seem to keep mine for more than five minutes.'

He nodded slowly. 'Thank you. When you put it like that I'm quite a catch.'

'Which is why I love you.' I looked at him from beneath my lashes and my heart beat a little faster. 'You may kiss me now.'

He didn't need asking twice. He cupped my face in his hands and lowered his mouth to mine. His kiss had an intensity that took my breath away. I responded in kind, delighting in the sensation of his stubble against my face, his tongue against mine, his lips gentle then firmer, sending darts of longing down deep inside to my core.

I melted into his arms, my body, tired only a few moments ago, alive and responsive to his touch.

'Sam.' I pulled away, breathless and looked into his eyes, holding this wonderful man's face in my hands. 'Life is a risk, *loving* other people is a risk. But this, us, I think it's a risk worth taking.'

'You're wonderful and wise and I can't believe my luck.'

And then we kissed again and we didn't stop kissing until we heard the rumble of a van pulling a trailer out of the garden and around the side of the building.

'Isn't that the hog-roast oven?' I said alarmed.

'Yep.' Sam wrapped his arms around me and kissed the soft hollow by my collarbone. 'The owner needs it back for tomorrow.'

'So how did you get here?'

'Motorbike,' he grinned. 'I won't bother asking if you need a lift home.'

My insides fizzed with what I was about to suggest. I was going to do it. It was time to get back in the saddle, in more ways than one . . . I'd overcome hurdle after hurdle this year and there was just one thing left. I trusted this man and I loved him, so . . .

I challenged him with my eyes. 'Have you got a spare helmet?'

He stared at me. 'Sure. I brought Annabel's with me.'

I grabbed his hand and began running across the grass, pulling him behind me. 'Come on then. What are you waiting for?'

He caught hold of me and lifted me off the ground, whirling me around before lowering me to him and pressing another kiss, at once tender and fierce, to my lips.

'You,' he said, huskily. 'I've been waiting for you. You make me the happiest man in the world.'

'Just as well,' I said, between kisses. 'Because as far as my happy list goes, you're my number one.'

Epilogue

The Enchanted Spa knew how to do Christmas, I thought happily, as I flumped down onto a comfy sofa, waiting for Laura. The foyer looked like a scene from Narnia: there were snow-tipped Christmas trees, fat fragrant candles giving off a festive scent of juniper and pine and miles of fresh evergreen garlands intertwined with tiny white lights which sparkled all day long.

The latter had been made by me and my students. I had a weekly slot here teaching mindful flower arranging and we'd been making Christmas wreaths and swags for the last six weeks. It was a wonderful environment and made a nice change from working at home. Plus, I could only get four students comfortably around my kitchen table and so being here gave me a chance to teach larger groups. The autumn had been fine because when the weather had been warm enough, we'd worked in the garden under a canvas sail which Sam had put up for me.

Next year would be different. In all sorts of ways, and I couldn't wait. Sam and I were looking at properties together, with bedrooms each for the children, space for a workshop in the garden for my flower courses and a big enough kitchen for him to be able to expand his business.

He'd set up Diamond Spices, his new barbeque marinade venture to sit alongside his hog-roast business. I'd sent some to Nina in Australia, where she was waitressing in a restaurant in Melbourne at the moment and it had gone down a storm with the chef. Today Derbyshire, tomorrow the world! Both of us had exciting work plans. But not today; today was all about relaxing.

I was having a spa day with my best friend, the first time we'd both been here together since that fiasco in the spring.

A movement outside caught my eye; she was here. I waved and then I jumped off the sofa to greet her as she huffed and puffed her way through the revolving doors.

'Sorry I'm late.' She kissed my cheek, her hand on her bump. A honeymoon baby, she told everyone who asked proudly. 'I think Baby McNamee played football all night and then I overslept.'

Her cheeks were plumper since the last time I'd seen her, but the happiness which shone from her eyes was unmistakable and I was so pleased to see it. Terry had passed away only a few weeks after her and Hamish's wedding, which had taken the shine off their honeymoon glow for a while.

'No problem.' I looped my arm through hers and led her towards the ladies' changing rooms. 'There's still time.'

We put our bags into lockers and left again. I pointed along the corridor towards the dance studios.

'This way.'

She gasped in horror and stopped in her tracks. 'I know I promised to do hula hooping next time we came but . . .'

We both looked at her rounded tummy and giggled.

'Don't worry, I think you'd freak the instructor out if you turned up to her class.'

She breathed a sigh of relief. 'Thank heavens for that.'

'Besides,' I added, 'I think you'd probably get stuck in the hoop.'

'Oi.' She nudged me. 'I'm not immune to comments about my size, as Hamish will confirm with the bruise on his arm sustained from a marital pinch.'

'What did he say?' I probed, my eyes twinkling.

'He's started to call me Laa Laa.'

I frowned. 'Sounds like a cute nickname for Laura, to me.'

'It's also the yellow Teletubby,' she said drily. 'Not so cute. Anyway, enough about me, how are you, how was the christening?'

'Christenings, plural,' I reminded her. 'First it was Rosie and Gabe's little girl, Eleanor-Mae. She entertained us by laughing all through hers, even when the vicar tipped cold water on her head. The whole congregation ended up giggling along with her. Noah looked so proud of his little sister and Rosie and Gabe seem to have adapted to life with a new baby without turning a hair.'

'Are you listening?' Laura said to her tummy. 'That's what we're aiming for: a happy, fuss-free baby. Did you all go back to the café afterwards?'

I shook my head. 'We went back to Stanley and Maria's bungalow for champagne and cake.' I winced. 'Maria got the limoncello out and Stanley insisted on everyone trying his pickled walnuts. Never again.'

Yasmin had asked me to be Inca's godmother and when Sam and I and the children had arrived at Inca's christening, she'd sprung a surprise request on me.

I smiled proudly. 'My goddaughter is a delight and it was a wonderful day. If a little emotional. And guess what? Her middle name is Frederica after Freddie, as if I didn't adore her already.'

'Congratulations!' Laura squeezed my arm. 'And what a lovely tribute to him.'

445

I stopped at the door to the dance studio and grinned at my friend. 'Ready?'

'Really?' she stared at me blankly.

I opened the door and nudged her in ahead of me, hoping she'd be pleased with the surprise session I'd organised with the wonderful Maureen, who was now a colleague of mine. The scent of cloves and eucalyptus filled my senses, sending a rush of well-being to my heart.

Laura looked sideways at me, nodding slowly. 'Good call, Lovage.'

'Oh my!' Maureen's face lit up as we entered the room and she pointed at Laura's tummy. 'Look at you!'

Laura laughed in surprise. 'You remember me!'

My fingers found the crystal in my pocket and I wrapped my hand tightly around it. *Selenite: to help someone who is grieving.* I'd always grieve for Freddie but I'd learned to live with the loss, to remember him with love and happiness. And when a wave of guilt passed over me for living when he no longer was, I'd think of his letter and about living with no regrets and I'd feel proud because I was doing that every single day.

'Of course,' Maureen said with a secret smile. 'Although you're both almost unrecognisable from the first time we met.'

She wafted us into the circle of chairs just like before and tipped a pile of crystals into the centre and invited us to choose one to hold.

'I need one to give me an easy labour,' Laura said, struggling to lean forward to see them.

'And I need one which gives me purity of love,' I added.

'That would be a diamond,' said Maureen, 'but I'm afraid I don't have one of those.'

'That's OK,' I said, thinking of Sam Diamond's marriage proposal that morning, which I'd accepted and which we'd sealed with a kiss. 'Because I do.'

Acknowledgements

The Thank Yous

I am very fortunate to have a wonderful team behind me, helping to make my books as good as they can be. Massive hugs, as always, to my eternally sunny agent, Hannah Ferguson and her colleagues at Hardman & Swainson. Heartfelt squeezes to my boss-lady editor, Harriet Bourton, literally the best person to have on your team. And thanks too to the amazing Orion team. They are listed in the acknowledgments but a special HURRAH to Victoria Oundjian, Olivia Barber, Katie Moss, Britt Sankey, Alainna Hadjigeorgiou, Rabab Adams, Paul Stark and Amber Bates. You guys are the bee's knees.

A number of people have been extremely helpful to me while I researched this book: Cath Cresswell, Dickie Hallam, Linda Jenkins, Jo Eustace, Lisa Thompson and Nicky O'Driscoll. An extra special mention to Susan Martorano from Rose Cottage Floristry and Flower School. Thank you for teaching me all about working with flowers and helping me with my many subsequent questions. A huge thanks to Lucy Felthouse and her dog Scamp. Lucy's dog is THE Scamp in *My Kind Of Happy* – I hope I've done him justice! Thanks to Liz Clark who runs Lizian Crystals in Nottingham's Victoria Market for helping me with the crystal healing scenes and for the beautiful gift of a labradorite crystal to energise my imagination, I will treasure it.

Thank you to Kim Nash for posting a video on Facebook by a man called Sebastian Terry. This man provided the inspiration for the novel. Following the tragic loss of a friend at the age of twenty-four, Sebastian asked himself if he was living a life which made him happy. After having decided he wasn't, he changed everything. *My Kind of Happy* takes Fearne on this journey and I hope, in some small way, it might encourage my readers to do the same.

Thanks and much love to my family who do their best to look interested when I'm telling them, in great detail, my latest plot problems; your support means the world to me.

Thank you to my wonderful readers for brightening my day with kind words and lovely photos (especially the ones with dogs in them!). It means such a lot to hear from you.

Finally, a huge thank you to Fiona Wilson who bid in the Get In Character campaign run by CLIC Sargent to have her aunt, Maureen Sinclair as a named character in *My Kind Of Happy*. Thank you both for helping us raise money for children with cancer.

Credits

Cathy Bramley and Orion Fiction would like to thank everyone at Orion who worked on the publication of *My Kind of Happy* in the UK.

Editorial
Harriet Bourton
Victoria Oundjian
Olivia Barber
Lucy Frederick

Copy editor
Sally Partington

Proof reader
Laetitia Grant

Audio
Paul Stark
Amber Bates

Contracts
Anne Goddard
Paul Bulos
Jake Alderson

Design
Rabab Adams
Rachael Lancaster
Joanna Ridley
Nick May

Editorial Management
Charlie Panayiotou
Jane Hughes
Alice Davis

Finance
Jasdip Nandra
Afeera Ahmed
Elizabeth Beaumont
Sue Baker

Production
Ruth Sharvell

Curl up with Cathy this Christmas...

Turn the page for an exclusive
SNEAK PEAK
from the new heart-warming
novel from

Cathy
Bramley

The Christmas
Project

Coming October 2021

Chapter One

High up in the Derbyshire Dales, the air smelled sweet and fresh: of the free-range cattle which dappled the slopes below, meadow flowers on the hillside and blackberries growing wild amongst the hedgerows. It was late summer, the August bank holiday weekend, both Daniel and I were in our T-shirts and shorts and my face and arms were already tingling. My lungs were working hard to keep pace with him, and my heart was full to bursting with the simple pleasure of being together, out in the countryside.

With one last surge of effort on my part, I reached the summit only a second or two behind my much fitter boyfriend.

'Look at that view,' I said, taking Daniel's hand.

The landscape spread out in front of us was breath-taking, literally in my case. When did I get so unfit? 'Aren't you glad I prised you out of bed this morning for an adventure?'

Daniel slung an arm around my shoulders. 'Yes, I bow to your superior wisdom; we *should* make the most of sunny days when they come along. This is a great start to the Bank Holiday weekend. And you were right; who needs a lie-in anyway?'

'Not us, that's for sure.' Love for him swelled inside my chest and I leaned against him, tucking my head under his chin.

Daniel was easy-going and kind and infinitely patient where my spur-of-the-moment ideas were concerned. He had to get up at the crack of dawn every day in order to open his specialist greengrocers in the little market town of Wetherley. Today was a rare day off; his assistant manager would be looking after the shop in his absence. Daniel would have been completely within his rights to turn his nose up at my suggestion of a picnic in the Derbyshire Dales. But here he was.

We stood together, arms around each other's waists in a silence broken only by my wheezing chest and the occasional brush of wings from birds flying overhead. The scenery looked almost too beautiful to be real. The deep, deep blue of the wide sky, the lush green hills which seemed to stretch into infinity, intersected with ribbons of silver, streams heading downhill to join up with the wide river in the valley below. Far, far in the distance was Wetherley, the town I called home.

Home. Me, Daniel, my new business . . . Life was every bit as good as I'd hoped.

It had been a hectic couple of weeks. It had all happened in a bit of a rush and although I couldn't be happier about it, my head was spinning with all the upheaval. Being here, out in the countryside just him, me and miles and miles of green was perfect.

'Quite a nice surprise actually.' He took a swig from his water bottle and passed it to me. 'In the year we've been together, you've never once suggested going for a walk, let alone a hike. I didn't have you down as a hiker.'

'Nor me,' I said. The only time I'd ever done anything which could be classed as a hike rather than a walk was during a geography field trip to Wales. I'd had to borrow kit from school lost property. The boots gave me blisters after five minutes and the cagoule had a large rip in its hood which I only discovered once it started to hail. Then

Robert Mason, the boy I'd had a crush on, had dared me to run across the river using the steppingstones. The chance to impress him had proved too tempting and I'd hurled myself onto the first stone only to find out first-hand how slippery green moss was when wet. Robert Mason had roared with laughter and called me an idiot and I'd had to squelch along next to the teacher after that in disgrace. It wasn't an experience I'd wanted to repeat in a hurry.

I drank some water and handed it back to Daniel. He wiped the lid on his T-shirt and I stifled a giggled. I wasn't insulted, there was nothing wrong with being hygienic, especially when you worked with food all day and I didn't think he was even aware of the implication that I was germ-ridden.

'Some kids have outdoorsy childhoods,' I added, 'Camping holidays, Sunday walks and family hikes. I didn't grow up in that sort of environment, so I thought it wasn't for me.'

'I know you didn't get the sort of opportunities I had.' He smoothed the hair back from my face gently. 'And I can't begin to imagine how hard it must have been for you growing up, but that's behind you now, you don't have to let your childhood hold you back. You don't need permission, or to wait to be asked. There is nothing that is *not for you*. You're a gorgeous, intelligent young woman in charge of her own destiny.'

I took a breath, about to argue with him, but I opened my bag and took out some sun cream, rubbing it onto my face instead. My chaotic childhood wasn't something I could just cast aside in adulthood; it was part of me. But he meant well.

'I know.' I managed a smile. 'Not that thirty-five is young. Besides I had two ideas for today and I thought you'd prefer this one.'

'And the other one was?' He raised an eyebrow, amused.

'A visit to an animal shelter to look at kittens. Choose our first pet.' It was on the tip of my tongue to say, 'Our first fur baby', but something told me that that would make Daniel itch.

I'd wanted a pet all my life and now that I'd be working from home, setting up my handmade candle company, Merry and Bright, it seemed the perfect time. This morning while he'd still been asleep I'd been searching online and found a litter of abandoned kittens liberated from terrible conditions and it had been all I could do not to email the shelter immediately and offer a home to the whole family.

'You chose well.' Daniel's eyes shimmered with laughter. 'There's no way I'd trust you within five miles of an animal shelter.'

'Why not?' I protested.

'Because you'd want to bring them all home. And instead of a small kitten, you'd fall in love with a great big hairy hound with halitosis and only three legs. Tell me I'm wrong.'

'Hmm.' I couldn't hold back my smile. He had me there. Those adverts about dogs who'd been living in shelters for years because no one wanted to adopt them broke my heart. It crossed my mind to point out that he'd just said I didn't need permission to do stuff. Mind you, it was his house, I supposed, he had the final say. 'Just so you know, what I'm hearing is that a kitten would be preferable to a dog.'

'I'm starving,' said Daniel, with a deft change of topic. 'Shall we climb up on there and have our lunch?'

He hopped up effortlessly onto a large rock and extended his hand to help me up beside him. Daniel was fit in all senses of the word. His face was boyishly handsome and with his pale blonde hair and blue eyes, he could be mistaken for being Scandinavian. He was lean and lithe too, thanks to his daily run or cycle. I admired his self-discipline. I tried to do a twenty-minute online yoga every morning but invariably I ended up watching it while I got dressed and hunted down a matching pair of shoes.

As far as I could make out, we were now officially at the highest point at Wysedale Peak. I dropped my rucksack to the ground and sat down beside Daniel. My legs were aching from all that climbing and I massaged my thighs and tilted my face to the sun while he unpacked the picnic.

'About getting a pet,' he said, inspecting the contents of several plastic tubs, 'I've just about got used to sharing my bed with you every day, let alone anything else.'

A dart of panic pierced my happiness. 'Are you regretting it? Because if so—'

He cut off my protests by kissing the ticklish part of my neck below my ear. 'Not at all. You're a great housemate and you make the best . . .' he sniffed a sandwich. 'Peanut butter and . . .?'

'Nutella,' I supplied with relief.

He laughed, shaking his head. 'You make the best peanut butter and Nutella sandwiches in the world.'

'Phew.' I needed to hear that; it made me feel less like I was imposing on him. I leaned against him, relishing his strength and solidity. New beginnings, I thought again. Hopefully the last new beginning I'd have to go through.

We shared the sandwiches in comfortable silence, and I poured us both some tea from a flask.

The bed he was referring to was his double bed, in his master bedroom, in his home. Technically mine too now, but I was merely the lodger and currently living rent-free. It was a neat-as-a-new-pin townhouse on the modern estate which nudged the little town of Wetherley ever closer to its big sister, Bakewell, famous for its delicious tart. The house was perfect for Daniel; it was decorated in a neutral and sparse way, nothing you could possibly fall out with, but nothing to fall helplessly in love with either. My choice, when I was in a position to buy a home of my own (or our own), would be something quirky and brimming with colour, with nooks and crannies, uneven floors and creaking pipes. I'd discover decades-old newspapers in the loft left there by goodness knew who, apple trees planted years ago by children who'd poked pips into soil; I'd sense the echo of generation after generation of family life and I'd take up the baton and put down my first proper roots, live by my own rules . . .

But for now, I was extremely grateful to Daniel for making room in his house for me. Moving in together hadn't been one of those carefully planned scenarios where two grown-ups talk about taking their relationship to the next level. It had come about because a few weeks ago I'd left my job at Tractor World, clutching a small redundancy payout and a vague plan to turn my hobby of candle-making into a business.

Daniel had helped me go through my household budget and we'd quickly established that I'd have to make significant savings somewhere along the line. I would have to sell an awful lot of candles to cover my rent on my flat, let alone the rest of my living expenses. Even though on paper the business didn't look hugely profitable, the more time I thought about it, the more certain I was that working for myself, relying on my own ingenuity and creativity, was right for me.

'I'll throw all my energy and enthusiasm at it,' I'd told Daniel. 'And if I can't make it pay in a year, I'll go back to having a nine-to-five job.'

'I love your determination,' he'd said, 'And I'm sure you'll be a great success, but in the meantime, why don't you move into my house to reduce your outgoings?'

I'd hardly been able to believe my luck; one of the first things he'd told me when we got together was that he'd never lived with anyone because he valued his own space. It had taken me a few weeks to get out of the lease on my flat but now I was fully set up at Daniel's house. He'd even offered to clear out the shed so I could use it for the business. I was nicely set up: an electric cable ran from the garage, down the garden and into the shed, giving me light and power, and the outside tap meant that I'd have easy access to water too. Setting up a business was a risky move, but risks never bothered me. Besides, was there ever a right time to take the leap? Like having a baby or getting a kitten. My friend Nell thought I was barmy. And in truth I'd have been in a bit of a pickle if Daniel hadn't been there to prop me up. But I had a feeling that starting Merry and Bright was exactly the move I needed.

'I'll have to do some work tonight when we get back,' Daniel said. 'I'm not complaining about being busy, it's a good type of busy, but if I don't keep on top of it—'

'I know,' I supplied, 'You'll be playing catch up all week.'

Not keeping on top of things was his perennial concern. Despite being outwardly laid-back, Daniel had an ambitious streak, he'd always wanted to run his own business. With a small investment from his parents, he'd taken over an out-dated greengrocers a few years ago and had done wonders with it. He sold all manner of fruit and vegetables with a focus on local, seasonal produce plus little extras such as local honey, fresh farm eggs and artisanal chutneys. His plan was to open another store in the next town and if that did well another and another. I wasn't at all ambitious, but I admired his doggedness to succeed.

The careers advice I'd been given was that I'd never amount to anything. At the tender age of sixteen, I believed it. I'd come a long way since then but at the time this was all I'd needed to hear to give up on any academic aspirations I might have had. Not that I could have afforded to go to university; I might not have wanted much, but I'd rather have starved than go into debt.

So instead, at sixteen, I enrolled at college to study childcare and got a part time job as a carer in a retirement home. I wasn't driven by money or status. I didn't feel the need to strive for more, have more, be more. I was more about the simple things in life: a place where I'd belong, family to love and who'd really love me, a home to feel safe in.

I stole a look at Daniel. He was making short work of his sandwich and staring straight ahead, a slight frown forming a crease between his brows, an expression I recognised as work-mode. He was probably debating whether to add flat leaf parsley or coriander to next week's veg boxes. I'd have to get his attention, bring him back to the moment, or I'd lose him. I jumped to my feet, flung my arms wide and was about to give him a rendition of 'The Hills Are Alive' when my foot slipped on some loose stones.

'OUCH. Shit. Ouch.' I fell backwards, smacking my spine painfully against the rock behind me and twisting my ankle. I bit my lip and tried not to cry.

Daniel knelt beside me, blue eyes full of concern. 'Merry! Are you OK?'

'I didn't look.' I said blowing out in short bursts, breathing away the pain like I'd seen in birth documentaries.

'Before you leaped?' He teased. 'Not like you.'

'If giving birth hurts more than this, I'm not sure I can do it.'

His entire body went rigid. 'You're not . . . are you pregnant?'

'I'm not pregnant,' I said rubbing my back. 'It was just an observation.'

'Thank goodness,' Daniel pressed a hand to his chest, laughing with relief. 'That's alright, then. For a moment there, I was panicking.'

I blinked the tears out of my eyes, shocked at his reaction. I'd never come out and asked him whether he wanted children or not, but nothing he'd ever said led me to think otherwise. We were responsible adults, in our thirties, with a home (his), and income (also his, but I'd probably be earning enough once my candle business took off). A child, even an unplanned one, would have been something to celebrate, wouldn't it?

'So, for clarity,' I swallowed, fiddling with the turn ups on my shorts. 'You'd be unhappy if I'd brought you up here specifically to break baby news to you.'

He kissed my cheek. 'No, you silly goose. But you've just fallen on rocks two miles away from the car, twenty miles from the nearest hospital. And if you were pregnant, I'd be worried about what was going on in there.' He pointed to my stomach.

I leaned my head against him and let out a sigh of relief. 'Thank goodness.'

'Although the timing would be crap,' he said under his breath.

'If you wait for the right moment, you could be waiting forever.'

'Well, true I suppose.' Daniel looked uncomfortable. 'I just mean with you trying to get a new business off the ground and me putting all my time into the shop. Let's stay just you and me, shall we?'

'Good point,' I nodded. He was right but I couldn't help feeling oddly disappointed. 'And this fresh air is doing me good. I can already feel my brain pinging with all the extra oxygen.'

Daniel grinned. 'Watch out world. Merry is going to set you alight with her candles. Get it?'

'Very good.' I smiled, relaxing against him. What would I do without him? In the past I'd heard people say things like, I married my best friend, and I'd never understood that. Surely, your lover and your best friend should be two separate people? Then last year, I met Daniel and now I understood. He was my best friend, my partner, my family. My everything.

His phoned beeped loudly, the trumpet sound effect reserved for messages from his younger brother, Tom. My heart sank a little; once Daniel took his phone out of his pocket, it was game over: he'd end up checking emails, web orders, Facebook notifications, he couldn't help himself.

'I didn't think I'd get a signal this high up.' Daniel whipped his phone out with glee.

I pulled away to give him some privacy and while Daniel read Tom's message, I plundered the picnic for more snacks.

'Pickled onion or beef?' I asked, holding out a choice of crisp packets to him. 'Or would you like some hummous and carrot . . . Daniel?'

He was miles away, gazing out at the hills below us.

'Daniel?' I said again. 'Everything OK?'

He blinked a couple of times before looking my way.

'Um, yeah, yeah. It was just Tom.' He pressed the button on the side of his phone to lock the screen. 'Wetherley Primary School appointed a new head teacher yesterday.'

Tom was the deputy head teacher at the local school where both he and Daniel had been pupils many moons ago. The head teacher had had a personal crisis over the summer and consequently, a replacement had had to be found at short notice. Daniel and I had told him he should apply for the top job; he'd have made a great head. But Tom reckoned he wasn't ready for the responsibility yet.

'Ah, is he regretting not going for it?'

'I don't think so, he just wanted to let me know who'd got the job.'

'Oh? Anyone we know?'

Daniel scratched his beard and laughed awkwardly. 'Yes, actually. Well, I do. You don't. It's a girl I used to go to school with. Well, *woman*. Tasha Sandean.'

'Primary or secondary?'

'Both. She was in my form for the whole of my school life. She moved away to university and never came back. Very bright girl. Top set for everything and brilliant at French because her parents were from Mauritius. They moved back when they retired, I think. I haven't thought about her for years.'

Either Daniel was blushing, or he'd caught the sun. He might not have thought of her in a long time, but he was certainly thinking of her now. My interest was piqued.

'We can invite her round when she moves back, you can get to know her again,' I offered.

'Maybe.' He opened the beef crisps and chomped on a large handful. 'Funny story. When we were seventeen, we both got temporary Christmas jobs at a garden centre working in Santa's Grotto. I asked if I could kiss her under a bunch of plastic mistletoe, but she dodged out of reach.'

'Aw, poor Daniel,' I teased, dotting his nose with my fingertip. 'Spurned and still sore about it.'

'It took a lot of courage, I'll have you know,' he said, haughtily. 'It's not easy for boys trying to work out whether girls like them or not.'

So he'd had a crush on her. I felt a flicker of jealousy and quickly batted it away. This had happened more than twenty years ago; everyone was allowed a history. I'd even been married. Very briefly.

'But we made a joke of it.' Daniel polished off the rest of his crisps and pinched one of mine. 'She said if I wasn't married by the time I was forty, she'd kiss me then.'

'Like one of those pacts to marry if you're still single by thirty or whatever, that's so funny!' I laughed. Then I remembered. 'You're thirty-nine.'

He and rummaged in the rucksack. 'Where's the chocolate?'

'I ate it when you disappeared behind a tree for a wee,' I said, vaguely. Something twisted uneasily inside me.

He bit into an apple instead. Juice squirted onto my chin and he wiped it away with his thumb. 'Sorry.'

'It's OK. Back to Tasha Sandean.'

'What about her?' He crunched away on his apple looking unbothered.

'Well. If she is going to be back in Wetherley this Christmas, maybe she'll want to kiss you under the mistletoe. Because you'll be forty by then.' I wasn't the jealous sort as a rule. But I didn't want some very bright girl, top set in everything, former crush of my boyfriend thinking she could just turn up with a sprig of mistletoe and expect him to pucker up for old times' sake.

He looked at me, amused. 'I'm sure she won't even remember it.'

'You remembered it,' I pointed out.

'She might be married anyway,' said Daniel, laughing. 'Hey, let's change the subject. It was just a silly story;

I wouldn't have told you if I'd known you'd take it so seriously.'

'OK,' I said meekly. But my mind wouldn't drop it, because a thought had just occurred to me.

Tasha might be married, but Daniel wasn't. Yet. What was to stop me from proposing to him, right now? All it took was a question. Just one simple question. I felt heat rise to my cheeks and my insides began to tingle with adrenalin. Could I do it? This was the perfect setting, the perfect occasion. OK, I hadn't planned to ask him to marry me, but when did that ever stop me from doing something? I was a big fan of spontaneity.

I pushed myself onto my knees to face him and felt the crinkle of the empty crisp packets underneath my kneecaps and the ache in my twisted ankle. Blood pumped through my ears and almost without registering what I was doing I reached for his hand.

You don't need to wait to be asked. Those had been Daniel's exact words just a few minutes ago. I hoped he meant it.

I wet my lips. 'Daniel?'

'Yes, Merry?' He laughed softly. 'What are you up to now?'

I swallowed the lump in my throat, this was a lot harder than I'd thought. 'I love you with all my heart. I want to be with you for the rest of my life. I want us to be a family. So, Daniel Casey, will you marry me?'

The air around us was so still, the moment so heavy with tension that for a few seconds I forgot to breathe. I watched a succession of emotions cross his face.

He gave a short bark of nervous laughter. 'It's not February twenty-ninth, is it?'

I shook my head, my eyes not leaving his. 'No, but why should women only have one chance in four years to propose and men get . . . whatever it is?'

'One thousand two hundred and sixty five,' Daniel supplied quietly. He was brilliant at mental arithmetic. 'And you're right, of course.'

My heartbeat had gone into overdrive. We looked at each other and I could read his thoughts as clearly as if they were tattooed across his forehead. The fact was that all those possible days had gone by when he could have asked me to marry him. And he hadn't.

As the seconds ticked away, the size of my mistake grew bigger. I didn't know what to say. If I could take back my proposal I would, but now it was out there like a big embarrassed elephant flapping its ears in the breeze between us.

He reached a hand to my cheek and stroked it with his thumb.

'Oh Merry,' he murmured. 'I'm flattered, honoured.'

'Good, because I don't plan on ever doing it again; it's nerve-wracking.' I said brightly, ready to brush the whole fiasco under the carpet and rewrite it as a joke.

Remember that time I proposed to you and you thought I was serious, I'd giggle and look at him over the top of our newborn's head. Remember it? He'd smile at me lovingly whilst strapping the twin toddlers into the buggy and looking around for the dog's lead. Of course, I do! That was the day I realised you were the one.

'Now you know how I felt under that mistletoe.'

Why did he have to bring her up again, I thought miserably. I forced a lightness into my voice that I didn't feel. 'Except you were a boy asking for a sneaky kiss; I'm the woman you love asking you to be my husband. It's not in the same league of bravery.'

'I suppose not.' He nodded, examining his feet.

'So?' I looked up at him.

He nodded once as if making up his mind and finally met my gaze. 'Look, Merry, you're right, you are the woman I love, but . . .' He drew in a breath and rubbed his hand through his hair distractedly. 'I'm sorry, I don't want to be tied down at the moment. Not through marriage, or babies or even a kitten. And I'm not sure I ever will.'

'Oh.' I swallowed, my eyes hot with mortification. This was . . . earth shattering. Why had we never talked about any of this before? He didn't want anything that I wanted. Nothing.

'You'll make someone a wonderful wife.'

He didn't mention the fact that I was already divorced, that I'd already messed one marriage up; I was grateful for that.

'But not you.' I looked at the stony ground through eyes blurry with tears.

'Not me,' he confirmed softly.

I shifted from my kneeling position and sat back, peeling the crisp packets off my skin.

'What's wrong with me?' I said this out loud, but it was as much to myself as to him. Anger started to seep into my bones. We'd been having such a nice day, trust me to do something impulsive and ruin it.

'Nothing. Nothing at all!' He reached for my hand and brought it to his lips, kissing it. 'You're wonderful. This is all on me.'

I shook my head; there was no way I could accept that. Despite what he'd said about maybe never wanting to get married, a familiar feeling of rejection gnawed away inside me; I'd thought he was the one, I really did.

We both stood up and he took hold of my shoulders. 'I do love you though, you do believe me, don't you?'

I nodded, tears streaking down my face. He'd never done anything to make me think that he didn't, until today anyway.

He kissed my forehead. 'This doesn't have to change anything.'

'Sure,' I murmured, swallowing down the lump in my throat.

But of course, it did. Inevitably it changed everything.

See where Merry's story leads in
The Christmas Project!

Pre-order your copy of

The *Christmas Project*

ready to curl up with this winter, for a chance to WIN a Christmas hamper filled with festive treats.

Visit bit.ly/TheChristmasProjectCompetition for details on how to enter.

This prize draw closes at midnight on 13th October 2021.
Terms and conditions apply.

Can she find her perfect fit?

Gina Moss is single and proud. She's focused on her thriving childminding business, which she runs from her cottage at the edge of The Evergreens: a charming Victorian home to three elderly residents who adore playing with the kids Gina minds. To Gina, they all feel like family. Then a run-in (literally) with a tall, handsome American stranger gives her the tummy-flutters...

Before a tragedy puts her older friends at risk of eviction — and Gina in charge of the battle to save them. The house sale brings her closer to Dexter, one of the owners — and the stranger who set her heart alight. As the sparks fly between them, Gina carries on fighting for her friends, her home and her business.

But can she fight for her chance at love — and win it all, too?

'A book full of warmth and kindness'
Sarah Morgan

Also By

Cathy Bramley

Ivy Lane

Tilly Parker needs a fresh start, fresh air and a fresh attitude if she is ever to leave the past behind and move on. Seeking out peace and quiet in a new town, will Tilly learn to stop hiding amongst the sweetpeas and let people back into her life – and her heart?

Appleby Farm

Freya Moorcroft is happy with her life, but she still misses the beautiful Appleby Farm of her childhood. Discovering the farm is in serious financial trouble, Freya is determined to turn things around. But will saving Appleby Farm and following her heart come at a price?

Conditional Love

Sophie Stone's life is safe and predictable, just the way she likes it. But then a mysterious benefactor leaves her an inheritance, with one big catch: meet the father she has never seen. Will Sophie be able to build a future on her own terms – and maybe even find love along the way?

Wickham Hall

Holly Swift has landed her dream job: events co-ordinator at Wickham Hall. She gets to organize for a living, and it helps distract from her problems at home. But life isn't quite as easily organized as a Wickham Hall event. Can Holly learn to let go and live in the moment?

The Plumberry School Of Comfort Food

Verity Bloom hasn't been interested in cooking ever since she lost her best friend and baking companion two years ago. But when tragedy strikes at her friend's cookery school, can Verity find the magic ingredient to help, while still writing her own recipe for happiness?

White Lies And Wishes

When unlikely trio Jo, Sarah and Carrie meet by chance, they embark on a mission to make their wishes come true. But with hidden issues, hidden talents, and hidden demons, the new friends must admit what they really want if they are ever to get their happy endings...

The Lemon Tree Café

Finding herself unexpectedly jobless, Rosie Featherstone begins helping her beloved grandmother at the Lemon Tree Café. But when disaster looms for the café's fortunes, can Rosie find a way to save the Lemon Tree Café and help both herself and Nonna achieve the happy ending they deserve?

Hetty's Farmhouse Bakery

Hetty Greengrass holds her family together, but lately she's full of self-doubt. Taking part in a competition to find the very best produce might be just the thing she needs. But with cracks appearing and shocking secrets coming to light, Hetty must decide where her priorities really lie...

A Match Made In Devon

Nina has always dreamed of being a star, but after a series of very public blunders, she's forced to lay low in Devon. But soon Nina learns that even more drama can be found in a small village, and when a gorgeous man catches her eye, will Nina still want to return to the bright lights?

A Vintage Summer

Fed up with London, Lottie Allbright takes up the offer of a live-in job managing a local vineyard, Butterworth Wines, where a tragic death has left everyone at a loss. Lottie's determined to save the vineyard, but then she discovers something that will turn her summer – and her world – upside down...

A Patchwork Family

Gina Moss is single and proud, and her cottage is home to three elderly residents who feel like family. Then a run-in with a handsome stranger makes her tummy flutter, before a tragedy puts her older friends at risk of eviction – and Gina in charge of fighting for them, and a chance at love, too...

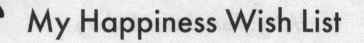

My Happiness Wish List

· ·

· ·

· ·

· ·

· ·

· ·

· ·

· ·

· ·

· ·

· ·

· ·

Share your wish list on social media using
#MyKindofHappy

 @CathyBramleyAuthor   @CathyBramle